T...
A...
SOME FO...
...ALL FOR KEEPS . . .

MARI McNICHOLS: To the world she's a beautiful, fearless investigative reporter. But no one knows the terrible secret that drives her from love—not even one very special, very precious man . . .

CHARLES MERRILL: A brilliant biomedical engineer, he's on the cutting edge of his profession. Then he meets the woman he can't live without, a woman who will drive him to his outer limits—to see if he is safe for her to love . . .

JANET McNICHOLS: Not even Mari guesses how much her mother sacrificed, how much she buried. But it's time for Janet to tell the truth—at any cost . . .

TRACY SADLER: The sexy new reporter is out to eliminate the competition, piece by piece. She's already conquered the boss. Now she's after Mari's territory: her on-air time, her job . . .

TONY ZUNIGA: The macho cameraman is in love with an older woman—and fiercely loyal to Mari. He'll even ride shotgun for her, as she takes on the mega-corporation that wants them off the air . . .

"A wonderful book . . . fascinating . . . I read far into the night."

—Roberta Gellis

Current
Affairs

CAROL
THURSTON

POCKET BOOKS

New York   London   Toronto   Sydney   Tokyo

An *Original* Publication of POCKET BOOKS

POCKET BOOKS, a division of Simon & Schuster Inc.
1230 Avenue of the Americas, New York, NY 10020

ISBN: 0-671-61912-8

First Pocket Books printing October 1989

10 9 8 7 6 5 4 3 2 1

POCKET and colophon are trademarks of
Simon & Schuster Inc.

Printed in the U.S.A.

For my daughter

Science doesn't explain at all how I as a thinking being exist and can do things. It is completely mysterious, this human existence.

—Sir John Eccles, Nobel Prize 1963 (for discovering how nerve cells transmit information from one to another)

PROLOGUE

She reached for the receiver on the first ring, without taking her eyes from the screen of the VDT.

"Mari McNichols." The words came automatically, like the reflexive jerk of a knee.

"You the woman who's been asking around about Pamezine?"

Her eyes went blind as she focused all her attention on the invisible caller with the genderless voice, the kind considered sexy in a woman but effeminate in a man.

"Uh, yes, I—"

"Why?"

"For a television program I'm working on." She pegged her caller as male, because women weren't usually that assertive on the phone, or so abrupt. "About women's health problems. Over two million women in this country are addicted to psychotropic drugs—Ativan, Elavil, Librium, Compazine, Etrafon, Stelazine, Tofranil, Norpramin, Vivactil, Asendin. The list is endless. And Pamezine is one of them, one of the most frequently prescribed. Reason enough to ask questions, I think."

"Yeah, a second dose is all it takes to get hooked, you know. Disrupts communication between the brain cells, which use chemicals as messengers. Neurotransmitters. Pamezine stimulates the synthesis of dopamine, which floods the receptor cells, makes the patient feel good. Until her brain runs out of the chemicals needed to make the stuff. Then she gets depressed again, starts craving more. But there's more to it than that—than addiction, I mean." His voice dropped suddenly, as if to make sure no one could overhear him. "It's women who're showing up with the worst side effects. Probably something to do with hormones. Not that we know all that much about how drugs are metabolized in women, how the effects are influenced by the menstrual cycle. Not enough research, even on female animals."

"Something besides addiction, you mean? What? And who are you?"

"Yeah, you have to be the one, all right. Heard you were full of questions." His breathy laugh rustled like dry leaves blown along the sidewalk by a gust of wind. "Sorry lady, but you'll just have to decide whether you want my name or what I can tell you about Pamezine. 'Cause you sure as hell aren't gonna get both! Ever hear of biting the hand that feeds you?"

Did that mean what she thought it did—that he was on the Pharmacol payroll? She'd already spent more than she'd wanted to of her own time and money on calls to the company that manufactured Pamezine, without learning anything more about the drug than she already knew from reading *Physician's Desk Reference*.

"And don't bother giving me any of that bullshit about how whistle blowers are protected by law, either," he added, anticipating what she was about to say. "They all catch it in the end, one way or another, no matter what anybody says about how upstanding or heroic they are. Remember that guy in the Pentagon who blew the whistle on the six-hundred-dollar toilet seats and the twelve-hundred-dollar hammers?" This time his short laugh sounded not only dry, but bitter. "And that engineer at Morton Thiokol, after the *Challenger* exploded? Hell, public as that story was, and despite all the orders from higher-ups in Washington not to retaliate, the company still managed to get him. I bet he never finds another job, unless it's collecting garbage! So let's not waste what little time I've got. You want to hear why I called or not?"

Words and phrases from the patient insert for Pamezine

flashed across her mind. "Drowsiness, dizziness, lighthead-edness, stuffy nose. Be careful going up and down stairs, avoid standing up suddenly. Get out of bed slowly and dangle your toes over the edge for a few minutes. Tighten and relax leg muscles. Avoid strenuous exercise, standing for long periods of time, hot showers, hot baths, saunas or Jacuzzis." And then the warning to "Call your doctor if you develop difficulty in breathing, irregular heartbeats, confu-sion, fainting spells or seizures." All of which meant to Mari that Pamezine was capable of some pretty dire effects on the circulation. Why, under what conditions, and exactly how dire, she hadn't been able to determine. A couple of the physicians she'd called said they didn't prescribe Pamezine, but none would say why. Just that they preferred one of the other drugs available for treating anxiety, depression, emo-tional distress, and other "nervous conditions"—symptoms they insisted were far more common among women than men, which only served to underscore what she already knew. When it came to female patients, the male medical establishment was still practicing nineteenth-century medi-cine.

"Yes, of course I want to know," she murmured, capitu-lating even though she knew she'd never be able to use the information unless she could get him to say who he was, maybe even give her some way to verify what he said, too. Because he could be just a disgruntled employee out to make trouble for the company in retaliation for not giving him the promotion or salary raise he thought he deserved. Nobody in the news business today would be idiot enough to air damaging product information without being able to back it up, in court if necessary.

"Anybody you talk to mention interactions?" he asked next.

"With alcohol? Yes. Even the patient insert carries a warning about that. And most pharmacists put a little yellow sticker or something on the bottle, as a reminder. Anyway, that's true of most of them so far as I know, not just Pamezine."

"You know that heavy smoking can block some kinds of drugs?" he continued, ignoring her comment. "Pain reliev-ers. Oral contraceptives. Beta-blockers like propranolol, which regulate the heartbeat and lower the pressure. And anticoagulants."

Mari's fingers brought the keyboard to life again, all her instincts telling her that what she was hearing was too important to chance leaving even the smallest detail to the vagaries of a subconsciously selective memory.

"We're not sure why exactly, but Pamezine seems to bring on a sort of clumping or thickening of the blood, which can be big trouble in the microcirculation—in the arterioles and capillaries. In some cases, even for perfusion of the vital organs. And it can block the primary anticoagulants, which makes it difficult to treat the very condition the drug seems to cause, the sluggish blood flow." He hesitated again, as if he were waiting for some sign that she understood the significance of what he'd just told her.

"You're saying that among heavy smokers the blocking effect is increased?" she asked, just to be sure she'd put the facts together right. "How much?"

"No way to answer that," he mumbled.

"Well, how bad *can* it get?" That was the sixty-four-dollar question, and both of them knew it. "Any fatalities?"

"In the field tests? Yes. Mostly in one group—women who are heavy smokers and also are on oral contraceptives. And Pamezine has an unusually long half-life, so there may be as many as three million women out there, right now, at risk for severe adverse effects. Stroke, maybe even death."

"How much at risk? What kind of numbers are we talking about, in that particular group, I mean?"

"Could be as high as one in six."

How many more brickbats could the pill take, Mari wondered distractedly, and still remain a viable option for women? A couple of million women had already quit taking it, resorting instead to surgical sterilization or having an irritant inserted into their wombs, in the belief that the pill caused cancer and heart attacks. The truth was that it was the safest and most effective contraceptive available. Women who *didn't* take the pill, in fact, were twice as likely to develop cancer of the ovaries and uterus lining than those who did. Some recent research even suggested that it helped build bone mass, which would be good for women later on, protecting them against osteoporosis after menopause. And now, just when the word was beginning to spread and the number of women taking the pill was on the rise again, some damned "unidentified source" was claiming it could kill you if you took it along with Pamezine and also happened to smoke a lot—even though everyone knew it could kill you just to smoke a lot, without any help from the pill or Pamezine!

"And you actually want me to believe that Food and Drug would okay a product with those kinds of figures?" Mari sounded every bit as incredulous as she felt. "Pharmacol had to have used a multiple-factor design, to look for interactions. At least for main effects."

"Yeah, we did." He knew for sure now that this woman's reputation was no fluke. The Kens and Barbies he was used to seeing on the local newscasts were real fluffballs, with their toothy smiles in place come hell or high water, blessed event or bloody head-on collision. And for the first time he experienced a sense of satisfaction, not only in what he was doing, but who he was giving it to.

"You're saying that the test data Pharmacol submitted to the FDA was purposefully falsified, that the company has known all along . . . ?" She let the words trail off and sort of laughed, letting her skepticism show.

"You got it," he breathed, relieved that she was the one to say it, and damned glad to finally have it off his conscience. He waited for her to digest all the implications, making no attempt to breach the brief, shocked silence that followed.

"How can you really expect me to believe that unless you tell me who you are? Why should I believe anything you say? Please, won't you give me your name?" She spoke hurriedly now, knowing he might hang up if she kept insisting. "Look, I can promise you confidentiality. Trust me. Give me *something* I can take to my news director."

"Sure." His raspy voice dripped sarcasm. "And I suppose you'd also go to jail for me when some judge orders you to reveal your source or face a contempt charge, right? At the risk of sounding like a B movie, lady, you can't squeal about what you don't know, to a judge or anyone else."

"Wait. Don't hang up yet."

"You know what to look for. What you do with it is your business."

"But how, if—"

"Take a look at the stuff we filed with the FDA, the interaction stats on risk factors. You know, heart disease, high blood pressure, smoking, the usual." He hesitated for a second. "I may try to get back to you later. Maybe. But don't count on it."

She heard the click when he broke the connection, but continued to sit there holding the phone to her ear, staring at the words on the screen in front of her.

CHAPTER
1

〜〜

"Morning, Sandy," Mari murmured as she passed the woman sitting behind the desk, sending a raised eyebrow along with her usual greeting. Jack Lunsford obviously was on some kind of a tear this morning, because she could hear his voice even out here in the station's reception area.

"Results of the February sweeps," Sandy said in a near whisper, answering Mari's silent question. "Arrived about thirty minutes ago." Sandy Pittman was not only the station's "front man," but always seemed to know what was going on behind the cameras at KPOC-TV as well. Mari continued on to the doorway to the news-division offices, then stopped and turned back, waiting for the other shoe to drop. Sandy shook her head. So the network hadn't come in number one in the latest national sweeps. And from the sound of Jack's voice, KPOC's news division hadn't done too well in the local ratings war, either.

Mari started toward her office, wondering who his victim was this time, just as Ron Bergner stepped out into the hall ahead of her, looking like a badly adjusted color set. His neck and face were bright red in contrast to his hair, which in the past year had begun to show a lot more salt than pepper. "Come have a cup with me, Ron," she invited before he had a chance to say even one word. They were too close to Jack's office, and the heat of his exchange with Jack was still riding him. They walked in silence to the coffee alcove, then on to Mari's office.

"I suppose you heard." The words swooshed out of Ron as he sank down into the chair beside her desk. He had the deep, resonant voice that marked every man she'd ever known who'd come to the business from radio. "We moved up a couple of points in both the six and ten o'clock slots. Almost nose to nose with KTRK. But that's not good enough for Jack. He's after top dollar. Threatening bastard says if we don't move out front next month, he's going to make drastic changes in the newsroom." Ron had been at KPOC even before the network acquired the station in the mid-seventies, which was a lot longer than most news anchors lasted in one place. "Acts like it's my fault, says I need to project more 'fire in the gut.' I should watch Mike Wallace, Sam Donaldson, see how they do it."

He took the time to draw a deep breath, then let it out in a long sigh. "Sometimes I wonder why the hell I don't get out. After twenty years, I'm just a parrot. Jack's making more of the editorial decisions all the time, too, shoving them down Ted's throat." Ted Calvacca was the executive news producer and had been with the station almost as long as Ron. "Until that bastard arrived on the scene, we all worked together, as a team." He shook his head, whether in disbelief or disgust, Mari couldn't tell. "Wants me to give that stupid slut he just assigned to city hall more time on-camera. 'Talk to her,' he says! She's been complaining, bending his ear while they're in bed, for christsake! Says she doesn't get enough exposure. Her 'sources' hardly know who she is when she walks in downtown." Ron looked up at Mari. "I told him to go to hell, that I wasn't going to pimp for him!" Saying it again didn't seem to make him feel any better. "Shit, maybe he's right, maybe I am losing it. I sure as hell never get into the field anymore."

"Did you say anything about that, suggest to Jack that you'd like to . . . ?"

"Yeah." He sighed again. "He just talked budget. And special beats with star reporters who can develop important contacts." Ron broke off, as if he suddenly realized how that might sound to Mari. "Oh hell, Mari, I didn't mean it the way— I wasn't talking about you."

She waved away his stuttered apology, but she did know what he was getting at. Jack Lunsford had come in as news director at KPOC a year ago with the general manager's promise of a sizable increase in the news-division budget, partly because they were under a lot of pressure from the medical community, an important audience in a city that was home to the largest medical complex in the world. The Texas Medical Center occupied more than fifty buildings scattered over 550 acres of prime city real estate—including twelve hospitals and nine academic institutions offering medical, dental, nursing, and allied health-science training programs—and transfused more than two billion dollars a year directly into Houston's economic veins. With the collapse of oil prices in the early eighties, TMC had become the city's single largest employer, a force to be reckoned with, which was the reason Mari had been hired as KPOC's first full-time medical news reporter.

Four months into her new job, when still another patient with the Jarvik heart started having strokes, she decided it was time to start asking why. And after a couple of months of lobbying by Mari and several doctors at the Texas Heart Institute, Jack Lunsford had given his reluctant okay to an hour-long look at the Jarvik and other artificial substitutes currently under development, one of them under the guidance of Houston heart surgeon Michael DeBakey. "Have a Heart" drew only a moderate audience, but about a month later the network had picked it up and put it on the national feed. The second time around, Jack had given it the local promotion the program deserved but didn't get the first time, and "Have a Heart" attracted more ad billings than any previous public-affairs program in the history of KPOC.

"You know, about every year and a half my life goes into limbo for six months," Ron mused out loud, gazing out the window behind Mari. "Contract-renewal time. Peg and I go on automatic pilot, start putting things on hold. We can't seem to make decisions about anything, even what bulbs to plant for next spring. I suppose it's because both of us are thinking maybe we won't be here when they bloom. I'll bet the neighbors wonder what the hell is going on with our yard. Flowers all over the place one year, and bare as an orangutan's rear end the next. Sometimes I wonder how she stands it." He continued to stare out the window, apparently lost in thought. Mari smiled and waited for him to come back. "I know it sounds trite, but she really does get better every year, like fine wine," he commented at last, almost wistfully.

Coming from Ron, it didn't sound as bad as it might have. Clichés were her mother's stock-in-trade, and usually they grated on Mari's nerves like the proverbial fingernail across a blackboard. A quick tap came on her door, and Tony Zuniga stuck his head around the edge.

"Oops, sorry. Wasn't sure you were in yet, Mari. I'll be out in the van, okay?"

"No, stay. I was about to leave anyway," Ron answered for her, rising from his chair just as the intercom buzzed on her desk. "I suppose the good word has made it around to everybody by now, huh?" Tony nodded and came on in, and spoke to Ron as Mari picked up the phone.

"We need to talk," Jack said over the receiver. He didn't waste time on the amenities, probably because he knew by now that they rarely saw eye to eye on anything, whether it was going to bed with him or what was important news. "Can you be at editorial today? One-thirty."

Mari still thought of the meetings as "budget," where it was decided what stories to cover and how much time would be given to them, but that was a hangover from her newspaper days. She glanced at her appointment calendar, then at her watch. "I've got a shoot at the med center at one. Why don't you go ahead and I'll come on as soon as I get back."

"Not another malpractice suit, I hope. Heard one, you've heard 'em all." She recognized the remark as Jack's back-handed way of letting her know what he thought of her Monday-night news segment.

"How about a dime a dozen?" she muttered under her breath, wondering if this was going to be one of those days when everyone she ran into felt compelled to spout all the shopworn clichés and homey homilies they could dream up.

"Telling stories on all the bad doctors in town is going to get you into a peck of trouble, Mari. Hasn't anybody ever warned you about biting the hand that feeds you?"

She straightened suddenly. Had Jack actually said that, the same words her anonymous caller had used last night, or was her imagination working overtime? That wouldn't exactly surprise her, not after the hours of playing everything he'd said over and over again in her head. It had turned out to be a long and restless night, a night that left her feeling wrung out in the morning.

"What's up?" she asked. "I haven't had a chance to scan the wire yet. Has something special come in?"

Jack had probably just come from morning editorial with Ted and Podge Pearsall, KPOC's assignments editor. Since coming to Houston, Mari had been deciding what stories to cover and air pretty much on her own, though she always checked with Podge just to keep him informed, and to make sure they weren't duplicating on what he called "stories of doubtful venue." Like the one about the new nontoxic biological insect lure. News judgment demanded that the story be covered, because the new chemical sent male cockroaches into a sexual frenzy that ended in death. And Houston was crawling with the creatures. It was just a matter of deciding who was going to do it.

"Not that I know of," Jack muttered. He sounded distracted and disinclined to answer questions. "We just want to look at what you've got coming tonight and for the next couple of weeks. So bring your futures file along." His voice started to fade, then came back stronger. "And get back here as soon as you can."

Mari watched Tony jockey the KPOC van across lanes to get into position for a right turn at the next intersection, onto the Southwest Freeway access road. Unlike Paris, "Metro" in Houston meant buses, not an underground rapid transit system. After a year, she rarely needed to consult a map anymore, but she still didn't know all the little shortcuts and alternate routes for avoiding the stack-ups on Houston's freeways the way Tony did. But then, he was a born and bred native, and at twenty-five had pretty much grown up along with the city. His family had been in Texas a lot longer, in fact, than the first "Texians," men like Sam Houston, Stephen F. Austin, and Mirabeau B. Lamar.

Mari began shifting mental gears, focusing on what she already knew about the government's effort to learn where and how fast the AIDS virus was spreading, to get ready for her next interview. The Centers for Disease Control in Atlanta had a program going to test blood samples for antibodies to the virus in several large teaching hospitals around the country. So far none of them had been named publicly, but that description fit at least two Texas Medical Center affiliates—Hermann Hospital and the University of Texas's M. D. Anderson Hospital and Tumor Institute. And Rachel Widener, the senior lab technician at Hermann, had let slip last week that a representative from CDC was due to be at the central clinical lab today.

"By the way," Mari advised Tony, "let's be sure not to let on that this is anything but a routine call. Wouldn't want Rachel to get into any trouble."

"Gotcha," Tony responded. The warning probably wasn't necessary, since he always played the role of cameraman to the hilt when they were in the field. He rarely uttered a word unless Mari ran into someone who couldn't speak English, which wasn't unusual in a city with a large Hispanic population, many of them illegal aliens fresh from Mexico. But Tony had developed a personal relationship with Rachel in the past few months, and Mari was afraid he might be tempted to say something he wouldn't around anyone else.

"I'm going to 'seize the opportunity' to talk to this guy from Atlanta, who just happens to be there when we make our beat rounds. Sneak up on his blind side and try to get him to tell me what he doesn't intend to." She didn't go in much for ambush interviews, but sometimes it was the only way to get information.

"Yeah?" Tony grinned lazily as he glanced her way, enjoying just the prospect. "Maybe you'd better give me my cues, then, to make sure I've got the camera rolling when he starts spilling his guts." The two of them had developed an almost instinctive rapport and often anticipated each other. He was so good at understanding what she wanted, in fact, and also the relative significance of what her sources were saying, that he did a lot of the editing with his camera, which could save time later at the studio.

"The CDC already has a relationship with the Institute for Immunologic Disorders at the Health Science Center," she explained. "They participated in a previous CDC study aimed at estimating the number of people with AIDS Related Complex. That's on the record and doesn't implicate Rachel or anyone else locally. So that's my lead-in—and your cue."

Tony peeled off the freeway at the Kirby Drive exit, headed south to Holcombe and then turned left, continuing on past the site of Glenn McCarthy's old Shamrock Hotel. A monolithic monument to the tastelessness of the Texas nouveau riche, it had for years been the scene of the glitziest livestock auction in the world, with all the oil, real estate, and cattle barons and their "ladies" arriving in big black Cadillacs, to mill around with the other cattle on the straw-covered ballroom floor, all decked out in their black ties and diamonds. But the Shamrock was gone now, bought and then torn down by the medical center to make way for still more hospitals.

It was a little after one by the time Tony slipped the van into the Hermann Hospital parking garage on Fannin. He spotted Rachel as soon as they walked through the door of the lab, dropped the Sony Betacam and power pack on the floor and began threading his way among the lab benches with the unerring instinct of a homing pigeon. Mari followed more slowly, sauntering through the room with a pretended show of interest in the centrifuges and cell counters, noting the two men she'd never seen before working at one of the benches along the far wall. She also couldn't help noticing how Tony's quite ordinary walk took on a certain bounce, almost a swagger, as he closed on the woman he continued to insist was "just a friend."

"*Buenas dìas, gringa bebê,*" Tony murmured, giving Rachel a smile that suggested she was a great deal more, then stretched himself taller and brushed his lips across her cheek, ending teasingly at the corner of her mouth. "Long time no see."

Mari doubted the truth of that, too, but it was a scene she'd witnessed too many times to waste her breath commenting on. Tony rarely resorted to bravado unless he felt uncomfortable or was trying to hide his real feelings, but when he did it with Rachel, she felt like shaking him until his teeth rattled. Given his ethnic identity, it wasn't difficult to guess that he might feel a little insecure once in a while, since Hispanics in Texas had been called wetbacks, grease-balls, and tamales for at least the past hundred and fifty years. Such overt displays of bigotry were "unfashionable" now, at least in public utterances, but that didn't mean they didn't still exist—only that they had become more subtle.

"Hi," the tall, fiery-haired woman responded with a smile, apparently unperturbed. Rachel was not only a fair-skinned "Anglo," a head taller and ten years older than Tony, but she probably earned at least twice as much as he did. Rachel seemed a unique combination of the intellectual and the sensual, which Mari thought probably scared the hell out of most men, including Tony. Either that or he just couldn't bring himself to believe that Rachel could be seriously interested in him, and so he fell into his adolescent macho routine at times just to show her that he wasn't really serious about her, either.

"How about some coffee?" she asked Tony. "If I can find you a cup that hasn't been used for urine samples." Mari nearly laughed out loud at Rachel's gentle but effective put-down of Tony's little display of Latino ego.

"Listen, Mari, you have to take a look at this instrument we just got in," Rachel began, then lowered her voice and dipped her head in the direction of the two men. "Let's sort of work our way over there—while you," she leaned closer to speak to Tony in a near whisper, "get your equipment ready to shoot, eh, Antonio? Because as the saying goes, 'Macho does not prove mucho,' *mi tamale calurosa.*" Her lips seemed to caress the Spanish word for a very different kind of "hot" tamale, and then she laughed softly as Tony's already ruddy complexion took on an even deeper hue. He didn't respond except to give her a slight nod and then a smile that spoke more of promise than acquiescence.

"We're just starting the clinical trials," Rachel explained as she watched Tony walk away, then commented, "Have you ever wondered how come it took millions of years to make men out of monkeys, yet it takes them only a few minutes to reverse the process?" She threw Mari a crooked grin and turned to the new instrument. "It's called the Vampire, and this little honey is probably going to revolutionize how we treat all kinds of diseases—cardiovascular, diabetes, who knows what else—because it can tell us what is going on in the blood before something happens, rather than after. If we knew that the red cells were beginning to harden or clump together, which can cause a blockage, then we should be able to do something about it before the patient suffers a stroke, for instance." Mari experienced a growing sense of déjà vu while Rachel talked. "It's so simple, it's positively elegant. Here, let me show you," Rachel suggested. "We just suck the blood up into this tube, like this." Three glass syringes were mounted horizontally across the top of the instrument, which was no bigger than a kitchen scale, and as Rachel slowly pulled the plunger out of one, a vertically mounted glass tube filled with blood. "Then we just flip this switch, and everything else is done automatically. You can't see it with the naked eye, but the blood inside that tube is moving up and down. The instrument determines the viscoelasticity of the blood by measuring the pressure drop and the volume of flow."

The word viscoelasticity was a mouthful, even for Rachel, but it had the effect of turning on a light in Mari's memory. Lots of materials were known to exhibit both viscous and elastic behavior, but it was Charles Merrill, a biomedical engineer at the University of Texas, who'd discovered that blood was one of them. "The readings are fed into this IBM PC-AT," Rachel continued, "which analyzes the data, stores it, and then prints it out. Or, if you want, plots the data points and draws the curves, there." She pointed to a small graphics plotter sitting next to the computer, then stood back to let Tony get an unobstructed view with his video camera. "The entire system's under pressure, so when it's finished with that sample, we just draw in de-ionized water to flush the tube in preparation for the next one." Mari watched while Rachel manipulated a different syringe this time, completing the operation.

"Charles Merrill?" she guessed, still not a hundred percent sure. This instrument looked so different from the one she'd seen in Austin six months ago. Rachel gave her an assessing look. "Yes. So you know him, huh? I suppose I shouldn't be surprised, but somehow I am."

"I interviewed him for my artificial heart program," Mari murmured, continuing to stare at the Vampire, remembering Charles Merrill's hands. And his voice. *"You have to look at viscoelasticity as a kind of physical metaphor, because it's really telling us something else. The red cells have to bend and stretch, change their shape in order to get through the smaller vessels and capillaries. So when they're even minimally harder than normal—as in sickle-cell anemia and diabetes, for instance—that causes real problems. Hardened cells also cause an increase in the viscoelasticity of the blood. Think of it in terms of a spring—a stiff one packs more wallop when it uncoils than a soft one."*

"A pretty interesting guy, don't you think?" Rachel asked, interrupting Mari's wandering thoughts. "Even his impressive knowledge of the field doesn't seem to bias him, just means he makes better guesses. He's open as a child. A natural experimenter. Nothing's too sacred or too far out to question!" She rolled her eyes suggestively, then lowered her voice. "An endangered species, in my book. Makes you wonder if he could possibly be like that outside the lab, doesn't it?"

Mari nodded absently, smiling as she remembered Charles Merrill's dark eyes. "Easy to talk to, too. Approachable, not stuck on himself, like so many." She turned and looked straight at Rachel with one eyebrow cocked. "I used to think it was just this profession. You know, the physician-god syndrome. Now I'm not so sure anymore." She glanced around at Tony, who was standing about ten feet away, behind the minicam, and eyed him up and down in a way he couldn't miss. "It seems to be more contagious than I thought."

Tony grinned, knowing she was ribbing him, letting him know she thought he'd acted the fool. But he'd learned too much since he started working with Mari, and not just about where and how to get information, to take offense. Truth be told, he admired the way she'd managed to slip it in, so smooth he hadn't even realized it was coming.

Mari was already thinking ahead, more interested now in Charles Merrill's Vampire than the limited information the man from Atlanta would or could give her. "What's he looking for in the clinical tests?"

"Correlations, between the viscoelasticity values and specific disease conditions," Rachel replied. "It's also being tested in two other hospitals, one in West Germany and the other in Sweden." She dipped her head in the direction of the two men who were now only a few feet away. "Should we move on?"

"Sure, just a second." Mari stepped over to speak to Tony. "Tag that Merrill and enter it into my futures file when we get back."

By the time Tony switched cassettes and was ready to shoot again, Mari was discussing the Centers for Disease Control–U.T. research with the man from Atlanta. It seemed perfectly natural for Tony to just keep shooting when she began to slant her questions in a different direction. "Dr. Levine, some sources estimate the number of Americans already carrying the AIDS virus at around a million and a half. Do you really think your sample of 163 patients, which produced a much lower estimate—around 300,000 as I recall—was large enough to be valid?"

"Well, I'd have to say yes and no. Depends on what you mean. It was a valid study, but it didn't have enough power—the margin of error was too large, you might say—to extrapolate what we found to the entire population. On the other hand, it was only intended to be a pilot study. With the average time between infection and diagnosis of AIDS thought to be five to ten or more years, knowing the extent of infection now will tell us what we may be facing down the line. That's why we've embarked on this new study, which also will provide a history of where and how fast the virus has spread."

"So these frozen blood samples you're testing here today, Dr. Levine, are part of the new nationwide study the Centers for Disease Control has under way to uncover just how far the AIDS virus has spread?" Tony hid a smile of admiration behind his eyepiece as he listened to her sink the harpoon. "Perhaps you could explain, for the benefit of our viewers, what procedures you're using to select these specimens, which I understand guarantee the anonymity of donors."

Mari had learned from experience to listen closely to the way her sources answered questions, because that, more than any other single thing, told her how reliable the information was. Most real scientists found it difficult to carry off a bald-faced lie when presented a direct question, and Dr. Levine sounded to her like a man who'd been socialized in the folkways of traditional science. So-called "pure" scientists rarely used personal pronouns, especially "I." They tended to qualify everything and were difficult to pin down, because to them nothing was ever really finished. At least not in the sense of knowing all there was to know about it. The research entrepreneurs, on the other hand, were really administrators rather than scientists, though they often carried the most impressive scientific titles. Like technocrats, they knew how to take personal credit for everything in sight, and were full of grand schemes and sweeping statements, but they didn't actually "do science" themselves. As a result, she felt compelled to verify everything they gave her, which took time she often didn't have before a broadcast. Medical doctors weren't true scientists by either education or instincts, in her opinion, despite the fact that they now were using some quite sophisticated technologies. They tended to be both secretive and elitist, characteristics that were inimical to scientific inquiry. The fact that Dr. Levine was using his own two hands to do a blood test suggested that he was probably a doctor of microbiology, not medicine.

"Well." Dr. Levine drawled it out slowly, his only show of hesitation. "In this laboratory, for instance, technicians have been freezing specimens from blood samples already drawn for other medical purposes, that normally would be discarded. Labeling them with the age, race, and sex of the patient. No names, nothing to identify whose patients they are. And once a month, in each of about twenty hospitals around the country like this one, a representative group of these specimens are tested. A statistically random sample of three hundred."

"Which means that you can't inform anyone if they do, indeed, carry the virus, isn't that so?" Mari injected.

"Yes, of course, because at that point we don't know whose blood we're testing, as I explained. There's really no practical alternative to doing this kind of study anonymously."

Mari probed a little more, but couldn't get anything about the results of the CDC study so far, which she really hadn't expected. She signaled Tony to switch off and begin folding up, while she thanked Dr. Levine. Instead he turned and walked toward Rachel, rolling up his shirt-sleeve as he went. Mari decided to stay and talk with Dr. Levine a minute longer when she saw Tony sit down on a tall stool and lay his arm out on the bench where Rachel was working. It was the third time she'd seen him do the same thing in the past two or three months, and though he never talked about it, she thought she knew what was going on, and why.

Without exchanging even one word, Rachel knotted a rubber tourniquet above his elbow, rubbed the inside of his arm with cotton, and then picked up a syringe. Tony's eyes stayed on her face while she inserted the needle, drew his blood into the syringe and then released the tourniquet, all so quickly done, it would be obvious to anyone that she was a highly practiced technician. His lips moved briefly while he touched Rachel's cheek with one hand, just before he jumped off the stool and started back toward his camera. Mari joined him, waiting for him to disconnect the power cord and fold up the tripod, which he handed to her to carry as they started for the door.

"See you next week, Rachel, if not before," Mari called to Rachel with a wave.

"Before," Tony said. "Much before. Seven?" he asked as he looked across the room at Rachel with a slow smile, which she returned, nodding at the same time.

"Whenever."

"We've got to start thinking like swimmers—shave our heads, in effect—to get every fraction of a point we can," Jack was saying as Mari walked into his office. He nodded to acknowledge her, but kept on talking. "Because sometimes that's all it takes to win." She noticed right away that Ron wasn't there, only Ted Calvacca, Podge Pearsall, and Lamar Kelso, the assistant news director. "I intend to beat the shit out of 'em in the May sweeps, because you better believe it, the network is going to be looking hard at their own. For where the profits are and where they aren't." Jack pulled hard on his cigarette, then swallowed the smoke. Mari watched, waiting, but none of it leaked back out. "Times are tough and getting tougher, and I'm not talking oil. I'm talking on-air television. So we're going to see to it we're the shiniest apple in the network's eye. And between now and then we're going to take the local market at six! Or else somebody's ass is going into the meat grinder."

Mari found it difficult to keep her mind from wandering whenever she had to listen to Jack for long. He was so predictable once you knew what fueled his engine—getting Jack Lunsford into the "big league," which meant network headquarters in New York. Her eyes wandered, too, over the framed photos covering the wall behind his desk, of Jack with his "good friend" Walter Cronkite, and a group shot with Jack standing next to the mayor, who was instantly recognizable even at this distance by her oversize glasses, man-tailored suit, and floppy bow tie. Was it because Dustin Hoffman used her as the model for "Tootsie" that she'd so drastically changed her appearance, switching to stylishly short hair and contact lenses? There had to be nearly a dozen shots of Bill Clements, the mean-mouthed nasty who'd become the state's first Republican governor in a hundred years, a "high roller" from Dallas, Jack's home-town. Defeated at the end of one term in spite of Ronald Reagan's coattails, Clements had returned four years later, when the Texas economy was no longer so hot, and—master of malaprop that he was—loudly proclaimed in his inaugural address that "the people of Texas want us to secede." His first official act had been to cancel a telephone hotline for runaway teenagers, which employed all of four people who took two hundred calls a day from troubled kids, even though it operated with federal funds. The second was to cut the state's AFDC payments to impoverished single mothers, which already were the third lowest in the nation. Bully Bill was, as Jack was fond of saying, "all heart, and one helluva grand guy!"

"We're going to review every goddamn second we're on air, see where we can beef it up, and that includes you, too, Mari. Can't have you getting overconfident, can we, just 'cause all those pill pushers down at the med center keep calling the station to say what a wonderful job you're doing?"

"As I recall, the last time you had me in here it was because you were getting complaints about 'that flaming feminist' and my biased reports." One corner of her mouth turned up a little. "That, and how I'd taken thirty minutes of some bigwig's time and then never showed his mug on camera."

"Yeah, well, we get a few of those, too. But like I told Ron, we're going over the top in this market or else. And we've got only one month to do whatever that takes. Most of the medics don't have time to watch television, anyway, which means what they think doesn't add up to shit when it comes to ratings." He took another drag on his cigarette, then glanced at her rundown for tonight. "Okay, let's have the details. But I have to warn you, there's a pisser of a story coming just ahead of you that's going to be one helluva tough act to follow." His grin was one of unadulterated pleasure.

The station's six o'clock newscast, which followed the network evening news, began with a twenty-minute round-up of local and national news, followed by two and a half minutes of weather, then three of sports. On Mondays, Wednesdays, and Fridays the final four minutes of the news were hers, a separate segment billed as "Health News with Mari McNichols." She covered breaking stories no matter what day it was, but they were integrated into the regular newscast on her "off" days. Jack was still chuckling and shaking his head when Podge started describing the news wrap for the night.

"Dave put together a package on the big gala last night, to raise funds for the ACLU fight against on-the-job drug testing. The Urine Defense Fund. We've got shots of people in costume, the MC with his zipper duck-taped, promising the crowd the show will go on into the wee wee hours, stuff like that. A bunch of music groups, one doing 'Mellow Yellow,' and the Uranium Savages, who changed their name to the Urine Savages, introducing their lead singer as Piss Pistofferson." Podge was as fair-skinned as she was, and his face was getting redder with each word. "And a bite of him singing 'Urine the Money,'" he finished apologetically.

21

"Sounds absolutely fascinating," Mari agreed with a crooked smile. "I can hardly wait to see it. It looks like I've got four segments tonight. At the top is the confirmation I just got that the U.T. Health Science Center is taking part in the CDC blood-testing program. Next is a bite from the AP wire on the just-released report on AMA-affiliated political-action committees."

Jack waved one arm in a dismissive gesture. "So what? Who really cares? Sounds like a real dozer to me."

There were times when Mari had to work hard at remembering what had really enticed her away from Denver: the freedom to cover the political stories she thought could have an impact on the medical profession and the way health care was delivered to the public, something she'd wanted a lot more than the increase in salary Jack had offered her. "So it turns out that the Texas committee is the second biggest contributor in the country, with half the contributions to state legislative candidates coming from the Texas Medical Association PAC," Mari answered. "And those same legislators are sitting up in Austin right now, deciding who can practice medicine in this state, whether midwives can deliver babies for poor families, and whether your insurance will pick up the tab if you go to a psychologist instead of a psychiatrist."

"Okay, but keep it short. And let viewers know up front what's coming down the line, which I hope is a helluva lot juicier than that one, or they'll be flipping the dial like crazy. Haven't you got anything sexier than those two?"

"Next one is about RU-486, the new morning-after birth control drug that's just gone on the market in France, with a sound bite from the wire plus one from a local gynecologist."

"Yeah, okay. Hey listen, that reminds me of a good one I just heard. You guys know what you call a Mexican who's had a vasectomy?" Jack grinned, waiting as if he actually thought one of them would make a guess. "A dry Martinez!" He laughed out loud, leaning back in his swivel chair, then glanced pointedly at Mari. "Remind me to tell that one to Tony some time." She just stared at him for a second, knowing that sarcasm was too subtle for Jack, then looked back at her notes.

"You're going to like this one. A Port Arthur woman let her physician spank her for two months as part of his pain research project, then made it all better afterward with sexual intercourse." Jack roared this time, and the other three men joined in. "Where the hell did you get that one?" Ted asked finally, still grinning.

"Seems he was late paying his bills. Promised her $2500 for participating in his 'research,' the woman said. So after two months of spankings and no dough, she called me. Said she'd already been to the police but they just laughed at her. She'd seen me on television and thought maybe I'd know how she could collect what he owed her."

"And?" Podge urged when she paused.

"I suggested she report him to the state Board of Medical Examiners. Gave her a name and number to call in Austin. A hearing officer is planning to recommend that they revoke the physician's license. Seems it was already suspended once before, five years ago, in Louisiana."

"Hey, what do you guys think about doing an advice program?" Jack asked suddenly, already enthused about the idea. "There must be thousands of people in our audience like that woman. Hell, newspapers do it all the time—what's the name of that guy in the *Post?*"

"Uh-uh," Mari injected before Jack could get too carried away. "That's asking for trouble, because people always want to know what to do about this ache or that sniffle. I'm not a medical doctor, so if I say anything except 'consult your physician,' I could be accused of practicing medicine without a license."

"Yeah, I suppose so. Why not get some doctor to answer their questions, then? A guy with a different specialty every week or something. You've got lots of contacts. Good advertising for them, ratings for us." He looked at them, waiting for some response, but no one had any words of encouragement. "Well, give it some thought anyway. In the meantime, what about a Saturday-night special, say a half hour, about what sex therapists do and how they do it? Let everybody in on a few of their secrets. And I'm not talking Dr. Ruth. I mean good-lookers, sexy, somebody viewers could see themselves getting it on with. Maybe run it right after the ten o'clock news, give them a few helpful hints just

23

before they jump into bed." The more Jack talked, the better he seemed to like the idea.

"Well . . . I . . ." Mari wasn't sure how to say what she thought. It was Jack's reason for doing the program that she objected to, and the sexual-fantasy approach he was talking about, not the subject itself.

"We could even shave it down to twenty minutes if it sells big. Hot damn, I bet it would attract billings like bees to honey!" He began flipping the pages on his desk calendar, thinking out loud. "Let's see. This is Wednesday. I want rough budget on my desk first thing Monday morning. And keep it tight, dammit!" When he looked up, it was obvious that he was speaking to all of them, not just Mari.

Mari watched the monitor mounted on the camcorder Tony had pointed at her, waiting for the signal for her wrap. She was vaguely conscious of the adrenaline letdown that always came toward the end of a broadcast. Like most stage performers, she was "up" at the beginning, then like a runner getting second wind, settled back to a level where she could go on indefinitely until she headed into the final segment, which somehow seemed to automatically switch off the hormones. As the last package wound down, she heard and saw herself on the monitor, talking about the big increase in hysterectomies, "the second most frequently performed surgery in the United States." Then she was asking Dr. Barbara Amaral what she thought about removing the healthy reproductive organs of all women at a certain age to prevent the development of cancer in the uterus and ovaries, an idea that was again being debated by gynecologists.

"Since the death rate from uterine cancer is lower than the mortality rate from hysterectomy, I hardly see how that idea has any merit at all," the young physician answered. "But if it did"—a soft smile appeared on her face now— "then we also should remove the prostrate gland of all males between forty and fifty, whether that leaves half of them impotent or not, because the same reasoning applies." Mari grinned, enjoying the doctor's response as much the third time as when she'd first heard it. Barbara Amaral was a maverick—Hispanic, young, bright, and beautiful—and she was taking on the Anglo-male medical establishment with a vengeance.

Mari caught the "live" signal from Tony and moved into her last "stand upper." Finally, she turned to Harley Caligan, Channel Five's weatherman, who led into the commercial break with the announcement that a thunderstorm was moving into the Houston area. As soon as the commercial hit the monitor, she unclipped her mike and moved away from the desk, leaving it to him. Her eyes were just getting adjusted to the dark behind the cameras when she glanced toward the door of the studio and saw Sandy, waving an arm to try to get her attention.

"Phone!" Sandy mouthed. Mari hurried toward her, wondering if it might be the Pharmacol whistle blower again, then followed her through the door. "Overseas operator," Sandy explained as they both started down the hall. "She's been holding awhile."

"Who's calling, did she say?"

Sandy just shrugged. "Couldn't understand her very well, but I think it's some kind of an emergency."

Now that she was outside the sound-insulated studio, Mari could hear Harley's thunderstorm, and as she entered her office, a flash of light exploded inside the dark room, lighting her way to the desk. An instant later a furious crack of thunder shook the glass in the window, then began to slink away in a long, low rumble, like a hound with his tail between his legs. She sank down into her desk chair and picked up the phone at the same time. "Mari McNichols." She waited a second. "Hello?"

"Is this Mrs. Ashmore speaking?" The female voice was distorted by distance, or perhaps electrical interference, but that didn't lessen the shock Mari felt, like an unexpected slap in the face, at hearing the name she hadn't used for almost ten years. Nobody here knew. Except Sandy. And that was only because she was the one who'd taken calls from—of course, that's who it had to be! "Yes, I'm Marilyn Ashmore," she answered quickly.

"One minute, please." It seemed a lot longer than that to Mari as she waited, hearing nothing but the blood roaring in her ears and the soft, steady drum of rain against the window behind her.

"This is Dr. Francisco Ibarzábal, in Torremolinos, Spain. Is this Mrs. Ashmore, please?" The words were soft, and accented.

"Yes. What's—"

"I am attending your mother, Mrs. Ashmore. She is quite ill, I am sorry to say."

Mari had to fight the urge to say he was wrong, to tell him about the postcard, just yesterday, from Portugal. "What happened?" she asked instead.

"She has the pulmonary edema. Fluid in the lungs. You understand?"

"Yes, but—"

"She should see a doctor sooner, I think, but I do not know all. One of her traveling companions say she has not been well for a week, that she is always very tired. I know this from the director of the tour group, who brought her to me two days ago, when they arrive in Torremolinos."

"You think she's been in heart failure for some time, then?" Mari asked as she reached for the switch on her flex-arm desk lamp and pulled it closer, subconsciously trying to shed more light on what he was saying. A cone of bright light flooded the light gray surface, pulling her eyelids tight in protest. She didn't need to be told that fluid in the lungs was the result of damage to the heart muscle, probably from a myocardial infarction, but she listened anyway, until she felt like screaming with frustration at how long he was taking to get to the point.

"That does not mean the heart stops, of course. Only the beat is not strong, so it does not do its work well. The beat also is irregular. But your mother, she say she cannot keep food for several days, even before I see her."

"You mean she's nauseated?" Mari asked. "But what could be causing that?"

"I cannot tell. We give her medication to reduce the amount of fluid her heart must pump, and to strengthen the beat, too, but—well, she does not respond well. But we have her in intensive care and are monitoring all things very carefully." He hesitated for a second, as if unsure what to say next. "So I thought to ask that someone from the family should be here. You can come?"

"I'll be on the next flight out of New York. But I doubt if

26

there is one before tomorrow night. Most flights to Europe leave New York early in the evening and arrive in the morning your time." March was off-season, so she shouldn't have any trouble getting a reservation. Her mind skipped ahead while he was giving her the name and address of the hospital, spelling out some of the words for her. It wasn't exactly the best time for her to be away, but not the worst either. Jack's special on sex therapists could wait, or else someone else could do it. She smiled slightly at that thought. Tony could edit the segments they'd already taped for Friday, and she'd probably have time to script them in the morning. Either Tony or Ron could read the bridges between sound bites, and with her gone, they'd probably integrate the stories into the regular newscast anyway. She wondered for an instant if it might be possible for Jackie to go instead, then realized it was mid-semester and dismissed the idea as quickly as it had come. But she'd have to call her.

What time was it right now in Spain? She glanced at her watch, then added six or seven hours, which made it twelve or one at night! "Isn't it late for you to be at the hospital, Dr. Ibarzábal?" she asked quickly, stumbling over the pronunciation of his name. It sounded odd even for a Spanish name.

"Yes. The nurse call me, because her blood pressure drops so low," he explained, answering her unasked question.

"Maybe it will help if she knows I'm coming. Can you tell her I'll be there soon? In another thirty hours or so. Sooner, if I can."

"Yes, of course," he murmured.

"And tell her I said to, to hold on till—no, I mean—"

"I will just say you are on your way, Mrs. Ashmore, and will be here very soon. We will do our best, but—you understand that she is very weak?"

"Yes," Mari whispered, nodding her head even though she knew he couldn't see her. "Well, I'll see you in a day or so, then."

She listened to his softly accented good-bye, then lowered the receiver and switched off the offending light. And simply sat there, letting his words really sink in, understanding at last what he'd really been trying to say.

He thought her mother was dying.

CHAPTER

2

Charles Merrill slid his overnighter under the seat, then reached up and shoved his briefcase into the overhead compartment before settling into the aisle seat with a sigh of relief. He fastened his seat belt while he glanced out the tiny opening to his right, past the turned-away face of the woman occupying the window seat, and saw that the plane was already moving away from the terminal. Running late was a way of life with him, but this was one time it had paid off, because he sure as hell wouldn't've made the flight if he'd had time in Austin to check his bag through. A flight attendant started down the aisle with her head on a swivel, making a quick check of passenger seat belts. Only half the seats looked to be occupied, probably because it was between seasons. Too late for the ski crowd and too early for the beach flies.

The big plane slowed, then pivoted slowly as it moved into position on the runway and stopped. A hushed expectancy settled over the cabin while they waited for clearance. And then, finally, the steady drone of the engines began to crescendo, rising in pitch until they were screaming for release. At last the big 747 began to lumber down the runway, quickly gaining speed until the occasional buildings on the ground blurred into a streak of color. He felt an

28

almost imperceptible instant of hesitation, followed by a sudden buoyancy as the flaps finally produced enough lift to overcome the force of gravity, and then they were airborne. The floor of the cabin tilted up at a steep angle and the lights of New York began to drop away. Within seconds he felt the wheels retract, jarring an otherwise perfectly smooth ascent as they snuggled into place, and then heard the No Smoking light ping off. He waited a couple more minutes, until the seat-belt sign went off, too, then got up from his seat to go do what he hadn't had time for in the terminal, before everybody else had the same idea.

As he neared the tail of the plane, a woman slipped into the aisle right in front of him and he had to slow his stride to avoid colliding with her. "Woman driver," he mouthed silently, though he couldn't help noticing the way her trousers shaped a very neat little rear end before she disappeared behind one of the tiny lavatory doors a few feet away. But when he reached for the handle of the door opposite and found that it was occupied as well, an audible "damn" escaped his lips.

Mari had no more than squeezed around the edge of the door and locked it behind her than she realized this was going to take real ingenuity. For maybe the tenth time today she wondered where her brain had been this morning when she was deciding what to wear. Because she was going to have to wrestle with her jumpsuit again, peel off the top and push the whole thing down below her hips while trying to keep it from dragging all over the floor—but this time she'd have to go through all those contortions inside a box built to accommodate a midget. She remembered worrying about what would get her through the weather in Houston, and New York and then Spain, even though she really didn't know what to expect there. Denim blue might be a seasonless color and the elasticized waist comfortable on a long flight, but it would have to be one cold day in hell before she'd ever put the damn thing on again! It was a strangely comforting thought, probably because it was the only thing she did feel sure about right now. She slid the zipper down and began to extract first one arm and then the other from the long sleeves, taking great pleasure in swearing quietly while wondering if she could survive if she didn't drink anything between now and Madrid. Then, without any warning at all, the plane lurched and she had to reach out and brace one hand against the wall to keep from being toppled off the seat. And the top of her jumpsuit, which she'd draped so carefully over her arm, fell to the floor.

Just when she was in the middle of doing everything all over again, this time in reverse, she caught a glimpse of herself in the mirror mounted over the tiny washbasin and broke up in giggles. *I should have run away to the circus. I could have been the rubber lady in the sideshow.* The thought was quickly followed by one that wasn't very funny—*then you and Dad wouldn't have had to stand by and be disappointed, over and over again*—which was the kind of game her mind had been playing all day. She pulled up the zipper and adjusted her collar, examined her eyes in the mirror while washing her hands, then pulled a couple of tissues from the dispenser and stuffed them into her purse, just for insurance, before digging for her comb and lipstick. Satisfied at last that the outside didn't look nearly as bad as she felt on the inside, she turned around and squeezed back against the sink, trying to make room to open the door. With one quick glance back at herself in the mirror, she started through the door. And ran smack into the man standing just outside.

He looked as startled as she was for a second, until his dark eyes lightened with recognition. "Mari! Well, I'll be damned!"

Surprise took Mari's tongue, and all she could do was stare at the familiar face in disbelief. "Dr. Merrill?" she stammered finally, still not quite ready to trust her eyes.

"Charles, remember?" He stood there smiling. She nodded, mute with disorientation and confusion, wondering again whether she might wake up to find that none of this was real. And then how Charles Merrill had managed to get a tan like that so early in the year. "Hey, this is great! It's good to see you. What are you up to in Madrid? Work or vacation? Are you alone?"

She nodded yes to his last question, returning his smile. "And you?" When he nodded, too, she took the plunge. "Then how about joining me for dinner?" Would he think she was being pushy? "I've got the entire row to myself, and I'd love to hear what you've been working on since I talked to you last." She felt the heat beginning to well in her neck and face. Maybe she *was* being pushy, or at least presumptive, but Charles Merrill was one of the most interesting men she'd ever met. Or was it his work? And she didn't know how she was going to make it through the next few hours.

"Sure, I'd like that," Charles answered immediately. "Been wanting to talk to you, meaning to get in touch ever since I saw the program, in fact. No sense in standing here, then, is there? Where are you sitting?" He sounded positively eager. Mari pointed to her seat, just a few rows away. "Okay, be there in just a minute."

It seemed more like a couple of weeks than seven months since she'd interviewed him for her program on artificial hearts, she thought as she refastened her seat belt, then loosened it. And time had proven Charles Merrill right on several counts. For one, the Jarvik heart itself, the pump, was causing clots and strokes in all the recipients. All, that is, except the last one, who had died of undetected internal bleeding because William DeVries and his team had turned into fumbling plumbers, even removing part of the man's sternum in their effort to fit the metal and plastic device into a chest cavity that wasn't big enough to take it.

"So what have you got going in Madrid?" Charles began, even before he settled into the aisle seat, leaving the one between them empty. "Hot on the trail of another story?" Mari watched his right hand grasp the arm of the seat when he sat down, then lift in a slow, graceful arc and turn palm up, pointing to her camera and tape recorder, which she'd forgotten were in the seat next to her.

"Oh—uh, no, not really. Just habit, I guess. Never leave home without them." She smiled apologetically.

"I see you've still got the Nikon, but the Sony's new, right? One of the new digital units?" She nodded, amazed that he'd remember the equipment she had with her in Austin. "How do you like it?"

She almost laughed with pleasure, recognizing his way of getting right to the heart of what interested him most without giving offense. "No comparison, really," she replied. "We've converted to the Mitsushita half-inch tape system at the studio, so things are better than they were. It's expensive, but doesn't stretch, which means no more stuck tape or wobbly sound. But the old tape technology's already dead, in my opinion. Just that little unit there gets me studio quality sound in the field."

"Mind if I take a look?" Charles asked, waiting for her nod before he picked up the Sony to examine it. Again she watched the way his hands moved, as fascinated now as the first time she'd noticed them. The cassette in the recorder happened to be blank, but she wouldn't have been worried even if it weren't. Charles Merrill's hands moved with the kind of deliberateness that said he never "fooled around" with any piece of equipment. "Neat," he agreed after he'd looked it over, then set the recorder back on the seat and looked over at her. "Not after a story, huh? Vacation?" The question brought her back to earth too suddenly.

"Actually, I'm going on to Torremolinos. How about you?"

"Microcirculation conference in Madrid. Starts tomorrow." It wasn't like her to be evasive. He glanced at her again, trying to assess what else was different about her. Maybe her hair. Still the same odd gray-blond color, which had to be natural judging by the fair skin that gave away so much about what was happening inside her head. It was shorter and fell free now, perfectly straight and shiny smooth until it curved inward at the line of her jaw, instead of being pulled back and fastened in a kind of knot. But it was more than her hair. She seemed oddly subdued, her eyes almost sad except when she smiled. And that was the other thing he remembered so well about her: the way her smile reached her eyes. What he remembered best, though, was the enthusiasm that seemed to just bubble up and out naturally, as if coming from some deep and limitless well. And the questions, every one of them cutting right to the point, keeping him on his toes. She seemed an unusual mixture, or maybe he noticed things in her that he hadn't in other women because she was playing in his ball park, and most of the females on the field sure as hell didn't look much like this one! He almost smiled at that, recognizing it as the understatement of the year. He guessed she was somewhere near thirty, give or take a couple of years, and she still wasn't wearing a wedding ring, though that didn't say a helluva whole lot, not with all the couples he knew who were living together, some just trying it out and others in apparently long-term arrangements.

"I sure am glad you ran into me." He grinned the words. "You know, until I saw the program credits, I didn't even know you spelled your name with an I instead of a Y." He remembered that particularly, because it had somehow struck a false note, like Luci instead of Lucy, and he hadn't figured her to be that type, in spite of the fact that she was involved in television. "I've been meaning to write you a note or call, ever since it showed, but somehow——"

"That's okay." Mari cut him short. She didn't want to hear any of the usual complaints from someone she liked to think of as different from the rest of the herd. Like most people, the doctors at the medical center simply weren't aware of how often they didn't complete a thought or a sentence, or how much time they wasted beating around the bush instead of answering a question. It was different with newspaper reporting, because you could correct the grammar or punctuation in a quote without changing the meaning, and still keep your source from sounding like an idiot. Not correcting the little errors everyone made in speaking, in fact, could make even a Phi Beta Kappa sound like an uneducated jerk in print. And she'd seen reporters do just that, intentionally.

"But I thought it was great, from beginning to end, the whole program. The way you kept it moving along conveyed the drama—suspense, I suppose you'd call it in that kind of situation. And it was jam-packed with good, solid information. I can't speak for anyone else, but you came out squeaky clean on my stuff. No strikes, no errors, no foul balls. And I know damn well how tough it can be to get some of that basic stuff across, even to most of my medical colleagues. If it doesn't tell you what pill to prescribe, who needs it, right?" He grinned as he said the last few words, expecting her to know exactly what he meant, and knew he was right when he saw her blue eyes light up with humor.

His comment reminded Mari that Charles Merrill held degrees in physics and engineering, not medicine. "What do you mean, no strikes, no errors, no foul balls?" she asked, wondering if he'd expected her to do something unethical, or perhaps blatantly sensational.

"Well, for one thing, you didn't quote me as saying anything I didn't. You'd probably be surprised at how unusual that is. Newspaper reporters are bad enough, but commercial television is—well, usually pretty awful." This time it was his smile that was apologetic. "Just about impossible, really, when it comes to almost anything to do with science. They either cut it short or else simplify until whatever you've told them gets all screwed up. And every time that happens to me, I swear I'm never going to talk to another reporter. Then I forget until the next time. Guess I'm just a publicity hound."

"Charles Merrill a 'grandstander'? Never!" She couldn't help laughing as she recalled his pithy remark about researchers who use press conferences to announce a new piece of data, "even though they don't know yet whether it's worth a shit or not." It was one of the statements she'd had to edit out.

He laughed, too, recognizing his own words. "I have to admit I did sort of worry about that afterward, thought you just might use it to liven things up a bit. How come you didn't?" He couldn't even guess at her academic background, but since seeing just that one program, he knew she was damned good at what she did. A different breed than any reporter he'd ever run into before.

"Your language was a little, uh . . . earthy, shall we say? Not that plain talk can't add punch to a piece, but I needed your research to shine in this particular case, not your flamboyant personality!" Charles watched one corner of her mouth curve up in a half-remembered crooked smile.

He'd noticed a couple of flight attendants working their way down the aisle with the drink trolley while they were talking, and now they were only a couple of rows away. "How about a drink before dinner? Or some wine?" Just asking caused him to remember something else—how she'd cut him off with a curt, non-negotiable, "No thanks, I always

34

pay my own way," that day in Austin when he'd tried to pick up the tab for her lunch.

Mari's first impulse was to say no, because of the problem with her jumpsuit, but instead she decided to throw caution to the winds. "Do you think they would have any Spanish wine?"

"On Iberia? You've got to be kidding," he chided gently. "Red or white?"

"White. I've been all over Europe, but never to Spain, wouldn't you know it? And now—well, I sure wish we were landing in Paris instead." Her voice broke suddenly and she looked away from him, studying her hands.

Charles watched her hair sweep forward, hiding her face. Had he just imagined the panic in her eyes? "Why, you speak French?"

Her hair swung back in one languorous, undulating wave as she glanced up again and then nodded.

He gave the attendant their order and then reached over to let down the tray table on the back of the seat between them. Mari watched the attendant's deft movements as she pulled the corks from two small green bottles, tipped a plastic glass over the neck of each one and then handed them to Charles, who held up a bill in exchange. He turned back to Mari, rewarding her with an infectious smile as he filled first her glass and then his own, simply because she hadn't made even the slightest move toward her purse, which was wedged into the seat beside her.

"How come you wouldn't let me buy your lunch in Austin?" he asked, knowing as soon as he said it that he probably was probing into something personal. But the habit of going after the answers he needed was strong in him, and it came out naturally, without premeditation.

Mari wondered if she'd heard him right at first, before it dawned on her that he meant why now and not then. And the incongruity of it—of this high-powered, big-reputation scientist asking such a silly, inconsequential question—hit her funny bone, and she had to take a couple of quick sips of wine to help squelch the impulse to giggle again.

"Because I never let myself get into hock when I'm working. Not to anybody," she answered honestly, forcing herself to a soberness she found difficult to sustain. "I just can't afford to get into that kind of position with someone I'm interviewing."

"Oh? What kind of position is that?" One eyebrow went up slightly, and humor was beginning to lighten his dark eyes again.

"Beholden. As if we have a special relationship of some kind. You know, where you might assume that I owed you something, whether you realized it consciously or not. Anyway, why should you pay for my lunch instead of me paying for yours in that particular situation, except for some outmoded social habit having to do with sex?" Realization of what she'd inadvertently said dawned almost as soon as the word was out, and she hastened to correct herself. "I mean gender."

"And now?" His question hung between them, pregnant with expectation.

"Now is different because I'm not working with you."

Charles waited, hoping for more, then pushed a little harder. "You meeting someone on the Costa del Sol?" He'd spent most of a day with her once before, and had come away with a renewed sense of purpose and enthusiasm for his work, as if hers had been contagious. He was discovering that Mari McNichols was both the same and different from the woman he remembered. Even then he'd been attracted enough to want to see her again, but somehow he'd never managed to find the time. And now he had the uneasy feeling that maybe he'd let something important slip away, something he couldn't even put a name to.

"Yes and no. My mother is ill," she answered quickly, then took another sip of her wine. Again Charles waited, but instead of telling him more, she switched subjects. "And I suppose you're reporting on your latest research in Madrid, something to do with capillary flow?" Her lips curved up in an encouraging smile, which pulled a fan of fine lines at the corners of her eyes. "Well, come on, aren't you going to tell me about it? Or are you keeping it under wraps until the news conference?" Her eyes flashed with mischief.

Charles shook his head, bemused, then capitulated. "Okay, but first I've got a confession to make." Mari stared at his hands as he talked, at the long straight fingers tipped by slightly squared-off nails moving with a coordination that spoke of deliberateness and control, watching him tip up the little green bottle to refill her glass. He crossed a leg toward the aisle and draped one hand over the curve of his thigh before looking over at her again. "I've been using your analogies—shamelessly I'm afraid—without even giving you credit. Especially the Velcro and yogurt. I get instant understanding now, the minute I mention yogurt. How'd you know it was thixotropic—what in the world ever made you think of it?"

Mari realized she was staring at his full lower lip, and knew, just from the sensation of heat she could feel spreading from her chest up into her neck and cheeks, that her genes were betraying her again. Charles was talking about yogurt, and here she was trying to keep her eyes from sneaking a peek at his shoes! His hands were the swami's pipe to her cobralike gaze, and they more than passed her test. She knew lots of other women who felt the same way about a man's hands. They either turned you on or were a turn-off. But shoes were something else! Not that she was actually "turned on" by them. It was just that she'd never run into a man with scuffed up shoes who she found the least bit interesting sexually. And she didn't have the foggiest recollection of Charles Merrill's shoes! Then, while her mind was still scrambling to find the answer to his question, Charles shifted in his seat, this time crossing one leg in the other direction, toward her. She caught a quick glimpse of warm mahogany leather, burnished to a soft satiny shine by repeated buffing.

Mari relaxed and threw him a smugly satisfied smile. "I guess because I like yogurt with fruit on the bottom, which is thick when you first open it but gets thinner as you stir it—just like blood," she answered. "I'm always dripping it down the front of me, so I figured I couldn't be the only one who'd notice how it changes."

He nodded sagely, pretending to consider seriously every word she uttered, though actually he was watching her mouth and her constantly changing face and eyes, animated by a life force he knew all about in clinical terms. It didn't prepare him one damn bit for what he was seeing, or feeling. Her skin was so fair, it flushed easily and often, allowing him to read more into her words than she probably realized. And every once in a while, without any warning whatsoever, something in her eyes seemed to flash out and touch him, and they'd laugh together or maybe just nod understandingly at something only the two of them shared.

"When you came out with, 'Blood is a complex material,'" Mari continued, trying to imitate his voice, "'at one time behaving like a thin liquid and another almost like a solid,' I could just see my viewers' eyes starting to glaze over. I think people ought to hear the big words, get familiar with them, but you didn't really expect me to let 'thixotropic' just lie there and die, did you?"

Charles started to laugh even before she finished, partly because she stumbled over "thixotropic," but also because he liked her unpretentious explanation. He'd listened to too many boring lectures himself to take offense at the way she teased him about big words and dry statements. But her direct answer also reminded him of her earlier response, when he'd asked why she wouldn't let him buy her lunch in Austin, and her admission that things were different now. "You really are good at what you do, Mari, you know that?"

If a thing is worth doing at all it's worth doing well! One of her mother's favorite truisms popped to mind without warning, unbidden and unwelcome. "Thanks," she muttered, almost under her breath, embarrassed.

"How about some more wine to go with dinner? They're already serving up front, so it shouldn't take long for them to get back here."

"No thanks, but you go ahead. I can't afford a headache on top of everything else." It just slipped out, before she realized she was even thinking it, but Charles didn't seem to notice. When the steward came with their dinner trays, she breathed a sigh of relief, glad for the distraction, and they ate in companionable silence for several minutes.

"What's your background in science, Mari?" Charles asked finally. "You must've studied more than journalism, or whatever you have to do to get into television."

"Oh . . . well," she stuttered, thrown off stride by the

unexpected question. "I majored in biology. For a while. That was after art and music, I think, and before political science."

"Why all the switching around?"

"The piano just isn't my instrument," she pleaded as persuasively as she knew how.

"It could be, if you'd work harder at it."

"But I want to try something different, Mom. Please?"

"Sometimes I wish everything didn't come so easily for you, Mari. You only want to stick with it as long as it's fun."

"What's so sinful about having fun?"

"You'll end up a jack-of-all-trades, master of none."

Mari now shrugged, trying to rid herself of the remembered exchange with her mother, one that had been repeated through the years with only minor variations, until it had become a too-familiar and hated refrain.

"You mean you never did—you've always known exactly what you wanted to do or be?" she asked.

"As far back as I can remember," he replied with a teasing smile. "But you bring something rare to your work, and I've got a suspicion there's more to it than you're telling." He paused, trying to find the right words to describe what he meant, then shook his head in defeat. "I'm not sure what it is. Understanding, I suppose, rather than just the simple reporting of facts. Something about the way you connect everything up."

His hands drew her eyes until she had to force herself to look away, for fear he'd catch her staring again. She couldn't think of anyone she'd encountered in the past ten years who attracted her in quite the same way she was drawn to Charles Merrill. Surely he couldn't be one of a kind! So often when she'd felt physically attracted to a man there was some mysterious "something" missing. Whether it was emotional or intellectual or what, she wasn't sure. And then after a while the physical attraction would disappear, too. She continued to glance at Charles from time to time while they ate, the whole idea just one more piece of craziness in a day that had seemed crazy and unreal from the beginning. His dark black-brown hair hugged his head, as curly as she remembered, though a little shorter. He was, in fact, a mélange of all the autumn colors she'd always longed to have herself—that and naturally curly hair—from his golden skin and warm eyes, dark lashes and thick, arching brows, to the chocolate flannel slacks and heathery tweed jacket.

Charles noticed the color in her face, and glanced down at her plate. "Feeling better? How about more coffee?" She began rearranging the dishes on her tray, trying to stack them into neat piles. "Sure, if someone comes."

"Why don't I get these out of our way," he suggested, lifting her tray and then his own, "and get coffee at the same time?" He waited for her to lean across the empty seat between them and push his tray table up out of the way so he could get out of his seat. As he walked away she could see that his entire body moved with the same deliberate control and coordination she'd noticed in his hands, lending a grace of movement that belied his size, though there did seem to be an odd little hesitation in his walk. An almost-but-not-quite limp that she hadn't noticed before. He'd taken off his jacket before dinner, and now her eyes swept quickly over the back of his seat-wrinkled shirt, down across his tan leather belt to the firmly rounded buttocks above long, straight legs.

Mari tore her eyes away and straightened in her seat, turning to look out the window, where it was too dark to see anything but her own reflection. A host of fragmented memories flashed through her mind, nearly overwhelming her with new-old sensations. And then she remembered something she'd read while trying to kill those four interminable hours between flights. "Patriarchy controls women by making them blind to their own desire, keeping their sexuality a secret from them." That certainly wasn't her problem! Here she was getting positively carried away with Charles Merrill's tush, while her mother was lying all alone in some hick-town hospital in Spain, dying or perhaps already dead. This was beyond the pale even for Mari, a past master of "inappropriate" behavior! Too lost in thought to notice Charles until he was back and handing her a cup, she tossed a smile his way but couldn't force herself to meet his eyes, afraid that her face would betray her thoughts. He set his cup on the tray table before settling back in his seat and stretching one long leg into the aisle, keeping it as close to the seats as possible, then loosened his tie and turned toward her.

"Now. Tell me about your mother." His serious, intense glance said the time for evasion was over. And all at once she wanted to tell him, needed to.

"She loves to travel. My father died six years ago, and since then she's been all over, to Peru, Australia and New Zealand, and now Spain and Portugal."

He listened closely, nodding his head from time to time as she told him about the doctor's call from Torremolinos. "How old is she?" he asked when she finished.

"Sixty-nine. But that's not really old, is it?"

"Hardly, but I suppose that depends on her health. The doctor didn't say what medication he had her on, besides the diuretic?"

"Something for her heart. Guess I was too rattled to think to ask what."

He lifted his shoulders in a dismissive shrug, then reached across the seat and covered her hand with his, enclosing it completely. "Doesn't matter. You'll find out soon enough. But he's right, it can be a difficult decision." His hand felt warm and reassuring, and when he took it away, her eyes began to fill with tears as a sense of loss washed over her. She needed to touch and be touched, now even more than usual.

"About eighty percent of deaths following infarction are due to either pulmonary edema or shock," Charles continued. "With one you want to reduce the volume of fluid the heart has to pump, but with the other you want to increase it. He's apparently targeted the edema." He paused. "She's probably on something like digoxin to enhance contractility, strengthen the beat. It's entirely possible, you know, that she had a heart attack years ago and just overdid on this trip." He pulled a ballpoint pen from his shirt pocket and reached for his jacket to search for a small notebook. "One of the best cardiovascular institutes in Europe is in Madrid, which is why this meeting is being held there. Maybe I can do something to help, at least get you some information, about who might be called in if needed and what facilities are available where she is." Mari gave him the name of the hospital. "Where are you going to be? Did you have time to get a hotel room before you left?"

"No, but the tour group is staying at the Bajondillo. If nothing else, I ought to be able to get her room. She sent me a complete itinerary before she left, with all the details. She's sort of compulsive about things like that." Her last few words were almost inaudible.

"Okay. I'll let you know what I find out soon as I can." Without warning he got up and reached into the overhead compartment for a pillow, then bent down and raised the arms separating the seats. "Time for me to go back to my seat so you can stretch out here and get some sleep."

"But I never can sleep on planes anyway," she protested, "and I'd rather you stayed. Unless you want to—"

"Okay, but at least put your feet up here and try to relax. You've had a rough day, and there's another long one coming up as soon as we touch down in Madrid, in about three hours." Mari nodded and slipped off her soft leather Campiones, then tucked her feet up on the seat between them and wedged the pillow into the corner.

The pale, cold glow of sunrise was slanting in under the half-pulled window shade when Mari opened her eyes again. She could hear the rising murmur of voices as passengers began to stir around. Her feet felt warm and heavy, and she lifted her head to see why. A wool blanket covered her legs and feet. Charles was leaning back in his seat, apparently asleep, with his right hand wrapped snugly around her ankles, holding the covering in place. She tried to stay still, but in the end couldn't resist wriggling her toes just a little, to relieve her cramped leg muscles.

His eyes flew open and he lifted his hand. "Get some sleep?" he asked, giving her a slow smile.

Mari nodded wordlessly, watching his face for a second before glancing down at her watch, oddly comforted to know that he'd been watching over her while she slept. "I think I'd better go comb my hair and brush my teeth before there's a mad rush to get in there," she whispered, indicating the rear of the plane with her head as she slipped her feet into cold shoes, wondering if she looked as rumpled and messy as she felt.

Charles rose to let her slide out. "I'll see if I can get us some breakfast while you're gone," he murmured as she brushed past him.

By the time she returned, the hum of conversation in the cabin was back to normal and the other passengers were beginning to mill around, stretching and talking with their neighbors. For Mari the continental breakfast came too close to dinner in the time-shifted night. She wasn't sure even the coffee would stay down, the way her stomach convulsed in silent protest every time she let her mind wander ahead to what she might find in Torremolinos. Charles seemed to sense that she wasn't up to making conversation, so he didn't even try. She kept glancing at her watch and then out the window, where she could now see mountains, which meant they'd already crossed the coast of Spain and were beginning the long descent into Madrid.

"I didn't realize Spain was so mountainous," she commented, just to make conversation. "I guess I never thought much about what it was like beyond the Pyrenees, at the French border."

Charles nodded. "More than any other country on the continent except Switzerland, I suppose," he said as he moved into the seat next to her and leaned closer, so he could see the peaks she was pointing to. "It's virtually ringed and crisscrossed with them. The Sierra Nevadas aren't far from the sunny coast where you're headed."

The plane intercom suddenly came alive, with instructions to buckle seat belts and straighten seats in preparation for landing, first in Spanish and then in English. It didn't sound much like the Spanish Mari was used to hearing in Texas, and she understood little enough of that. Her pulse began to race and she couldn't seem to get enough breath. And then she felt Charles's hand envelop hers again, as if he knew intuitively that she needed help to hold herself together. Madrid came into view with a suddenness that took her breath completely, with the sun rising red behind mountains peaked with snow.

As the plane floated lower and lower, the gray landscape turned into a colorful patchwork quilt. And then they were gliding over cluster after cluster of red-brick apartment buildings, all of them arranged in circles like children's building blocks. Within minutes they felt a slight bump as the wheels touched ground, followed by a huge rush of engine noise, much too loud to talk over, and that was quickly followed by the muffled shuffling of passengers preparing to leave the plane.

Charles stayed close to Mari while they waited for their luggage, then followed her through the formalities of passport control and customs, touching her shoulder or her elbow or, at times, sliding his hand down to clasp hers. Sure now that he hadn't imagined the panic in her eyes earlier, he felt a frustrating sense of helplessness, the like of which he hadn't experienced for a long, long time. Maybe since he was a child. What he didn't know was that Mari was fighting an internal battle of her own.

Torn between the pressing need to get to Torremolinos as fast as possible and the almost irresistible desire to stay with him, she felt a compelling need to find some way to hold on to whatever was going on between them, some indescribable thing she might just be imagining. Was it simply that he'd been there with a shoulder when she needed one so desperately? She tried to tell herself that she was indulging in girlish wishful thinking, that Charles Merrill might be entirely sincere in his concern right now, and might even call. Once. But it was far more likely that he'd get involved in his meeting and not give her another thought.

The Madrid terminal was strangely reminiscent of some of the "country" towns he'd flown into at home, like Lubbock up in the Texas Panhandle, Charles thought as he stood with Mari outside the arrivals gate—except for the low hum of foreign words that settled around them like fog. He watched her examine one face after another as people brushed past them. Was she hoping she could tell, just by looking, whether this one might speak English or that one French?

"Mari?" he began, then stopped. The time for making conversation was over. And it wasn't the right time to say anything more, either. "I'll be in touch soon, okay? Soon as I can." She simply nodded, avoiding his eyes. The relaxed smile was long gone, and her face looked pale in the white morning light. He wondered if she might be on the verge of tears again, and felt his gut tighten.

And then she really looked at him, searching his eyes and his face as if to memorize whatever she saw there. "I don't know what I would have done without you, Charles. Thanks." She stood on tiptoe and kissed him on the cheek, then tried to smile and failed. Charles nodded slightly, his eyes never wavering from hers. "Bye," she whispered, her eyes still on his for one last look as she picked up her bag, then turned and walked away.

He wanted to go after her, to stay with her wherever she went, whatever happened, just to be there. But first he had to find Rafael Prados. Pronto! And he had a talk to give in the morning. So instead he watched her walk toward the exit to the domestic-flights building, her stride determined yet subtly feminine. Her shoulders were broader than usual for a woman, he noticed, though he hadn't before, and her hips rounded nicely before straightening at the thigh, which he had. And then she was gone.

Charles continued to stand there for a minute, still feeling the pull, even though he could no longer see her, sure of only one thing as he turned to walk through the door to the row of waiting taxis. He wasn't going to make the same mistake twice.

CHAPTER
3
∿

The flight to Málaga was a carnival act Mari couldn't possibly have imagined, let alone anticipated, and her ears were still buzzing when she climbed out of the taxi in front of the Clínica Santa Elena. A small van had ferried the dozen or so passengers to the little Aviaco commuter jet sitting way out away from the terminal, and she should have suspected what was coming as soon as she saw the swivel-tail wheel—four hours of undiluted engine noise instead of what should have been one quiet hour. All because she hadn't been able to get a seat on the nonstop Iberia "airbus" on such short notice. But what fantastic scenery! Approaching Córdoba, the little plane had come down through the mountains, giving passengers the thrill of a lifetime, ready or not, as it wove its way around and between the taller peaks.

She dug around in her purse, extracted several bills and then took the easy way, holding them out to the driver to let him take what he needed. It was an act of almost instinctive self-protection, a way of saving her energy for more important things. Then, draping her trench coat over one arm, she picked up her suitcase and started toward the door, hardly noticing the green canvas canopy or the colorful flowers blooming along the edge of the sidewalk leading up to it. She'd long since lost track of the time of day, but she did notice the heat. Her heart sank the minute she caught sight of the ancient telephone switchboard set at right angles to the reception desk, dashing her hopes that she'd find any up-to-date technology here, while confirming her opinion that Spain was the most backward country in western Europe, thanks to forty years of General Franco.

"I believe my mother is a patient here," she began to explain in English to the young man behind the counter, though she had absolutely no idea whether he would understand a word she said. "Mrs. Janet McNichols. Dr. Ibarzábal's patient. I'm her daughter, Marilyn, uh, Ashmore." She shook her head and cleared her throat. "I mean Marilyn McNichols. From the United States."

"Just one minute, please," he answered, taking her appearance and her English completely in stride, as if someone like her walked in every day of the week. She watched him turn to the switchboard, grasp the old-fashioned plug and pull it up, then insert it into one of the two dozen or more holes in the upright board. In her mind's eye she saw Lily Tomlin as Ernestine, the gossipy switchboard operator, and came very near to smiling. A small light flashed on above the connection and he spoke into the mouthpiece of his headset, then just as efficiently pulled the plug, letting it retract into the base of the switchboard, and turned back to her.

"Dr. Ibarzábal is waiting for you on the second floor."

Mari looked around, spotting a stairway but no elevator. "Is there anywhere here I could leave my luggage?"

"Just there." He pointed to a corner of the entrance hall between the front door and what appeared to be a waiting room opening off to the left.

She pushed her bag as far out of the way as possible, then started up the white marble stairs. The hallway on the next floor was empty, and she didn't see anything that looked even remotely like an intensive care unit, so she just stood there, waiting and wondering. Every time a nurse came into the hall, or anyone else for that matter, she expected them to direct her to Dr. Ibarzábal, or at least to ask who she was waiting for. But no one did. So she continued to wait, shifting from one foot to the other and glancing at her watch from time to time. And then the number on the door across the hall finally hit home: 102! How could she have forgotten that on the continent they didn't begin numbering with the ground floor? She hurried back to the stairs and up another floor. Double doors at the end of the hallway opened into what looked like a large ward, and she headed in that direction, slowing only long enough to take a quick glance around inside before entering. The room contained about ten beds, some with white cloth screens set up around them. A nurse was sitting at one end of the room behind what appeared to be a bank of lighted television screens. Mari waited for her to see her, then hurried to meet her.

"I was directed up here to meet Dr. Ibarzábal. Mrs. McNichols is my mother. Do you . . . ?"

The nurse was blond and very thin, and the white uniform didn't do a thing for her, but at least she understood, and spoke, a little English. "Yes, she is just there," she answered, pointing to a bed at the other end of the room. Mari let out her breath, hardly realizing that she'd been holding it until now, and trailed along behind the nurse.

Janet McNichols lay against the slightly raised head of the hospital bed, hardly distinguishable from the white sheet that covered her. A thin plastic tube was taped above her lips, feeding oxygen into her nostrils. Small metal discs were taped to her chest just below the gaping neck of the white hospital gown, attached to wires running to the electrocardiograph that constantly monitored the electrical activity of her heart. Clear liquid dripped slowly from the plastic bag hanging on the stand next to her bed, and huge purple bruises marched up and down both arms, even the backs of her hands, in silent testimony to the repeated failures and reinsertions of the thick steel IV needle.

"She has the low blood pressure, and the needle works through the vein," the nurse explained. "The solution goes into the tissues, so we must move it to a new place each time."

Mari moved closer and laid her hand over her mother's, now pitifully thin, trying to understand how she could possibly have changed so much and so fast. At her touch, her mother's eyelids came up, slowly, and eyes that had always been a clear sky blue but now were a dim, almost lifeless gray, tried to focus on Mari's face.

"Marilyn," Janet whispered, trying to smile. "I knew . . . you . . . would come." Then her eyes closed again, as if just those few words had exhausted her small store of energy.

Mari continued to hold her mother's hand, trying to share her own warmth as she watched the rise and fall of the sheet pulled halfway up over her mother's pitifully bony chest and listened to her labored breathing, silently willing her to breathe. She had no idea how long she'd been standing like that before she felt a touch on her arm and turned to find a man in a white coat. He motioned for her to follow him, and led her to the bank of monitors where the nurse kept watch.

"Dr. Ibarzábal?" she asked huskily, unshed tears clogging her throat.

He nodded. "I am glad you are here, Mrs. Ashmore. You can see for yourself. This one is your mother's." He pointed to one screen with a hand that was as deeply tanned as his face. He looked to be about forty, and his hair was blond, which came as something of a shock. Weren't all Spaniards dark? Mari watched the curve snake its way across the monitor, realizing instantly what she was seeing. "Yes," he confirmed, "it beats too fast, and is irregular, as you see. I give her something to make it stronger, more regular."

"But why is she so thin?"

"We do not know for sure, but as I say to you on the phone, she has difficulty keeping food down. Perhaps because of the medication, but she tell me it is a trouble she has before I see her. Her liver is enlarged, which comes often with the edema. Because there is such poor circulation to other organs. You understand?"

"Yes, but if she doesn't get nourishment, or can't keep it down, how can you expect her to get stronger?" Certainly that must be as obvious to him as it was to her. "She's so weak. Can't you change the medication, if that's what's causing the nausea?"

"We have not so many choices, but I will have her blood chemistry again this evening, and decide then if it is possible to change. You may stay here with her for a few hours, but do not interrupt her rest."

"What kind of diet do you have her on?" Mari wasn't

about to let him get away so fast. "I know what she likes, so maybe we could change it, try something different."

"A low-sodium regime, of course, but she can have whatever she wishes aside from that."

"What about one of those nutritional supplements, like a milkshake, that comes as a powder you mix with milk or water? Maybe if I try giving her just a little at a time she could keep some of that down."

"I will leave an order with the nurse," he agreed, then turned to leave. "We shall see how she is in the morning, yes?" And with that he walked out, leaving her standing there staring at the monitor.

Mari sat holding her mother's hand, hoping Janet would know she was there even in her sleep. The nurse brought a small carton of milk and a glass, along with a vacuum-sealed envelope containing the nutritional supplement Mari had requested. And the first time Janet woke again Mari persuaded her to take a few sips. "If only I could have my regular breakfast," Janet whispered, too weak and short of breath to speak in her normal voice. "It's always sticky buns and sliced cheese and ham!" A small smile fluttered momentarily across her lips, just before she closed her eyes again. Mari wondered if her mother was hallucinating, or maybe trying to joke, because she couldn't believe that any hospital in the world would feed cheese and ham to a heart patient in intensive care!

The next time Janet woke, Mari managed to get a little more of the "milkshake" down her, and then Janet surprised her by asking if she could brush her teeth. "My brush is in that drawer, I think. I don't mean to complain," she explained breathlessly, "but I can't make the nurses understand. I even tried going through the motions. Do you think I'm not supposed to?" It was the first time Mari had really thought about what it must be like to be so sick and not be able to communicate with the people caring for you. She rolled up the head of the bed a little more, put toothpaste on the brush and handed it to her mother. Janet had to give up within seconds, because she was simply too weak, so Mari took the brush in her own hand and gently scrubbed a little longer, knowing that just the minty taste and washing out her mouth with water would help Janet feel cleaner and refreshed. Afterward Janet settled into what sounded like a more regular breathing pattern and dozed off again.

Mari continued sitting at her mother's side while the afternoon died quietly, letting her mind go back across time, to events and places she hadn't thought about for years—first to when she was in college, trying so hard to find her own special niche. But she never did, at least not until she met Phillip Ashmore. After that she simply majored in him, and four months later, when he had three days off between his first and second year of medical school, they'd gotten married. Her first surprise was seeing even less of Phillip than she had before, because even when he was home, he either slept or studied. She tried every way she could think of to be involved in what he was doing, even helping him to prep for exams. At times she'd try enticing his attention away with something special to eat, which wasn't exactly easy on their meager income. The second surprise had come a few months later, after she finished school and went looking for a job, only to discover that a bachelor's degree in political science wasn't worth a fig. When she did finally manage to find work, in spite of her lack of experience, it was because the restaurant manager thought she had a "classy" look about her. The tips she earned allowed them to live a little better, but her shift at the restaurant rarely matched his at the hospital, so all she really remembered about that year was being alone. That, and fantasizing a lot about making love.

It was the year after that that she couldn't forget, when Phillip was almost finished with his internship and the end of the constant grind was in sight. But by then he was so caught up in playing doctor that her little mishap couldn't even begin to compete with the really serious medical emergencies he saw every day. He'd never shown any real concern or regret, in either his words or his face. There was no admission that "I feel as bad as you do," or even a warm hug to say he shared her disappointment. In the end he'd resorted to the most unforgivable of platitudes—"I'm sure it's all for the best, anyway. You probably should have waited until I'm finished with my residency." As if he didn't have anything at all to do with it!

I wasn't any better at sticking with one man than with one

51

*musical instrument or a college major, was I, Mom? Not like
you, married to the same man for almost thirty-five years,
and I'll bet never even let another one kiss you. But it wasn't
for lack of trying. I did try, to be understanding and patient,
no matter what he said or did. I even read his textbooks, so I
wouldn't be one of those wives who don't know a damn thing
about their husband's work! But it wasn't enough! Nothing
was ever enough with Phillip!*

Silent tears streamed down Mari's cheeks now, blinding
her, forcing her to grope around in her purse for a tissue. *You
know what I finally figured out, Mom? I wanted approval so
much that all I could think about was what Phillip would like,
or think or say, what he wanted me to do. Hoping he'd notice,
at least once in a while. But he kept me on a starvation diet. I
actually was dumb enough to think we could work it out if
only I tried hard enough. Me, not him! Isn't that funny? I
know you think I'm flighty, changeable. But if there's anything at all I am sure about, Mom, it's Phillip Ashmore. And
nothing you say can ever change that. Later, after I lost the
baby, I almost hated you. And I'll bet you never even guessed,
did you? Mostly, though, I hated myself for being like you.
For believing in the old myths, about men and women and
wives and mothers, and that love makes everything come out
right in the end. So for years now I've tried not to think like
you, not even to sound like you. And now here I am, feeling
guilty again, like a child, because I'm thinking about making
another change in my life. Just when you thought I'd finally
"found myself" and would stop flitting from flower to flower
like a nervous butterfly. I know it sounds crazy, Mom, but I
wish more than anything in the world that I could have been
what you wanted. But I can't!*

She blew her nose and sat up straighter in the chair as she
consciously willed herself to stop blaming her mother. The
misfortunes and mistakes of the past were of her own doing,
just like her aching eyes were now, and it was time to stop
being so unfair and immature. *Isn't that what you always
called it, Mom—immaturity—the one thing I liked best
about myself? My adventuresome spirit!*

Mari saw herself walking home from school under a row
of huge red-gold maples, her head down and skirt pulled up

to cradle her treasures, with each step discovering another brilliant leaf more irresistibly beautiful than the previous one, forcing her to decisions she didn't want to and couldn't make. She could even smell the smoky haze of Indian summer as it settled over the field of corn stalks her father had stacked into teepees, where she and Mary Lou sometimes hid from Paul and Kenny, the neighborhood pests. And then she knew what it was like to be five again, riding her green-and-white-striped tricycle down the sloping sidewalk at breakneck speed, until an unseen rock jerked the handlebars out of her hands. Feeling the pain as the front wheel turned, catching her bare toes in the spinning spokes just before she was dumped off in a tangle of legs and wheels. Hearing the sound of her mother's voice as she wrapped gauze around Mari's big toe. Letting the pleased grin break across her face as she realized it would be days, maybe even weeks, before she would have to put on shoes again.

And now, years later, here in Torremolinos, it was as if her mother had become the child and Mari the mother, soothing Janet's fears and cajoling her to eat, worrying about her. Janet had always been quick to tell Mari that "you'll have one of your own someday" when she found her playing with one of Jackie's kids. *Only I didn't, Mom, much as I wanted that at one time. I thought I lost that chance, with Phillip, but lately, well, I've been thinking about that, a lot. A child of my own. And only mine.*

Like a flash out of the blue, she suddenly saw Charles Merrill's face. And he was talking to her. About yogurt! She jumped up and hurried toward the nurse's station. Yogurt, that's what Janet needed! It was supposed to be great for the digestive system because it contained exactly the right enzymes or something. Why hadn't she thought of it before?

Except for the short nap on the plane, Mari hadn't slept for more than thirty-six hours, and didn't much care what kind of room the Hotel Bajondillo gave her so long as it had a bed. She went through the motions of explaining who she was to the young man behind the desk while he peered at her—a bit like an owl, she thought—through round granny glasses. Wisps of wavy black hair curled around the edges of his forehead, lending him the air of an aesthete, perhaps a poet.

"My name is Juan Diaz," he informed her with a smile when he finally handed her a key. "I remember your mother, Miss McNichols, always with a smile and friendly word."

Mari had to blink back sudden tears, and for a moment all she could do was nod. "Do you know if any messages have come for me? Maybe a telephone call?"

"A minute please. I will look." He sorted through the odd slips of paper scattered across the top of the desk below the counter, then looked up and shook his head. "Sorry. But we will put a note in your box, there," he turned and pointed toward the wall of key boxes behind him, "if a call or mail comes for you. Perhaps in the morning you will hear something, yes?"

She felt a keen sense of disappointment, a dashing of dim hopes, at discovering that Charles hadn't even tried to call. But Juan Diaz was only confirming what she'd told herself to expect all along. She'd simply overreacted to Charles on the plane. But as she walked toward the elevator, she had to fight back the tears. Upstairs, moving along the dimly lit corridor, she was still searching for room 244 when the hallway went completely dark, and the tears overflowed in a rush, blinding her even in the dark. This was the last straw—just too damn much! Timed lighting might be a great energy saver, but why did it always have to go out at the wrong time? Dragging her suitcase behind her, she fumbled along the wall for the light switch, not caring that the tears were rolling down her cheeks and dripping off her chin.

Once inside the room she dropped everything, switched on the overhead light and began peeling off her clothes, letting them fall to the floor right where she stood. Soft music was coming from somewhere in the room, and she glanced around, searching for the source. Was that a Chopin étude? She noticed a sliding glass door opening onto a small balcony, and walked across the room to pull it open a few inches, to let in the fresh, cool night air, then turned around to survey the room. A big double bed with a little lamp on the night table next to it, a small breakfast table with two chairs, and a sofa and lounge chair. But no television set. A telltale round of cloth mounted flush into the wall next to the bed was probably a speaker, and the single knob below it had to be the on-off and volume-control switch, which meant no choice of stations. So the hotel probably was piping in its own music.

She went into the bathroom to wash her face and hands, decided to leave unpacking until morning, and climbed into the bed. Tired as she was, sleep proved elusive, perhaps because it was too quiet. So she raised up and turned the music back on, then snuggled down under the blanket and lay there, remembering all the nights when she'd gone to sleep to the sound of the piano, because it was the only time her mother could find to practice back then.

Janet McNichols had made her husband and two children, her house and even her church her life's highest priorities. She'd allowed the society of her youth to trample her dream of becoming a concert pianist, which Mari had never really been able to understand. How had her mother endured giving up so much of what she wanted for herself, for all those years—until it was too late? Feminists liked to point to women like Janet as object lessons, casualties of what they called "patriarchal sexual arrangements," lumping them all together as stereotypes rather than treating them as individuals. But in Mari's opinion, women like her mother had been ostracized and victimized twice over, first by the male power structure and then by the "sisterhood."

She'd be the first to admit that she *did* want the same feeling of closeness with someone special she'd seen between her mother and father—but without all the one-sided compromises. Like the running cliché of the eighties, she wanted it all. A companion and lover, a child or two *and* her own work, whatever that might be at any given time. And that's where the real world and the world of fantasy always collided head on. Charles Merrill seemed proof enough of that.

With that thought—so unutterably weary that she hardly made sense even to herself—Mari allowed the tears to well over again, running from the corner of her eye into her hair, and down her cheeks to the corner of her mouth, where she tested the salty taste with her tongue. Then she simply couldn't fight the effect of jet lag and lack of sleep any longer, and drifted slowly into unconsciousness.

The sun glinted off a glassy sea, turning it from steely blue near the shore to blinding white where it merged with the hazy horizon. Only an occasional taxi moved along the broad boulevard edging the sand, breaking the early-morning quiet as Mari stood watching a small fishing boat tack back and forth just a little way offshore, casting out and then winching in its heavy net. Off in the distance, to the north, a range of mountains jutted out into the sea to form the bay of Málaga, the big coastal city where she'd landed yesterday. And just below her balcony, in the U formed by the two wings of the hotel, was a brilliant blue swimming pool, where a few guests were already basking in the early-morning sun, including a woman with a deep tan and no swimsuit top. Mari finally glanced at her watch, then turned to go down for breakfast, scooping her sweater out of the chair as she headed for the door.

She was feeling more hopeful by the time she got to the hospital, which was its own testimony to how much difference a little sleep could make. But when she stepped inside the door of the ICU she stopped short. Her mother's bed was empty! Had she stopped on the wrong floor again? No! Everything was the same, except the sheets had been stripped from her mother's bed and wadded into a loose roll. She looked around quickly, to see if they might have moved her to another bed, then hurried to the nurse's station. It was a different one today, who didn't seem to understand anything except the name McNichols. Waving one arm toward the door, the nurse motioned her out, or down the hall, or somewhere. Mari started partway down the hall, trying to find someone who could tell her something, anything, a rising tide of fear and dread already threatening to suffocate her. Then she saw a man emerge from one of the rooms at the opposite end of the hall, and she almost ran.

"Ah, Mrs. Ashmore," Dr. Ibarzábal greeted her, smiling. "Your mother is so much better this morning, I moved her to a private room, where you can spend as much time with her as you like." Mari peeked into the room behind him and saw her mother halfway sitting up in the high hospital bed, her eyes and face surprisingly alert. The oxygen tube and chest electrodes were gone, though the IV stand was still there. Janet saw her, too.

"You're up early, Mari," she whispered, still a little breathless, revealing a weakness it wasn't possible to recover from overnight.

Mari rushed around the doctor and into the room to give her mother a hug. "Boy, do you ever look better, Mom!" She glanced down at the breakfast tray cantilevered over the bed in front of Janet. "Think you can eat some of this?" She didn't know the Spanish word for oatmeal, so didn't know if the nurse had really understood her yesterday.

Janet tried to laugh and failed, mostly because she couldn't muster enough breath. "The woman who brought it called it baby food. I know that much Spanish! Seemed to think I don't have any teeth, treated me like I was positively ancient."

Mari laughed, beside herself with joy at the unexpected change in her mother's condition. "Rest a minute, okay? I'll be right back to help you, but I want to talk with Dr. Ibarzábal before he gets away." She found the doctor out in the hall instructing the nurse who was accompanying him on his rounds.

"As you can see, you are good for her," he observed, anticipating her questions. "She is still very sick, of course, but her blood pressure is up, which means the heartbeat is stronger. That is why she is more awake. Sometimes it happens that way. We cannot explain the power of love." He shrugged his shoulders slightly. "Though I did start her on a different medication for her heart last night, and already she is responding. A colleague from Madrid called, I understand at the request of a friend of yours."

"Charles Merrill?" Stunned by the unexpected revelation, his name exploded from her lips.

"Perhaps. I'm afraid I do not remember. We put our heads together on your mother's case and decided perhaps the quinidine makes her sick, so we must try something else to regulate the heartbeat." He searched through the mobile file for Janet's records. "Here is the X ray of her lungs, and the latest report on her blood chemistry." She ran her eyes down the list of factors and corresponding numbers, but nothing really registered. Instead, her mind was scrambling to make sense out of what had happened. And why Charles hadn't called her last night.

"But I don't feel like eating," Janet protested weakly when Mari tried to persuade her to take just a few more bites of oatmeal.

"I know, Mom. But the sooner you get your strength up, the sooner you can go home."

Mari couldn't help smiling at the look of almost childish determination that appeared on her mother's face as she accepted another spoonful of baby food. By the time they were finished, she was exhausted by the effort, so Mari lowered the head of her bed a little and then moved to the easy chair in the corner of the room near the window, so her mother could nap.

When she looked at her watch again it was nearly eleven. She decided to go for a short walk, just for the exercise. The Clínica Santa Elena was located in a residential area, with apartment buildings all around it, and less than a block away she came across a tiny café with two tables outside, both of them shaded by blue-and-white-striped umbrellas. Next door was a small neighborhood grocery with fruits and vegetables displayed in boxes stacked out front. She walked closer and spied a bucket filled with cut flowers tucked between the tomatoes and oranges, and couldn't help smiling at the thought that perhaps her luck was beginning to change!

Mari spent the next couple of hours in her mother's room, listening to her relate bits and pieces of what she remembered from the days prior to arriving in Torremolinos, when she'd obviously been too sick to travel but simply wouldn't "give in," as she called it. When lunch came, Janet was amenable to the soup and yogurt, but waved away the stewed chicken and rice. Once again Mari cajoled her into trying at least one bite, "so we can get you back to the English-speaking world." And then one more.

Because she didn't want her mother to tire herself talking, she told her about her first meeting with Charles six months ago and about his research on blood. By the time they finished, it was obvious that just the effort it took to eat had exhausted her again. "Time for another nap, Mom," Mari suggested. "I'll just sit over there and read while you get your strength back for supper."

"An orange is not enough lunch, Mari, but if you won't go back to the hotel for a decent meal, at least go walk down to the beach. It can't be far from here, if I remember correctly from the trip out from town."

Mari waited until her mother dropped off to sleep, then went to the reception desk to ask directions to the beach and also about another little restaurant she'd noticed earlier, this one just across the street from the hospital. "La Coquina? It has only fish," the young man answered as he pulled a plug from the ancient switchboard, "but perhaps you like. Or you can have a coffee and pastry in the afternoon." It sounded a less than enthusiastic recommendation, so Mari decided to head straight for the beach. Perhaps she would stop for coffee on the way back.

She walked briskly, enjoying being alone. The sun was high and caressed her bare arms with a gentleness that felt so different from the harsh Texas sun. Rows of apartment buildings gave way to individual houses after a few blocks, all of them surrounded by whitewashed plaster walls about five feet high, protecting yards filled with lush flowering shrubs and succulents. Bougainvillea vines clung and climbed everywhere, and she could only guess at several flowers she'd never seen before, even in Houston. Then the houses and street ended abruptly at a low curb edging an apparently empty beach that stretched endlessly, to both the left and right. And dead ahead, just about thirty feet from where she was standing, the blue-green Mediterranean was lapping gently at the steel-gray sand.

She kicked off her sandals, leaving them right where they fell, and started across the sand, rolling the sleeves of her moss-green shirt even higher than they already were. The warm sand between her bare toes felt so good, and then the cool, gentle water rolling over the tops of her feet as she walked the line where sand and sea met, even at times rising to her ankles when she didn't guess the waves quite right. The empty beach and quiet sea fit her mood, soothing her seesawing emotions. Once in a while a tiny pebble caught her eye, wetted by a wave to a short-lived brilliance of color, and she would bend down to pick it up. Before long she had her hands full, and without thinking, she lifted the hem of her skirt to form a pocket, because she couldn't bring herself to throw any down quite yet. And that was the first time it even occurred to her to look back at how far she'd come. She saw a woman and a small child off in the distance, near where she'd left her shoes, and she stood watching for several minutes while their German shepherd caught the child's yellow sand bucket in his teeth and dashed into the water with it. Then he would bound back to drop it at the child's feet, as if asking him to come play, too.

She turned back to continue on in the opposite direction, still following the water-smoothed pebbles marking the wave line along the beach. The touch and sight of the dark, granular sand, cool water, and intense blue of the sky and sea, seemed to intensify all her senses, making her more aware of the changing light, even the distant sounds. Suddenly she turned back again. And this time she saw a tall figure, still way off in the distance, but headed in her direction. An intruder on my beach, she thought, feeling mildly put out, but as she continued to watch him come toward her, she was nearly overwhelmed by an inexplicable sense of the familiar. She'd been thinking about Charles, puzzling over what he'd done for her mother and why he hadn't called, wishing he could be here to share this place with her—and now she was imagining that he was!

She looked away quickly, trying to rid herself of the image, and let several minutes pass before turning to look back down the beach again. She watched him come closer and closer yet still stay distant, as if she were seeing him through a cinematic telephoto lens—until all at once, as if he'd crossed some threshold to come into focus, she recognized the slight hesitation in his walk. And then the questions came, like a flash flood. How could he be here, in Torremolinos? How could he possibly know she would be here, on the beach? And why had he come?

Then her momentary paralysis disappeared with a rush of happy relief and she dropped the edge of her skirt, heedlessly spilling out all her carefully chosen treasures as she raised one arm to wave it back and forth, wildly, giving away how she felt about seeing him again. She saw his face break into a smile as he raised an arm to wave back. And then his name exploded from her lips in a whoop of joy, just before she ran to meet him.

"Charles!"

He opened his arms and caught her on the run. "Mari!" Her name swooshed out of him as he swung her around, giving her a quick hug before letting her feet touch the ground again. "I knew that solitary wanderer had to be you!" Her almost childish show of enthusiasm delighted him, and when he pulled away, his smile was at least a match for hers. His hands stayed at her waist, and they just stood there for a couple of seconds, looking at each other, smiling, too satisfied with what they saw to even speak.

"How did you know—" she began, just as Charles exclaimed, "Hey, I thought your eyes were blue!"

Mari laughed, letting her pleasure at seeing him bubble out. "I know. They can't make up their mind, either. Depends on what I wear. How did you know where to find me?"

"The fellow behind the reception desk at the hospital. Try the restaurant across the street, he said, or else the beach," he answered without thinking about it, his eyes still on hers. She was right, they did match the silky blouse. "How about when you wear red?" he teased.

Mari shrugged and the shiny fabric reflected flashes of sunlight off the slope of her breasts. "I don't. Can't compete." She hardly thought about what she was saying, either. All she wanted to do was look at him, and touch him, to know that he actually was here.

Charles felt an almost irresistible urge to reach up and smooth his hand over her windblown, sun-streaked hair. "You knew I'd come, didn't you?"

She shook her head mutely, letting the happiness his words brought wash over her. Her judgment wasn't all skewed and crazy after all! "When you didn't call, I—"

"You really thought I'd just walk away, that I didn't . . . ?" She could hear the disbelief in his voice. "I tried to get you last night, at the Bajondillo. The guy on the desk said nobody by that name was registered. The hospital was the only way I had of finding you." Was she just imagining the hint of desperation in his voice? "How's your mother?" he asked finally.

"Much better, thanks to you—and your friend in Madrid." A relieved smile lifted the corners of her mouth. "He and Dr. Ibarzábal 'put their heads together' last night and decided to change her medication. By the time I got back there this morning, she was a different person! The medicine of love, Dr. Ibarzábal calls it, but I know better."

"You don't believe love can work miracles?" he asked, only halfway in jest, though he was smiling again.

"Maybe, but in this case I suspect it had a lot more to do with the new medication. That and the yogurt I managed to get down her yesterday. The poor woman was starving to death! And I have you to thank for that, too, because I probably never would have thought of it if we hadn't just been talking about yogurt a few hours before."

"You look better, too. But I think you may be—" He touched her face from forehead to chin with one long-fingered hand, smoothing her hair back from her face in order to test for sunburn, which was just a convenient excuse. The heat she could already feel in her skin intensified, gentle as his touch was.

"I sunburn fast, especially near water." He glanced down at the sand stuck to her plaid skirt, which picked up not only the gray-green in her blouse, but also the blue of the sky, and then at her bare feet, and she saw the beginnings of an amused grin. "I was, uh—" She stopped, suddenly self-conscious about how unkempt she must look, and simply waved one hand back in the direction she'd come from.

"How about something to drink at that little restaurant up by the hospital? Get you out of the sun." He was grinning now, somewhat indulgently, she thought. "Think you can find your shoes?" She returned his grin, pointing back toward the road, then grabbed his hand and swung it playfully as they began retracing their steps. "What about your meeting?"

"I gave my talk this morning. Nothing but sightseeing and 'entertainments' scheduled for tonight and tomorrow," he explained, turning to look at her as they walked side by side. "I'd rather do my sightseeing here with you."

"Oh. Well, I'm not sure how much time I'll have for—" she protested, taking him literally.

"You'll do for now," Charles murmured as they came to her discarded shoes. He extended an arm and she grabbed hold, to stand on first one foot and then the other, brushing off the sand before slipping on her sandals.

"I must look awful, but maybe they'll let me in—with you. At the restaurant, I mean," she ventured, making an overt show of looking him over. He was dressed casually in stonewashed blue jeans and a white knit shirt, though they somehow stopped short of true informality. Probably something about the way the pants fit, she thought, and the sharp crease down each leg. The front pocket linings as well as the smooth-fitting yoke across the back were a darker blue, and his burgundy leather belt matched the cordovan brogues. Cool as they were, the blues and white seemed to enhance the warmth radiating from his tanned skin and brown eyes.

"I've always envied people like you, with skin that tans to such a wonderful color, instead of always turning pink or red like mine," she commented as they left the sand behind and started up the street toward the hospital.

He dropped her hand, draped one arm across her shoulders and pulled her closer for a second, as if to share a secret. "You'd prefer a mask to hide behind, huh? That doesn't sound like you, Mari," he chided gently. "Your skin has a clarity mine will never have, even without a tan—so it shows the life processes going on inside you, which I find infinitely interesting to watch."

"Always the scientist, huh?" she acknowledged with a wry grin. "And I'm just one more specimen for your microscope?"

He gave her shoulder a squeeze and laughed, shaking his head, then dropped his arm and took her hand again. "Every scientist worth the name is a sensualist, Mari, so be forewarned. It comes naturally to us—observing, using every scrap of sense data that's available. Sight, sound, pressure, temperature, resistance, velocity—you name it."

She took her time responding, really thinking about that. "You're always on the outside, then, the observer, never a participant?"

Charles recognized the old argument she was alluding to, which had grown out of the myth of "two cultures"—the idea that "reality" in physical science was different from human reality, whatever that was. But he also suspected she was using it to cloak what was, in fact, an entirely different and quite personal question. He shook his head. "You really think it's possible for me not to be involved, when I both choose and respond to what I observe?" Like her question, his answer carried the harmonics of another meaning. Her smile confirmed what he'd already guessed—that she enjoyed fencing with him, and might even be testing him.

"Sounds to me like you've been spending too much time around the guys in white coats," Charles added when she didn't respond, flashing her a quick grin. "Now Rafael Prados, my man in Madrid, is not only the best cardiologist in Spain, but a very different breed of cat—uses his head instead of going by the bible."

"He's the one who called last night?"

"Yeah, we've been working on some research together for the past couple of years. He spends holidays near here and knows Ibarzábal. Says the hospital care is pretty good, in spite of how it may look. God, I haven't seen a switchboard like that in years, have you? How's intensive care?"

"A strange mixture. Electrocardiograph signals are displayed on a bank of monitors at the nurse's station, but apparently they don't have guardrails for the beds, because one of the patients rolled off onto the floor last night. Caused quite a stir. The whole place is spotlessly clean, of course. You can hardly go up and down the stairs without stepping around some poor woman down on her knees scrubbing the white marble. It's the same at the hotel. Between the floors and the church, Spanish women must spend their entire lives on their knees!"

The little white café was situated on the corner just across from the hospital. A continuous ribbon of windows opened onto the esplanaded boulevard, and to one side an outside terrace was protected from the street by a three-foot-high, white stone wall. An overhead trellis of dried palm fronds shaded the tables. "Let's sit outside," Mari suggested. "It's shady enough and I love this air, don't you? It must be the sea."

One of the men watching a domino game at another table sauntered over. Charles looked at Mari. "Something to drink? You have had lunch, haven't you?" She nodded and shook her head, confusing him.

"We have baked apples, from Ronda. *Peros.* A specialty." The waiter, or whoever he was, spoke in nearly unaccented English, surprising them both. He wore gray slacks and a light yellow V-necked sweater over a gray shirt open at the neck. But no white apron. Mari smiled at him, feeling inordinately pleased that he spoke English, and he returned her smile, almost shyly, she thought.

"Yes, that sounds good," she decided. "And coffee."

"A beer for me," Charles said. As the man walked away he leaned over and whispered, "I say he's the proprietor, what do you think?" She nodded, enjoying the fact that, at least here in this strange place, he was guessing just as much as she was. The whole thing suddenly felt like an adventure, now that Charles was here.

"It's even bigger than a Texas grapefruit!" Mari exclaimed when she saw the huge yellow-skinned baked apple. "No wonder it's called a *perro*—doesn't that mean dog in Spanish?" She dropped a cube of sugar into the tiny white cup of espresso, added a little thick cream and gave it a quick stir. "Ahhhh, yes." She closed her eyes and swayed with pretend rapture as she savored the taste. "It's true." By now she had both Charles and the proprietor thoroughly bemused by her performance. "'The Italians make the best espresso machines, but it's the Spaniards who know how to use them.' I read that just this morning, in my mother's travel guide." The man left with a smile on his face.

"Think I could get a room where you're staying?" Charles asked as soon as he was gone. "I left Madrid in kind of a hurry, and came straight to the hospital. Didn't want to take the chance on missing you."

"They had rooms last night. And it's actually pretty nice. Right on the beach, with a wonderful view of the sea."

"Okay. What do you say we go back to the hospital next, then, and you spend however long you want to with your mother. Don't worry about me, I always have something to read with me." He paused to tip up the last of his beer. "Your mother doesn't need more visitors today. Maybe tomorrow. Then we'll go back to the Bajondillo and you can rest awhile. I'll bet your biological clock is still upside down, right?" He seemed to be taking charge, but it was a relief to relinquish the burden of making all the little decisions, so she really didn't mind. "After that I'm taking you to dinner, to a place Rafael told me about." He reached across the table and picked up her hand, threading his fingers through hers.

"And then, if you're still game, I'm going to show you some Spanish women who very definitely are *not* on their knees!"

CHAPTER

4

The waiter poured red wine over the sliced orange and lemon, added a generous dash of brandy, and then upended a small bottle of soda water into the multicolored faience pitcher. Mari watched him, making a mental note of every ingredient and how much he used, storing it away for future use. He gave the whole thing a quick stir, then poured the deep red mixture into two stemmed balloon glasses already half filled with ice.

"Rafael says the paella here is good," Charles commented, "but the sangria alone is reason enough to come." He lifted his glass to her in silent salute but waited for her to take the first taste.

"Wonderful," she agreed immediately. The Restaurante El Roqueo was in the Carihuela district, the old fishing village a little way up the coast from the modern town. Rather than the flashy tourist place Mari expected, it was small and quiet, even intimate in the shadowed corner where they were seated. "I could get addicted to all this in a hurry!" she whispered, leaning across the table as if to impart a secret she didn't want anyone else to hear. She had an almost overwhelming sense of well-being and pleasure— in the place, the cool fruity-tasting drink, the balmy evening air, the way Charles looked, who he was and the way he responded to her. Everything combined to create a lush sensuality that seemed to saturate the very air she breathed. "Tell me about your meeting in Madrid," she suggested, groping for some way to moderate the intensity of her feelings.

"Not now. Maybe later." He dismissed the suggestion with a curt sweep of one hand. "Tell me how you got into television, instead. I would've pegged you for a writer. Not that I'm putting down what you do. I meant what I said about your program. But I have to confess I have a hard time making you fit into all the show-biz television stuff." He caught the nearly imperceptible lift of her eyebrows. "It's so damned superficial and fragmented, at least most of the time. But maybe you don't agree." His quick smile was almost apologetic.

"As if Gutenberg had invented the printing press and then printed nothing but comic books, is that what you mean? That's what Richard Lamm says about television."

"Who's he?"

"The governor of Colorado, or he was back when I was working in Denver. I grew up there. My mother and sister both still live there." Sister or not, Charles couldn't believe there was another woman anywhere in the world with the same hair. It made him think "honey" every time he looked at her—not just the color, but the way it moved in languid, sweeping waves, flowing like a highly viscous material.

"I could tell you weren't one of us, just from the way you talk, maybe even from the way you look." He tilted up his glass without taking his eyes off her face. There was a glow about her tonight, which he supposed might be due to the light sunburn she'd picked up this afternoon, or maybe even the candlelight, though he preferred thinking it might have something to do with being here, with him. The dress she was wearing was khaki, a near match for her hair, and at first glance seemed simple and plain. But the longer he looked, the more he noticed. The cotton fabric had a coarse texture to it that made his fingers itch to touch—just as her shiny hair did—and served as a foil for the necklace that looped around her neck, a motley collection of beads, charms, and coins. Much as he tried *not* to look at it, because he didn't want her getting the wrong idea about why his eyes were constantly on her chest, the temptation was there, because he kept discovering one curious little object after another among the intermingled strands of amber, lavender, blue, and green beads. A tiny pewter armadillo, a pair of Dutch wooden shoes (except they were silver), and a gold "key" with Greek letters on it, which he guessed was the symbol of some scholastic honorary. And dead center, hanging at the bottom of the longest strand, was a jade monkey with both his hands clapped over his mouth.

Mari wasn't sure what he meant by "the way you look," so she picked up on his earlier question instead. "But I *am* a writer, in spite of what you think of television. That's still mostly what I do. And I got into television when one of the local stations asked me to do an occasional on-camera report for them, back when I was working at the *Denver Post.*" She paused to take a sip of sangria. "But you're right, in a way, because it is a constant fight to keep them from turning everything into fluff. Most of the news directors I've worked with think viewers just won't watch unless we make it fun and games for them. That they're all a bunch of stupid, uneducated slobs. Even most newspapers aim their stuff at the ninth grade, you know, except for maybe the *New York Times* and the *Christian Science Monitor.* A few others. But TV reaches so many people. And it has—oh, immediacy, I guess, a quality of being alive. And visual impact. That's why it's such a mover and shaker."

"And that's what you really care about most, isn't it? Reaching a lot of people?" he asked, surprising her with his perceptiveness.

"Maybe. To be uninformed about your body and how it works sets you up as victim. Doctors are like politicians. Both prefer to operate in secrecy, and they will if we let them. The more ignorance among all us peasants, the greater their power, because controlling information is the ultimate position of power, whether you're trading arms for hostages or treating menopause. So they'd like to have us believe that medical professionals are the *only* source of reliable information, that we have to get it straight from God's mouth. Unfortunately there are too many people around who are still buying into that crock of horsefeathers."

Charles laughed, though he didn't think what she was saying was particularly funny. "I'm on the outside, too, you know, so you're not alone." He caught her disbelieving look. "You don't think so? Remind me to tell you about my experiences with the NIH sometime. Talk about the blind leading the blind!" Mari knew the National Institutes of Health in Washington was the major source of government funding for research in the biomedical sciences. "But not tonight," he added, as the waiter appeared with two oval platters, one heaped with lettuce and chunks of ripe tomatoes topped with Spanish onion rings and thin, elongated red radishes with the leafy tops still on, and the other with thick slices of crusty bread. The waiter hurried away, then was right back with a bottle of white wine and a big platter of rusty-red shellfish, the likes of which Mari had never encountered before. A half dozen made a heap that filled the plate from edge to edge.

"Can you believe this?" she gasped. "What are they?"

"*Carabineros.* Want me to show you how?" Charles picked one up with his fingers, dropped it on his plate, and then separated the head from the tail before peeling off the shell. Next he squeezed a wedge of lemon over the big hunk of white tail meat and then cut off a piece with his fork. "A cross between shrimp and lobster, I'd say." Mari quickly followed suit, swept away by the fun of trying something entirely new, and for the next few minutes they occupied themselves with eating.

Charles watched her, delighted at how openly she seemed to enjoy the whole messy business, almost like a child. So different from the woman he remembered seeing on television, talking about the problems created by the Jarvik heart. And then suddenly he realized that she wasn't being childish at all. She was one of the rare ones who'd somehow managed to grow up without losing the fresh eye and unique sense of wonder all children seemed to have. The very qualities he searched for in graduate students but seldom found, and almost never in females. He was still puzzling over that when Mari asked, "What do we do now, teach?" wiggling wet fingers stained fish-pink, and making a silly face to go with them. But before he could answer her, the waiter appeared with two bowls of warm water, more lemon wedges, and clean linen napkins. "He must have been watching me," she commented as she squeezed juice into the water, then dipped her fingers in and swished them around, completely at ease as she smiled engagingly at Charles.

A few minutes later the waiter came scurrying again, and set a big, shallow iron pan of steaming paella smack in the middle of the table. Mari moaned exaggeratedly and touched the back of a limp hand to her forehead in a melodramatic gesture of feminine distress. Charles tried to keep a straight face but failed. "You don't have to eat it all yourself, you know." They took turns dishing the saffron-tinted mixture onto their plates.

"Okay, here goes," Mari said. She took one bite, then closed her eyes and pretended to swoon.

"What?" Charles asked, not entirely sure this time whether she was acting. Her eyes flew open.

"It's just fantastic, that's all! Mine never came out anything like this." They ate in companionable silence for a minute. "This is one of the famous dishes that had its beginnings with the poor, did you know that? They used whatever was available and cheap at the market, which is why it varies from place to place. The only constants are saffron rice, chorizo sausage, and green peas." She paused thoughtfully, fingering the little jade monkey. "Common people everywhere are creative in spite of their limitations, maybe even because of the constraints on their lives. I guess that's one of the reasons I like folk art so much. Do you think maybe there's something innate in humans that pushes them to try to transcend being human, to try to overcome having feet of clay?"

"You just did it again, Mari! What I was trying to describe before, on the plane, about the knack you have for putting things together."

"What? Cooking isn't folk art?"

"Sure, I suppose. But that's not the point. So you can cook, too?" he teased.

"Don't start with that. It's no joke," she admonished with a grin, then began telling him about a job interview she'd had with a newspaper editor. "He thumbed my résumé and clips, said I looked good on paper, but—well, 'all that

71

science and medical stuff is pretty esoteric. What I need to know is, can you cook?' What he meant, of course, was could I cover the cop shop and city hall. I figured 'esoteric' was the biggest word in his vocabulary, and he dragged it out just to impress me. Or put me down. I'm never sure which, with some of the Neanderthals in the newspaper business."

"You're not kidding, are you? He wanted *you* to cover crime, the police—what'd you call it?"

"Police blotter, the cop shop?"

"Whatever." Charles shrugged, indifferent to the press jargon, shook his head in disbelief and glanced at his watch. "Coffee now or . . . ?"

"Don't even ask."

"We could get dessert later, maybe somewhere down along the paseo," he suggested as he signaled the waiter. "It's nearly ten and— But maybe you're tired, would rather go back to the hotel."

She shook her head but refused to give him the satisfaction of asking again where they were going. She'd already tried that once. Her hand strayed to the little monkey.

"Where the hell did you get that necklace?" he asked suddenly, his curiosity finally getting the better of him.

"What? Oh!" she almost stuttered, then smiled as she looked down at it. "My fetish necklace, you mean. Actually, I got it in Austin, at Old Time Teenie's on West Sixth Street. A woman named Sandy Hale makes them. She did this one using my own things. Mementos, I suppose you'd call them, from various places I've lived or traveled, little things people have given me over the years. A few are old, like my grandfather's gold baby locket. He was christened in it."

He reached across the table and lifted the little figure to take a closer look. "And the monkey?"

She gave him a few seconds, then took it back, smoothing her fingers over the little figure in a gesture that was already familiar, though he hadn't consciously realized it until now. "He's to remind me that there are times when I should keep my mouth shut!" She laughed self-consciously, but Charles assumed she was joking.

* * *

Mari glanced around at the shops and cafés edging the plaza, while Charles paid the taxi driver. She had no idea where they were in relation to the beach, whether the Plaza Andalusia was the center of the business district or even if there was such a thing. She knew very little about Torremolinos, in fact, beyond its reputation as a tourist center. Then Charles took her arm, guiding her down the sidewalk toward a bright blue awning. Las Chinitas. She didn't recognize the word, but it appeared to be a restaurant, except for the words TABLAOS FLAMENCOS printed on the blue awning. Inside, a performance had already begun, and the meaning of the words finally hit home.

The crowd and the smoke were thick, and she and Charles were seated at a table so tiny that their knees touched no matter which way they turned. Charles scooted his chair around as close to her as he could get and put his lips to her ear. "What to drink?" His breath was like a summer breeze on her hair, and his lips brushed her ear, sending an involuntary shiver skittering up her spine. Mari stared at him for one brief second, then mouthed, "Anything, or nothing," before turning back to the dancers, letting herself get caught up in the aura of excitement that permeated the room.

She could hardly take her eyes off the brilliant figures, turning and circling each other in time to the almost strident, high-pitched voice of a male singer. The women's dresses shaped their bodies from breast to hip, then flared to the floor in widening tiers of frilly ruffles, while the men wore wide-brimmed hats, short black jackets over ruffled white shirts, and high-waisted, torso-molding black pants. One in particular caught Mari's eye as he preened himself like some beautiful exotic bird, arms raised to extend the sinuous line of his body, hands clapping constantly as he turned, slowly revealing the curve of his back, buttocks, and legs. And all the while his boots sent a fusillade of sharp, staccato signals to his partner—insistent and compelling.

Charles was torn between watching Mari and the dancers. He saw her lips curve momentarily and then straighten again, leaving behind the ghost of a smile, and he found himself wishing he could hear whatever was going on inside her head. The tempo began to pick up—the guitars, clapping hands, and jingling tambourines mounting in a crescendo of sound—and he was aware of the quickening of his own heartbeat as well when the lead dancer, a woman named Galiana, moved out away from the others. A mass of vibrating motion from her tapping heels to the clattering castanets in her curving hands, her head was thrown back and held aloof between the archway of her arms. Dramatic was the only word Charles could think of to describe her face—all planes rather than soft curves, creating shadows that enhanced her already intense expressions. Her dress was a gray and black flowered print rather than the brilliant reds, blues, and greens of the other women in the troupe. And as she danced, Galiana's face revealed some deeply felt emotion, provoking a kind of kindred agony in her audience, affecting the crowd as nothing had before, forcing them to give voice to their own pent-up emotions. An almost palpable tension filled the crowded room as her partner began to edge closer and closer, keeping his back to her as they wove in and out and around each other in an intricate dance of invitation and denial. Her hands came down to grasp the ruffles at her hips, then lifted them toward him in an act of explicit invitation, while the noise and rhythm continued to intensify, binding the crowd in one collectively held breath.

Charles turned to look at Mari, only to find her eyes already fixed on him, and sparks seemed to explode between them, as hot as those from any real fire. And they knew, without understanding how, that the music and movement of the dancers' bodies were tapping into the same deep emotion in each of them—earthy, stripped naked, raw—creating a startling awareness and deep joy in simply being alive, a kind of singing sensation in the blood. The tension in the room continued to mount, and the audience grew restless as the anguished cries of the singer came faster and faster. Then, without any warning at all, there was silence. Sudden and complete. A silence that sounded loud. Until it was ripped by a single plaintive cry of nearly unbearable ecstasy.

The crowd exploded in a frenzy of clapping and yelling as they jumped to their feet, released at last from the nerve-shattering tension. Charles rose and pulled on Mari's hand, breaking through the spell that held her immobile, somewhere between the present and some distantly glimpsed past. Or was it the future? "Let's get out of here, okay?" She could only nod, then follow behind him as he opened a path for her through the crowd.

They walked a full block in silence, her hand tightly enclosed in his, letting the night air cool their aroused bodies and emotions. Charles couldn't bring himself to break physical contact with her. And Mari didn't want to talk, at least not about what they had just seen and felt.

"Galiana was the name of a Moorish princess who was the great love of Charlemagne's life, more than a thousand years ago," she mumbled finally. "I suppose it's probably a common name here."

Charles thought about that for a minute. "Yeah, I think I know what you're trying to say. The sense of time you feel here, history. And more. Maybe something to do with what Rafael was trying to explain to me about flamenco. Flamenco is the soul of 'al Andalus,' he said—Andalusia, that's what the Moors called this part of Spain. Not exactly restful, was it?" He threw her a wry smile, which she returned with an understanding one. They came to a tile-paved street open only to pedestrians, and he stopped abruptly, realizing for the first time where they were.

"Hell, I'm sorry, Mari! Guess I wasn't even thinking. You're probably too tired to walk back to the hotel."

"No, let's, unless it's miles and miles. Do you know where we are?"

"Sure." He dropped her hand and reached for her sweater, which she was carrying on one arm. "This is Calle San Miguel, the main drag, at least for tourists. Lots of shops, galleries, restaurants, all bunched in around here." They started walking again. "I looked around this afternoon, cased the place a little while you were napping. Spotted a little grocery store back there, by the way," he turned and pointed in the opposite direction, "with all kinds of imported stuff. Thought you might want to come back in the morning and take a look, see if you can find anything there your mother might like to eat." He smiled, beginning to feel more relaxed. "The town is built on cliffs overlooking the sea, and also down the rocky slopes from here to the beaches. Six miles of beaches. The Bajondillo is down there, just over the edge of the cliff." He pointed in the direction they were already headed. "One of the old mills is still there, built into the slope along the edge of the stairs down to the beach. Guess that's where the name Torremolinos came from—mill towers. There's a great view of the sea from the stairway, but probably not much we can see tonight, in the dark."

The stairway he was talking about wasn't exactly what she expected. As wide as a two-lane street, it tacked back and forth down the side of the cliff like a mountain road or path, but was edged on either side with shops and restaurants, even a hotel or two. "Ships, tankers, probably," Charles said when they stopped about halfway down, pointing straight out from the edge of the cliff to the few scattered lights way off in the distance. "And that's the Paseo Maritimo—the boulevard running along the edge of the beach," he added, pointing to the line of brighter lights.

"Could we walk down there?" she asked. "To the beach, I mean. I doubt I could sleep yet anyway."

"Sure, whatever you want." They continued on, strolling hand in hand in silence until they reached the wide walkway bordering the lighted paseo, then turned left. On one side was a row of big resort hotels, and on the other, sand and water. As they walked down the sidewalk on the beach side of the paseo, one cabana and umbrella concession after another began to block their view of the sea. Charles touched Mari's arm, guiding her through a break in the curb edging the sand, down the hard-packed path that wound between stacks of folded beach chairs and ended only a few feet from where the waves rolled in to a thin white edge. A half-moon illuminated the broad, open expanse of sky, sea, and sand, and they had it all to themselves. Charles draped an arm around Mari's shoulder, turning her to look up the beach, at the same time sheltering her face from the light coming from the paseo.

"See that tall rock abutment way down there?" He slid his hand across her shoulder and wrapped his fingers around the back of her neck as he bent down to her eye level, pointing off down the beach.

"Where the cliff looks like it's pushing out, intruding onto the beach?"

"Yeah, it does look natural, doesn't it? But it's not. That's all there is left of one of the watch towers the Moors built along this coast, every two miles, to warn against attacks by pirates coming up from North Africa." He slid one arm and then the other around her from behind, pulling her back against him, laid his cheek against her hair and slowly began rocking his head back and forth against the silky moonlit strands. He recognized the scent she used, though he'd never consciously thought about it until now, and closed his eyes, the better to relish the shape of her under his hands and against his body. Mari turned in his arms, brushing against his body as she rotated. He was about to step back and release her when he felt her arms sliding over his rib cage, under his jacket and around to his back. He stroked his palms over her hair, gently smoothing it back from her face, then stilled as their eyes met and held. His mouth came down on hers, hungry, searching, and she opened to him, eagerly, letting his tongue slide between her lips, ending the waiting and wanting. And then they both were exploring with tongues and hands, over firm muscle and soft hollows, from cloth to skin to cloth, their breath mingling, racing hearts beating against each other.

In just the few short hours they'd spent together, Mari's awareness of his hands had turned to longing as she watched them sketch and shape invisible objects and ideas. And now she was experiencing an even more intense awareness of herself as his hands shaped and caressed her body, evoking a kind of consciousness she'd never known before.

As his lips slipped away from hers and into her hair, Charles whispered, "Do you ever have nightmares?"

He still held her close, but Mari pushed away so she could see his face. "Sometimes. Why?"

"Because I haven't had a decent sleep since I got on that damn plane the other night!" She thought he was teasing at first, though he looked perfectly serious, even a little worried. "There you were in Houston, only a hundred and sixty miles away. But I had to come to Spain to find you, and I almost decided at the last minute not to come. Too busy with mid-semester exams, graduate students. And then I

77

was late getting to the airport. What if I'd missed my flight? I wake up in a cold sweat, thinking about it. What if I'd missed you, Mari?" She heard the desperation in his voice as he pulled her into his arms again and just held her, as if trying to reassure himself that she was real. He couldn't resist the urge to touch her hair, and cupped the back of her head with one hand, holding her against the curve of his neck as he let the smooth strands slip between his fingers.

Mari moved her head and lips against his neck, and felt a shiver ripple over his skin just before she pushed away. "You're not the only one. Nothing about any of this seems real to me. One day I'm in Houston and Rachel Widener is showing me your Vampire, and the next my mother is dying and I'm on my way to Spain. And there you are! She's probably going to be okay again, because of you. And now . . ."

He waited for her to go on, growing impatient when she didn't. "Now?" he urged.

"Well, you sort of appeared out of nowhere. I'm afraid maybe I just conjured you up out of my imagination, because I needed—because I was feeling so alone." She wasn't even sure what she was trying to say, much less how it might sound to him.

"You think you're imagining this?" he murmured, brushing his lips across hers between each word, "or are you trying to tell me it was just gratitude?" Now he was butterflying soft kisses from one corner of her mouth to the other.

"No, not exactly," she whispered, letting a slow smile take her lips as she reached for more.

"You don't sound too sure. Maybe we should try again, just to help you make up your mind."

Charles was standing at the desk talking with Juan Diaz. Apprehensive already about how he would take the fact that she was almost an hour late, Mari couldn't help noticing the way he was tapping a rolled newspaper against his thigh. Then he turned and saw her, and the worried expression vanished. He tossed a quick word to Juan and came toward her, wearing a smile that made her want to throw her arms around his neck and give him a big hug.

"I overslept," she confessed, returning his smile. "I hope you went ahead without me."

Charles simply bent forward to brush her cheek with his lips. "Every minute you're not with me seems like an hour," he whispered, without even a hint of impatience, then took her arm, keeping her close to his side as they started toward the hotel bar. Last night when they'd come in from the beach, it was filled with middle-aged German tourists listening to a male vocalist belt out a schmaltzy rendition of "Besamé Mucho," but this morning it was the breakfast room, and was set up with a self-service buffet.

A huge basket of fresh oranges stood at a tilt next to a noisy do-it-yourself electric juicer, while smaller baskets were filled with soft-boiled eggs wrapped in a linen napkin to keep them warm, croissants and hard rolls, and foil-wrapped squares of butter. There was a big platter of sliced cold meats and cheeses, which reminded Mari of her mother's complaint about breakfast at the hospital, and little bowls of jam were crowded in wherever they would fit. Off to one side stood three stainless-steel urns, like a row of sentinels, ready and waiting to dispense coffee, hot milk, and water.

Charles slid his hand from her waist to the back of her neck and let his thumb play along the line of her jaw, creating a shockwave of sensations that caused her cup to rattle against the saucer while she spooned powdered chocolate from a brown earthenware jar and then filled her cup with hot milk. She stole a quick glance at his face to see if he'd noticed, but he'd already turned away to fill his own cup with coffee.

"Looks like a perfect day for a swim," he commented as he stopped at a table near the floor-to-ceiling glass wall opening out onto a wide brick portico edged with flower beds. A well-kept lawn stretched toward the pool. Charles swigged down half a glass of fresh orange juice as soon as he sat down, then started on his egg, but his hand kept straying to hers from time to time as they ate, whenever it could find hers idle.

"Look at the pool. See how the brilliant blue rectangle shimmers, seems to hover just above that sea of green?" Mari asked. "Like a Rothko painting." Beyond the pool was the paseo, busy with cars now, and then the vast expanse of the Mediterranean, which this morning was bright white under the early-morning sun, making it almost impossible to look at, especially without sunglasses.

"You have your suit on?" Charles asked, turning to look at her. He'd suggested they sandwich visits with her mother around a swim and lunch at La Coquina, but the beach near the hospital was fairly remote from both the Playa Bajondillo and the Playa Carihuela, the two major beaches in town, and wasn't outfitted with facilities for changing.

"Yes, but are you sure you wouldn't rather do something else today, Charles? I wish you wouldn't feel you have to—"

He cut her off with a mumbled, "I thought we settled that last night," and a look that challenged her to continue the line of thought, which had everything to do with what was happening between them and nothing at all to do with feeling beholden or trapped by her need to spend time with her mother.

She gave in, nodding again, then began twirling her glass of tomato juice, first to the right and then to the left, keeping her eyes glued to the turgid liquid as it slowly followed the direction of the twist she gave it. Charles recognized the self-conscious gesture and reached out a hand to cover hers in an almost instinctive act of reassurance. As a result, the look on her face when she glanced up at him came as a surprise.

"It's viscoelastic, isn't it?" Mari blurted, without a trace of self-consciousness. "The tomato juice. Look! When you twist the glass it moves with it, but slower, almost like it's being dragged along." She showed him. "That's the viscous part, right? But when I stop turning the glass, it slows. And now, watch! It starts to reverse itself, recoiling like a spring! That's the elastic part, isn't it?"

Charles grinned and nodded, sharing her delight in the moment of self-discovery. "Yeah, you've got it. It both dissipates and stores energy, which means it's . . . viscoelastic." They said the last word in unison and then laughed together, too.

After breakfast they headed for the stairway up the side of the cliff, retracing their steps of the night before, through the narrow street from the hotel, past vendors hawking everything from handmade leather sandals and lace tablecloths to flowers and rotisseried chickens. Midway up the cliff Mari pulled Charles to a stop, both to get her breath and to look at the view of the sea. She spotted a little cinnamon-colored dog racing around the edge of a red-tiled roof they now could look down on, and as they stood there watching him, a crowd began to gather. The little dog picked his way across a narrow catwalk connecting the house to another building and began to bark excitedly, voicing his objection to the invasion of his garden, fifteen or more feet below, by two white cats.

All the shops on the Calle San Miguel were open, even though it was Sunday. Mari noticed the hours posted on several shop windows—nine to one, and then four-thirty to eight. As if jet lag wasn't enough, the entire day was shifted here, even at the hospital. Lunch was the big meal of the day, and wasn't served until two or two-thirty. Supper came around seven-thirty. She saw a sign for a used-book store written in both English and Spanish, with an arrow pointing to a stairway leading up to the second floor, and made mental note of where it was. A block farther on Charles stopped in front of a pharmacy. "You go on to the grocery," he said, pointing to a shop just a few doors away, "while I go in here and get you some sunscreen. I'll be there in a minute." He waved away her protest before she could get out more than two words. "Forget it. We're not working together, remember?"

They found Janet sitting in the overstuffed chair near the window, wrapped in a soft white cotton blanket, but she was still attached to the transparent bag of fluid by the thin plastic "umbilical cord" snaking down to the needle taped to the back of her left hand.

"Come in. Both of you," she called as soon as she saw them, lifting her free arm as Mari hurried across the room to accept her hug. Even Janet's voice sounded stronger this morning, though her body felt unbelievably thin and fragile to Mari, and she had to blink rapidly to disperse a quick rush of tears.

"This is Charles Merrill, Mom," she explained as she straightened slowly. "I told you about him yesterday, remember?"

"Of course I remember." Janet spoke softly, conserving her breath. "But I would have recognized him anyway."

Charles looked puzzled, and Mari hurried to explain, so he wouldn't think her mother's mind had been affected by her illness. "She's seen you in 'Have a Heart' who-knows-how-many times! Has her own copy of the videotape, shows it to all her friends, like home movies."

"Maybe you're the one to clue me in on how I can get a copy to show to my classes, then." Charles moved closer so he could hand her the flowers they'd brought. Mari had picked out the colors—yellow, orange, and violet—but Charles was the one who'd insisted they be fragrant, to help dispel the antiseptic smell of the hospital.

Janet's blue eyes sparkled with pleasure as she lifted the flowers to her face, using both hands in spite of the intravenous needle. "Freesias," she breathed, closing her eyes momentarily as she inhaled their aroma.

"We brought you some goodies to eat, too, Mom," Mari added. "Jell-O, for one thing, from a store up on the Calle San Miguel that has stuff from all over the world. And Charles brought you the *Tribune,* so you can catch up on what's going on in the world. But maybe I'd better go find Dr. Ibarzábal before he finishes his rounds, get him to leave instructions for the kitchen. Otherwise I doubt they'll be willing to prepare it for you."

"Yes, of course, you go on. Charles and I will talk." As Mari left the room she heard her mother ask, "Can you imagine a hospital that doesn't serve Jell-O, Charles?"

"That bad, huh?" He plucked at the knees of his trousers and squatted down beside her chair to be at her eye level. Janet McNichols was smaller than Mari and they didn't look much alike—Mari's cheekbones were more prominent, and Janet's hair was a reddish brown, now streaked with gray—but he caught a fleeting glimpse of a familiar expression every time she smiled.

"Actually, I don't remember too much before Marilyn came, except for this blamed thing!" The blanket fell away from her arm as she extended her hand to show him the hollow steel needle, and Charles almost winced when he saw all the purple hematomas, some of them beginning to turn yellow around the edges. "Seems like the nurse was forever pulling it out just so she could stick it back in, in a different place." She couldn't have learned much from the nurses about what they were doing or why, Charles thought, when she could hardly communicate her most elementary needs to them. He took her hand, placed it in the palm of his own and held it, slowly stroking the fragile skin with his thumb.

"Marilyn?" he asked with a grin. "So that's it! I wondered—"

"Where the Mari came from?" she finished for him. "Marilyn was a big mouthful for Jackie, my other daughter, when she was little. So of course we all ended up calling her that." She stared at her hand in his for a couple of seconds, apparently lost in her memories. "Mari was so, so adventuresome, so curious. So . . . special." Charles thought she might be on the verge of tears, but when she looked up at him he saw a smile in her eyes. "But then, I'm not exactly an unbiased source, as Mari would say."

"That's okay, Mrs. McNichols, I'm not, either," he assured her with a grin.

"Oh, let's not be formal with each other, Charles. Call me Jan. Anyway, I feel as if I already know you. Mari told me about your friend from Madrid, the one who called my doctor the other night. I hope you will thank him for me." He shifted his hand while she was talking, just enough to slide one finger over the pulse in her wrist.

"My pressure was ninety-eight over fifty-four this morning," she told him immediately, letting him know that she was perfectly aware of what he was doing. "Not too bad, but not good enough to get me home, is it?"

"But better than a couple of days ago, I bet," Charles answered. "How are your ankles?" Janet began pulling at the blanket, so he could see for himself. They were thick and puffy, swollen with fluid, just as he expected. "It will help to move around, but you're not up walking already, are you?" He rewrapped and tucked the blanket under her feet while he talked.

"No. A therapist came in this morning to begin exercising my legs. In bed. Then he just swooped me up, plunked me down over here, and wrapped me up in this cocoon. What a relief it was to get out of that bed! His name is Antonio, and he doesn't speak English, but he pointed out the door, hummed the wedding march, and said, *'Mañana.'* So I know he means for me to walk down the hall tomorrow. So I'll soon be ready to go home." Charles saw the sparkle of determination in her eyes. "Now, I want to hear what you've been doing in your research, since Mari interviewed you, I mean."

Mari spotted Dr. Ibarzábal at the far end of the hall, talking with one of the nurses in the little closetlike room that passed for a dispensary, and stood outside the door for a minute, waiting for him to see her.

"Ah, Mrs. Ashmore, your mother is better again today, yes?" he commented as he came out into the hall to join her.

"Yes," Mari agreed quickly, "but my name—" She hesitated, knowing her tongue was going to trip, even before she tried to say it. "Would you mind calling me McNichols instead of Ash—Ashmore, Dr. Ibarzábal? That was my married name, and I know my mother still uses it, but I'm . . . uh, not married now. Better yet, how about just Mari?" She didn't wait for his answer. "I bought some food in town that I thought might help her appetite, but I knew you'd want to check it over, make sure there isn't something here she shouldn't have."

"Yes, of course." He smiled suddenly, which changed his entire demeanor. "I will call you Mari, and you will call me Cisco, all right? That is the name my friends call me." His request took her completely by surprise, since he'd always been so formal up to now, as if he wanted to keep a proper distance with his patients and their families. "Your mother and I, we speak for a time this morning. It is the first time she is able, I think. And she says she is from Denver, which I know very well because I go sometimes to Aspen to ski."

"Really?" She smiled the word. "When you have the mountains right here behind you? I've read that you can ski them almost all year 'round."

"Yes. Some of the peaks are more than three thousand meters—eleven thousand feet you would say. Mulhacen, which you can sometimes see from here on a very clear day.

I go to the mountains every weekend I can be away from the hospital. But I have a fondness for your Rocky Mountains, too. I sometimes visit my relatives who live in Wyoming—they go there many years ago to herd the sheep."

"Artzainak?" Mari asked, using the Basque word for sheepherders. "You're Basque?" Why hadn't she thought of that before? The "zabal" ending was common among the people who called themselves *euskadi* in their own language, which was still something of a mystery because it wasn't related to any known linguistic family. Even the word Basque had come from French, and ultimately from the Latin *vascones*.

"You speak Euskara?" he asked, his voice wavering with surprise.

"Oh no!" she denied with a little laugh. "Only a few words that I learned several years ago when I visited some of the sheep camps in Wyoming for a newspaper story on the Basques who settled those remote areas. It's slowly dying out as a way of life now, but I expect you know that."

He nodded thoughtfully, staring out the window into the parking lot behind the hospital. "Yes, but the customs stay—the holidays, the games and dances—at least in a few towns."

"Yes, I remember seeing one dance that was done with bent wooden hoops. And another with the Basque flag." She paused. "I suppose you know that the Basques have the highest incidence of Rh negative factor in their blood of any population in the world—along with some of the Berber tribes in Morocco, which of course is just a few miles away across the Strait of Gibraltar. And I'll bet that some day soon," she continued nonchalantly as she handed him the paper bag from the grocery store, not even noticing his look of surprise, "someone's going to figure out where you Basques and your language came from, just from that one piece of information alone."

"But I do not understand how a newspaper reporter knows about such things. Or cares!" He stared at her with a puzzled expression as he opened the bag without even being conscious of what he was doing.

"A *medical* news reporter, Cisco. And I work in television now, in Houston."

As understanding dawned, he gave her a smile that stripped ten years from his age. "Ah, I see. Then perhaps you will have lunch with me one day. You can tell *me* about the famous Houston Medical Center, and I will tell *you* all about the blood of the Basques, eh?"

"You've got a deal!" she agreed, laughing, then waited while he looked over the food she'd brought for her mother. "My friend who asked Dr. Prados to call you, from Madrid, is here today. He's a biomedical engineer. Perhaps you'd like to meet him, if you have time," she ventured while he scribbled a few words on a slip of paper.

Cisco leaned back into the dispensary to hand the nurse his written instructions for the kitchen, then for answer took her arm and began to guide her back down the hall toward her mother's room. "For you and this mysterious friend of yours, Mari, I make the time."

CHAPTER

5

"You sure are a fast worker," Charles teased, swinging Mari's hand as they walked toward the beach. "Did you see your mother's face when you called him Cisco?"

"No, but I can imagine. She's one of the ones I was talking about, who put doctors up on a pedestal, never question anything they say or do. And from what I saw back there, she accepted you into the priesthood, too. All that stuff about diuretics leaching potassium out of the system, which is needed to 'fire' the heart. Bet she eats a banana a day from now on. I've never been a reliable source, maybe because she still sees me as a child. Do you have that problem with your mother?"

"Not that I know of," he answered with a laugh. "Cisco has her on a supplement, but I figured it wouldn't hurt to give bananas a plug since you're trying to get her to eat more, especially low-fat stuff with enough calories to give her energy."

Suddenly aware of how she must sound to him, she mumbled, "I'm sorry, Charles. I meant to thank you for being so kind, and patient with all her questions. Instead, I end up sounding resentful, and childish."

"No need to thank me for liking her, *Marilyn.*" He emphasized her name on purpose, to let her know that he

87

knew. "She's sharp, and still has a sense of humor in spite of everything. Wanted to know how come engineers could build an artificial heart but not a decent bedpan!" He chuckled, remembering, then thought of something else. "She probably needs more touching, by the way." He grinned at her. "*She's* interested in my research, too. You two are a lot alike."

"Oh no, Charles," Mari protested. "My mother and I are about as different as any two people can possibly be, which I guess is why we don't get along very well. Never have."

Charles pulled her to a stop. "You're serious, aren't you?" he asked incredulously.

"Oh, we're civil enough to each other, at least on the surface. But we operate under a sort of uneasy truce, and have for years. We used to battle all the time, until I finally started to practice avoidance, learned not to talk to her about what I really thought, or how I felt." She looked down at her feet. "I suppose that hurt her, when she realized what I was doing. But we just couldn't seem to agree about anything, whether it was politics or religion, how much play is enough to how much work isn't. I know she means well, but you name it, if it has anything to do with how I live my life, what I really think or feel, we argue about it."

Her eyes were brimming with tears, which to Charles meant there was still a lot of anger and frustration, sadness, and perhaps even a sense of loss behind her half-hearted attempt to make light of the conflict with her mother. "What about your father?" he asked, more out of curiosity than anything else.

"Nothing wrong with debating the issues, he used to say. I don't know what I'd have done without him. He was the one who kept everything on an even keel, in balance."

"Yeah, well, I guess that happens sometimes." They walked on in silence for the next couple of blocks, both pretending an interest they didn't have in the gardens they were passing.

"What did you mean when you said she needs more touching, Charles?" Mari asked then, her voice so low that he could barely hear her. He was still holding her hand, hadn't let go of it, in fact, since they left the hospital, and she'd become intensely aware of how important that contact was to her. And also of how much she was dreading the time when he would leave.

"Weak as she is, she held on tight when I took her hand, like a swimmer going down for the third time. So I pulled the pulse routine and some other stuff, just to have an excuse. I'll bet she needs that kind of medicine as much as the other, probably has been missing it ever since your father died." Mari squeezed his hand because she suddenly couldn't speak, and then the tears began streaming down her cheeks. She tried to laugh at herself and couldn't do that, either, which only made her feel worse—silly and inept, and embarrassed. Charles stopped and wrapped his arms around her, right there in broad daylight in the middle of a public sidewalk, cupping the back of her head with one hand to hold her close. He waited a couple of minutes, then smoothed the hair back from her face and handed her his handkerchief. "Better?" he asked with a half smile as she dabbed at her eyes and sniffed.

She nodded and smiled back. "Sorry about that, too."

"No problem," he answered easily, taking her hand as they began walking again.

The bright, warm day had turned out a scattering of sunbathers even on this remote section of the beach. "Probably residents of the apartments around here," Charles guessed as they walked along the firm sand near the edge of the water until they'd left everyone behind. "How about here?" Mari suggested. She took two big bath towels out of the oversize leather shoulder bag she used as a carryon when she traveled, spread them on the sand and then kicked off her sandals.

She wasn't embarrassed about undressing in public, but couldn't help worrying about whether Charles would find her body attractive. Her winter-white skin always made her feel so naked and exposed, especially when she was with someone darker. He stepped out of his pants, folded and then dropped them near one of the towels, and straightened. She'd expected him to have more hair on his body, maybe because it was so thick on his forearms, but there was only a light scattering of dark hair across his chest and down his legs. One leg seemed to bend in slightly at the knee, but perhaps that was just the way he was standing—facing her, waiting. For what? Her approval? The thought that he might be as apprehensive about her response as she was about his came with startling awareness. Certainly the fear of being inadequate had to be a two-way street, though she hadn't really thought much about that before. But Charles had nothing to worry about. She could hardly keep her eyes off him, in fact. His body exuded a subtle aura of strength, without any of the ostentatious bulging muscles that came with pumping iron, and his torso was flat and smooth both above and below the lean black trunks.

"Not that I really mind, but the top of you is going to be well-done before you even get your skirt off if you stand there much longer," Charles teased, then laughed out loud when her face began to turn red without any help from the sun.

"May your tanned hide burn in hell for all eternity!" Mari muttered darkly as she began unbuttoning the waistband of her skirt. Charles heard her and burst out laughing all over.

"What'd you do with the sunscreen?" he asked finally, still chuckling.

"I will do it myself, thank you," she muttered as she unzipped her skirt and let it fall to the sand, then stepped out of it, still chafing at being caught staring at him.

But now it was Charles's turn to stare. Her suit was a sort of bluebonnet-blue flowered print, elasticized so it hugged every curve and hollow of her body, revealing it in a way that made her look smaller and more fragile than he expected. Maybe that was because she gave the impression of being so strong in ways that had nothing to do with physical strength, he thought. Her breasts were small, yet were rounded and full, just right to fit into the palm of his hand. He liked what he saw so much, in fact, that he was having one hell of a time controlling the urge to touch, and at last gave in to it by extending an open palm and repeating his demand. "Sunscreen?"

"I can do it," she repeated, just as insistently, as she dug into her shoulder bag.

"Okay, if you insist, but I've got something else, when you finish with that."

She spread the sunscreen between her palms, then rubbed

it over her neck and chest, up her arms and over her shoulders, and finally on her nose, chin, and cheeks, then held the tube out to him. "Here—you can do my back, where I can't reach."

He covered every inch of exposed skin, then picked up the small plastic bottle he'd gotten from the pharmacist on Calle San Miguel. "Spanish women have been using this for centuries, or so I'm told, and swear it's better for their skin than any modern cosmetic preparation. I thought maybe you'd like to try it."

"Smells wonderful. What is it?" She turned to look at the little bottle he held up.

"Aceite de Almendras Dulces." He pronounced the Spanish words slowly, trying to get them right. "Oil of sweet almonds, from the orchards growing on the hills all around here." He waited a moment before touching her again, trying to stifle the nearly overwhelming urge to reach out and wrap his arms around her, to protect her from the sun or from whatever might hurt her, whether real or only imagined.

Mari searched his eyes, so deep and penetrating she couldn't help wondering if he could see into all the dark corners of her soul. She found it impossible to look away. And this time she didn't care if he knew it. Charles brought his hand to her cheek, smoothing and spreading the almond oil over first one and then the other with a feathery touch. Her eyelids closed, and she was aware of nothing but the touch of his fingers, tracing the edge of her jaw, the hollow underneath, moving to her chest, stroking the exposed tops of her breasts, curving up and over her shoulders, sliding down her arms to the tips of her fingers, tugging at them to pull her down onto the towel. Circling her ankle, over her calf and under her knee, inching up her thigh, slowly, until he reached the edge of her suit. Then beginning all over again on the other leg.

When he finished, Charles ran a forefinger down the ridge of her nose, and Mari's eyes flew open to find him staring at her lips. Then he smoothed oil there, too, just before he framed her face between his hands and slowly brought her lips to his. After only a few seconds he broke the kiss, still trying to restrain a hunger that was threatening to rage out of control, and hugged her close. "I can't seem to get enough of touching you," he whispered, burying his face in her hair.

Desperate for some way to break the intensity of the feeling that was building in both of them, Mari said the first thing that came to mind. "Mae West was right. Give a man a free hand and he'll run it all over you!"

Charles caught the familiar sparkle of mischief in her eyes as he pulled away, and matched her grin as he rose. Mari watched him stride through the shallow water, then lean into an incoming wave and move away from shore with a strong crawl stroke. His arms cut the water with the same, almost lazy deliberateness that marked his every move, which she now recognized was simply part of who and what he was. She had no thought of catching up with him, especially when she discovered how cold the water was, but she moved quickly, seeking the warming that always came with exercise. Battling the waves had an exhilarating effect, and by the time she climbed out, she felt invigorated and refreshed, though she hadn't stayed in long, mostly because she hadn't wanted him to see her weak, amateurish efforts, especially in comparison with his. She got out another towel, dried her face and arms and then wrapped it around her body like a sarong, tucking the corner in over one breast, before settling down to watch Charles again. How good and right it felt, being here in this particular place, at this moment in her life, with Charles Merrill. He came dripping out of the water several minutes later, to flop down on his towel next to her with a sigh of satisfaction.

"You swim as if you were born near water."

"Nope," he laughed, "just a tough coach. He really worked our butts! Almost everything I've tried since has seemed easy by comparison. But I didn't have any choice. It was either swim or sell real estate."

"How come?"

"That's how I got through undergraduate school—on a swimming scholarship. Broke my leg when I was thirteen. Riding my bicycle. Dark night. Raining. Hit by a car. A woman. Didn't see me." He was still breathing fast, and the words came out in short bursts. He pointed to a round depression in the skin high up on the outside of his left thigh, then a matching scar on the inside. "They pegged the femur, then added a cast, hip to heel, just to be sure. And I wore that damn thing for six months. By the time it came off, the muscles were atrophied. Started swimming for therapy. Turned out to be my ticket to the university." He leaned back on his elbow in a half-reclining position and stared out over the water for a minute, then down at the sand, lost in thought. Mari was silent, waiting to see if there were more to his story.

She'd done her homework before interviewing him and knew he'd started the university at sixteen. The loss to everyone, had Charles Merrill been forced to drop out because he couldn't swim well enough, just didn't bear thinking about. Because so much of what was known today about how the blood moves through the body had come out of his laboratory.

"See that?" he asked, drawing a squiggly line in the steel-gray sand with a forefinger, then pointing to where the grains were piled up at the edge. "I think we've got to change the way we think about blood, see it as a granular material, instead of like water. Because the red cells move like grains of sand edging past each other." He paused, then went on to explain what he meant. Mari let the towel slip down so the sun could dry her suit while she listened, fascinated by this unexpected glimpse into the way his mind worked. She remembered the video of Charles in his lab, and her voice-over. *The red cells are covered with tiny fiberlike projections, like Velcro, that tend to become attached to each other. And these clumped cells have to be broken apart in order for the blood to flow.* And then Charles's voice. *"In pathological blood those 'hooks' are stronger than in normal blood, so the heart has to work harder to maintain flow."*

"You should have seen the exhibits at the meeting in Madrid," Charles commented, bringing her back to the here and now. "The drug companies make it all sound so damned simple. Most of the medics, too, especially the guys who are on their payrolls as consultants, not to mention the ones they recruit with research grants."

"You mean the drug companies buy off researchers so they'll manipulate their data to support claims for the company's products?" she asked, sitting up straight.

"Not any I know of personally, at least not malicious falsification of data, if that's what you mean. More a matter of finding pretty much what you're looking for, I suppose." He glanced at her shoulders. "Did you put more sunscreen on after you got out of the water?" She handed him the tube. "I suppose manipulation is the right word," he continued, starting on her arms, "though the kind I'm talking about is more subtle. But the net effect can be pretty broad, because certain areas of research get singled out, and attention and funds are focused on problems of interest to these companies. The really big money goes where the opinion leaders go, the big boys, so the strategy of the big pharmaceuticals, as I see it, is to either get to these so-called stars or build new ones, which they do with both money and ego gratification. Some companies put out tabloid 'news' sheets that pump up not only their products, but the stars they're building, who then get onto the boards of professional journals and societies, which in turn puts them in control of who gets published, who presents invited lectures at meetings, whose students win awards, stuff like that. Hollowell's fingerprints are all over this meeting, for instance, underwriting everything from cocktails to the gold medal for outstanding work in clinical hemorrheology—blood flow—which goes to an under-forty researcher. They fund the award, they get a man on the committee to select."

He nudged Mari's shoulder to indicate that he wanted her to lie back on the towel so he could do her legs and thighs next. She obeyed without even thinking, anxious for him to continue. "Another multinational had equipment set up to show how long it takes a 'normal' red cell to drip through a special millipore filter, claimed that's a measure of cell deformability. No mention of the force exerted by the heart, or that the cells stack up and block the pores of the filter almost immediately. And several companies were pushing drugs to restore 'proper' deformability, even though we still don't know what that is! Organon's got Fludilat, and Hoechst has Trental."

"I remember Hoechst from somewhere."

"Probably those television ads they ran, where an older man gets pains in his legs whenever he goes walking with his wife. Discovers he has intermittent claudication—

inadequate circulation of blood to the legs. An attempt to psych up the public at the same time they started distributing Trental to the medics."

"But doesn't your own research show that how soft or hard the red cells are is important, especially where the passageways are so small the cells have to be able to bend or stretch to get through?"

"Sure. Unfortunately the problem isn't that simple." He grinned, appreciating her question and the quick mind that produced it. "Watching it drip through some damn filter doesn't have anything to do with the real world. Red-cell deformability depends on how fast it's moving. Did you ever play with Silly Putty when you were a kid?" His grin was so infectious, she couldn't help matching it as she nodded eagerly. "Usually it's soft enough to mold with your fingers, right? Left alone long enough, in fact, it takes on the shape of whatever container you put it in—or don't. I remember once when I forgot to put it back in its little egg. Did I ever catch hell, 'cause it flowed right into the rug!" She matched his grin and nodded understandingly. "But do you remember what happens when you form it into a ball and throw it down on the sidewalk?"

"It bounces," she answered immediately, her eyes never leaving his face.

"Same thing with the red cells. Push them fast enough and they act like they're hard, too, which means they're not going to bend or stretch very easily." Mari understood the analogy instantly, but also that she was getting only a glimpse of the complexity of the problem he was working on.

"But you're one of the big boys, Charles. Isn't there anything *you* can do about what's going on?"

"I'm under forty and I've never won the award, so it would sound like sour grapes. Besides that, I've always refused to do time on committees, and anybody with half a brain knows what that means—I'm either some kind of freak or not to be trusted." She missed the touch of his hand the instant he finished with her legs. Charles edged closer and peered into her face. "Hey! You know you're putting wrinkles in your forehead with that frown?" She dropped her head back on the towel and closed her eyes, but only because she couldn't keep them open against the bright light.

"That's unbelievable," she muttered.

"What? You thought I was over forty, or I'm not a freak?" He smoothed the wrinkles in her forehead with his fingers, applying the sunscreen there, too. She could tell from his voice that he was teasing her again.

"No, you fool, I know exactly how old you are. And the fact that you've never gotten the award is all the proof anybody needs to know there's something really rotten in Denmark!"

Charles's fingers stilled, then both hands framed her face for a second before he began smoothing back her hair. It felt like a caress, and when he bent down to bestow a soft kiss on her surprised lips, she knew that's exactly what it was. "Maybe I'm just hearing what I want to, but backhanded as it was, that sounded like a compliment to me." His words whispered across her lips just before she circled an arm around his neck and pulled his mouth back to hers.

The sky was overcast and the water had turned gun-metal gray by the time they left the beach. When they arrived at La Coquina, the outdoor terrace was completely deserted. "We're in luck," Charles commented, urging her ahead of him toward the only empty table inside, next to the windows looking out on the wide boulevard. A variety of fresh fish were laid out along the bar today, for all to see and choose from. Once again the proprietor came to wait on them, probably because he was the only one who spoke English, Mari decided. "Would you choose for me?" she asked him. "Fish, but something light."

"I fix just for you, very simple," he assured her, then turned to Charles.

"Same for me, but something different. And whatever wine you think goes with it. Surprise us."

The proprietor smiled. "I see to everything," he agreed.

"From what I can see at other tables, this promises to be another fantastic adventure," Mari whispered as soon as he was gone.

"It's been an adventure for me, Mari, an exploration into

uncharted territory, ever since I set foot on that plane in New York," Charles answered, completely serious as he reached across the table and covered her hand.

A parade of waiters began to arrive then, first with a bottle of white wine, then an earthenware pot filled with gazpacho—a cold tomato soup with chopped cucumber and parsley sprinkled on top—along with the usual crusty bread. And finally, the proprietor himself appeared with the fish course.

"The *dorada* is for you," he announced as he set a plate in front of Mari, then turned to Charles, "and for you, the *boquerones.*"

She tried a bite, then looked up at him. "Sole?"

He nodded. "Pan-fried in butter, sprinkled with just a little garlic and parsley." He looked at Charles next, and saw he needed help. "It is not impolite to eat *boquerones* with the hands. Like there." He pointed toward a table in the corner where a man was nibbling on the small deep-fried fish just as if it was corn on the cob.

Charles did the same. "Yeah, it's great! Here, you try one, Mari."

She did, laughing her delight with still another new taste experience, and then Charles had a bite of her sole. They tried guessing what the little fish was called in English, laughing at themselves and each other at the same time. "Smelt," Mari suggested, only to have Charles accuse her of making up the name. "Sardines" was Charles's entry, though he'd never had any except from a can. The proprietor finally left them to it, wearing a small satisfied smile.

"Tell me why you refuse to work inside the scientific organizations, Charles," Mari asked. "I realize you're not going to win all the time, but if you disagree with what's going on, wouldn't it be better to at least be in a position to argue your views rather than sit back and say nothing?"

It took him a second to figure out what she was talking about. "Boy, once you get your teeth into something, you really do hang in there, don't you?" He sort of halfway laughed, admiring her tenacity even though it meant postponing what he really wanted to talk about.

"I'm sorry, Charles, I wasn't thinking. It's really none of

my business—" Two red smudges appeared on her cheeks, and Charles hunted quickly for some way to make amends. He reached across the table for her hand again.

"And I didn't mean that the way you took it, Mari-Lynn." He pronounced her name as two separate words. "How many people do you think I meet who give a damn one way or the other, who are interested enough to ask a question like that?" She didn't answer him, but the look in her eyes softened perceptibly. "You think maybe I'm running from a fight, huh?" he continued, his expression thoughtful as he stroked his thumb across the back of her hand. "I guess I like to think that my data is a lot harder to ignore than anything I could say. That what I *do* is a better way to say what I think the really important problems are, even if they don't agree."

She watched his face for a minute, then gave him a little nod. He breathed a sigh of relief and released her hand. "So how come you didn't tell me you used to write for the *International Herald Tribune,* Lynn?" he asked with a perfectly straight face. "More I learn about you, the more impressed I am, but you sure don't let on much—"

"Lynn? Mari-Lynn? What are you doing?" she asked finally.

"Just experimenting."

"How about 'Mac'? Or another one of my favorites—M and M? 'She melts in your mouth instead of your hand.' I've heard them all. What's wrong with Mari?"

"Nothing. I like it. Like Marilyn, too. Like everything about you." What had started as a tease suddenly turned serious, surprising them both. He hesitated only a moment, then reached for her hand again. "You know I have to go back to Madrid in the morning, don't you?"

"I suppose," she admitted with a sad smile. "I'm so glad you came, Charles. I'm not sure if it's this place—the air and water, the flowers, and the light—or some magic spell you've cast, but I can't remember ever having such a . . . such a wonderful time."

"Then go with me to the Alhambra. I can be back here Wednesday night or early Thursday morning. We could drive to Granada, spend the day. It's only eighty miles." He felt a rush of excitement at finally giving voice to the idea he'd been bouncing around in his head all day.

"I'd love to, but—" Mari felt her pulse quicken, and turned away to look out the window in case it showed on her face. Until now she'd refused to let herself think about when, or even if, she might see Charles again. Or how she could bring herself to interview him about his Vampire, six months or more from now, just as if nothing had ever happened between them. She only vaguely noticed how the palm fronds were whipping around in the wind.

"Your mother's going to make it, Mari," Charles continued. "More important, she believes she's going to get home now, since you came. And I'm guessing that Jan can be a pretty determined lady." Mari couldn't help smiling at that, because he was so right. "I wish I could stay longer, but one of my students has her oral exam Saturday morning, and I must be there." He waited, hoping he'd persuaded her.

"Yes, let's," she agreed with a rush of eagerness, then remembered to add, "If Mom continues to improve like she has, that is!" She gave him an impish grin. "I hear the Alhambra is like no other place in the world! I've always wanted to see it." The excitement he saw in her eyes took his breath. His laugh, when it came, was a mixture of both relief and surprise.

They finished off with huge bowls of fresh strawberries topped with whipped cream, and were sipping espresso when the proprietor reappeared. "You enjoy?" he asked softly.

"More than that," Mari answered for both of them. "It was an experience."

He smiled his appreciation. "Then perhaps you would let me bring you a brandy, with the coffee?" Charles knew from the way he asked that he meant "with my compliments."

"Only if you'll join us," Charles suggested.

"I am Fernando Ramos."

He turned and waved to one of the waiters, extended his hand first to Mari and then to Charles before sitting down. Mari asked where he'd learned to speak English, and he told them about the restaurant he'd operated in England, on the coast near Brighton. They talked over coffee and brandy for several minutes, until a sudden gust of wind rattled the windows.

"It looks like we are in for a good storm tonight,"

Fernando observed. "So you should get inside soon, before the rain begins."

By the time they arrived back at the Bajondillo it was just beginning to rain, and what was left of the daylight had taken on an eerie, greenish cast. The soft, caressing air of Andalusia had turned sharp, causing them both to shiver as they ran the few steps from the cab to the hotel entrance. They separated at the door to Mari's room, to go wash off the saltwater residue and put on warmer clothes.

Mari ran a quick bath, submerged her body until only the tips of her breasts rose like small peaked islands in a tropical sea, and closed her eyes. In her mind she could see the scene in the little restaurant, and hear Charles's slightly husky voice. She could feel his hands, too, circling her calf, sliding into the sensitive area behind her knee, up to her thigh, over her shoulders and across the tops of her breasts as he spread the almond oil, caressing her face or enclosing her hand in his, always so warm, wherever he touched her. And then everything went black.

She tried blinking her eyes a few times, just to confirm that she did have them open, which meant that the lights had gone off, undoubtedly due to the storm. She waited, staying exactly where she was for a couple of minutes, to see if the electricity would come back on, but lying naked in a tub of water made her feel vulnerable, too unready for whatever might happen next. She felt for the lever to let the water out, turned on both faucets as she stood up, adjusted the temperature, then sent it to the shower head as she reached for her bottle of shampoo.

The blackness lightened slightly when she came out into the bedroom, mostly because of the diffuse greenish-yellow light coming through the glass door to the little balcony. She put out an arm, just in case, and went to see what was happening outside. The sky and sea had simply disappeared, and in their place was an amorphous, hazy sort of mist. And in front of that the palms and streetlights lining the Paseo Maritimo were partnering each other in a frantic dance. She heard tapping at her door and turned to make her way back across the room, trying to "see" the furniture in her head. She felt to make sure the night chain was in place—which she'd trained herself to use wherever she was, at Tony's insistence—before easing the door open.

"It's me." Mari closed the door, slid the chain back and then pulled it open. Charles stepped into the room and wrapped her in his arms, all in one motion. "Are you okay?" he whispered into her damp hair.

"Sure, but everything is such a strange color. Looks eerie, doesn't it?" She whispered, too, against his neck, feeling warm and secure again. "I was in the tub when the lights went."

"You should see it from my room! The sea has come alive!" He gave vent to his building excitement as he peered at her, trying to see her face. "It's really fantastic out there. Look!" He extended a hand. "I got a candle from Juan, and a bottle of Manzanilla from the bar. How about a come-as-you-are party?"

"But my hair is still wet," she protested, even though she wanted to rush to her room right away. It was on the same floor as hers, but fronted the beach, with windows opening to the sea in a broad semicircle. "And I'm not dressed."

"I don't mind, and no one else will know." She could hear the smile in his voice, even if she couldn't see it. "And I'll dry your hair with a towel while we watch." As an answer, she simply made her way back to her cosmetics case and searched for her hairbrush, then felt around on the top of the chest for her key.

"Juan says lines are down all over the place, so it may be morning before the electricity is back on," Charles said as he took her arm to guide her down the hallway.

"I don't care," she whispered conspiratorially, "so long as it isn't while I'm walking down the hall in my robe with a strange, fully dressed man!"

She noticed the music as soon as she stepped into his room, though she didn't know where it was coming from. "How appropriate," she commented as she walked toward the glowing wall of windows to watch the sea.

"You recognize it?" he asked, a little surprised.

"Yes," she answered, without turning around. "Frank Bridge's 'The Sea,' isn't it?"

"Yeah. I forgot, you were a music major—for a while. What instrument do you play?" He filled two glasses. When he looked up again, she had her brush out and was trying to get the tangles out of her hair. He could see now that her velour robe was sort of a dusty-pink color.

"Cello, a couple of others, none of them very well." He got the impression that she didn't want to talk about it.

"Here, just what we need for a stormy night. The real stuff, from Sanlucar." Mari turned to accept the glass he held out. He cupped the side of her face with one hand, then smoothed it over her damp hair as he watched her face in the flickering candlelight. "Cold? Want me to brush it for you?"

She shook her head, sensing intuitively that it was nearing decision time. "It will be dry in a few minutes." She sipped at the sherry and turned back to look out at the sea. She heard him set his glass down, and then his arms came around her from behind, overlapping just under her breasts as he pulled her back against his body.

The tall yellow streetlamps marking the wide paseo lit a scene of unrelieved fury. The beach was gone, drowned in the raging waves that came crashing against the low seawall. And everything else—blue sky, green sea, and gray sand, red tiles and stark white walls—all seemed to have been painted with the same brush, transforming the scene into a sepia-toned photograph. Balls of sea mist lifted by gusts of wind rushed at them, here and gone again in the blink of an eye as they passed under the lights.

Charles tightened his hold and rubbed his cheek against her hair, and then his lips began murmuring words and kisses against the curve of her face, along the line of her jaw, and down into the concave hollow below. "You feel soft as a puppy." She smiled at the childlike words, but there was nothing childish about the response of her body when one of his hands moved up to cup her breast. A simmering fire blazed to life somewhere deep inside her body, fanned by more than the picture of his hands that she carried with her everywhere, inside her head. He stroked her emotions and her mind as well as her breast, all in one huge engulfing wave as overwhelming as those crashing against the seawall outside. His lips moved back to her temple, walking kisses from her chin to her hairline and then back again, only to stop teasingly at the corner of her mouth.

Mari's eyes opened onto the misty, colorless, unrecognizable world outside, and then the flickering candlelight inside as he turned her to face him. She loved being touched by him, and she loved touching him, too, she realized, as one arm curled around the back of his neck so she could run her fingers through the springy curls there, while the other slipped around his waist and up under his sweater to his warm back. His lips sought hers, caressing, asking, seeking, and finding the answer he wanted as her lips parted to admit him. Their tongues flirted, then blazed a trail of discovery, creating their own language along the way.

His hands began a voyage, too, from her breasts to her rib cage, dipping into the curve of her waist and then down over her hips to where her thighs straightened, searing the imprint of her body into his memory. Her hands left off playing over the muscles of his back to move down to the belt circling his waist, to his firmly rounded buttocks, holding him while she swayed from side to side, rubbing against his hard flesh. Charles moaned an agonized breath into her mouth, straining his hips against hers, then forced himself to break contact so he could reach down between them and loosen the tie of her wraparound robe. As it fell open he knew for certain that she was a natural blonde.

He caressed her body with his eyes, from the valley between her small, full breasts to the smoky curls where her thighs joined. "I've read about it," he said wonderingly, "but I've never seen it firsthand." Mari felt disoriented at first, then as if someone had thrown cold water on her heated face. "The sexual flush . . ." He let the words trail off as he sensed her begin to withdraw, closing him out, even before she pulled nervously at the edges of her robe, trying to cover herself. Her eyes shifted away from his to focus instead on the dark nothingness above his left shoulder.

And all of a sudden it hit Charles that he was standing on the brink of disaster. It simply hadn't even occurred to him that she might find his words offensive or embarrassing. He searched frantically for some way to make her understand as he pulled her into his arms again, just to be sure she didn't get away from him. "Your flushed body is the most beautiful thing I've ever seen," he whispered into her hair, struggling to find the right words.

"It's all right," Mari murmured quickly, instinctively trying to help both him and herself, wishing she could just push away the embarrassment and forget it. "It's just, well—" She sighed. "It's been so long. I didn't know what you were talking about at first."

"You still don't, but I'm going to make sure you do, if it takes me all night." He loosened his hold so he could see her face. "It's one thing to 'know' something in the abstract, and another to experience it." He took her head between his hands and looked directly into her eyes. "And what I just saw happening to your body is the result of what you're thinking and feeling about me. *Me! I'm the cause of all that!* Can't you guess how that might make me feel?" He saw her beginning, slow smile even before he finished, and then her little nod of comprehension. But he wasn't through yet.

"Your skin gives new meaning to old words, like peaches and cream, and dynamic flow." He grinned, suddenly a little self-conscious about letting those last two words slip out. "Your silky, shiny hair, your broad shoulders, and how straight you are here." He let one hand drop, to run it up and down over the place where the curve of her hip straightened. "And your eyes—hell, do you have any idea how much fun I'm having just trying to guess what color they're going to be next?" He lowered his voice. "I love everything about you, Mari honey, don't you know that?"

By the time he finished, Mari was grinning, too, and they just stood there, looking at each other. The endearment Charles had used was nothing short of commonplace, but the way he said it made her feel as if the sun had just come out. And suddenly she knew that if ever there was going to be a right time and person, it was now—with Charles. Mari moved toward him, to meet him halfway as she lifted her lips to his.

The desperation drained out of him like a sigh, and he cupped her face with his hands, cherishing the very texture of her as he accepted what she offered, then took more, and still more, from her mouth, vaguely aware of the contrasting coolness of her damp hair and warm skin as his hands slid down the sides of her neck, inside the collar of her robe, pushing the fabric ahead of them to the very edges of her shoulders.

"Mari?" She heard the question in his voice, and it was the last thing she needed from him—the asking, and then listening to her answer—because she could never again as long as she lived allow herself to be a passive receiver.

"Yes," she whispered, burying her lips in his neck, taking soft nips and tastes as she felt her robe fall around her bare feet, and then the rough surface of his sweater against her breasts as he pulled her close. The incongruity of her smooth nakedness next to his rough, fully clothed body struck her as funny, and she laughed, backing away from him at the same time. "Now you." She ran her hands under his sweater and began to lift. Charles smiled, raised his arms and let her pull it over his head. His eyes caressed her while she attacked his shirt buttons, with almost the same effect as if he'd used his hands. He watched as her nipples hardened and the pulsebeat in her throat became visible. And then she backed away again to stand perfectly still, waiting, not touching him anywhere. Because anticipating the moment when their bodies would meet was too delicious to relinquish so soon.

Her body felt languid, sort of like the almond oil Charles had smoothed over her skin earlier in the afternoon. And then the remembered touch of his hands flooded her consciousness, pushing out everything else, and her legs began to tremble with the effort it took to remain where she was. Charles saw only her bright, glistening eyes and the stillness of her stance, which served to enhance his awareness of the subtle changes taking place in the color of her skin, from chest to abdomen, which in turn told him what he wanted to know—that her pulsing blood was rushing to fill sensitive tissues, causing them to swell, that a warm, slippery fluid was beginning to seep to the surface of her most delicate membranes, preparing the way for him. For the first time in his life Charles Merrill wished he *didn't* know something, and tried willing himself not to think about it. Because if he did, he was going to lose control the instant he touched her again. He stripped off his pants and undershorts, then straightened to stand before her in the shadowed candle-light, trying to match her restraint, letting her see what she did to him, which was much more obvious than her flushed skin.

They moved as one, and as Mari sank down on the edge of the bed, Charles went down on his knees and buried his face in her breasts, inhaling the fragrance of her heated skin. As his lips closed over one nipple, she gasped in surprise at the flash of sensation. But it was as nothing next to the tormenting pleasure that came when he began to suckle, drawing the heat from her breast down to the core of her very soul, setting her entire body afire.

Clasping him to her breast with tight arms, she fell back across the bed, bringing him with her, wanting more. More what, she wasn't sure. Just more. Mari heard a low, keening moan coming from somewhere off in the distance. "Did I hurt you?" She heard his whispered words, too, soft lips murmuring against her neck, his breath a cooling breeze against her hot skin, but could only roll her head back and forth. When he stretched out beside her, she knew what "more" was—the touch of his hands and his body, anywhere and everywhere—while his tongue stroked hers. Her legs moved with a mind of their own, enticing him until his hand found the sensitive skin of her inner thigh. Attuned to every nuance of response and change, his touch grew more and more knowing, sending wave after wave of agonizing pleasure through her body. She opened to him as a flower to the sun, taking everything he was willing to give until torment turned to nearly unbearable ecstasy—which she now wanted to give to him in return. Her hand curved around his hip, then slowly began sliding down.

Before she could reach him, Charles had her fingers in a viselike grip. "I'd like that—too much right now," he whispered into her hair between quick breaths. "You've turned me into a teenager." She felt his smile against her mouth and knew what he meant, because she felt exactly the same way.

"Then come to me . . . now." Cool air hit her heated skin as he moved away from her.

"Be back in a second," he whispered, just before he bent to brush his lips across one nipple. It wasn't until she felt the mattress rise and heard the tiny sound of crinkling foil that she realized what he was doing.

"Oh Charles, please, you don't need to—" She almost cried with frustration. But he was quickly back, catching her before she could fall too far. She reached for him as he came up over her, guiding him with her hand while she covered his face and neck with kisses, and ran her tongue over his lips. He followed her lead, copying the movement on her other lips with a very different "tongue" before pushing into the warm, moist place where she wanted him. Charles stilled his movements as she tightened around him, and held even his breath in anticipation, giving her complete ownership of this moment of exquisite pleasure.

He knew the exact instant she crested the wave, taking him with her in one headlong, unstoppable rush toward a shattering climax of his own. And then she was keening softly in her ear, rocking him in her arms as the waves of pleasure flowed together, joining and intermingling to become indistinguishable, one from the other, hers or his.

I t was still raining outside, though the wind had died down. Mari lay quietly in the curve of Charles's arm, wondering at the sense of harmony and closeness that seemed to saturate every cell in her body. His breathing had settled into a slow, steady rhythm, which probably meant he was asleep. Even his portable radio was silent now, so the station must have gone off the air for the night.

At thirty-eight Charles had to be fairly experienced sexually; she wasn't kidding herself about that. And like most men, he apparently didn't like to talk afterward. But that's where the generalizations had to come to a screeching halt. She remembered what Rachel had said about him, that day in the lab. "A natural experimenter, nothing's too sacred to question, or too far out to try." But how much more there was to it than that. Not only eager to experiment and to learn, he was so "tuned in" to her every response—as if her pleasure was as important to him as his own—that her body had become a source of wonder to her as well as to him. Phillip's idea of learning had been to look, and then to identify and put the right name to all the parts. She nuzzled her face into the warm curve of Charles's neck as she took a perverse pleasure in knowing just how wrong Phillip had been, and how much he'd missed—which brought a little smile to her lips. But when she stretched lazily, reveling in the thought, Charles's arm tightened and she realized he was as wide awake as she was.

"You did expect me to use a condom, didn't you, Mari," he murmured, "even if you are on the pill?"

"But I'm—that's not what I—" she blurted without thinking, then fell silent. What could she say? That the response he'd called from her body was a revelation, unlike anything she'd ever experienced before? That his sudden withdrawal had come without warning, plunging her into the black hell of remembered disappointment and failure? That she'd considered all the possibilities and decided to take the risk because she was thirty-four and he offered the kind of gene pool she wanted for her child? That she wanted, even hoped, to get pregnant? And had no intention of telling him if she did, so there was no need for him to worry? There was simply no way she could even begin to explain, or hope that he might understand. Not when she didn't even know herself, when echoes of the past continued to shadow the present, hiding the truth from her as well as from him.

Charles hadn't expected it to be her first time, but he hadn't expected her to be on the pill, either—otherwise why the "you don't need to"—which meant she probably was involved with someone in Houston. But then why . . . ?

"What did you mean, 'it's been so long'?" he ventured.

Mari almost laughed at the irony of wishing Charles wasn't so alert and sensitive, that he didn't catch and hold on to every word she uttered. "Just that I forgot about my body, what you called the sexual flush. I was married once, back when I was, uh, too young. My husb—" She couldn't bring herself to say the word, and Charles felt her stiffen against him. "He teased me unmercifully at first, said I was such a prude that even my body blushed with embarrassment. Later he decided there had to be something wrong with me, that the blood went to all the wrong places, or something."

"What the hell is that supposed to mean?" Charles asked, incredulous. He held her away a little, trying to read her face.

"He thought it had something to do with why I was . . .

frigid, or almost." Her throat was so tight now she could hardly speak. She refused to meet his eyes, even in the dim light that already hid so much from him.

"My God! What a stupid jerk!" Charles blurted with sudden, hot anger, then pulled her close again and wrapped both his arms around her, as if even now he could protect her from the cruel taunts of the past. That anyone could think she was unresponsive, let alone frigid, was simply beyond the pale!

"He was a medical student." She had to whisper because Charles was holding her so tight she could hardly breathe.

"Which was why you believed him!"

"Yes. Maybe. Oh, I don't know! Can't we just not talk about it anymore, please?"

That little anecdote alone was enough to explain why the marriage had failed, Charles thought. "How long were you—?" He stopped as he felt the quick shake of her head.

"I refuse to remember," she said, her voice entirely free of uncertainty as she broke his hold and rolled away.

"That's nonsense, Mari. How can anyone just 'refuse' to remember something, as if you have a choice? You either do or you don't."

Mari didn't agree, but she had no intention of arguing the point, so there was nothing more to say. The silence stretched into minutes, until she was beginning to wonder if he really had gone to sleep this time. And then Charles raised up on one elbow and turned toward her, peering down at her face as he brushed the hair back from her temple, curling it behind her ear. She waited, barely able to make out his face in the dim light, wondering what he was thinking.

"It doesn't matter, Mari. Nothing before you and me matters. I love you."

In contrast to the weekend with Charles, the three days he was gone felt like three weeks to Mari—like watching a film in slow motion. She walked to town to get something to read to her mother, and also picked up several paperbacks for herself at the bookstore on Calle San Miguel. Janet preferred nonfiction, particularly history, or the kind of philosophical reflections on the human condition written by

Loren Eiseley. But Mari was a fiction addict, requiring big doses, and often, because indulging in the fantasy of other lives, other places, and other times fed her imagination and, like sleep, helped her stay sane. She also bought two books about the Alhambra.

Charles called Tuesday night to let her know that he'd be arriving early Thursday morning, and by mid-afternoon on Wednesday she was as nervous as a cat, unable to sit still or concentrate on anything for long. She tried reading to Janet, but her mind's eye kept straying to the clothes hanging in her closet at the Bajondillo. Finally, after she read the same paragraph through twice without even realizing it, her mother sent her away with the admonition to "get to bed early tonight, and enjoy yourself tomorrow."

Mari decided on the khaki skirt and blouse she'd already worn once, to dinner at El Roqueo, because she could do the most to change it with different jewelry and shoes. She did try to go to bed early, but couldn't sleep, so got up and brushed her teeth again, then hunted up the historical novel she'd thrown aside the night before. Wordy unto death, it was fat with details that said nothing and went nowhere, boring her into drowsiness. And then she kept waking up every hour or so through the night, anxious that she might oversleep and not be ready when Charles arrived.

She was among the first down for breakfast, and headed for one of the tables near the glass wall facing the sea. Isolated from the rest of the room by the high U-shaped back of the booth, she sat motionless for several minutes, consciously letting herself feed on the scene spread out before her.

What was it about this place that had such a profound effect on her? Was it the warm, soft winds that seemed to caress the skin, the golden light, or some vague sort of awareness of the past, of the endless stream of people who'd been here before her? Was the light and air the same today as it had been when the Moors came out of North Africa and landed on this sunny coast, a thousand or more years ago, bringing with them an advanced understanding of science and medicine, a system of education and laws, and a whole new concept of agriculture—using aqueducts to carry water from the mountains, and waterwheels and engineered irrigation ditches? And also the lute, and paper and glass, cotton and rice, and sugarcane and palm trees. How was it possible for such a people to be swallowed up among the barbaric tribes of North Africa? Or for those who stayed, to be persecuted and their "heathen" culture systematically obliterated by the "civilized" Christians after Ferdinand and Isabella combined forces to overwhelm their last outpost—Granada and the Alhambra?

A slight movement on the edge of her vision caught Mari's attention and she glanced up into Charles's smiling face. And judging from his slightly indulgent grin, he'd been there for some time. She scooted over a little and he slid into the seat beside her, curling his right hand around the back of her neck to hold her still while he sought her lips with his.

"Where were you?" he asked as he pulled away.

"With the Moors, at the Alhambra. James Michener was right, Spain *does* intrude into the imagination." Her hand touched the side of his freshly shaved face. "I missed you," she whispered before brushing his lips again. He had on a bittersweet-chocolate gabardine suit today, and a light beige oxford cloth shirt with a heathery knit tie.

"Me too," he mumbled, "so much, in fact, that I almost packed it in yesterday and came on. Couldn't seem to keep my mind on 'erythrocyte deformability' for some reason." Nuggets of turquoise swung from her ears, a match for the rope of graduated stones that looped down into the valley between her breasts. He noticed the quickening pulse in the hollow of her throat and the rosy tint rising in her cheeks, and felt an answering fire in his own blood. But now wasn't the time. "Looks like you're just starting. Let me go get a roll and some coffee. Be right back."

His quick "be right back" echoed across the days and nights as if he'd never been away, while Mari watched him walk toward the buffet, admiring the easy motion of his body and the now-familiar hesitation in his walk. Her stomach tightened as she remembered the little round scars, one on each side of this thigh, as soft as silk to the touch.

"What have you been up to while I was gone?" he asked as soon as he sat down again.

"Well, I bought some shoes." She stuck one foot out from under the table far enough for him to see one of the tan sandals she'd found up on the Calle San Miguel. "And I'm keeping the secondhand bookstore in business—oh, and I had lunch with Cisco one day."

"Yeah?" His glance was appraising. "You let him pick up the tab, too?"

She was about to object when she realized he was teasing. "I think there may be more there than meets the eye," she said, deciding to ignore his little joke. "We talked about the Basque country. He's from Guernica."

He wondered what was significant about that. "And?"

"The Basques have a long history of being at least semi-independent, even had their own special legislative assemblies for several hundred years. When the civil war broke out in the thirties, they tried to stay neutral by organizing an autonomous government, at Guernica. You must know the famous painting by Picasso. Franco's forces practically wiped out the town and everyone in it, to crush the separatist movement. Except it won't stay dead."

"So what'd you mean there's more there than meets the eye?" He knew too well how inquisitive she was, and he didn't want her getting involved in something that could mean trouble.

"It's just, well, Cisco seems so different from most medical doctors at home. While we were talking he said something about Picasso that really intrigued me. 'His ability to see is Andalusian.' I asked him what he meant, and he said civilization in this part of Spain goes back to the time of the Minoans, three thousand years, maybe more, and that the Andalusians have some unique consciousness of the past. 'They do not have a linear sense of history, like you and me,' is the way he put it. And suddenly I understood. You can see it in Picasso's cubist paintings, for instance, where different views of the same object are presented simultaneously. He portrays another reality, which makes us question our own."

Charles didn't much care about Picasso or anyone else at the moment, but he was fascinated by the twists and turns her mind took, along pathways that were entirely foreign to him, to arrive at some unexpected insight. At the same time he breathed a figurative sigh of relief at hearing that she hadn't been digging around in the Basque political mess.

"I stopped to see Janet on the way in from the airport, by the way," he said, changing the subject. "She's a lot better, isn't she? Insisted we shouldn't 'waste' time stopping there on our way out of town. Said she can do perfectly well without us for a day, or however long we want to be gone."

Mari nodded. "Sounds like her. Which reminds me, thanks for leaving your radio. She really has enjoyed it. And the soap." Charles had taken the time to stop at the hospital Monday morning, on his way to the airport, though he'd never mentioned his plan to Mari. And, as usual, he'd delivered the *Tribune,* along with a special bar of soap. "I think Mom knows how close she came to not making it. Anyway, she commented that it made her feel like a woman again, not just a sack of bones and bruises."

"Hospitals are bad enough anywhere, and when you can't understand most of what's going on, it must be a special kind of Hell. But she always seems to have something or someone else on her mind, not herself. You, for instance. She worries about you, you know. Says you're so busy chasing stories, you don't have time for a . . . for much personal life."

Mari almost snorted at that. "Fat lot she knows!"

"Not that she doesn't think what you do is important," Charles continued, ignoring her outburst. His lips broke into a broad smile as he began rubbing his thumb over the back of her hand. "You're about the best there is, anywhere, to hear Jan tell it."

"And I think you're a little confused—she can do that to you at times." Mari pulled her hand away under the pretext of using it to pick up her cup, uncomfortable with the direction the conversation was taking.

"Uh-uh." He sounded adamant. "She ran across an article in the *Trib* about a fatty acid in fish oil that's supposed to reduce the risk of heart attacks. Asked what I thought about it. The damn thing was loaded with claims, all of them unproven—that it made the platelets, the cells involved in clotting, less sticky, and therefore prevents the clumping that leads to a heart attack, for instance, which is just a lot of shit! Clotting and red-cell aggregation are two different things. Besides that, most clots form *after* an insult to the heart, not before. Anyway, the piece was riddled with misinformation." He glanced at Mari. "You know what she said?"

She shook her head, though she could guess. Janet could be pretty intolerant of what she called "careless errors."

"'Marilyn doesn't make mistakes like that no matter what her sources claim, because she researches everything, knows what questions to ask. This kind of mindless propaganda never appeared in the *Tribune* when she was writing for them.' Her exact words, I swear it." Mari looked at him wonderingly as he repeated Janet's praise, too surprised to think of a snappy comeback.

"Speaking of which," Charles went on, "you never did tell me how you happened to go to Paris, or how long you were there." He felt an urgent need to know everything about her now, to fill in all the years before they met, though just the idea that she'd existed without him knowing it still made him feel anxious for some reason.

"You want the story of my life, huh?" She flashed him a grin, then took a quick sip of hot chocolate. "You have any idea what a great job you can get with a bachelor's in political science, Charles?" she asked. "I finally figured out that I'd better go back to school if I ever wanted to live above the poverty level. Which is when I discovered journalism, the glue I could use to stick all the mishmash of stuff I knew or was interested in together. I could write about all kinds of things, something different every day if I wanted to, dig around on my own and find out things, and nobody would think I was being—oh, you know, frivolous. Flighty. Fluff-brained." Just telling him about it brought color to her face, leaving no doubt in his mind that she was still as enthusiastic and excited about her discovery now as then. And about her work. "I got an internship at the *Tribune* because I happened to know French. Started taking it in high school, then kept on with it in college." She tossed him a slightly apologetic grin. "Mostly because Mom wanted me to take German. Anyway, after I came back I went to work for the *Denver Post*. Not a very glamorous story, I'm afraid."

"Nor one that explains how you got into medical reporting, either," Charles pointed out.

"Oh! Well, I just happened to be in the right place at the right time, I guess—when the big fight started over who discovered the AIDS virus. I'd already done one story about some research at the Pasteur Institute, in Paris, which came about when my editor found out I'd taken some biology courses in college. The French yelled foul, because the Americans were trying to patent the AIDS antibody test developed by Gallo at the National Cancer Institute, after he'd agreed to use the materials and information supplied by the Pasteur Institute only for research. They filed suit against the U.S. government, and it turned into a running story. I made the *New York Times* several times with that one. After that the die was cast. I got all the science and medicine assignments." She straightened suddenly and looked at her empty plate, then at him. "I'm through, you're through, so why are we still sitting here?"

His arm came around her and he nuzzled his face into her hair, whispering into her ear, "Because there's so much I don't know about you. I've got so much to catch up on." He gave her shoulder a quick squeeze, then moved to get up. "Maybe I should speak with Juan about a room before we leave, and get my stuff out of the car." He reached back down to pull her out of the cushioned booth. As they walked toward the desk, Mari tugged on his hand, trying to slow him down.

"You could stay in my—with me, if you want to, that is." He had to bend down to hear her. "Unless you'd rather . . ." The words dwindled, and she looked anywhere but at him.

"Mari." He smoothed a hand over hers and waited, until she was forced to meet his eyes. "You're sure?" He was asking because *he* had to be sure.

"Yes!" She grinned like a mischievous elf, and started pulling him toward the elevators, freeing him to reveal his own eagerness to participate in whatever she was plotting.

"Not so fast," he protested, "let me get my stuff out of the car. You go on and call the elevator." He went for his overnighter and was back just as the elevator doors opened. The lift crept up two floors, taking what seemed an impossibly long time, while they took turns inching closer and closer to the doors. Then Mari was hurrying down the hall ahead of him, key in hand.

Just inside her room Charles dropped his bag and pushed the door closed behind him, leaning back against it as he ground out a gruff, "Come here." His fingers curled over her shoulders then slid up to circle her neck, thumbs stroking the line of her chin as he held her still, his eyes caressing her face for a moment before he bent to cover it with kisses. As his mouth moved over hers, Mari wrapped her arms around his waist, shutting out everything but the growing urgency of her body against his, seeking some elusive configuration that would allow them to fit still closer together.

"I just want to hold on to you for a minute," Charles whispered finally as he slid his mouth free and buried his face in her satiny hair, reveling in the feel and the scent of her while trying to slow his breathing. Then he tilted her face up to his, and his smile set her pulse racing. She thought he was going to kiss her again, but he didn't. Instead, his lips teased all around hers, nibbling at the corner of her mouth, then skimming the line of her jaw. And try as she might, she could never quite catch them.

One of his thighs pressed against hers, urging her away from the door, and then he was slowly walking her backward. Mari hardly realized where they were until she felt the mattress against the back of her knees. But instead of urging her down onto the bed, he began working at the buttons of her blouse, so she undid the little buttons down the front of his shirt, without taking her eyes from his face. But when she got to his tie, she only succeeded in pulling it tighter. Then her blouse was open, and off, and he was reaching around for the clasp of her bra. Tossing it onto the nearby chair, Charles took a step back from her and just stood there, feasting on the sight of her fully exposed breasts, with the string of turquoise nuggets exactly where he'd imagined them. She felt her nipples contract and harden in response to the touch of his eyes, and saw the urgency blossom in his face. And then he was slipping out of his jacket and pulling at his tie, tossing it to join her bra while working at the recalcitrant button underneath. His shirt fell away, too, and then Mari joined him in the sensuous dance, zippers purring in unison and fabric whispering to the floor, stepping out and away, leaving everything behind where it fell, as if they were shedding unwanted and outgrown skins.

Charles's eyes swept over her thighs and hips, stopping momentarily at the patch of smoky curls, then up across her flat stomach to her full, taut breasts, rising and falling rapidly now with her quickened breath. Mari lost awareness of everything but the swelling warmth radiating from the center of her being and the aching need to be touched. It took all the willpower Charles could muster to keep his hands away from her, to stand back and watch the faint rosy blush surface across her chest, then inch down over her breasts and abdomen—until a spark leaped across the gap separating them, igniting a rage to know the feel of her heated skin against his again, to be inside her loving body.

He took a step toward her and they fell across the bed together, lips parted and tongues seeking, hungry for the taste of each other, letting the massive need to touch and be touched have its way. She writhed beneath him, wanting more. Not knowing what. Her hand stroked down to the small of his back, kneading the tight muscles there while pressing him close. But that wasn't enough, either. His mouth left hers, trailing a path to her breast, to alternately suckle and circle the nipple with his tongue, while his hand slid down over her abdomen, leaving tremors in their wake. A long, inarticulate moan escaped her lips when his fingers slid through the wiry curls between her legs to caress and tease, creating fevered, nearly unbearable sensations of pleasure. She strained against his hand, then drew away, closing her legs in silent denial, torn between the urge to completion and the equally strong urge to prolong and savor the moment.

"Mari?" She knew he was puzzled, maybe even worried, but she didn't have time to answer his question, at least not with words. Instead her mouth tasted his skin while her hand moved to enclose him, letting her fingers gently and gradually strengthen their grip as she tested his response, moving up and down the length of him. His eyes fluttered closed as he rolled to his side, giving her greater access yet keeping her close.

Now it was her turn to be fascinated by the response of his body. She noticed the strong pulsing of blood through every visible vein, and the way his entire body shook with each beat of his heart, and couldn't help wondering if she was endangering his life—she'd heard of men dying while

making love, probably due to the rise in blood pressure—
but he sensed her hesitation instantly.

"Don't stop." The words were tortured, his eyes slitted
and unseeing, and his jaw looked rigid, though his lips were
parted slightly. And she could hear a little hissing noise as
his breath passed through his teeth, all visible evidence of
what *she* was capable of doing to *him*.

Mari's heart missed a beat, then fired again with a violent
kick, plunging her into a fury of motion. She pushed him
over onto his back, swinging one leg up and over him at the
same time, guiding him with her hand, allowing his silky tip
to tease her, reveling momentarily in the anticipation of
what was coming. His eyes flew open, glittering in the early
morning light as he watched her face, and then he was
thrusting up to meet her as she slid down over him. But he
made no attempt to reverse their positions, or to take
control. A trilling laugh of pure joy burst from her lips at the
realization, and then she concentrated on watching and
listening, using every nerve in her body to sense what was
happening to him, to learn just as he had learned from
her—from the sound and length of each shaky breath he
drew, the slight flutter of his eyelashes, from the tensing of a
muscle and the increasing pressure she could feel inside her
own body.

"No more . . . Mari . . . honey. . . . Wait . . . no more
. . . please," he pleaded at last, forcing the words out in
spite of the intense pleasure he was experiencing at her
hands.

Mari refused his request, knowing instinctively that he
was trying to hold back for her, and instead carried him
along with her, waiting until the last possible instant to still
her body, suspending them both for one long, exquisite
moment of anticipation. This time when she began to move
again, he matched her with a fury of thrusts, until a shower
of sparks exploded inside her brain, sizzling and dancing in
her blood like ice on a hot griddle.

She knew when Charles joined her a few seconds later,
and though her mind wanted to shutter her eyes, to close out
everything but the delicious river of warm honey flowing
through her veins, she forced herself to watch this, too—the

way his expression changed from intensely felt pleasure to sublime release—before allowing herself to fall forward over his heaving chest.

As soon as she could get her breath, Mari rolled away, to lie quietly, staring up at the ceiling. "Have you ever tried to duplicate the conditions in the blood, measure the viscoelasticity right at the peak, at the very moment of—" Charles whooped with laughter, cutting her off, and reached over to grab her in a bear hug, then rolled with her back and forth across the bed, rocking her playfully.

"Ah God, Mari honey," he breathed, suddenly not laughing anymore. "How did I ever live without you all this time? I haven't been able to think about anything but you, and this, for three whole days! The strangest damn thing happened to me in Madrid. I'd be sitting in one of the sessions, listening to a talk—who the hell knows what about?—and all of a sudden I'd 'come to,' as if I'd been unconscious or something, realize where I was and feel sort of surprised. Thought I was going a little crazy. But the second time it happened I knew damn well what was going on. I wanted to be here, with you, so much that in my mind I was."

"I know, I thought about you all the time, too," Mari murmured, skimming her lips over his jaw, catching a whiff of after-shave or soap, which reminded her of her mother. She raised up on one elbow so she could see his face. "What did you take to her this time?"

"Who? Oh, Jan." He matched her grin. "Today's *Tribune*, and a jigsaw puzzle. A picture of the Alhambra."

After Málaga they turned northeast, into the lush green velvet foothills of the Sierra Nevadas, climbing higher and higher as the curving, hilly road wound between slopes alternately covered with silvery-green olive groves or the deeper green of almond orchards. Thirty minutes farther along they began to catch an occasional glimpse of massive mountain peaks in the distance, dwarfing the rolling hills they were passing through. "That must be what the Moors could see from the Alhambra," Mari commented. "One of the books I bought talks about 'peaks capped with eternal snow.'"

"Yeah, why don't you tell me about it before we get there,

since you've been reading up," Charles suggested as he reached for her hand, placed it on his thigh and covered it with his own.

"Uh-uh. I think it's more fun if you don't know exactly what to expect. The palace and gardens were started in the thirteenth century on the site of an old fortress, but that's all I'm saying right now. Maybe as we go along."

Thirty minutes later they walked hand in hand from the wooded car park to the ticket office, where Charles picked up a brochure and map of the grounds. Built along the very edge of the Sierra Nevadas, Granada presided over the richest vega in the country, a huge agricultural basin that had been irrigated since the days of the Moors. And the Alhambra, the fortress castle of the Moorish kings, occupied a thirty-five-acre plateau, a spur of the mountains that jutted out to overlook it all. The Gate of the Pomegranates, the fruit that had given Granada its name, built in the 1500s, was different in feel as well as style from the horseshoe-shaped arch of the first Moorish gate, which Mari noticed a little farther along up the inclined path. They stopped from time to time to look at the map, trying to identify every building in sight, until they came to an old, anything-but-grand-looking structure with two crenelated towers. The ocher plaster was worn away in spots to reveal sections of thin horizontal bricks alternating with patches of round stones. Unprepossessing as it appeared from the outside, Mari guessed this had to be the castle itself, though it looked nothing like what she'd been expecting.

"The name means red, or reddish, palace," she commented, "but maybe the color has faded with time." Charles stopped to glance at the map again. "This is the entrance to the public rooms of the castle. The Hall of the Ambassadors first, it says here, where the sultan held public audiences." He took her elbow as they passed through a long, dim corridor.

As they emerged from the shadowy hall into the high-ceilinged square room, the thought that hit Mari first was that no amount of reading or looking at pictures could possibly prepare anyone for the opulent light and riot of pattern and color that literally enveloped them. Arabesque! The word bounced around in her head.

Every inch of wall and ceiling was either carved, painted, or glazed to create line and movement, whether geometrical designs, plantlike shapes, or continuous calligraphy. And the flowing gilt lines stood in relief against rich burgundy, browns, and blues, intricately intertwined, running riot in horizontal bands and borders, setting the eye into constant motion, relieved only where double-arched windows were cut into alcoves projecting out beyond the outer walls. And even those were wainscoted with the sapphire and cobalt-blue ceramic tiles the Moors had brought to Spain, which the Spaniards would take with them to Holland a few centuries later. Mari walked over to one of the alcoves to look out at the city and plain spread out all around them, and Charles followed.

"If the king wanted to impress his visitors, this must have succeeded beyond his wildest dreams," he commented. They turned back and discovered the dome overhead at the same time. "Wow!" was all Charles could say. *Mocarabes* dripped from both the dome and arched openings of the room, carved out of layered and built-up plaster, then gilded and painted in brilliant colors to create a frosty lacework of delicate icicles.

"The room is alive with motion," Mari murmured, hardly able to believe what she was seeing. "Yet nothing intrudes, everything belongs. They created harmony out of contrast and conflict."

Up to that moment Charles had registered the colors, and even that the room had a certain tranquility about it in spite of the "busy" designs covering everything in sight. He'd also been guessing at how the stalactites might have been constructed, but now he stepped into the middle of the room and slowly turned, trying to see what she meant. After a couple of minutes he looked back at the brochure. "It says here this is the only room that's been completely restored. They're still working on the rest. Maybe we should leave, quit while we're ahead," he suggested, only half joking, "because it can't get any better than this. We probably should have seen this one last." He turned for a final look. Mari slipped her hand into his as they started for the door to the private rooms of the royal palace, but kept turning back for one more look. "Maybe we can come back again later, take another look," Charles suggested, sensing her reluctance to leave.

"Okay, on to the seraglio, then," she agreed. "Don't you love that word? It just seethes with mystery and intrigue, passion, romance, betrayal. Calls up images of voluptuous harem ladies in flowing balloon trousers and brief little boleros, their fingers and toes dripping with jewels. Darkly handsome and very, very virile sultans, striding through these airy halls with their curving scimitars swinging at their sides."

Charles couldn't help laughing. "As in *Abduction from the Seraglio?*"

"Yes, abduction is the natural twin of seraglio, but Mozart's style doesn't really fit this, do you think?" she asked, pleased that he was going along with the game. They emerged into an open courtyard and Mari recognized it immediately, from a picture in one of her books. "It's the Court of the Lions, the heart of the family apartments," she told Charles.

In the center of the court a huge alabaster bowl rested on the backs of a dozen sturdy stone lions, already ancient when the Alhambra was begun. Water spouted out of their mouths into a round pool at their feet, then flowed away in four different directions through shallow troughs cut into the stone pavement, to silently disappear into the adjacent rooms. "The lions used to be a sun dial," she explained. "At each hour of the day the water would flow from the mouth of a different lion." She paused, watching the water bubble up from the spout in the center of the bowl.

Charles guessed at the question she was mulling over in her mind—was modern technology unable to duplicate the skills the Moors had possessed seven hundred years ago? "Maybe they didn't even try to make 'em work that way when they restored it."

Double marble columns surrounded the court on all four sides, forming delicate arches and a wall as light and airy as lace. Small pavilions at either end were topped with tiled roofs, but a dark recess above the filigreed wall made each pyramid-shaped roof appear to float, as if levitated by the magic of a genie. Mari reached for Charles's hand, drawing him along with her as she started around the edge of the court under the gallery, absorbing everything in silence. Charles kept watching her bright eyes, wishing she'd speak so he'd know what was going on inside her unpredictable head. When they reached the pavilion at the opposite end, she started through the door, apparently already anxious to go on to other places, still without uttering a single word.

"I think we should go on to the other rooms, get a better picture of the whole place, and then come back here," she explained when she noticed that he was reluctant to leave so soon.

"Okay, you lead and I'll follow," he agreed, "wherever."

From the Hall of the Two Sisters, which also had a fountain in the center and a domed ceiling that was honeycombed with tiny cells, they passed into the dressing room and bedroom of the sultana, a secluded section set out like a big bay window from the rest of the rooms, which flowed from one to another without interruption. Low double-arched openings on all three sides of the room were edged with a frame of frost, as if a clear space had just been scraped clean of its coating of icy crystals.

"Can't you just picture her in front of this window, lounging on a pile of thick, jewel-encrusted and embroidered pillows, gazing out over her garden to the purple mountains in the distance," Mari mused. They were alone, and it was so quiet they could hear the water playing softly in a fountain outside, just below the window. She slipped an arm around Charles's waist, to pleasure herself with the warmth of his body as well as the pictures in her mind's eye. His lips touched her temple, then tickled her ear. "Who could help trying to imagine what it was like to be a woman," she continued, "here in this place, seven hundred years ago? The wife of a king—probably one of several—or one of his harem?"

"Tell me what *you* imagine it was like," Charles urged, a little surprised by her unexpected flight of fancy.

"Did you know that the Moors came to the Iberian peninsula without women?" she asked, turning to look at him for the first time. "So the second generation of Moslems here were already half Spanish. In those early years, two or three hundred years before the Alhambra was built, the caliphs and emirs enforced a tribute of female slaves for their harems. *Gallegas*—blond women from Galicia, a region in northwestern Spain—were in great demand, which resulted in blue eyes among some of the later caliphs.

"But history really doesn't tell us much about what the women themselves were like. What they thought, or felt. And I doubt that my twentieth-century American imagination is any match for them, any more than the modern Spaniards were able to restore the Lion fountain to its former glory. But certainly the man who started all this," she waved an arm to indicate the building, "had to have been unique, even by today's standards. Alhamar, his name was, and he built schools, even colleges, and hospitals and public kitchens, to care for old people and to feed the poor. Then made surprise visits to see that they were run right."

"Sounds like a big spender to me," Charles decided, the first really pragmatic thought he'd had all day. "How did he manage to pay for it all?"

"He developed a merit system, rewarded excellence and gave special privileges to the best artisans and thinkers, who developed a silk industry and fabrics that were more in demand than those from India or China. They also were the first to mine silver and gold in the mountains near here."

"Okay. But didn't most of his treasury have to go to fighting the Spaniards? I thought they were at war for about two hundred years before Ferdinand and Isabella defeated them. The same year she sent Columbus to the New World in search of gold, wasn't it? I know the Spaniards sure as hell were broke."

"Yes," Mari agreed. "But Alhamar sort of rose from the ashes of war, after the Moors lost the rest of Spain, and united Málaga, Almería and Granada. And the first thing he did was negotiate peace with Castile. He lived to be nearly eighty, and had peace all that time, which must have been a special kind of 'Golden Age' for the Moors."

Charles had both arms around Mari now and was watching her face, not the gardens or the opulent decoration. "The story really appeals to you, doesn't it?" She nodded. "I'm sure it's been romanticized over the centuries, because it's almost too good to be true, isn't it?" She tried to pull away but he wouldn't let her go.

"Just think," she mused. "He found a way to live in peace,

made it possible for people to develop their minds, and rewarded those who did well. He raised the standard of living for everyone, took care of the old and the poor." She looked into Charles's dark eyes. "But there was something else," she said slowly. "They say he treated his wives as 'friends and rational companions.' Which seems easy to believe now, here in this place, doesn't it?"

Charles was mesmerized by the parade of emotions he'd seen cross her face, and in her eyes, since they first walked into the Hall of the Ambassadors—an awed wonder, with perhaps just a tinge of disbelief, followed by serious and thoughtful, then mischievous and playful, and now serious again, maybe even a bit sad.

"I think I'm beginning to understand what you mean about the 'feel' of the place," he told her. "It's one thing to know about their marvelous feats of engineering, how they brought water from the mountains and pumped it up here for fountains, reflecting pools, baths, and all that. But that doesn't tell you what it was like to live here in these water-cooled rooms in the summer, to feel the mountain breezes, or hear the slow trickle of life-giving water. To be surrounded with such serenity! Do you think they were different because of it?"

Now it was Mari's turn to be surprised, and she laughed her delight with his response. "You're as much under the spell of the place as I am."

"The place—or you," he murmured, bending to touch her lips with his own, letting her go only when they heard other visitors approaching.

They strolled hand in hand through the Royal Baths, with its marble tanks for hot and cold water, and walls perforated to let steam and perfume vapors escape; a Turkish bath; and finally, an area called the Hall of Repose. Here, too, a riot of color and pattern covered the tiled walls. Three-cornered figures in black, gray, and brown curled and danced around the room like cresting waves. High overhead, wooden grills covered openings to a gallery surrounding the central rectangle, supported by four majestic pink-marble columns.

"Legend has it that blind musicians played sensuous melodies from up there for the ladies of the harem, down here in their perfumed baths," Mari told him with a perfectly straight face.

Charles looked equally serious, and let out a pained sigh. "All those beauties languishing here, waiting for a call to their lord's bed. How in hell did we ever let things get so out of hand!"

Mari laughed and pulled him with her into still another room, which contained what she claimed was a flush toilet. "Aw, you're letting your imagination run away with you now, Mari honey," he teased. So she led him closer, to show him where at one time there had been a constant stream of water running below the seats.

The Court of the Lions was empty of tourists when they went back later in the afternoon, to sit in cross-legged Spanish Renaissance chairs placed around the edge of the court, soaking up the elegance and serenity of the place. Mari was the first to break the lengthening silence.

"It took the Moors a hundred years to build. And then the Christians destroyed most of what they found here. The rest they changed, covered over the incised decoration with plaster." Looking at it now, that was almost impossible to imagine. *And immoral,* she thought. "In the end it was because the Moors were weakened by dissension among themselves that the Spaniards were finally able to defeat them. Love, and the jealous wrath of one woman, changed the course of history." She paused, thinking about that. "The next to the last king of the Moors, who already had a wife and two sons, fell in love with a beautiful young Christian captive named Isabella de Solis. Changed her name to Soraya. Morning star. Isn't that beautiful? He took her for his second wife and had two more sons. But his first wife plotted her husband's downfall, because she was afraid her son would be cut out as heir. In the end he deposed his father, but was too young and weak, and within ten years the Spanish army marched into Granada."

The story was complete, so Charles let the silence spin out, more than content to simply sit quietly, holding Mari's hand. He could sense that she wasn't ready to leave yet, though the sun had long since dropped below the edge of the roof, casting the entire court into shadow.

"It's hard to find words to describe it, isn't it, even inside your head?" Mari asked at last. "Maybe because it's both delicate and voluptuous at the same time, fanciful and functional."

"Maybe," Charles agreed. "But it's strange that they left nothing at all of themselves." The question had been in the back of his mind all afternoon. "No statues, of either sultan or serf. Not much like the Romans, were they?"

"Because the Koran forbids it. Moslems believe that God alone can bestow life, so to recreate human or animal forms is to usurp God's role. But don't you feel you know them anyway, even without seeing their faces? Can't you deduce the kind of people they were, just from all of this?"

Her question piqued more than his curiosity, because he considered himself something of an expert at the deduction game she was playing now. "Well, let's see." He tossed her a quick smile. "They obviously were superb craftsmen and architects, so they had good minds. And they were spectacular farmers, gardeners, and engineers. With this climate, fruits and vegetables would have been available most of the year, so they had a balanced diet, should have been pretty healthy. Judging from the baths, they also were clean, hygienically speaking. Those two things alone would mean their life expectancy was probably longer than in other cultures of the period." He paused. "Okay, I'll give you a turn now, but no cheating. You can't use anything you've read, only what you can see here."

"They raised civilization to new heights, because they were tuned in to the senses, not just because they developed sophisticated technologies," Mari answered without a moment's hesitation. "And they understood that the senses serve the soul as well as the physical appetite. They knew, for instance, that the serenity you mentioned is a state of mind *and* body."

"Where the hell did you get all that from? Come on, let me hear what your evidence is for that." She was just off on another flight of imagination, which was okay, but he wanted her to play by the rules this time. So he was calling her bluff.

"You hinted at it yourself, just a minute ago. Listen to the fountains, the murmur of running water, the rustling of the trees. Watch how the colors around us change as the sun moves across the sky. Think of seeing the shimmering landscape of the vega and mountains change with the seasons. All of that is built into this structure, is part of it, which says as plain as any words that we are part of nature, not outside or above it—that we can't separate ourselves from nature without losing the very qualities that make us human. It's a miracle of art and craftsmanship. But for all its splendor, the Alhambra doesn't attempt to belittle us humans, to overpower or reduce us with massiveness or grandeur. Instead, it enlarges our experience. Everything here is calculated to enhance our consciousness of being alive."

Charles stared at Mari as it slowly began to dawn on him that his own awareness of the world around him was being changed irrevocably and forever by every minute he spent with her, and every experience he shared with her. He'd recognized well enough her special talent for synthesizing information, for making unlikely, sometimes even profound, connections. But now he suspected he didn't know even the half of it. And he was beginning to feel like a detective on the trail of some mysterious something or someone, without a single clue as to how or where to proceed next.

CHAPTER

7

Mari came awake when Charles switched off the motor. She'd been dozing against his shoulder for the past hour, drifting in a dim, shapeless euphoria of hands and mouths on bare warm skin, nude curves sinking into soft, lushly embroidered pillows. Only half awake, she turned against him, seeking his mouth almost instinctively, letting her hunger blossom into arousal. Taken by surprise, Charles smiled against her lips, then sobered as her hands sent blood surging through his veins. His own shaped her ribs, then one breast, before his arm bumped against the steering wheel.

"Come on," he urged, laughing as he broke away to open the car door. "Let's get out of here." She scooted across the seat after him, fully awake now and aware that they were in the parking lot at the Bajondillo.

"I guess I was dreaming," she mumbled, in an attempt to explain away what she'd just done.

"No complaints here. Must have been some dream." He slipped his arm around her waist as they walked toward the main entrance of the hotel. "Why don't you go on up to the room while I get a bottle of wine? Unless you'd prefer something else before dinner."

"No, that's fine. I want to take a quick shower, get rid of the dust. And the cobwebs." She glanced at her watch. It was almost nine. "How about we just stay here? I'm sort of walked out, aren't you? They've got a salad bar and the steaks aren't bad."

Fifteen minutes later she came out of the steamy bathroom dressed in nothing but her robe, to be greeted by a tableau that was even better than her dream, because it was real. The parchment shade on the bedside lamp cast a yellow-orange glow around Charles, sitting in the lounge chair with his long legs extending straight out in a vee that crossed at the ankles, one arm hanging relaxed over the arm of the chair. His eyes were open but he stared into space, apparently lost in another world. He'd already filled two stemmed glasses and they waited on the little table beside his chair, while de Falla's "Nights in the Gardens of Spain" flowed softly from the speaker in the wall next to the bed.

Mari hurried toward him on silent feet. He looked up with a smile when she snaked an arm around his neck and dropped down onto his lap, opening his arms to enclose her in a tight embrace, as if he hadn't seen her for days. Her skin rippled into goose bumps as his lips moved against her neck. He smoothed one hand over her damp hair and she closed her eyes, savoring his touch, the way he made her feel, even inside. Pictures of the Generalife Gardens on the hillside facing the Alhambra crowded her mind. She imagined she could smell the roses and jasmine, see the orange trees loaded with ripe fruit, their branches bent low over pots of bright red geraniums, and the lazy spouts of water playing all down the long length of the soft, green reflecting pool edged with myrtle.

"I'll never be able to listen to that music again without seeing the Generalife," Mari whispered, caressing his temple with her lips. "Thank you for a wonderful day, Charles."

"Yeah, it *was* special, wasn't it?" he agreed with a small smile, leaning away a little so he could see her face. "Here." He reached for one of the glasses and handed it to her, then waited for her to taste it. "We need to talk, Mari."

"Later. Right now I'm going to relax, sip my wine and listen to the music, while you go shower——if you want to get to the dining room before it closes, that is," she said, gave him a quick kiss and climbed out of his lap. He shook his head, but went to rummage around in his suitcase for clean clothes without protest. A couple of minutes later she heard the shower running, and let her mind wander back to the Generalife and the Alhambra.

Before she knew it, Charles was standing in front of her with his curly hair dripping onto his bare shoulders and chest. Her eyes caressed every contour and shadow down to the belt of his navy trousers, then his smiling face, watching her watch him. She rose, drawn toward him as if by a powerful magnetic force, and without a word took the towel from his hand and ruffled it over his hair, soaking up the glittering drops, then draped it around his neck before slipping her hands around his waist to pull him closer.

"Uh-uh," he insisted, putting her away. She wasn't the only one who could play that game. "Can look, but no touch—if you still want to get downstairs before the dining room closes." Mari broke away with a little laugh, letting her hands tickle a trail across his ribs.

The dining room had an air of informality about it, even in the evening, and Charles directed Mari across the plush carpet toward a small alcove of glass set between narrow strips of polished wood, where the dark outside provided the privacy he sought.

"The service has been Americanized." She pointed to the lighted table along the far wall. "If you want salad, you go get it yourself. There's also a huge pot of gazpacho down at the end, though I don't think it's as good as what we had at La Coquina." Sitting directly across from him gave her the chance to revel in looking without being obvious about it. He was dressed casually, yet there was something rich about his camel sweater over a burgundy, navy and tan plaid shirt, probably something to do with the colors next to the warm tones of his skin and eyes.

They ordered and then went to the salad bar, where Mari heaped tomato wedges and cucumber slices on top of romaine lettuce, then reached for a long-handled wooden ladle sticking out of a stoneware crock. Charles watched the purplish liquid run out through round holes in the bowl of the spoon, revealing gray-green olives blushed a delicate pink here and there. Returning to the table, they ate ravenously for a few minutes, then both started to talk at once. "You first," Charles offered.

"No, you go ahead," Mari demurred. She really didn't want to know what time his plane was leaving tomorrow, at least not yet. Her earlier carefree mood was becoming more and more difficult to sustain as the time with him flowed away like waves ebbing with the tide.

"Have you talked to Cisco yet about when Jan may be able to make the trip home?"

"Another week, if she continues to improve at the rate she is now, with no setbacks." Her fingers played nervously with a spoon, and Charles reached across the table to hold it still.

"I don't know exactly how to say this, Mari, but—well, are you involved at home? With someone else, I mean."

Taken completely by surprise, she stopped eating. "What a quaint way to put it. I don't know whether to answer yes or no," she teased, her eyes bright with mischief. "If I answer no, you'll begin to suspect I have some fatal flaw, otherwise someone would've snapped me up before now, right?" She hurried on without giving him a chance to answer. "And if I say yes, you'll think I'm, uh, promiscuous, I suppose is the word. I'm thirty-four, Charles. Were you expecting a virgin?"

"You know damn well that wasn't what I meant at all!"

"No, I don't, but I'm relieved to hear it. Virginity is a state of mind, you know, one I wouldn't wish on my worst enemy. Unawakened, naive, unknowing. No woman—or man, for that matter—could possibly be a good journalist *and* a virgin. It's a contradiction in terms." She straightened and slipped her hand out from under his on the pretext of scooping up a bite of salad. "I'd be happy to satisfy your craving for a lengthy discourse on virginity, but some other time. It's not a subject that interests me greatly."

He looked at her, exasperated and amazed at the twist she'd given his question. "Will you stop that and be serious? We need to talk, damn it!"

Mari looked down and began toying with an olive. "I know," she mumbled on a sigh. "No, I'm not involved, or attached, or whatever it was you asked." She glanced up with a wry smile. "Am I supposed to ask the same of you?"

"Of course not!"

"I shouldn't ask, or you're not involved?" She couldn't keep the corner of her mouth from twitching.

"Why are you doing this, Mari?" He was more than a little put out, because she seemed intent on trying to distract him from the subject no matter what tack he took. Maybe he'd read her response to him all wrong. "I thought we had—" The waiter arrived at just that moment with his filet, so he leaned back from the table to wait. Mari hadn't ordered anything besides the salad, and now it looked like she wasn't going to eat even that. "Don't you want more than that?" Charles asked, though the waiter was already walking away.

"Yes, a lot more," she whispered urgently, leaning toward him. "I want this day to go on and on, for it to never end." As if they both were at the mercy of someone else's perverse whim, now it was Mari who needed to be serious. "Everything seems larger than life here, have you noticed? The colors of the sky and the sea, the way the air feels and smells."

Charles watched her expressive face. She was wearing the same silver earrings he'd noticed the day he found her at the beach—and they flashed blue from time to time, reflecting the color of her chambray shirt—and a chain of silver-washed filigree beads looped twice around her neck, matching in delicacy the blush of pink on her cheeks.

"Maybe it's just too good to be true, too much like a fairy tale, a fantasy. Perhaps it's only . . . al Andalus!" She saw that he was about to interrupt. "No, let me finish. I'm suspicious of my sense of reality, of my judgment, maybe because too much has happened to me in the last week. I'm not sure I should trust my feelings, or what's going on in my head."

"I'm having to learn my way, too, Mari. But just because it's new to us doesn't mean it isn't real. The important thing is that it feels right—you and me." This wasn't exactly the place, or the way, he'd planned to say it.

"Maybe, here, away from your work. And mine. Away from the constant pressure, and all the mundane but frustrating little things that have a way of making everything not so . . . so right."

Charles reached for her hand again, giving in to the

overwhelming urge to touch and hold onto her. "You may need more time, Mari, but I don't." The slight hesitation she'd heard in his voice a moment ago was gone. "I love you. No ifs, ands, or buts, no strings attached. You'll see. It's going to be the same wherever we are. Or better." His sudden grin was infectious.

Mari wasn't sure what being in love meant to her, let alone to him, and she couldn't even begin to guess what he meant by "no strings attached," but she held onto his hand as if it were her only link with reality. "Your mind does crazy, shocking things to me—did you know that, Charles?" He could hear the smile in her voice even before he saw it in her eyes. "But when you touch me, it really gets out of hand. And I can't get enough of touching you, either, even if it's only with my eyes."

His eyes never wavered from her face while she spoke, until he became aware of the color rising in her cheeks. Suddenly he reached back for his wallet, pulled out a couple of bills, and tossed them down on the table, then picked up the half-empty bottle of wine and grabbed her hand as he rose from the chair, heedless of his uneaten steak.

"Come on. Let's get out of here."

Janet's physical therapy sessions were getting longer each day, which also meant she was getting stronger, though she had to rest in bed for a while after each one. But Friday morning was her first try at taking a tub bath. They talked as usual, while Mari ran the water and then helped her in.

"If you get to town today or tomorrow, would you get some candy for me to give the nurses, Mari? You know, for Easter," Janet explained. "They've all been so nice to me." Mari thought of Charles's comment about how her mother didn't spend much time thinking about herself. "Mabel Carrothers was here yesterday. She says the group is going to Ronda tomorrow, just for the day. If you'd go to town this afternoon, you'd have tomorrow free. It's an interesting old town, Mari, sits way up high on a cliff that's split by a deep gorge. Bullfighting originated there almost three hundred years ago. I know you're not very interested in that, but Mabel says they're also going to the Pileta Caves, just a few miles outside of Ronda, which are older than the ones at

Altamira. The oldest pottery fragments in Europe were found there, and red and black drawings on the walls, one of a fish that's nearly fifty feet long."

"Maybe," Mari mumbled, refusing to commit herself as she helped Janet stand up in the tub, averting her eyes from her mother's sagging flesh while she wrapped her in a thick white towel, then reached for a second towel and began patting her arms and shoulders. Mari wasn't used to seeing her mother even partially dressed, let alone nude, and her pathetically thin, wrinkled thighs and buttocks, and her shriveled breasts, now little more than pockets of skin, shook her more than anything since that first day in the intensive care unit. Mari thought of all the women milling around in the locker room at her health club in Houston, so nonchalantly nude, and realized that a lack of physical self-consciousness epitomized the difference between her mother's generation and her own. It was one thing to hear the words from Cisco, and something else entirely to confront the reality of her mother's mortality, to know without any doubt that the time was nearing when Janet would no longer be a physical presence in her life.

"I've been reading up on the flamenco, trying to learn more about it since I saw that performance with Charles," Mari told her, trying to shake off the disturbing thought. She helped Janet step over the edge of the tub, then dried her feet and slipped a fresh gown over her head. There'd never been a time when they didn't talk to each other. Only what they talked about had changed, so gradually at first that neither of them noticed, at least not in any conscious way. After years of sometimes noisy, other times silent resistance to almost everything Janet suggested or told her to do, Mari had fallen into the habit of focusing on impersonal subjects that didn't lend themselves to debate, until Janet had finally acquiesced and adopted the same "rules." During her marriage, Mari's need to avoid confrontations with her mother had intensified, because she simply couldn't handle any more conflict or disapproval than she already was getting. Afterward, she'd purposefully stayed away from Denver, and her mother, for almost two years. By now the impersonal mode was as much habit as intent.

"They can trace it back to the time when the Romans

were here, to the famous dancing girls of Gades—Cadiz—who were known for their musical ability and their provocative, arousing movements."

"I know," Janet sighed, still slightly out of breath from exertion as Mari helped her back into bed. "I saw a performance in Seville that was electric, to say the least." Mari uncapped a bottle of moisturizing lotion and began to smooth some over Janet's hands and arms. "And I've seen pictures of the wall paintings at Pompeii, of dancers in similar poses, engaged in some sort of ritual dance to their fertility god. The position of their arms and castanets, movements that suggest they're skilled in the art of love, loud music and hand clapping, the beating of the feet, overpowering emotion. All calculated to arouse the audience to a sexual frenzy. The duality of the sacred and the profane." Mari glanced at Janet, expecting to catch a moue of disapproval or distaste, but instead found her thoughtful. She couldn't remember ever hearing her mother talk about such things before. Was that why she'd always assumed that Janet never had any truly "sexual" thoughts at all?

Massaging Janet's arms and legs had become a daily ritual to help return venous blood to the heart, which could be a problem in patients unable to take much exercise on their own. The lotion also was an excuse to touch her, a need Mari knew something about from personal experience. She'd once done a report on the health benefits of pets that could be stroked and loved, especially for the elderly, who were severely deprived when it came to touching. So why did it come as such a surprise when Charles had pointed out that her own mother suffered that same deprivation! Had she actually believed that Janet didn't have the same needs as other women? Or was it that she'd always equated touching with sexuality, and had never thought of her mother in that way, at least not in the same sense that she considered herself a sexual person?

"Cisco says civilization here in Andalusia is the oldest in the western world, that it goes back to around one thousand B.C., perhaps to the time of the Minoans," Mari continued.

"Yes, because of the metals—silver and gold, and also copper, which they used to make bronze."

"Then perhaps the roots of flamenco go back even further than the Romans. To Crete," Mari suggested.

"To the snake goddess?" Janet not only read a lot, but had an unusually retentive memory, so her quickness had to be a sign of a good strong heartbeat and improved circulation to the brain.

"Yes," her daughter answered. "Certainly the flounced skirt is similar, and she holds her arms aloft kind of like the flamenco dancers. She's also got what you might call a 'transfixed' expression on her face."

Janet smiled at that. "Maybe so. Dance has been associated with religious celebrations from ancient times, as a way of expressing sexuality and fertility, death and resurrection. Pagan dancing never really died out, you know. It was assimilated by the Church. Sensual experience as religious ritual. Today it's the 'born-again' Christians who are transformed in spirit, who experience religious 'ecstasy,' though I doubt most of them would admit that what they feel has anything to do with the flesh. I expect the flamenco is a similar combination of the sensual and spiritual."

"Maybe," Mari mumbled distractedly. The ideas were coming fast now, tumbling over each other. "Cisco used the word *duende* the other day when we were having lunch." Mari could tell from the flicker of Janet's lashes that she still wasn't used to hearing her doctor referred to by his given name. "When I asked him what it meant in English, he said 'the spirit of flamenco,' but that it didn't really translate. I got the distinct impression that he was talking about a different kind of knowing, more like intuition." She went into the bathroom to wash her hands, but raised her voice so Janet could hear. "According to what I read, it was the Gypsies who were the connecting link over time. They picked up erotic Oriental dances as they moved through Persia, western Russia, and eastern Europe over a period of about five hundred years before they arrived in Spain. The *zarabanda,* for instance, is a combination of ancient dances with those the Gypsies were doing back in the 1700s. And of course here they found Islamic culture, another Oriental society. They put it all together—the singing, playing, and dancing—even took the Moors' cithara and added a sixth string, to make the flamenco guitar."

She made several trips back and forth to the bathroom to change the water in Janet's flowers, talking all the while. Potted plants and vases of cut flowers crowded not only the table next to her bed, but also the windowsill, most of them from members of the tour group.

"How I wish you could go to Huelva, Mari," Janet sighed, relaxing back into her pillows. "The Tarshish of King Solomon's time. A shipping center for copper that was mined inland, a port already old when Columbus sailed to the New World from there. At the mouth of the Rio Tinto, about fifty miles from the Portuguese border. I saw round *crótalos* in the Museo Arqueológico there, bronze castanets that were dug up somewhere along the river, dating back centuries before the Romans ever set foot in Andalusia. Yet they're almost exact duplicates of the ones the flamenco dancers use today."

Half-formed images gradually began taking distinct shape in Mari's mind—a priestess to the snake goddess metamorphosed into Galiana the flamenco dancer, and the youthful bull dancers of ancient Crete filing into the bullring at Ronda—until her fingers itched with the urge to put the images in her head on film or videotape. And it was at that moment that she made the decision to go to Ronda the next day.

Janet was just finishing the grilled sole Mari had brought to her from La Coquina when Cisco came breezing into the room with a big smile on his face. "So you're back! I hear you went to Ronda yesterday," he began, only to be interrupted by a nurse who handed him a gift-wrapped package the size of a shoe box.

"This was delivered to the hospital, for both of you, it says," he explained, handing it to Mari. She didn't recognize the name on the sticker, but it was from a store in Torremolinos.

"Why don't you open it?" Janet suggested, since Cisco was taking her pulse. Mari slid off the pink ribbon, opened the box and found a small white envelope on a cloud of yellow tissue paper. She peeled back the layers of tissue to expose two intricately decorated candy Easter eggs, then set the box down where Janet could see them. "They're from

Charles!" she exclaimed as she slid the card out of the envelope.

"Might have known," Janet murmured, the corners of her mouth curling up in a delighted smile.

Mari read the message aloud. "Only in al Andalus! Another wedding of the Christian and Moslem." She looked at Cisco with a quizzical lift of one eyebrow. "Do you know what he means?"

"The egg of our Christian Easter is a symbol of resurrection and life, but it is made of marzipan, the almond and sugar candy brought to us by the Moors."

"Even the egg as a symbol of fertility and renewed life," Janet chimed in, "goes back to the ancient Egyptians and Persians."

Cisco bent to look closer at the eggs. "When I was a boy there was always a marzipan egg waiting when we woke on Easter morning. But my family was very poor, so sometimes it was only a little one, and never so grand as these. Afterward there was church, and in the afternoon we play pelota, my brothers and cousins, and all the boys in my school. You know pelota, Mari, from when you visit the Basque towns in your country?" Mari nodded. "But perhaps what you see there is not the same. In my town, Guernica, we play the *cesta punta* style, with a scooped racket." His hands moved rapidly while he talked, wrapping the blood pressure cuff around Janet's upper arm. Mari suspected his storytelling was partly intended to help Janet relax so he could get an accurate reading. "It is a new town, for Spain, and my oldest brother is on the town council, so now we have a magnificent covered pelota court that holds three thousand people!" He gave Janet a big smile.

"Your family was in Guernica when it—during the civil war?" Janet asked.

He nodded. "My father lose a leg in the bombing. Many people were gathered in the center of town at that time, in the open market. It took only three hours, to kill more than two thousand." He pumped the rubber bulb attached to the pressure cuff, then inserted the stethoscope into his ears. The room was unnaturally quiet for a few seconds, while he counted the arterial pulse in Janet's arm and watched the needle on the pressure gauge fall. "One hundred twelve over seventy-six," he announced as he released the pressure in the cuff. "At this rate you will soon be home. Yes, those who lived through the bombing of my town will never forget. My brother is fifty-six, so he was only a child, but . . ." He paused. "Afterward it was a very hard time, with the country devastated by war but little materials to rebuild because of the international blockade. And now, for eighteen years, we have the fighting again. A different kind of warfare, perhaps, but war all the same. Some of my old school friends are involved in the separatist movement."

"But I thought the Basque provinces have their regional parliament and government back, since Franco died," Mari injected.

"Yes, since 1980. And a military governor to head it, appointed from Madrid."

"You actually know some of the ETA guerrillas?" Mari asked, another idea beginning to take shape in her mind. Cisco shrugged before answering, and for a minute she thought he wasn't going to.

"It is not for me to say who are the guerrillas. Some say the delegates to the regional assembly from the Herri Batasuna party, the political arm of the ETA, are guerrillas, though they are legally elected."

After he left, Mari put the eggs on the table and straightened Janet's blanket. "Would you like to be quiet for a while now, Mom, maybe take a nap, get rested up for supper?"

Janet matched her wry grin, but shook her head. "You rest for a change. Sit down. I want to talk to you for a minute." She waited for Mari to pull the lounge chair closer to her bed. "Have you heard from Charles?"

"He called last night. Said to tell you he's coming to Denver next month for a meeting and is counting on taking you out to dinner." Mari smiled to herself, recalling the nearly overwhelming urge to call him last night, to tell him about her trip to Ronda, just to talk, and then hearing the phone ringing as she came out of the shower.

"Scientists aren't all alike, you know," Janet said in a soft voice.

"You can say that again!" Mari agreed with a little laugh, beginning to feel a little wary. Certainly Janet wasn't going to go digging into her personal business after all this time.

"Charles is different."

"Yeah, I guess so. He's good at explaining about his work, isn't he? Some of them are slippery as eels, or else obtuse. But not him. He's not all puffed up about himself, either." She'd tried to push Charles out of her thoughts after he left, telling herself she needed to back off and get things in perspective. But he just wouldn't go. Instead she kept reliving the night of the storm, the two of them sitting together afterward in the quiet dark, hands entwined while they sipped Manzanilla and watched the crashing waves and clouds of sea mist. His physical presence seemed to follow her wherever she went, whether it was wandering through the crowded streets in town or alone in her room, and at times she would glance up, almost expecting to see him.

"I meant he's not like Phillip," Janet said, jolting Mari out of her reverie.

"Phillip is not a scientist, Mom. Not by any stretch of the imagination," she shot back firmly. "He may be a fairly skilled artisan by now, but he has neither the instincts nor the motivations of a scientist. But how could you possibly know that much about Charles on such short acquaintance?" She didn't even like to think about her former husband, let alone talk about him, especially with Janet, so her question was a little like a bullfighter coaxing the bull to charge the cape.

"He cares about others, for one thing, in a way that Phillip Ashmore wouldn't even begin to understand. Oh, Phillip can give the appearance of caring, on the surface, because a doctor is supposed to. But it's all facade. Phony." Janet's perceptiveness surprised her. "Charles puts himself in the other person's place. I could tell, just by the way he always took my hand and held it. He knows how it feels, to be in a hospital, I mean." She pointed toward the bar of Spanish Macedonia soap, a beautiful mélange of opaque green, blue, and lavender chips suspended in a transparent gel, which she kept in a dish on the table next to her bed. "Not only the smells, but, well, how impersonal everything is! I know he brought that soap to remind me that at least one person is thinking of me as *me,* not just a body to be washed or fed, or a pulse to be counted."

Mari thought about the Guerlain cologne she'd bought herself, that year she was in Paris, and how it made her feel. Even now she could hardly put it into words, but that particular fragrance possessed some indefinable sensuality that seemed to suit her, and she'd used it ever since. There had been a time when she would've dismissed all such superficially "feminine" things as frivolous and inconsequential, but she knew better now. In some intangible way, that cologne had helped her become consciously aware of herself, which, she supposed, was another kind of a loss of virginity. Because for the first time in her life she'd seen herself as a separate and complete individual, not part of someone else—her mother or father, or her husband.

"He's quite taken with you, Mari, you realize that, don't you?"

"He told you that?" Mari asked. *Taken with you!* Who but her mother would use an old-fashioned phrase like that?

"Of course not! He didn't have to, though he did say he admires your work. You will see to it that he gets a copy of your heart program, won't you?" Mari nodded, trying to think of some way to change the subject without being obvious about it. "He's trying so hard not to make a mistake with you, and he's a little unsure of himself."

"Wherever did you get that idea? Charles Merrill is about as sure of himself, as self-confident, as anybody I've ever met in my life!"

"Maybe, about his work, but—"

"And that's why you think he's not like Phillip?" Mari asked, incredulous. Never in her wildest imaginings could Janet even begin to guess at the damage Phillip had done to her ego, or how she had hated herself for what she'd allowed him to do to her, which had been the most difficult of all—learning to accept and understand that. And to get over the grieving. Like Phillip, Charles had all the earmarks of a workaholic. She'd found no wife or children listed in his *American Men of Science* entry, only the "facts" of his academic and professional life—a B.S. in physics from Texas at nineteen, a master's from Washington University in St. Louis, and Ph.D. in biomedical engineering from the

University of Wisconsin, followed by a two-year postdoc at Stanford before joining the faculty at Austin, and a list of research contributions and awards that filled half a page. All of which meant that he'd probably never been able to tear himself away from his work long enough to become deeply involved with anyone.

She'd fallen in love once before, or thought she had, and it had turned into a disaster. So thinking she was in love with Charles, or being attracted, or whatever it was, wasn't enough to push her into a commitment. Anyway, for a woman, commitment was just another word for giving in to someone else, giving up the right to make decisions about her work and just about everything else. A man might call it compromising, but it was the woman who was expected to do it. She sometimes thought of the book *Smart Women, Foolish Choices,* and worried that she might be one of those women who were doomed to repeat the same mistakes over and over, to always be attracted to the wrong kind of man. Truth be told, that was one of the reasons she didn't trust her own judgment with Charles. For all she knew, she might even be confusing admiration for his work with admiration for the man. Was she simply in love with his work?

"You can't really know he lacks confidence, Mom, and neither do I."

"I'm not as good with words as you are, Mari. What I meant to say is that I hope you'll give him a chance, that you should stop letting Phillip cast a shadow over your life. Charles isn't rigid, like Phillip. I suspect he's quite imaginative, in fact."

The word brought a little smile to Mari's lips. How right her mother was about that! Phillip would never even consider making love at seven-thirty in the morning, because his mind and body were already paying homage to a different mistress the minute he opened his eyes. And not until she was finished with him, had wrung him dry of all gentleness and caring, did he come back to his wife—tired, impatient, needing only to empty all the frustration of the day into her body. In the end, sex had become a duty, a chore to be dispensed with as quickly as possible. He hardly even touched her there, let alone wanted to look. *I spend all day putting my hand into one cunt after another. What makes you think I want to look at another one when I get home?* Over the years, she'd tried to forget the hateful words, and the man who used them to punish her, by suppressing the restless stirrings of her body. But with Charles it was so different, an adventure in pleasure that provoked an intense awareness of how her own body responded, as well as his. Was it possible to become addicted in such a short time? she wondered. Because just thinking about making love with him brought a physical response that left her swollen, wet, and aching for the touch of his knowing hands. And his mouth.

"You need someone to share your life with, Mari, a partner. Someone to love who loves you." Janet sighed and turned her head enough to gaze beyond Mari, out the window.

"Someone to take care of me? Every woman is incomplete without a man, right?"

"As every man is incomplete without a woman. I know you don't agree with me about many things," her mother answered, turning her eyes back to Mari. "But in spite of what you may think, I know you're lonely. You need more than just your work. Which reminds me of what I really started out to say. You must need to get back home to your work, and I'm stronger now, so you don't have to stay here any longer, waiting on me."

Mari started shaking her head before Janet was finished. "Uh-uh. We're going home together, Mom. You don't need to worry about me or my job. Or Charles." She couldn't help smiling when she said his name.

"I didn't mean to interfere. It's just that—well, I want you to be happy."

"That's okay, Mom, I'll think about what you said," she answered, more to appease than to promise.

While Janet rested, Mari walked down to the beach, then on the way back stopped for a cold drink at La Coquina and to talk with Fernando Ramos for a few minutes. As the afternoon wore on she found herself thinking more and more about the idea that had come to her while Cisco told her mother about his childhood in Guernica. The ETA was constantly in the news because of a barrage of hit-and-run terrorist attacks, especially against the French. They'd bombed about thirty French-owned businesses in the Basque provinces, burned French-registered cars, and destroyed a French-Spanish chemical plant in just the past few months, to protest France's deportation of suspected separatist guerrillas back to Spain, where they'd been imprisoned. It wasn't always front-page news, at least in the United States, but the story would be far more interesting to viewers if there were a different kind of information, instead of just the usual brief paragraph or two that came over the wire. Presented with the right visuals of places and people, it would be more real and meaningful to viewers. But she needed equipment. And she needed Tony. It was time to check in with Jack, anyway, to let him know she would be back in about a week, if her mother continued to progress. What was the best approach to take, to get him to okay what she wanted to do? Talk up the likelihood that the network would use the story, at the same time enhancing KPOC's national and local reputation by demonstrating their ability to contribute to the network's international news operation?

Later, standing under the green canvas canopy outside the hospital, waiting for a taxi, she glanced down at her watch, then did a quick calculation—barely noon in Houston, time enough for Tony to catch the Iberia flight out of New York tonight. Or if not, tomorrow night for sure, which meant he could be here no later than Tuesday morning.

CHAPTER
8

~~~

The two seemingly endless hours of waiting in Denver were almost over, but Charles continued to pace the long corridor, glancing at his watch every minute or two. The Stapleton terminal was a seething mass of humanity, as always, but he was hardly aware of the shifting scenes of greeting and parting as he walked past one gate and then another. Too restless to sit still even if there had been an empty chair in the boarding area near Gate 24, his mind wandered too, refusing to settle anywhere for long. But it wandered in the past rather than the present. The past two weeks.

It was Mari, not Spain, who intruded into the imagination, he thought wryly, remembering her comment. He sensed her presence everywhere he went now, no matter what he was doing. Sometimes, like a needle stuck in the groove of a record, his memories got stuck, too, replaying the same scene over and over again. Other times, without the slightest warning, she would sweep him away with her into a world of fantasy, where he was the novice—a world he'd only begun to glimpse, through her eyes, that day at the Alhambra—and he'd remember how impoverished his own response was by comparison with her fantastic sensitivity to both feeling and knowing. She'd become a distraction he couldn't afford but never wanted to be without again.

Like that last morning, in Torremolinos, slowly coming awake to the gray light of dawn, only dimly aware at first that something unusual was going on, even before he was sure what. A silky brush stroked his bare skin, feathering over his shoulder, across his chest, cresting the cage of his ribs to slide down the slope of his stomach. And then a picture of Mari's smooth, straight hair, swaying in languid fluid waves as she moved, exploded in his head, bringing a surge of blood to his loins. He'd cupped a hand over her head, allowing his fingers to thread through the slippery strands, recognizing that for him her hair was a kind of sensual Achilles' heel.

"Mar?" he whispered. If he sounded tentative, it was because he wasn't sure she was awake. But her quiet "Ssssh" had come with only the briefest interruption of her caressing exploration of his body. Nothing was left untouched by her thick sweep of hair, questing fingers, or gentle lips as her head moved inexorably lower, blazing a trail of anticipation with her tongue. And his breath would stop again, as it had at that unforgettable moment of exquisite pleasure, and his body would ache as if it, too, could remember.

He'd arrived back in Austin eighteen hours later to a cold, empty house, and then a grueling three-hour oral exam the next morning, which left him feeling more than a little dissatisfied, not to mention irritated. Lupe Gonzalez had done a good job of fielding most of the questions put to her by members of the qualifying committee, and they'd passed her to candidacy on condition of another course in fluid mechanics. But as usual, Sam Roth had played devil's advocate, taking great pleasure in ferreting out Lupe's weak point and then hammering away at it until the small hole in her preparation gaped open like some damn bleeding wound. Sam's biting comments had become increasingly vitriolic and personal, and nothing Charles tried in order to divert him had done one damn bit of good. What Charles really couldn't understand, though, was how Lupe could just stand there, taking one abusive comment after another without uttering a single word!

As it turned out, the exam had been the opening salvo in a week filled with more than its usual share of faculty meetings and forms to be filled out. The ravening bureaucracy in the dean's office wanted a list of specific things he'd done in the past five years to improve his "teaching skills"—as if every minute he spent thinking and working in the lab, trying to find answers about what was going on in the blood, had nothing to do with what or how he taught. He'd gone home Tuesday, physically and mentally exhausted, only to find the videocassette with Mari's artificial heart program waiting in his mailbox. Hearing her voice and seeing her on his television screen had done more to remedy his fatigue than several hours of sleep.

He'd waited until noon the next day to call, seven in the evening there, figuring she'd be back from the hospital by then. But she wasn't, nor could he reach her any of the zillion other times he tried over the next twenty-four hours. Cisco Ibarzábal wasn't around, either. The hospital told him Janet's condition was "satisfactory," which he had to believe since she didn't have a phone in her room. In the end he left messages at both the hospital and the Bajondillo, asking Mari to call him whenever she came in, no matter what time of day or night it was. But when the call finally did come, late Thursday night, it was from Rachel Widener.

He shook his head in wonder and glanced at his watch, then hurried back toward Gate 24. The plane was already in and the first few passengers were beginning to drift into the loading area, to be greeted by someone in the crowd gathered around the opening to the gangway. Janet probably would be among the last off, not the first, he thought, just as he caught a glimpse of Mari behind a bunched knot of exiting passengers. She looked surprised at first, then smiled and waved, and another picture surfaced in his mind—of her waving and running to meet him on the beach at Torremolinos. It was nearly nine o'clock, and long past dark outside, but to Charles it felt as if the sun had suddenly come out after days of dreary gray clouds.

She came into his arms with a little laugh and a breathless "What a delicious surprise!"

He hugged her wiggling body and nuzzled his face into her hair. "God, am I glad to see you. You really had me worried."

She pulled away, a puzzled look on her face. "Worried? Why?"

Instead of answering, he took her face between his hands to give her a quick kiss, just as one of the hurrying passengers jostled them in passing, spoiling his aim, and his lips whispered against the corner of her mouth instead. "Guess we'd better save it for later. How's Jan?"

"Tired. Exhausted, is probably more like it," she answered quickly. "I've got to see about a wheelchair for her. Jackie called you? Have you talked with her? Tonight, I mean." She started walking again, and he followed without thinking.

"I've got a chair and an attendant, and a car just outside, in a loading zone. And yes, I talked with her when I got in, a couple of hours ago. She's waiting for us at the hospital, has everything arranged there." He was grinning while he talked, so happy to see her that he couldn't even keep a straight face. Without any warning at all she stopped and reached her arms up around his neck to give him a tight hug, a spontaneous embrace that told him all he wanted to know.

"I didn't mean for Jackie to ask you to come, but I'm glad," she mumbled against his neck.

He shook his head, sliding his cheek back and forth against her hair. "She didn't. I came because I wanted to, needed to, couldn't wait any longer. And thought maybe I could help." He held her away from him for a second so they could simply look at each other. "How about you go alert the attendant with the chair? You'll spot him standing by the check-in desk, or at least that's where he was last time I looked, in a uniform. I'll go get Janet."

He could tell the moment Janet recognized him, which was about as soon as he entered the cabin of the plane. "Charles. How nice." It seemed to take a lot of effort just to whisper those few words, and judging by her wan face and tired eyes, Mari was right. She was just about at the end of her meager physical resources. He reached down and scooped her up in his arms.

"You are one heck of a determined woman, aren't you?" he said, giving her a gentle squeeze. "But you can relax now, Jan, leave the rest to us. A few more minutes and we'll have you tucked into a nice warm bed so you can get a good night's rest." He started down the aisle of the plane with her, the shock of how small and light she was registering someplace on the fringes of his mind.

They hardly talked at all on the way to St. Anthony's, mostly because he didn't want Janet to even try to make conversation, and he needed privacy for what he wanted to say to Mari. She glanced at him from time to time and smiled, but seemed content with the silence.

He drove directly to the emergency entrance, where he lifted Jan out of the car. "I'll see you tomorrow," he said as he settled her into the waiting wheelchair, then planted a quick kiss on her cool cheek before turning to Mari. "I'll move the car, come to the waiting room in the cardiac unit, be there whenever you get through." He grinned and gave her a quick kiss. "Take your time. I'm not going anywhere." A nurse was already pushing Janet through the swinging doors.

An hour later he looked up from his magazine and saw Mari coming down the hall. The woman with her had to be her sister Jackie, though they didn't look much alike. She was taller, and her hair was dark brown, streaked through around her face with gray, but it was their eyes and mouths that accounted for most of the difference. Oddly enough, Mari had a stronger look about her, even though Jackie was the larger of the two. He rose quickly and went to meet them.

"Charles?" Jackie queried with a smile.

"Jackie?" he answered, and then they both laughed and shook hands.

"Mom's already asleep," she said. "Dr. Richardson thinks she weathered the trip okay."

"He put her on the EKG," Mari added, "wants her to rest tonight. Plans to run some tests tomorrow, decide then whether she needs a change in medication." They started down the hall toward the bank of elevators.

"She asked us to thank you, Charles," Jackie remembered as they got into the elevator, "and said to tell you she wants to see you tomorrow, if you have time."

"For her, Jackie, I've always got time," he mumbled without looking at Mari.

"Why don't you stay with us tonight? We've got room, if

you wouldn't mind sleeping on our glassed-in porch. It won't be very private, or quiet, after the kids get up in the morning, but—"

"That's okay, Jackie, I can—" He stopped when he felt Mari jiggle his arm.

"I've got to get to bed, and soon," she pleaded. "Feels like I haven't slept for a week. But we'd have more time together tomorrow if you stayed at Jackie's." Just one look at her face was enough to persuade him.

"Sure," he agreed, tossing Jackie a quick smile. "Anyway, I can sleep through just about anything." He wrapped an arm around Mari's shoulder just as the elevator doors opened, and felt her body go rigid. He shot a quick glance at her—and saw that her face was as pale as death.

"Marilyn. Jackie. Nice to see you," the man in a starched-white coat greeted both women. "None of the family in trouble, I hope." He had the hearty manner and broad smile Charles had encountered in so many practicing physicians. Probably something they were taught in medical school, but he'd always found it slightly irritating, not to mention inappropriate.

It was Jackie who answered. "Mom's in the cardiac unit. Mari just brought her in, from Spain."

"From Spain? Still likes traveling, does she? Is she all right?"

Jackie darted a look at Mari, then at Charles, who thought she looked positively uncomfortable. "Yes, Dr. Richardson thinks so."

"Well, I'm glad to hear that, anyway. I'll stop in to see her tomorrow. Right now I have a baby waiting for me upstairs, so I'd better get on up there. Once they decide to come, there's not much we can do to stop them, middle of the night or not." He laughed, but it was sort of a dry, mirthless sound.

Mari had already begun to edge her way down the hall toward the main entrance, anxious to leave. Her face was so white Charles wondered if she were going to be sick, and he was just moving toward her when the doctor spoke again. "Oh, Mari!" Charles saw her flinch. "I understand you're working in Houston now. And doing very well, too. I've seen a couple of your reports, on the network news."

Mari glanced back once, then mumbled, "Sorry, I have to go," just before she turned and ran for the door.

Charles muttered a quick "Excuse me," then followed her without a backward glance, really worried now.

He looked around outside, in the dark, and found her leaning against the wall, several feet away from the door, her mouth open, gulping deep breaths of the cool night air like a fish out of water. Her forehead was beaded with perspiration and she was trembling, but when he touched her arm, she drew away from him.

"Do you feel sick?" he asked, trying to think what to do for her. "What's wrong, do you know? Your stomach?"

She moved a little farther away, still leaning one shoulder against the wall as if she couldn't stand alone. "Its nothing," she mumbled, "I just needed . . . some air." And then she covered her face with both hands, as if she didn't even want him to see her, turned toward the wall and began to sob.

Charles rolled over and stared at the beaded ceiling for a few minutes, listening to the murmur of voices somewhere in the house, probably in the kitchen. He glanced at his digital watch and then threw back the covers, moving quickly because it was colder out here than inside the house. He stepped into his pants and pulled on a shirt, grabbed up his shaving kit and headed for the bathroom, hoping that everyone else had already beaten him to it. Halfway across the living room he heard a growl and turned to see a small black and white collie just a few feet behind him, crouched low, apparently undecided about whether to attack. At almost the same time a boy's face peered around the edge of the door to the next room, to see what was going on. He saw Charles and came into the room to put his hand on the dog, which seemed to cause the dog's tail to wag.

"Hi. He doesn't bite, just likes to make noise," he explained. "His name is Pepper. Mine's Alan."

He looked to be about ten, Charles decided, nodding to acknowledge the introduction. "Mine's Charles. Think it will be okay with him if I go shave, in the bathroom, I mean?" By the time they'd arrived last night, Jackie's two kids had been in bed. And apparently the dog, too.

"Sure. You can go anywhere now that he knows you're

okay. My aunt's still asleep, in my room. I had to sleep on a cot in my mom and dad's room. Mom says we should be quiet."

"Right. I'll watch it," Charles agreed. "Thanks for warning me."

Twenty minutes later he'd shaved and showered, dressed in corduroy slacks and a thick cotton sweater, and was straightening his bed on the porch when Alan reappeared. "My mom wants to know if you're ready for breakfast yet. She says you can come any time. Kitty and Dad and I already ate."

"Kitty your sister?" Charles asked as he followed Alan toward the kitchen. The house was a long, rambling ranch-style, with the kitchen end a pretty fair distance from the bedrooms. The glassed-in porch where he'd spent the night was just off the family room, which was next to the kitchen, so he'd been aware for quite a while that someone was up.

"Yeah, she's thirteen. My dad took her to her dancing lesson, so you lucked out. They won't be back for at least an hour." He threw Charles a devilish grin as they entered the kitchen.

"Sleep okay?" Jackie greeted him.

"Never better. Can I help?" Charles wasn't sure what the protocol was here, but he was more than willing to learn.

"Pour yourself some juice, or coffee, whatever you want," she suggested. "How many eggs and how do you like them? Sausage or bacon, or both?"

"Two over easy and sausage, if you don't have to cook it just for me. Sure I can't help?" He poured himself a glass of orange juice and took it to the breakfast table. "Here?" he asked, just to be sure, and waited for her to nod. "Alan says Mari is still sleeping." He tossed a quick smile at the boy. "I think maybe she was about as exhausted last night as your mother."

"Yes," Jackie said. "It must have been a terrible strain on her. Anything's easier when there are two of you. I feel guilty about not going with her."

"Don't," he advised. "You'll have enough to do here until Jan gets back on her feet. Mari tells me you're in school."

"Yes, I decided to go back last year, to try to finish what I started before I got married and dropped out."

"Mom, I'm going down to Jake's for a while," Alan interrupted. "How about ringing the cowbell if you want me?" Charles suspected Alan had only stayed around this long to satisfy his curiosity about the stranger sleeping on the porch. Jackie nodded absently, hardly noticing when Alan left. Everyone in the neighborhood would know it, Charles thought, if she rang a bell to call him, which probably made it doubly effective.

Jackie slid two eggs out of the pan and onto a plate, added several small link sausages and then pulled open the oven door. "I've got to tell you that I'm the one feeling guilty now," he said, watching her reach for a pan filled with thick, golden biscuits. "I hope you didn't do that just for me."

She looked up, puzzled for a second. "What? Oh, these. No, I didn't. Nick makes them whenever Mari comes. Worries that she doesn't eat right, or not enough, or something. You probably noticed how he is with her."

"Yeah," Charles agreed. He concentrated on eating for a while, recalling how careful Jackie's husband had been with Mari when they arrived last night. He'd teased her a little at first, affectionately, trying to draw her out of her almost catatonic silence, then shut up and fixed her a cup of hot chocolate instead, adding a wallop of brandy, even handing it to her as if she were a child, making sure that she held it with both hands and guiding her fingers around the cup to warm them. He seemed to sense that something had gone terribly wrong, though no one said a word about what had happened as they were leaving the hospital.

"Who was he?" Charles asked Jackie at last, unable to push away the need to know any longer.

She sat down suddenly, right across the table from him, and didn't even try to pretend that she didn't know what he was talking about. "Phillip Ashmore. Her husband. They were divorced ten years ago." She might as well've thrown a bucket of ice water in his face, and it showed. "You didn't know?" she asked quickly.

He nodded slowly. "Yeah, she told me she'd been married once. When she was 'too young,' was the way she phrased it." He reached for his coffee cup, needing a little time.

"It was rotten luck for her, running into him unexpectedly like that, when she was already worn out, on the edge. He's an obstetrician here. Mari used to say, 'What else would you expect from Phillip, since for a man, delivering a baby is the ultimate ego trip.' As you may have guessed, she's not very fond of him."

Charles wasn't so sure about that. He couldn't help remembering all the old clichés about love and hate being two sides of the same strong emotion. "If that's the case, I wonder why a reaction like that."

"Maybe it's like cigarettes are to a smoker who's quit. The longer you're away from them, the more likely they are to make you feel sick, even to smell one." She paused, then took a sip of coffee. "She's never really talked about him, or what happened between them, with any of us. Says they just grew apart, but I don't know. Maybe you—with you she seems to feel—" Jackie broke off her stumbling attempts at whatever she'd been trying to say and jumped up from the table just as Mari appeared in the doorway. In the mauve robe he remembered so well. Judging from her tousled hair and bare feet, she'd climbed out of bed and come straight to the kitchen.

"Morning," she said brightly, coming right toward him, dropped down onto his lap, wrapped her arms around his neck and squeezed hard. His arms accepted and enfolded her almost automatically, as if he'd had a lot of practice at it. He squeezed back.

"I came to see if you were real or imaginary," she whispered in his ear. "Thought maybe I might have dreamed you up." She felt warm and soft, and was behaving as if last night had never been. "And to get one of Nick's biscuits, to hold me while I shower," she said out loud as she jumped back up and reached around Jackie to grab a biscuit. Then she disappeared again.

"Be back in a minute, piglet," she called back from somewhere off in another room.

Jackie tossed him an indulgent smile and shook her head, then began busying herself refilling his cup and flipping switches on the stove. "I have the feeling I've seen you someplace before, Charles. I know that sounds trite, but—"

"Maybe on her heart program. I'm amazed at how many people remember seeing me on television."

"Then you may get even more 'famous.' I understand

they've submitted that program for some kind of national award. So you two met before Spain?"

Charles nodded. "It was pure chance, running into her again on the plane." Missing the plane and Mari had become a recurring nightmare over the past couple of weeks, one that brought him fully awake with his heart in his throat. He watched Jackie lay raw strips of bacon in the frying pan for Mari.

Mari was back again in minutes, with her hair brushed until it was smooth and shiny, but still without makeup. He loved seeing her like that, without any mascara to darken her light lashes. "Worst thing about the whole two weeks was wearing the same rags over and over. I'm taking everything to the women's shelter as soon as I get home. Never want to see any of them again." She was wearing a navy sweater with faded jeans and loafers.

"I've never seen that before," he commented, rubbing his hand over the line of white roses intertwined with green vines running from wrist to shoulder.

"It got cold in those mountains, so I finally broke down and bought this sweater, in Vitoria," she confessed with a grin. "Which reminds me, where are the kids, Jackie?"

"Alan's gone to Jake's. Think he got tired of waiting for you to get up." She brought Mari's plate, with bacon, two eggs, and two biscuits. "I'll call him as soon as you finish eating. Nick took Kitty to her dancing lesson, but they should be back any time now. When does your plane leave?"

"Four-eighteen. I hate to eat and run, but—" She grinned at Jackie. "I've got to get back. I'm on tomorrow night."

"So soon?" Charles objected. "I was going to talk you into coming back to Austin with me for a couple of days, rest up, loll around my pool and get fat eating my barbecue. I can't match Nick's biscuits, but—"

"Speak of the devil!" Mari trilled, rising to greet Kitty and Nick as they came through the door from the carport. "Hi, kitten," she murmured, hugging the blond girl, who looked a lot more like Mari's sister than her mother did. They had the same coloring and eyes, but the younger girl was long-legged and willowy, with the erect posture and fluid body mannerisms of a dancer.

"You feeling better this morning?" Nick asked Mari quietly.

"You bet," she answered breezily, "thanks to your magic potion." She gave him a hug, too, then returned to the table to finish eating. "And these fantabulous golden nuggets."

"I've got to go change," Kitty said to Mari. "See you after, okay?"

Mari nodded and watched her leave the room with a wistful look on her face. "Sure."

"So tell us about this trek into guerrilla territory you made, you and your intrepid Tejano," Nick suggested while he got a cup out of the cabinet and poured himself some coffee. Charles was a little surprised that Nick would know what most Texas chicanos called themselves.

"Not much to tell. Mom's doctor, Cisco Ibarzábal, happened to know some of the guys in the ETA, the Basque separatist organization, because he went to school with them. Two of them are delegates to the provincial assembly, from the party that's the political arm of the movement. He called, and they agreed to talk to me. Like I told Jackie on the phone, it just seemed too good an opportunity to pass up, since I was already there and Mom was so much better. But I needed someone who could speak Spanish, and I didn't have any equipment with me but a tape recorder. So Tony caught a direct flight into Málaga, arrived Tuesday morning. With Rachel." She snuck a grin at Charles. "I was as surprised as you were. She stayed with Mom while we were gone. Tony and I flew into Bilbao, in Vizcaya province, then rented a car. Bilbao's the largest port in Spain, though the city is actually a few miles inland at the end of an estuary, built up against the mountains. Beautiful views of the Basque coast as you go up, and pine forests. We also went to Guernica, San Sebastian, Vitoria, and a whole bunch of little towns."

Everyone at the table waited for her to take a bite and finish chewing, so she could go on with her story. "Tony and Rachel are staying on a couple more days, to go to Seville and Huelva." She looked down at her plate, wishing she could have gone with them to the archeological museum, and particularly to Crete.

"So why do *you* have to get back in such a hurry, then?"

Charles inquired. He glanced at Nick. "Says she's going back to Houston this afternoon."

"Because all kinds of crazy stuff hit the fan after I left, from what Tony told me. I'm not even sure I still have a job. Jack Lunsford, the news director, knocked Ron Bergner out of the evening-news slot, assigned him to the five-minute news breaks in the network's morning program, and hired a woman from Chicago to replace him. Bought her a bright red Mercedes convertible, is redecorating the studio to 'set her off' properly, and God only knows what all else he may have promised to get her to come." She looked at Charles with a crooked smile. "I had to use all my 'wiles' to persuade Jack to let Tony come over. He actually had the nerve to tell me we didn't have the money to throw around on foreign travel—when I was offering him interviews with people the networks haven't even been able to identify, let alone talk to!" She sighed, then sipped at her coffee. "Besides that, I need to get back to my work at the shelter, and the group is supposed to play for a wedding later this week. I've already missed two practice sessions, probably more."

"The group?" Charles felt as if he'd missed something.

"You mean you've known this woman for a whole week and haven't heard of the group?" Nick teased. "The hottest bunch of women musicians playing today, to hear her tell it—all four of them!"

"Don't start again, Nick," Mari warned, though it was obvious she wasn't in the least offended.

"You play in a quartet?" Charles asked, still wondering.

"Yeah, they call themselves the High-Strung Women," Nick explained before Mari had a chance. "Two violins, a cello, and a flute."

Charles started to laugh, then glanced at Mari and thought better of it. He was just beginning to realize there was a helluva lot about her he still didn't know. "I suppose you're the cello. But what's the flute doing in there? I'd guess from the name that you'd all be strings."

"We lost our viola, tried the flute one time and liked it a lot. I think we sound even better now, in fact. Wish we could find an oboe, break another stereotype." Mari glanced at her watch, then at Jackie. "Listen, we need to get this show on the road. Dr. Richardson is going to be at the hospital by two with Mom's test results, so maybe we could go early and visit with her first. I might as well get my stuff together, go on to Stapleton from there. How about you, Charles?" she asked as she started to get up from the table.

"I'm going to see if I can change my flight," he answered with a wry grin, "take the long way home, through Houston. At least I'd have someone to talk to, help sort of pass the time of day."

Mari ran around the table, wrapped her arms around his neck and gave him a loud smack on the cheek. "Would you, really?" she asked, giggling like a little girl. It wasn't hard to tell she was pleased.

She straightened and turned to Nick. "You get one, too, for the biscuits, and everything," she explained, knowing he'd understand, then gave him the same treatment. There were tears in her eyes when she looked at Jackie. "Now how about ringing that damned cowbell of yours for Alan, so I can at least see how big he is before we have to leave? In the meantime, I'm going to be in with Kitty. I brought her something really special." She stopped in the doorway and looked back at Charles, a slight smile curving her soft, pale lips. "A set of castanets I got from a flamenco dancer named Galiana."

"We just let your segment slide, Mari, didn't even try to cover your beat for two whole damn weeks. And it didn't make a shit of difference to our position in the ratings," Jack said, trying to justify what he was proposing—to cut her news segment from five to three minutes and to twice a week. "Which only confirms what I've been saying all along. The audience for the kind of esoteric crap you're putting out is insignificant. The great mass of humanity wants the old heart strings plucked—more pathos and more excitement, the highs and the lows of life."

Mari was beginning to feel as if she'd never been away. "That's not what the audience research says."

"That's just because people always say what they think they *ought* to, not what they actually do when it comes time to turn on the set," he shot back in a loud voice. "If we were sitting at the top, I could see taking a don't-rock-the-boat position. But we're not, and I intend to do whatever it takes to get there! So give me one good reason to stick with the old format."

Mari had negotiated the terms of her contract to protect herself as much as possible, and not only from the "sudden death" syndrome that had ended so many broadcast-news careers. He was going to have to come up with more evidence than he'd laid on the table so far if he wanted to avoid a suit against him and the station, which would cost the network money for sure, and might even cost Jack his reputation as a top news director. And she needed to get that message across to him somehow, even though she'd had no warning that he was going to hit her with this the minute she walked in the door.

"News isn't just what people want to know, Jack, it's also what they need to know. Besides," she went on, trying to ignore his derisive shrug, "you know as well as I do that with the oil industry on the ropes, the medical center is even more important economically to this town than it was before, not to mention that new developments going on there all the time give us opportunities for input into network programming that we otherwise wouldn't have, except when there's a damaging hurricane or an explosion in the ship channel. But the best reporters in the world can't cover disasters that don't happen."

"Maybe, and maybe we just haven't been trying hard enough, haven't had the right personnel to bring it off. Hard-hitting and hungry. Beautiful, to boot. But we do now." He grinned suggestively.

Mari purposefully skipped around what she knew he was alluding to, instead using his point to make one of her own. "I agree. With people like Bill Kurtis moving from the network to Chicago, Steve Bell to Philadelphia, and Sylvia Chase to San Francisco, the trend definitely is toward more hard news at the local level, not more ambulance chasing and happy talk. Which also means the networks will be using more locally produced segments, because that's going to cut their costs. The whole industry has seen big drops in ad revenue, which is due at least as much to the inroads cable and VCRs have made into our audiences as to the state of the economy. Cable is one of your 'facts of life,' Jack, that we're going to have to learn to live with. And how we do it may well determine whether we survive."

"Survive—whadda ya mean?" he jeered, trying to maintain the assurance he'd exhibited earlier. "That's going a bit overboard, even for you, isn't it?"

"No. The local station landscape has changed already, because of the technology available. What we're seeing is only the beginning. I'm talking about local station networks like Conus, Jack, which are taking a big bite out of network ad revenue. Conus already has over fifty stations around the country tied together—using microwave vans and transmitting to each other via satellites—which is breathing new life into local news coverage. One station can't afford to send reporters all over the country, but Conus has begun to compete with the big networks for national stories, sometimes even beating them with live coverage. Look at KTLA, in Los Angeles, which picks up stuff from all kinds of sources, including CNN." Mari had Jack's full attention now.

"This network just dropped a hundred people from the news division and canceled their weekly news magazine. The New York office has announced that it plans to do a half-dozen documentaries instead, which could mean opportunities for us, if we're good enough. The way to go is to do an even better job on the hard news, to look less like our local competition, not more. Let me put it this way—how do you think Marvin Zindler would go over in Chicago, or Philadelphia?" Zindler was Channel Two's consumer "investigator," the white-wigged zany who'd blown the whistle on the "Chicken Ranch"—a bordello operating in La-Grange under the benign eye of law-enforcement officials—only to be immortalized in *The Best Little Whorehouse in Texas*.

"Right now, except for my medical-news segment, the stations in this town are all doing essentially the same thing, night after night. We're just beginning to become a news and documentary source that no half-assed local independent can come even close to. Network stories are getting longer and fewer per broadcast, an economy because it means not having to be in as many places as before, which also means more in-depth coverage, not less. As I see it, Jack, we either continue to go in that direction or we'll end up one of the faceless crowd. It's quality that's going to make the difference. Anyway, the viewers who only want fluff have probably already tuned us out. They're watching Vanna White flip the cards on cable."

"I'm not so sure I buy that, Mari. Viewers who want the kind of in-depth stuff you're talking about are probably already getting it from *MacNeil/Lehrer,* or the *New York Times.*" That was an argument Mari had heard before, most recently from Ed Princeton, an assistant managing editor at the *Houston Chronicle* she'd gone out with a few times. He was a nice enough guy, but cleaning her apartment was more exciting. All Ed wanted to talk about was the power play going on between editorial and advertising at the paper. The *Chronicle* thrived on a thirty-percent news hole, which included Dear Abby, Ann Landers, Miss Manners, horoscopes, a crossword puzzle, and the comics, which didn't leave a whole lot of space for hard news. In Mari's opinion, the paper had been a textbook case of how local ownership compromised news coverage via the good-ole-boy power structure—until it was sold. And Ed Princeton had been one of the first to go.

"How about the blacks in those shacks down by the University of Houston, with nothing much but a TV set?" Jack continued. "You think they give a shit what the commies are doing in Afghanistan? Or the guy who just got laid off at Exxon? He's not tuning in to be told what lousy shape the economy's in!"

"That's a cheap shot, Jack. I'm not suggesting we do away with entertainment programming, and you know it. Have you even considered the possibility that our marketing strategies are off target? The over-fifty segment of the population holds half the discretionary income and more than three quarters of the financial assets of this country. They're the ones who are experiencing more health problems, too. If we developed more programming to attract those viewers, we'd have an unbeatable pitch to make to advertisers."

Jack looked thoughtful for a few seconds, then seemed to come to a sudden decision. "Okay, I'll tell you what. I'll give you one month. One, no more. And then I'm taking a real hard look at the ratings again—final-decision time. So you'd better get on the stick, get some color into your stories, see if you can come up with something a helluva lot juicier than what we were airing before you took off for Spain. I'm not asking you to do another Dr. Red Duke. Anyway, you haven't got the East Texas twang or the Wyatt Earp mustache to pull it off." He grinned to show her that he meant it to be a joke.

The folksy emergency-room surgeon's one-minute health reports from the University of Texas Health Science Center were syndicated to local stations around the country, but watching him on television, Mari always got hung up on wondering what his scraggly mustache must look like when he was eating. He'd also sold a half-hour series called *Bodywatch* to PBS, which ended with him getting on his horse and riding off into the sunset. Most professional medical reporters considered him a joke, but she believed a subliminal message was implied in everything he said— "Gee, gosh whiz, look how wonderful all us medical doctors are." Still, he'd been responsible for starting Life Flight, the oldest and safest air-ambulance service in business, and she didn't begrudge him the credit for that.

"But for God's sake," Jack pleaded, serious again, "at least try taking a look at some of the sad and dirty, grungy stuff that goes on in the real world. Maybe even show us a little violence now and then."

He jumped up from his plush desk chair to signal the end of their meeting. Mari nodded, trying to keep her face as neutral as possible, and got up to start for the door. Jack hurried to open it for her, pulling his solicitous-gentleman act. What a hypocrite, she thought. He hadn't even asked if her mother was dead or alive.

"Guess you haven't met Trace yet, have you?" he inquired.

"No." But she knew who he was talking about. Tracy Sadler, the news anchor he'd hired while she was gone.

"Yeah, well, she doesn't usually come in until after lunch.

Why don't you come to story meeting this afternoon? I'll introduce you."

"Sure, if something important doesn't break," Mari agreed.

Back in her office she hit the power switch on the VDT and then swiveled around in her chair to look out the window. Maybe if she looked out at the bright daylight long enough, it would convince her biological clock to reset itself. Anyway, she needed to clear her head. It was more chaotic in there than usual this morning, with all the voices colliding into each other in the process of saying new things about old subjects—not only Jack Lunsford, but Phillip Ashmore and Charles Merrill. And her mother.

She stared out at the elevated section of the Southwest Freeway, with its blurred line of traffic and the tinted glass facade of the Greenway Plaza building rising behind it. There was one inescapable social leveler in this town—the grinding traffic jams that clogged freeways and city streets alike. The conspicuously wealthy might fly their helicopters from downtown pads to weekend playhouses on the coast or to the highland lakes near Austin, but that didn't solve the problem of how to get out San Felipe to Chimney Rock.

"So you're back at last!" Mari swung back to see Ron Bergner peering in around her half-open door. He wore a big smile as he came toward her, and she got up to walk into his quick hug.

"How's your mother? You get her back to Denver okay?"

"I think she'll be all right, in time. What about you? Tony told me—"

"Yeah, I can imagine!" He grinned again, and she wondered if his ebullience was real or just a defense mechanism. "I'm rising with the chickens for those damn morning breaks, but I'm also back out on the street. A beat reporter. Jack tell you he assigned me to city hall, got rid of that bitch he was sleeping with? I'm working my damn tail off, and feeling better than I have for a long time. Is Tony in yet?"

"He won't be back till Tuesday night. We got two good packages, Ron, or they will be when we finish editing. One with the Basque contacts, and the other one—well, it's going to be a surprise. We want to show instead of tell.

Tony's picking up a few more location shots while he and Rachel are seeing the sights. I brought back the Basque cassettes so I can start scripting, but I need him for voice-over translations, and I don't want any of the editors even touching the tapes until he's here." She barely paused before plunging on. "Tell me what you think of Tracy Sadler, Ron."

"She's good. You'll see for yourself tonight. And a good looker," he answered without hesitation. "Guess she should be, for a hundred and fifty thou. But Jack's probably right. We needed a change of face." His refusal to say any more whetted Mari's curiosity, and she decided to make the editorial meeting in Jack's office at two, whether she could afford the time or not.

She worked at her terminal until after one, breaking only to fetch a carton of yogurt from the refrigerator down the hall, which she ate while scrolling through the wire- and news-service listings, trying to keep in mind Jack's edict about juicy stories. Occasionally she'd stop to call up an abstract, if the headline sounded even remotely interesting, or even an entire article. The A wire carried a story by Jane Brody, the *New York Times* health writer, whom Mari rarely cited, though she checked her stories just to see what topics she was covering. Brody's writing was so dry and lifeless, and the information so predigested, that it was impossible to evaluate, which was also the reason Mari worked almost entirely with primary sources. She was struggling through Brody's piece on leg pain when her phone rang.

"Mari McNichols." She spoke without taking her eyes off the screen.

"I'm just checking—to see if you're real or imaginary, maybe just one of my better dreams."

Mari burst into delighted laughter and pushed back from her desk. "Charles! Yes, I'm here, have been since before eight, as a matter of fact. Couldn't sleep any longer. Guess the bod is still halfway between here and Spain."

He dropped his voice. "Do you realize how ridiculous this is?"

"What's ridiculous? Did I miss part of this conversation?" She was more than pleased to hear his voice and was still laughing a little.

"That I'm here and you're there. Have you changed your mind yet? About coming to Austin this weekend?"

"I don't see how I can, Charles. But I may be footloose and fancy-free a lot sooner than I thought." She gave him a blow-by-blow description of her meeting with Jack Lunsford, ending with the one-month reprieve she'd talked him into.

"Christ!" Charles swore as soon as she finished. "You're too good for the bastard! If he doesn't have enough sense to recognize what he's got, why the hell do you waste your time working for him?"

"Because I can reach a lot of people with information that's important, Charles, many of them people who won't get it anywhere else. Houston is the fourth-largest city and one of the biggest television markets in the country. That's why I came here, that and a couple of other reasons. Anyway, don't you think maybe you're just a little bit biased, about me, I mean?"

"No!" he shot back, but she could hear the smile creep into his voice when he added, "At least I don't think so."

"I was just thinking about you when the phone rang—was reading a piece from the *New York Times* about sources of leg pain, which mentions claudication as a symptom of cardiovascular disease. It says fifty million Americans over fifty have it, that the most effective treatment is to quit smoking, lose weight, start exercising, cut out saturated fats, and—get this—'take a drug like Trental to improve circulation to the legs'!"

"Well, maybe it doesn't matter as long as it doesn't do them any harm."

"You know what I was thinking about when you called? Taking a closer look at the path a drug follows from the time it's just a gleam in some researcher's eye to acceptance by not only the medics, but the media, who I suspect act to reinforce acceptance by practicing physicians, in spite of their protests to the contrary. It's the old vicious circle. First the drug company's sales rep gives them a spiel, backed up by technical scientific articles they don't have time to read, and then they see a brief report in the newspaper which includes quotes from 'experts,' who of course are their professional peers. After that it's okay for them to jump on the bandwagon. Is it really impossible to find anyone who hasn't already accepted this drug, who will question it? Are you the only one, Charles?"

"Maybe." He laughed. "Have you considered that I might be the one who's off base? That you might be just a little bit biased in my favor?"

She smiled at him, not caring that he couldn't see her. "I'm willing to admit to a very definite tilt in your direction, but it's based on solid evidence and logic."

He laughed again. "If you say so, Mari honey."

"I've got an idea, Charles. I'm going to look at the effectiveness of another drug I've been hearing about, not Trental. A tranquilizer that's prescribed mostly for women. Then the possibility that I'm biased won't even come into it, because I'll have to find another source as convincing as you are, won't I? It might not turn out to be juicy enough for our television audiences—that's Jack's word, not mine—but maybe I could use it in a program on women's health problems I'm working on."

CHAPTER

9

Come on in, Mari, you're just in time. Tracy's got a great idea, and she was just starting to lay it out for us. Oh yeah, I forgot, you two haven't met yet. Tracy Sadler, our new anchor from Chicago." Mari walked straight to the small group already arranged around the coffee table in the informal, conference end of Jack's big office.

"Mari," Tracy murmured. "I've heard a lot about you." She looked to be about twenty-eight or -nine, Mari decided as she shook hands with the tall, tanned brunette. Unlike Nancy Reagan, Tracy had the personal presence or charisma, or whatever it was, to dominate the bright red she was wearing, which also made Mari feel positively mousy in her natural raw silk.

Jack waited while Mari responded to the murmured inquiries about her mother and her trip to Spain from Ted Calvacca and Podge Pearsall, before introducing her to the man sitting on the couch next to Tracy. "Oh yeah, and this is Lou Slocum, our new program director, who also came on board while you were gone. He's taking some of the load off Podge." Lou looked to be about forty, had thinning sandy hair and a freckled, chubby-cherub face. Mari extended her hand to shake his briefly, then sat down on the couch, next to Podge.

"Trace wants to initiate an update on AIDS as a regular part of our newscast," Jack explained. "An AIDS Watch, something like what Ted Koppel did with the hostages in Iran, only we wouldn't air it that often, which I think is one terrific idea. What I want from you, Mari, is how much really gritty stuff on AIDS is coming in, so we can get some idea how often we'd need to air. We're trying to get a handle on whether we're talking once, twice a week, or what."

"I like the idea," Mari answered honestly, without hesitation. "It's a subject that merits up-front treatment in our primary news slots. The CDC in Atlanta estimates one and a half million already are infected with the virus. Ninety thousand cases of AIDS have been reported to the federal government so far, two thirds of them are already dead— that's more than fifty thousand! The numbers have been going up fast since we broadened the definition of AIDS. Up to now we haven't really been calling a spade a spade. Regular reports would be a way for us to make a real contribution to educating the public, especially with condom ads and PSAs still so controversial. As for how many stories are coming in . . ." She paused to think about that. "A lot."

"And so many of the victims are famous, aren't they, like Rock Hudson, and fashion designers Perry Ellis and Willi Smith?" Tracy volunteered. "Who else?" She looked to Mari to answer her.

"The congressman from Connecticut, and quite a few others. I agree that reporting names and numbers makes a point, but I'd hate to see us do nothing but obituaries— viewers would soon be calling it the Death Watch. And there are plenty of other things we need to be telling viewers about."

"For example?" Lou queried.

"New research results, like the recent report from England on a genetically inherited protein that appears to determine your susceptibility to the virus. We have an expert on that very same protein right here in Houston, Dr. Stephen Daiger, a medical geneticist at the U.T. Health Science Center. He says this protein is going to tell us how the AIDS virus attacks the body. We're also finding out more about different strains of the virus, some more virulent than others so they kill quicker. New viruses are turning up, too, slightly different from HIV but just as deadly. How come—because we're just getting around to detecting them, or because they're mutations?"

"Uh-uh, that's too technical, would be the kiss of death," Tracy objected. "Not what I want at all."

"Maybe the protein story," Mari agreed, "but what about other research reports, like whether it's possible for insects to play a role in transmitting the disease? That ought to interest almost everyone. And there are policy issues galore you could cover. AIDS is already a political hot potato. How we deal with this disease is going to be a major story for the next decade, maybe longer."

"Give us a for-instance," Jack ordered impatiently, tossing a quick glance at Lou. "Lay it all out in black and white, everything you can think of."

"Well, right now we've got more questions than answers. About the role of federal regulatory agencies, and the media. What about health-care costs? We've got a good case in point right here in Houston, with the Institute for Immunological Disorders closing its doors due to lack of funds—in a state with the fourth-largest number of AIDS cases in the country. Reported cases may be leveling off in New York, but not in Texas! It's the only AIDS hospital in the country, not to mention a center for research and testing experimental treatments. Peter Mansell, medical director at the Institute, thinks the number already incubating the virus is closer to five million, by the way. How much money are we going to put into research? And what's the best approach—build big centers, support individuals, or both? Are we going to continue the obscenity of our current defense budget, spending three billion dollars a year on Star Wars, a system reputable scientists say is folly, while hundreds of thousands die of AIDS, not to mention other diseases?"

Mari paused to catch her breath, halfway expecting someone to make some sort of rebuttal to her last question. Lou was writing furiously, and the others seemed to be waiting for more. "We're already considering mandatory testing, which raises questions about privacy and discrimination. The most widely used screening test we've got at the moment, the ELISA, doesn't tell us whether there's active infection present or whether a given subject is capable of transmitting the virus."

"Why in hell does everything associated with a disaster always have to be named after a woman?" Tracy complained, breaking the building tension. "It's a goddamn conspiracy."

"ELISA is an acronym," Mari explained with a quick smile, "for enzyme-linked immuno-sorbent assay. The ELISA also produces a high rate of false positives, twenty-five to thirty percent, though the Western blot, which is used to confirm the ELISA, is more accurate. But it's expensive. It's also unlicensed and unregulated by the FDA. Even if the confirming test is done on all positives, if the accuracy rate is extended to the entire population—as opposed to the high-risk groups—one third of positive responses will still be false! That may be a relatively small number of cases, but let me give you a for-instance of what could happen if we elect to do mandatory testing right now.

"How would you like to lose your job and your medical insurance, Ted, maybe your wife and most of your friends, your place to live, and be shunned by your church—all because of the doubt and innuendo resulting from a positive test that turned out to be false?" Mari knew that Ted belonged to an evangelical group that had been violently opposed to the city ordinance giving equal antidiscrimination protection to gays. "Or maybe you'd just never get another raise or promotion, but never know why." Ted squirmed in his chair, pulling his shoulders together in an almost-shrug, so she knew her words were hitting home. Everyone in the room seemed caught up by the picture she was painting, except Tracy, who wore an unvarying faint smile on her face.

"How do *you* feel about mandatory premarital testing, Lamar?" Mari asked the assistant news director. She'd watched him in meeting after meeting, and knew his real forte was bootlicking, not thinking, because he always stayed silent as the grave when something even remotely controversial came up. "What if Sherry tested positive, then on follow-up tested negative?" she asked, knowing he was planning to get married in about a month. "How many retests would it take before you'd feel really sure?" She didn't expect an answer, nor was she surprised at the pained look on his face, probably because she'd breached the etiquette he lived by in putting him on the spot. "Even a negative test may not mean much, since it looks now like the virus can be present for a year or more without being detected by any of the current testing techniques. In a nutshell, we're talking about mandatory testing when our screening tests are ambiguous. And when we don't have any real privacy protection in place."

"Seems like I remember running across something about a new and better test, just recently," Podge volunteered.

"Yeah, one that detects infected cells, rather than antibodies. And it looks like it may be both faster and more accurate. But it's still being tested and probably won't be available for at least a couple more years, maybe longer. Another policy issue," she continued, "is how we're going to deal with flagrant sexual misbehavior by those already infected, who still have human sexual urges and needs. Are we going to round them up, build huge holding pens to incarcerate them until they die, put the energy and intellect of this nation into dreaming up punishments that are worse than death? How is AIDS already affecting marriage and divorce rates, our so-called permissive lifestyles, teenage pregnancies? Are all the changes women have worked so hard for going right down the tubes? Will we see higher premium put on virgins than ever before, this time because they're the ultimate in safe sex?" Mari stopped, realizing that she might be committing overkill with her impassioned questions. "Well, those are just a few of the questions I think we'll see debated, or reported, in the news media."

She glanced around at Podge, then Ted and Jack, ending with Lou Slocum, who was still scribbling madly. The others seemed to be waiting for him to finish. Lou's position was a new one, so she wasn't sure exactly what role he was to play. As editor, it was up to Podge to pull wire stories, decide about graphics, assign associate producers and writers to stories, edit and approve scripts, and to keep the producer informed about breaking or developing stories. Ted coordinated the entire newscast, on the set and in the control room, with the aid of a floor director and engineers.

"A lot of food for thought in all this, Mari," Lou agreed

finally, giving her a quick, impersonal smile before turning to Jack and Tracy. Mari felt like a puppy who'd just been given a pat on the head and told to go lie down. "We probably ought to talk to our audience-research people about best night of the week," Lou went on, "but I'd say let's try it a couple of times without putting a name on it. Just script it in, see how it goes before promoting it as a regular feature. Mari could cull the wires for us, A and B, and pass on what she finds there as well as the local stuff." He didn't even look at her when he mentioned her name.

"Yeah, that's a good idea," Jack agreed. "You pass on the really hot stories to Trace, use the other stuff for your segment, Mari. Better yet, how about you script the stuff you pass on."

"Aw, come on, Jack," Podge objected. "We've got plenty of writers. We ought not to ask Mari to script stories for Tracy. Besides, why should she waste time scripting before we know if we're going to even use a story?"

"She's the one with all the ideas, isn't she? Besides, she's our health guru, knows more about it than anybody else around here, so her script might be the deciding factor in whether we use the story. Then whatever Lou decides, he'll have the benefit of her expertise before doing final edit on Tracy's copy."

"I guess I could give it a try," Mari agreed hesitantly, taken aback by Jack's suggestion yet not wanting to dampen anyone's enthusiasm for the AIDS Watch idea. "See if it works timewise." She knew her cheeks were flushed, because her face felt warm.

"Okay, let's go with it for the next couple of weeks, then, get the bugs out and have it ready to promote big before May One, next national-sweeps month."

"It's just wonderful to work with such a decisive director, Jack," Tracy gushed, rewarding him with the first real smile Mari had seen. "I don't know how to thank you enough for working all this out for me. You, too, Mari," she added, glancing briefly at Mari. "I'm so glad we're all going to be working together as a team." She gave Jack and Lou another smile. "Now, can we get on with the lineup for tonight?" she asked, though it sounded more like a command than a question.

Mari took advantage of the change of topic to mumble something about having a lot of work still to do before tonight's broadcast, and got up to leave. There were times when she could be as confrontational as anyone, maybe more than most, especially when dealing with a source she knew was trying to withhold information. But that decision was hers to make, a lesson she'd learned at considerable cost, and this time she was choosing to walk away. She wasn't sure what was going on—only that something was—but she also wanted out because she felt uncomfortable in Tracy's presence, which she recognized as nothing less than a childish feeling of inadequacy. It probably would only get worse if she stayed. The fact that she'd allowed Tracy and Jack and Lou to make her feel that way generated both frustration and anger, but the anger was directed inward, at herself.

"By the way, Mari," Tracy called out just as Mari was about to go out the door, "I'd like to get some input from you later, if you have a few minutes, on a five-part series we're airing next week."

"Sure," Mari answered breezily. "Any time. I'll be in my office most of the afternoon, or in editing."

It was nearly midnight when Mari got home Tuesday night and found Charles's message on her answering machine. She tried calling him Wednesday morning before she left for the station, but got no answer at his house. Later, at work, she found a big brown envelope from him in her mail, containing several copies of *The News,* a tabloid put out by the pharmaceutical company that manufactured Trental, along with a couple of journal articles. After lunch she tried calling him at the university, but his secretary said he was in a meeting and she didn't expect him back until late afternoon. She hung up, feeling strangely disappointed, and sat thinking for a few minutes, then made a quick decision and lifted the receiver again.

Tony came in just as she was putting down the phone, his eyes a match for the brilliant flash of white teeth. His skin looked darker than usual, which made Mari wonder how Rachel had fared under the Spanish sun.

"It was good, huh?" she asked, matching his grin.

"Better than good. Fantabulous, as you'd say. But too short. I'm going back, first chance I get."

"They let you shoot at Huelva?"

"You betcha, bebé. By the time I got through sweet-talking 'em, they were ready for me to shoot the whole damn museum!"

"Must be all that practice you've been getting, on Rachel," Mari shot back.

"Not practicing, bebé, that was real. *Is* real." He dropped like a stone into the chair next to her desk, his face suddenly serious, and sat staring down at his hand as if he was trying to read his palm. "Rachel's the best thing ever happened to me, I guess. Maybe too good to believe. What do you think, Mari?"

The direct question took her by surprise. It had been apparent for months that Tony was serious about Rachel, in spite of his breezy refusals to admit that she was anything more than "a friend." Mari also knew that the courtship he'd been conducting for the past three or four months—a Jekyll-Hyde performance that alternated between macho chest-beating and gentle, loving persuasion, between youthful exuberance and a maturity and sensitivity beyond his years—included having Rachel test his blood for antibodies to the HIV. And the minute they'd stepped off the plane at Málaga, it was obvious that their relationship had changed, that there was a new closeness or intimacy that Mari hadn't seen between them before. They'd stopped fencing with each other.

"I don't think Rachel is the type to play games, if that's what you're asking. Why do you find that so hard to believe?" she asked, feeling her way.

"Oh, you know." He paused, but Mari kept quiet, waiting him out. "She's always got something cooking. Lately she's talking medical school, or maybe graduate school, so she can get more into research."

"And you'd prefer someone who wouldn't rock your boat, some little mealy-mouthed teenager you could order around, who'd be there waiting for you every night, keeping your enchiladas hot?"

"Come on, Mari, you know better than that. It's just that, well, what the hell am I going to do, if—when, if she decides to—" He stopped again, unable to bring himself to actually say what he was thinking.

"To what?" Mari thought she knew what was bothering him, but she wasn't about to put words in his mouth. What Tony truly cared about he pursued with a dedication and inventiveness Mari found both rare and unique—and she suspected that Rachel did, too. But she'd also seen him flipflop from an open-minded, rational professional to a strutting stud, the stereotype of the macho Hispanic male. So she couldn't help wondering if he'd ever be able to really accept a woman like Rachel. More than that, would he ever let himself believe that such a woman could possibly love him the way he loved her?

"I keep trying to convince myself—uh, that we could ignore all the usual, uh, crap—the age stuff, and, well, you know, me being Mexican, and . . . if we tried hard enough."

"You can sit there and stammer and stutter about trying hard enough—after waiting months and going through all those bloody tests just to convince her it's safe to go to bed with you? Have you ever discussed whatever the hell it is you're *not* saying with her? Or are you letting your anticipator run away with you?"

He shook his head. "Talking about it might give her ideas, might make it happen."

Mari just gaped at him for a second. "For God's sake, Tony, that's about the most ridiculous, adolescent thing I've ever heard out of you! If you can believe that kind of garbage about Rachel Widener, you're right, you'd better live it up while you can, 'cause you're way out of your league!"

Tony stared at her for a couple of seconds, his dark, sad eyes reflecting the torment going on inside his head, until she wished she could take the angry words back. Then he began to grin, sheepishly this time, the infectious little-boy grin that appeared whenever he knew he'd acted the fool. "You like her that much, huh?" He jumped up from the chair, too happy to sit still another second.

"Yeah, I do. And you, too, you lucky dog! Now, when are you going to be ready to start work on those tapes? I want to do two different packages, have them ready to go by Monday, if possible, even if we have to work all weekend. One to show to Jack and Ted, and Podge." It occurred to her that she ought to ask Tony what he knew about Lou Slocum, since he hadn't even mentioned the man in Spain, but decided not now. "And a longer one to feed to the network. They'll probably just file it away, since there's no news peg to hang it on, then cannibalize it for background and visuals when the need arises. But that's okay. They'll know where it came from, which will add to Jack's credit chips in the New York office."

"You telling me that all this was just a devious plan to make him look so damned good someone will hire him away from us, or else move him up and out of here to the network?"

"Dream on, my Latin Lothario! Unfortunately, the world is getting 'realer' and 'realer' around here all the time." And then she did tell him about the session in Jack's office, and some of the worrisome thoughts she was having about Tracy Sadler and Lou Slocum.

Mari stopped on the way home to buy groceries, and was fumbling with her key when she heard her phone ringing. She dropped the sack just inside the door of her apartment, hoping it might be Charles, and dashed through the living room, flipping on lights as she went. "Hello!"

"Why didn't you just call if you wanted to talk?" He was holding the little white card in his hand, staring at the "Just needed to talk to you."

"Charles!" She was out of breath but managed a short laugh anyway. "You don't like getting flowers?" Some men, she knew, would consider it "sissy."

"Sure." He glanced at the half-dozen blue irises sitting on the corner of his desk. "But I needed to talk to you, too. Where the hell have you been? And why didn't you return my call?"

"I did, but you weren't home. Or at the university. Then I got busy."

"What about this weekend? You change your mind yet?"

"No. Tony and I will be working through the weekend on the Basque tapes, so we'll have them ready by Monday, one to air locally and one to send to the network morgue." She didn't tell him about the flamenco tape, because they were planning to surprise both Charles and Rachel with it.

178

"You're going to broadcast it Monday night, then?"

"I don't know. Probably sometime next week, if or when Jack and Tracy decide to use it." She didn't want to even think about that now. "But I should be all caught up by the next weekend. Don't you need to come to Houston to consult with Rachel about the trials with your Vampire, or something?"

"You think I need an excuse? You're not reason enough?"

"No. Yes." Neither answer fit the positive-negative way he'd formulated the question. She laughed again. "We'd have the whole weekend, if you came Friday night." She was breathless for a different reason now, and her pulse was noisy in her ears. "If you could get here early enough, you could even come to the studio, get an inside look at the newscast." She was only trying to mask how eager she was to see him. "And on Saturday I thought I might ask Rachel and Tony to dinner, try my hand at paella again."

"I'll be there. If I can stand to wait that long." He sounded perfectly serious. "I want to be with you right now." The line hummed with silence for a second, and then he cleared his throat. "But maybe it's a little late to make it tonight. Talk to you tomorrow, okay?"

"Yes, okay." He could hear the smile in her whispered words.

Everything and everybody in the studio trailed cables, connecting them to the semidark control room, where Ted Calvacca and several engineers hovered over the banked monitors and control panels. Standing in the shadows behind them, Charles watched and listened. Mari had gone to "fix" her face, leaving him in Tony's care.

"That's the on-air monitor," Tony explained, pointing to the largest screen, which showed an on-going commercial for Advil. "The others are picking up from the studio cameras—see the three shots of Tracy, from different angles—a couple of live remote setups on location around town, sound bites that probably are going to run with voice-overs, commercials coming down the line, and that one's a still from the wire, probably for a chromakey."

"Chroma-what?" Charles injected. Tony was moving too fast for him.

"You know, the little photo that comes up on your TV screen while the anchor is reading a story, usually in a rectangular box in the upper right corner?" Charles nodded. "The wire services feed stills or slides to us via a telephone line, so we can use them to illustrate stories. They're inserted electronically."

The lights came up on the set at that moment and two images from the studio cameras brightened. One was a tight shot of Tracy Sadler and the other a more distant view of the news set. Big red plastic hoops dangled from Tracy's ears, matching a wide band of flowers across the front of her bright royal-blue sweater, which camouflaged the fact that her breasts were meager, at best. Carefully arranged to look casual, her dark hair waved loosely to her shoulders, framing a face that was all angles and planes, and high color. She was, Charles supposed, the epitome of the dramatic look Mari envied. Yet to him Tracy looked, well, costumed. She was the kind of woman he rarely even noticed anymore, at least not consciously, though he could remember a time when he used to wonder what they were like under all that carefully contrived decoration. Disappointed too often, he'd long since lost interest in trying to find out.

"She's watching Ed for the on-air signal," Tony explained. "He's the floor manager. She can see what's actually being aired, all the time, on the monitor mounted on the camera-two dolly." Tracy straightened and looked directly into the camera, wearing an expression of pleasant alertness, halfway between a smile and dead sober, as the bumper shot of the studio came up on the monitor. The camera moved in on her, and on cue she launched into a quick read of headlines of the major stories to come. Images on the on-air monitor changed quickly, to another commercial, followed by a voice-over station identification accompanied by logo visuals and theme music. Then it was back to Tracy with the lead story.

"Hispanic groups marched in protest against the new immigration-reform law at immigration centers all over the country today, criticizing the provision in the law they say will split the families of illegal aliens. Here with a report from the new immigration center in Houston, which was set up in a northside barrio specifically for the purpose of accepting applications for legal status, is Jorge Esposito."

Charles turned to where Tony was pointing, in time to see a picture of a reporter standing in front of a picket line come up on the monitor. He looked to be standing in the parking lot of a rundown strip shopping center. The sound bite was short, and then Tracy came back on with the tag, before moving on to an equally brief voice-over shot of a plane crash in Florida, followed by two other short national stories before she turned to a different camera.

"Locally tonight, two people were killed in a three-car accident on I-ten near Dairy-Ashford." A series of short video bites followed as she read from the teleprompter, about a second accident, then a murder trial, and then the cause of the food poisoning that put forty-three people in the hospital, the last accompanied only by a chromakey. When another commercial flipped up, Tony nudged Charles toward the door of the control room. "Let's go watch from behind the cameras. Anyway, Mari ought to be back in a minute."

The studio reminded Charles of a darkened theater, with all the lights concentrated on the stage, and he could hardly make out the big cables trailing across the floor. He stopped well back behind the cameras, to let his eyes get used to the dark, rather than take a chance on stumbling over one.

"At a press conference in Austin today, Governor Clements finally revealed his long-awaited plan for solving the state's budget crisis without raising taxes," Tracy began next, turning to face camera one on cue from Ed, which lent emphasis to the switch from local to state news. "The governor is calling for major cuts in spending all across the board, from mental health and human services to highways and education."

Charles moved around a little, so he could see both the news desk and the on-air monitor, as a shot of the press room in the state capitol came up.

"Are you aware, sir," a female reporter was asking the governor, "that the hundred-million-dollar cut in state AFDC funds you're asking for means a loss of $124 million in federal matching funds?"

"Well, that is something we are going to have to look into, of course, but I doubt that will happen." The governor let his voice trail off as he turned to take a question from another reporter. "Are you also *unaware,* sir," the woman reporter called out, refusing to let him cut her off and emphasizing the word to make her point, "that your proposal would cut welfare grants by fifteen dollars a month, when Texas already ranks forty-seventh among the states? And how can you justify cutting funds to investigate child abuse at a time when we're seeing a huge increase in cases of abuse? Aren't you telling the Department of Human Services to simply ignore most reported cases of child abuse?"

"Well, as usual, you people are getting this all out of context. It is our intention to put people back to work, not on the public dole. Let me assure you, young lady, that child abuse is just as *repungent* to me as it is to you. But we don't need to have the state sticking its nose into every little family dispute that comes along! And that's the last question I'm taking on that subject."

Charles felt a hand slip under his elbow and heard Mari's half-laughing whisper at the same time. "He's the one who's 'repungent,' with his dumb malapropisms!"

He mouthed a silent question, but she just shook her head, setting her hair into the languid fluid motion he loved to watch. She'd been gone only a few minutes, but he felt the same exhilarating lift at seeing her now as he had an hour ago, when he first arrived. She hugged his arm tight against her breast, pulling him down a little so she could whisper in his ear.

"I'm so glad to see you."

He seized the opportunity to swipe his lips across her cheek, not caring how many times she repeated herself when it was such an obvious expression of the same rush of pleasure he felt. He had to force his eyes away, back to Tracy and what was going on in the studio. Mari began telling him about what he was seeing, but from an entirely different angle than Tony had. Whenever possible, she explained, they led off the six o'clock news with a national story that had some local tie. Generally the story lineup followed a format referred to as peaks and valleys, which meant alternating national with state and local stories, all with the mandatory commercial breaks woven in between. And for the first time he began to get a sense of the complexity involved in putting together a fifteen-minute newscast, which at a station like KPOC meant taped segments from the daily network "feed" as well as local and state stories originating both in the studio and live from remote locations around town and from their capital bureau in Austin.

A Toyota ad came up next, followed immediately by one for Cardi-Omega-3, and then one for Black Flag Roach Ender. Lou Slocum took advantage of the break to scuttle to the news desk to hand a sheet of paper to Tracy, say a few words, and then fade back into the shadows behind the cameras. The commercials were followed by teasers for three network programs scheduled later that evening, and then Tracy started on the final segment of a running story on single-mothers-by-choice.

"A million families in this country today are headed by mothers who have never married. Though only a small percentage of these mothers deliberately set out to have a child alone, their number is growing. And sociologists say many more women are thinking about becoming single-mothers-by-choice than ever before. Most of them are women in their thirties who are economically sure of themselves. Many say they are simply refusing to settle for just any man in order to get married and have a baby, that they're tired of waiting for Mr. Right. Time is running out for them, biologically speaking, and they want a child. The fathers of their children may be transient lovers, selected friends, and even strangers. Or sperm donors. In some cases the fathers know, but often they don't. In France, for instance, where the average age at marriage is closer to thirty than twenty, what these women are doing is called 'stealing children from men.' We talked with Houston psychoanalyst Dr. Richard Hampton, who believes there is a lot more to this bizarre behavior than these mothers are willing to admit."

Mari straightened abruptly, releasing Charles's arm. "Bizarre!" she exclaimed softly.

Tony leaned forward, caught a glimpse of her eyes,

flashing with quick anger, then offered an explanation to Charles. "She ain't too hot for that kind of editorializing in the news, in case you're wondering."

Charles nodded, his eyes glued to the monitor. Dr. Hampton sat behind a big walnut desk, the usual black-framed diplomas and licenses carefully arranged on the wall around and behind him. "I would say it's more likely that these so-called elective mothers, especially those who opt for artificial insemination," Dr. Hampton opined in a deep voice, speaking slowly and ponderously—which Mari recognized was calculated to lend importance to his words— "are simply acting out their unconscious desire to conceive a child with their own fathers."

That did it! Too agitated to stand still now, she began combing the fingers of one hand through her freshly brushed hair. "Far more likely, I'd say," she muttered angrily, leaning toward Charles and Tony, "that the reason these mothers make Hampton, and most men, so damned uneasy is that they've taken the absolute power to decide when to have a child into their own hands!"

Charles reached an arm around her shoulders to pull her closer. "Hey, you're on in a couple of minutes, remember? Cool down." His lips moved against her ear, bringing a different kind of heat to her cheeks, and she turned her face into his neck for a second. Then, without even thinking about it, her tongue darted out to taste him as she brushed her lips across the concave curve just below the line of his jaw. She felt his involuntary response to the unexpected caress just as she heard her own name, and realized that Tracy was bridging from Dr. Hampton to her.

"We asked Mari McNichols, Channel Five's medical news reporter, about the health risks these elective mothers may be taking, since most of them are past thirty-five." Mari revolved inside Charles's arm, to watch herself on the monitor as the tape began.

"New methods of detecting birth defects and monitoring the well-being of both mother and child have taken most of the health risks out of child-bearing for women in their thirties, even for women in their early forties. Instead, we're discovering that the problem is getting pregnant. A study just out indicates that fertility drops off sharply between the ages of thirty-one and thirty-five—much earlier than we thought. More than two thousand women were artificially inseminated in one study, some as many as twelve times at peak fertile periods over a year's time, yet only sixty-one percent of them got pregnant. And only half of the women over thirty-five got pregnant. The other major problem single parents face, of course, is finding child care, which also may affect their children's health."

Seeing Mari like this, on the screen, next to another woman, Charles was newly aware that she had a style that was hers alone. More than just her blond hair compared with Tracy's brunet; it probably had something to do with how she dressed, he supposed. Certainly she had a special knack for combining colors and textures in a way that made him want to touch or feel, that promised more than could be seen on the surface or from a distance. He was conscious even now of the slightly nubby texture of the fabric under his hand. Nearly the same color as her hair, her dress was elegant in its simplicity, but he recognized her own unique touch in the matching piece of fabric twisted into a thick rope at her waist—and the string of turquoise nuggets he'd seen before, in Spain, which set off tantalizing visions inside his head. In the clip he was watching, though, she'd swept her hair back behind one ear and was wearing a silver ear cuff set with a matching stone. Charles was analytical enough to realize that part of how she looked had to do with motion, from the fluid swing of her hair to her walk, from her expressive hands to the constantly changing color of her skin. Her mind and her emotions spoke to him through her body, and in spite of her light coloring, there was a passionate intensity about her that was almost tangible. And when he was with her, the world seemed a more exciting place—he simply felt more alive.

During the next commercial break Mari stepped a little away from Charles, moving ahead in her mind as she glanced over the pages of script, to reassure herself that she was ready. Tracy had only one more story now, the second of the AIDS updates Mari had scripted for Lou, before her lead-in to Mari's health news segment.

"Federal officials today revealed that three health-care workers were infected with the AIDS virus when their skin was briefly exposed to blood from infected patients—the first documented cases that did not involve either direct injection or prolonged exposure. Each of the three workers had small breaks or other abnormalities in the skin, through which the virus may have passed, Dr. James Hughes of the Centers for Disease Control in Atlanta said, so there is still no evidence that the AIDS virus passes directly through intact skin. In none of the three cases, however, have investigators been able to determine the exact mechanism of transmission of the virus."

A video bite came up on the monitor. "In one case," Dr. Hughes said in reply to a question from a network reporter, "a hospital worker was exposed to blood while she was pressing gauze against the arm of a patient who was bleeding. In the second case, a rubber stopper popped off a glass tube, spattering blood into a health-care worker's mouth, where the virus might have passed through mucous membrane. And in the other case, blood spilled onto the hands and forearms of a worker who was manipulating a machine used to separate blood into its components."

Mari glanced at the clock on the studio wall, noting that Tracy was cutting it close, and felt the rush of adrenaline that always came just as she was about to go on camera. The camera picked up Tracy again, for her wrap, Mari thought. But instead she bridged to another short bite.

"Officials are urging strict adherence to the federal guidelines for health-care workers, which include wearing gloves when handling blood, and in cases of more extensive exposure, gowns, masks, and goggles. Captain Marvin Wilson, an EMS technician who is president of the Firefighters Association in Charlotte, North Carolina, says that employees in hospitals, clinics, and fire stations across the nation are expressing increasing anxiety."

"Our guys wear rubber gloves," Captain Wilson explained, "but we are getting to be paranoid about pulling bloody people out of cars in traffic accidents."

Mari was really getting itchy as the time to end the newscast came and went, eating into her own time, which meant she'd have to adjust her lineup at the last minute, unless Ted intended to cut the weather or sports. Tony caught her anxious glance and sent her a shrug.

"Underscoring Captain Wilson's concern," Tracy continued, "is the case of a retired Houston man, a Methodist bishop who was active in ministering to people with AIDS. His family has just revealed he died of AIDS."

Mari crossed in front of Charles, to stand next to Tony. "Where in hell did she get that?" she asked in a whisper. "That case hasn't been documented! We have no idea whether he got it from working with AIDS patients or from—"

"And in Washington today, Democratic senators introduced the first comprehensive national anti-AIDS legislation," Tracy went on, giving no indication at all that she was about to close out the newscast. "Senator Edward Kennedy of Massachusetts, chief sponsor of the $900 million plan, criticized the administration for what he called a leadership vacuum. The bill calls for spending $450 million on education, prevention, and risk reduction programs, $100 million on developing better treatment and care for AIDS patients, and $350 million on research to find new treatments and a cure."

"When in hell is she going to quit?" Mari asked no one in particular, angry disbelief taking the place of her earlier puzzlement.

"Here in Texas, the House passed a bill to quarantine AIDS carriers who are a proven threat to public health. The bill carries an amendment that would require AIDS testing for couples who want to get married. And in a related development, the contraceptive sponge approved for use in the United States in 1983 has been found to offer women protection against chlamydia and gonorrhea, two sexually transmitted diseases that public health workers say have reached epidemic proportions."

"Damn! That really rips it," she whispered angrily.

"Want me to talk to Lou?" Tony ventured.

As soon as he said the name, Mari knew. Lou had to have known that Tracy's lineup was not only long, but overlapped Mari's, because the program director was the last link in a chain that began with the assignments editor—which meant that Lou had final approval on the edited copy book. But why? Especially without even telling her!

"What you gonna do?" Tony asked anxiously.

Mari was still shaking her head in disbelief. "What I have to," she decided quickly. "The same viewers who heard her have to hear the rest of the story on the sponge. I suppose the difference between protection from and reducing your risk of getting a disease is too fine a point for her—too 'technical'!" She threw a quick glance at the wall clock again.

"I'll do a quick bridge to the toxic-shock statement, then take it as scripted from there. But she went so damn far over, I'm going to have to pull one of my stories." She glanced through her pages of script, then made another quick decision. "But I don't have time to refigure my back-timing. Get with Ted, will you, Tony? Tell him what I'm doing, then cue me at thirty seconds before wrap and again at fifteen seconds, okay? I'll fill in with a brief from my pad copy."

"Sure," he assured her, as they both heard Tracy say, "And now, stay tuned for Health News with Mari McNichols, coming up next." Tony moved toward the control booth while Mari started toward the news desk, picking her way carefully over the cables strung out across the floor.

Charles didn't have the slightest idea what was going on, so could only stand by and watch, and wonder.

Mari didn't look at Tracy as they exchanged places during the commercial break, knowing that if she did, she wouldn't be able to resist making a scathing comment, which was a distraction she couldn't afford at this point. She spread her sheets of script across the top of the desk, quickly marked two sections of pad copy—the brief extra stories she always carried into a broadcast in case she should come out short, because all kinds of things could throw off the timing—and a couple of paragraphs in the story on the contraceptive sponge. Then she scribbled a big number one in the margin, and when she got her cue from Ed, started off almost exactly where Tracy left off, adding only one sentence by way of introduction.

"We have more for you on that contraceptive-sponge story. While the sponge does appear to reduce the risk of contracting chlamydia and gonorrhea, it also turns out to be far less effective as a contraceptive than the manufacturer claims. We talked earlier today to Dr. Barbara Amaral, a Houston gynecologist who says she has been advising her patients against using the sponge since it was first approved by the FDA in 1983."

Charles moved closer to the monitor. Mari was talking to Dr. Amaral, at Women's Hospital. "Why is it you're not recommending the sponge, Dr. Amaral?" Mari asked.

"First of all, it simply is not acceptable as a contraceptive because the failure rate is much too high. All women do not have the same size cervix, especially after childbirth, so the one-size-fits-all concept predicts a high rate of failure, which several studies now confirm. Among women who have borne a child, the failure rate is twenty-eight percent, not eighteen, as claimed on the package. And even among women who have not had a child, the failure rate is eighteen percent, not eight, as claimed on the package. In addition, women who use the sponge put themselves at higher risk for toxic-shock syndrome, which is a potentially fatal infection. The only study we have that found to the contrary was financed by the manufacturer of the sponge. And I find that—well, highly suggestive." She spoke softly but confidently and smiled from time to time, as when she mentioned the manufacturer-supported study. "Users also are more prone to yeast infections, which may not be serious in most women, but are lingering and unpleasant, partly because they require dietary and other constraints that affect the quality of life, sometimes for quite long periods of time. To put it plainly, there is no compelling reason to use the sponge and several good reasons not to."

The video switched back to Mari in the studio, where she moved into another voice-over, this one about the new blood test for cancer, followed by a report on lubricants used with contraceptives. "Researchers have found that many of the commonly used lubricants—including Wesson oil, baby oil and Vaseline Intensive Care lotion—can cause condoms to break within sixty seconds after application. Bruce Voeller, of the Mariposa Research Foundation, says packaging directions should warn users against any product containing mineral oil."

There was a short commercial break, and then she continued with a story on popular fish-oil diet supplements, again sandwiching together pieces of interviews with a Houston physician, a dietician, and a pharmacologist. All three were pretty much of the same opinion. "Take ten grams of fish oil every day for a month," the pharmacologist concluded, "and you will have an effect that is no greater than taking a single aspirin."

Back on camera at the news desk, Mari was wrapping up the story when Tony gave her the fifteen-second cue. She picked up a page of script, glanced at it quickly, and turned toward camera one, which had moved in close. "And this just in, from the *Texas Observer.* The EEOC is bringing suit against a subsidiary of Johnson and Johnson, one of the biggest pharmaceutical companies in the country, because its hiring directives discriminate against women and stereotype them as inferior. The company's hiring guidelines include this profile of the ideal female worker, and I quote.

"'She's not pretty, she's not sexy, she should be neat, clean, and without frills. She should have the look of someone who might clean her bathroom or kitchen on her hands and knees.' End of quote." Mari smiled for the first time, looking straight into the lens of camera two.

"That's it for tonight. Join us again on Monday, for another edition of Health News. This is Mari McNichols. Good night, and good health."

Charles was wearing a huge smile long before she finished, and so was just about everyone else in the studio, including Tony, who was also shaking his head in amused admiration.

CHAPTER

10

W hat the fuck are you trying to do to me, for christsake!" Jack yelled as Mari came through the door of the broadcast studio. He was still about twenty feet down the hall, but the words hit her like an unexpected slap in the face and she slowed under the impact, causing Charles and Tony to bunch up close behind her. The fleeting thought that at least her back was protected was vaguely comforting.

"I might well ask the same of you," she shot back as soon as Jack was within speaking distance. Jack and Podge always watched the newscast on a monitor in Jack's office, so she knew he'd seen and heard everything. "Just what the hell did you think was going to happen in there, when you let her cut into my time like that—and without any warning? I had to cut and then pad, at the very last minute. Minute, my foot, more like a couple of seconds before I went on the air! What are you trying to do, up our ratings by turning us all into clowns?" Just thinking about it was breathing new life into her still simmering anger.

"So somebody slipped up someplace." Jack jumped in when she stopped to catch a breath. "It happens all the time in this business, Mari, you know that." He never knew when she was going to grab the ball and run with it, put him on the defensive, instead of trying to protect her own tail, like any normal person would. "I sure as hell didn't know, and I doubt Ted did, either."

"Podge knew I was doing the contraceptive sponge story tonight," Mari continued, unwilling to let Jack get away with the "it just happens" excuse. "You're trying to tell me that Lou Slocum didn't know, that the left hand doesn't know what the right is doing? Is that the way you run a news operation?"

"Why the hell are you in such a snit, anyway? I never figured you for a prima donna, Mari. Besides, it all came out okay in the wash, right?"

"Yeah, right, no thanks to anybody but Mari," Tony tossed in. "But next time we might not come away so lucky. You mess up in front of viewers one time, and they'll remember it forever, probably take a clean sweep of the news team to make 'em forget. You'd have to buy out Mari's contract—and Tracy's. Is that a chance you want to take?" Jack glanced at Tony but didn't bother to answer him.

Charles still wasn't entirely sure what was going on, but he did know that Mari was mad as a hornet. Her whole face was flushed now, and he could see the blood pulsing in the big artery in her neck.

"But I *do* know how it happened, Jack, even if you don't, 'cause Lou let the cat out of the bag in there. I suppose he and Tracy figured I'd just cut the sponge story completely. You asked me to script the stories I pass on to Lou because I'm the expert, which is the only reason I agreed to do it, by the way. I tried to make my follow-up sound like an addition or continuation, rather than a correction, so she wouldn't look bad. But she didn't leave me any choice, Jack, not after the misleading impression she left with viewers. The stuff she put out on the sponge was, was, uh—"

"A lot of crap!" Tony supplied cheerfully when she hesitated, relishing the word.

"She never even mentioned the increased risk of toxic shock," Mari continued. "And I suppose the difference between protection from and reducing your chances of contracting a fatal disease must be too subtle for Lou. Or Tracy."

"Whadda ya mean, Lou let the cat out of the bag in there?" Jack asked, as if that was the only thing he'd heard.

"He's really a sweet guy, your new program director. Came up just as I was leaving the news desk, I thought maybe to apologize for the mix-up, but was I ever wrong about that! Called me 'little girl,' said if I ever pull a trick like that again I'll be lucky to get a job waiting tables in Dime Box!" The corners of her mouth tucked in, but she wasn't really smiling. "I'm wondering what makes him think he can threaten me like that. Somehow I get the feeling there's something going on I don't know about, Jack. What do you think?"

"I think you're paranoid as hell, McNichols, and you've gotta helluva lot of nerve criticizing the way I run my news operation! You just axed one of our biggest accounts with your cute little story knocking fish-oil supplements, right after we run an ad for one."

"I don't check my stories against the commercials, Jack, and I wouldn't pull a story for an advertiser anyway, you know that." Mari also knew that advertising ruled the roost in broadcasting just as it did in the newspaper business, sometimes even more so, one of the inescapable "facts of life" no reporter could ignore completely and hope to survive. "What I would be willing to do, though, is switch a story to another night, so it doesn't hit one of our ads head on, unless it's an emergency and viewers need to get the information immediately. But I'd need to know ahead of time, not after all the scripting and editing is done."

"Okay, I'll look into it, see what we can work out," Jack agreed, accepting the olive branch she'd extended. He sounded relieved, in fact, though he still wasn't ready to let her think she'd managed to get the upper hand.

"But you be in my office first thing Monday morning. We're going to straighten this thing out, one way or another!"

"I'm sorry, Charles," Mari mumbled as she rolled away, feeling both embarrassed and guilty. She sought the far edge of the bed, wanting to hide her face even though the room was dark. But Charles refused to let her go. His arm tightened and he pulled her back against his body, fitting himself around her. She could feel his erection against her buttocks, and felt a sudden urge to apologize, or at least to try to explain why she couldn't respond, in spite of his tender, patient attempts to arouse her further.

"I—I just can't get my head turned on to the right frequency, or something. It's nothing you did—or didn't do," she whispered. "It's not that I'm not aroused. I just seemed to reach a plateau, then sort of leveled off. Can't go forward or backward." For a man, she thought, it was always all or nothing, never halfway in between.

"I know." Charles raised up enough to lay the side of his face against hers. He could hear the frustration in her voice. "Too many things are going on inside there tonight, right?" His lips moved in word kisses against the corner of her eye.

She nodded, feeling even more miserable because he didn't sound the least bit irritated. "I tried to concentrate. Really I did, but—"

"Maybe that's the problem. Trying too hard."

And now you're going to suggest that you'll just go ahead without me, that I can't possibly mean to leave you in this condition! Mari held her breath, silently chiding herself for waiting and hoping that he wouldn't, even though she fully expected that he would. Knowing, too, that she could never again offer herself as a passive receptacle for a man to use. Not if she wanted to keep her self-respect or her sanity. Charles would never understand why, just as no man seemed capable of understanding how or why just the *idea*—that a woman should "service" a man no matter what her own desire or state of arousal might be—could generate an anger so deep and intense that it completely eradicated all sexual desire. It was never a matter of noblesse oblige, either, because such behavior was only considered the "honorable" thing to do in a female, never in a male. Otherwise why all the worry among women about premature ejaculation, or all the fantasies about men who could wait?

"Don't worry about it," Charles murmured in her ear. "Happens to everybody at times." His lips stretched into a smile against her cheek. "I think I may live—if you don't wiggle around too much." Mari didn't know whether to believe him. Maybe he was only trying to make the best of an embarrassing situation, get through it somehow until tomorrow, when he could plead the press of work as an excuse to cut short the weekend and go back to Austin.

"Couple of things I forgot to tell you earlier, by the way," Charles continued, interrupting the silent stream of doubts. "For one, that bastard at the station deserved everything he got tonight, maybe more. You did a good job on him, had him on the ropes the whole time." He chuckled a little, remembering the sense of pleasure and satisfaction he'd felt watching and listening to her turn into a little tiger, so passionate in her defense of viewers and the need to give them accurate information. She might look cool on the outside, but there was plenty of fire and heat on the inside. She'd knocked Jack Lunsford off balance by attacking Tracy's distorted report on the contraceptive sponge, and while he was still trying to figure out what hit him, tossed him a compromise, a face-saving way out he couldn't possibly turn down. Charles also had a much better idea now of how it was possible for a reporter to get the full story about something yet fail to get it on the air, or into print.

"But right now you need to let it go so you can relax and go to sleep." He hugged her close one last time. "The other thing was, I love you, little girl." Mari could hear the smile in his voice, knew he was picking up on the epithet Lou Slocum had thrown at her earlier in the evening, on purpose, to try to take the sting out by turning it into an endearment. It was an hour or more before Mari was able to drift off, though, long after Charles's breathing had settled into the regular rhythm of sleep.

Full consciousness always came suddenly, even after a short night, and within seconds of waking Saturday morning, Mari's mind was seething with activity, going over everything that had happened the night before, again and again, beginning with Tracy's segment on single-mothers-by-choice. The more she thought about it, the surer she was that her instincts were right, and had been from the beginning. The fish-oil thing was just a coincidence, and it was out in the open, where she could deal with it. But it had nothing to do with the real problem. Tracy Sadler was out to eliminate the competition. She was after Mari's reporting territory and her broadcast time. In short, her job! The AIDS Watch idea had been nothing more than the opening salvo in the battle to make Mari's presence at KPOC superfluous, first on AIDS and then on other health stories, gradually shrinking her time until no one would even notice when Mari quietly disappeared entirely.

Mari thought it all over a little longer, until she had everything sorted out in her mind, then threw back the covers and slipped out of bed, planning ahead while she brushed her teeth and then her hair. She decided to make pancakes, and maybe bacon and eggs, too, depending on how hungry Charles was, mix up the batter and put it in the refrigerator. And also save dressing until later so she wouldn't disturb him. She slipped on a short gown and matching robe and started for the kitchen, her bare feet silent on the polished oak floor, but then couldn't resist stopping to look at Charles on the way. A shade paler than usual in sleep, his skin nevertheless contrasted sharply with the light blue sheet and blanket. She stood watching the life pulsing through his torso, neck, and arms for a couple of minutes, watching his body throb with each beat of his heart, until at last, with an unconscious sigh, she turned to leave the room—only to be jerked off balance when his hand snaked out and grabbed her wrist. Too startled to do more than protest "Hey!" she stumbled sideways against the edge of the bed, then fell across him, into his waiting arms.

"Where'd you think you're going?" Charles grumbled, his voice still husky with sleep as he wrapped his arms around her.

"I *was* going to fix pancakes, until you manhandled me into your bed," Mari replied, rubbing her wrist.

"Let me," he ordered, turning her to fit better into the curve of his arm, then lifted the inside of her wrist to his lips. Mari snuggled her face against his neck, teasing the warm skin with her lips and tongue, indulging herself while his hand kneaded her lower back for a second, then shaped her buttocks to pull her hard against his quick arousal.

"Charles?" It sounded tentative because she wasn't sure exactly what to say.

"Mmmmm?" was all the answer she got because his lips were already busy.

"About last night," she began, "I don't know——"

"Forget it, it's not important," he interrupted quickly, while his hands continued to roam. "Anyway, after all the shit they threw at you down at the station, not to mention the kind of hours you work, it's no wonder." It hadn't been until he heard Mari and Tony talking with Jack and Ted last night about the changes they needed to work out before ten o'clock that he realized she was going to have to be back for the later newscast as well. They usually taped her segment, Tony told him later, but it wasn't unusual for her to spend all day developing and taping stories and then work straight through the ten o'clock broadcast.

"You're a great one to talk!" she protested, raising her head so she could see his face. "I figure that's just about all you do, work."

"Yeah, but I'm not marching to someone else's orders, except for a few hours a week, when I meet classes. When and how much I work is up to me. And just so you'll know that's not all I do—ever hear of climbing right back up on the horse?" he asked, grinning lecherously.

Mari couldn't help laughing. "How come I never noticed you do that before, the clichés, I mean?"

"Saves a lot of time, like shorthand. Gets you instant understanding, and don't tell me you didn't understand!"

Mari loved Charles's body, but the way she felt about him was more than just a physical thing. It was all mixed up with who he was—his reasoned deliberateness, his curiosity and compulsion to experiment, the way he could look at things with a fresh eye, his unembarrassed honesty about what he *didn't* know, and his sensitivity to her feelings—and she responded to his touch with a fast-rising warming in her blood, as eager for it in her head as in her body. Last night her head had kept her body from responding the way it wanted to, and she'd been helpless to do a damn thing to change that! And then he'd made no attempt to push her, or to—

"Aaaah!" Charles froze suddenly just as he was starting to roll over, pulling her with him, and let out a low, involuntary groan. Then he slowly and carefully straightened out his legs.

"What's wrong?" Mari sat up, to get out of his way.

"Just a catch in my back. Happens sometimes when I spend too much time bent over a lab bench. Need to stretch out for a minute, that's all."

"I know just the thing," she muttered, already jumping up from the bed. Before he realized what she was doing, she'd tossed the pillows onto the floor and pulled the covers down to the foot of the bed, letting them drape off to the floor. Then she helped him turn over onto his chest and stomach, arranging his arms and head so he was as straight as possible yet could relax. "Be back in a second," she whispered, brushing the edge of his ear with her lips before she ran into the bathroom to get her bottle of almond oil, the one Charles had gotten her in Torremolinos. She set it on the table near the head of the bed, where he could see it, along with a little white porcelain won-ton soup spoon, then loosed the tie of her robe and slipped it off, tossing it onto the chair as she walked to the foot of the bed and wrapped both hands firmly around one of his ankles. "Relax," she ordered as she leaned back, letting her entire weight pull on his leg.

"What in the hell are you doing?" He raised up carefully and turned his head, trying to see her. "Thought you were going to give me a massage. My anticipator was already engaged." His mouth curled up in a twisted grin.

"Sssshhh. Just do as I say. Relax. I'm going to stretch you out first." She leaned back again, slowly pulling on first one leg, and then the other. Then she climbed back onto the bed astride his thighs, poured oil into the palm of one hand and rubbed her hands together before skimming them over his back to coat his skin with the light lubricant. She picked up the spoon and began running it firmly but gently in straight lines across his back and down his arms. Then she switched to her hands, starting just above his buttocks, her thumbs tracing small circles over the bones and muscles as they moved upward, fingers fanning out around his waist and then his rib cage, smoothing and warming as they progressed. When she reached his shoulders, she cupped her hands and began to squeeze lightly, sliding down his arms to the elbows, then back up again, to knead the muscles at the base of his neck, before her fingers crept higher, into the curling edge of dark hair, to soften the tight tendons there.

Mari's short camisole gown bared most of her body, but

already she could feel the heat of her exertions, and would have stripped it off except for the oil on her hands. She moved down his body, gentling her touch at the bony pelvic area just below the small of his back. Even so, the pressure was enough to sink him deeper into the mattress with each rhythmic push. Skipping quickly over his buttocks, only because they were sheathed in knit briefs, she scooted herself down to the foot of the bed as she began on his thighs, spreading them apart slightly in order to reach the inner muscles. At last she moved off the bed completely, to finish her ministrations to his calves and ankles, finally ending with his toes. When she finished, she stood there for a second, watching him, wondering if he'd dozed off again. He hadn't made a sound the whole time, or moved of his own volition. Suddenly, without any warning at all, Charles flipped over and leaped off the side of the bed, all in one fluid motion, and there was a demonic gleam in his eyes as he stalked her.

"Witch! Thought you could get away scot-free, did you, with torturing me like that?" Too startled for a moment, she could only stare at his glistening body. But one glance was all it took. And then she began backing away. But she was grinning now, too. He reached for the lower edge of her gown and with one swift jerk had it up and over her head. He tossed it aside with complete disdain for where it might fall. Then, turning her to face him, he began inching her backward, toward the edge of the bed, thigh to thigh, until one shove was all it took to topple her—an act that was both rough and gentle since he caught her as she fell, lowering her slowly onto the mattress and following her down with his own body. She lay across the bed with her legs bent to accommodate the mattress, her toes barely touching the floor.

Charles seemed intent on wreaking his revenge in kind, but face to face, and he was using his lips and tongue as well as his hands. "No fair," she protested weakly, going along with the game while he licked and nibbled his way from the base of her throat down the valley between her breasts, to the concave slope below her rib cage, causing a flood of swelling sensations. His hands followed just behind his mouth, and she turned into them, trying to give him access to even more of her body. One long-fingered hand engulfed her breast completely while his tongue circled her navel, before slowly working its way lower, continuing the siege on her senses. Then, before she knew what he was about, though he was still following the pattern she'd set, Charles backed off the side of the bed between her legs and was urging her knees apart. She felt the heavenly soft, slippery slide of his tongue over the one place he hadn't even tried to touch, and knew that nothing else in the whole world mattered but this, and now.

"Oh God, Charles!" she sighed softly, as the icy-hot sensation flared out of control, and she was unable to hold back any longer, to contain the blossoming ecstasy that shook her entire body. Charles had held back purposefully until now, pushing her ahead of himself because he was determined to wipe last night from her memory. He raised himself enough to slide into her slowly and carefully, afraid that he might hurt her, though it was all he could do to keep from exploding in those first delirious moments as she tightened around him, again and again. The effect of her hands had been to somehow produce pictures in his head that seemed to intensify the sensations in his body, even before the arousal that always came with just looking at her body. There were times, in fact, when the looking created such an agony of anticipation that he could barely keep his hands, or body, from reaching out for her. And then with one deep thrust he gave himself up to the exquisite agony of release, knowing somewhere way out on the edges of his mind that what he was feeling was some unique combination of feelings and thoughts and sensations he'd never known before.

The rich dark aroma of freshly brewed coffee filled even the bedroom, confronting his senses anew as Charles came out of the shower. Vague memories of longings and feelings long denied began to haunt him, bringing the here and now into even sharper focus. Here, this morning, with Mari, he knew a sense of peace, of fit and rightness, of being home—feelings so strong that he stood perfectly still for a moment, letting both his mind and body enjoy the inexplicable pleasure of it.

A quick glance out the window told him the sun was already high and hot, so he pulled a clean short-sleeved shirt out of his overnighter and stepped into a pair of jeans, his usual garb when he was away from the university, often even when he wasn't. The informal campus environment had been one reason he was attracted to academic work in the first place, and even now he didn't much like the idea of having to conform to what he considered unnecessary constraints that only wasted his time, which reminded him of the growing pile of bureaucratic busywork piled up on his desk in Austin.

He was just starting for the kitchen when he recognized the tiny blue and white porcelain bowl sitting on one end of Mari's chest of drawers. Last night, after not seeing her for two long weeks, his mind had been on only one thing, and he really hadn't noticed much of anything about her apartment or this room. He smiled, remembering the shop where the little hand-painted dish had set him back all of two dollars! And how smug he'd felt about her willingness to let him pick up the restaurant tabs in Torremolinos. How long ago all that seemed now, though there still were times when she didn't seem to trust him—times, in fact, when she reminded him of a prize fighter, bouncing around on her toes in order to present a moving target, as if to keep from getting punched or pinned against the ropes.

The bowl was filled with little water-polished pebbles like the ones Mari had been collecting in her skirt that day he'd found her on the beach at Torremolinos. Next to it was a lacy frond of fern, dried and bleached to a delicate ivory color, along with a twig the size of his finger covered with circles of rust- and cream-colored lichen. As he straightened, his eye was drawn to the wall above the low white chest, where several small scraps of fabric were tacked up with almost invisible pins. He leaned closer, examining the sculptured surface of one small rectangle, patterned all over with tiny gold and orange stitches between and on top of layers of faded turquoise and white, which had been cut through in a geometrical design to reveal the pink underneath. And then a frayed square of coarse olive-drab cotton, alive with multicolored chainstitching in an asymmetrical design that never repeated itself. The largest piece, also a cut-and-stitched relief but with saw-toothed edges, was bright orange, white, and black, in a design that hinted of some animal form. All had undoubtedly come from some "undeveloped" culture, yet there was an abstract sophistication about them that was anything but "primitive." Charles groped to remember Mari's exact words that night at El Roqueo, about how the creativity of ordinary people and their urge to embellish their lives, to do more than simply satisfy their need for food, clothing, and shelter.

"Any time you're ready, C.B.," Mari called as she came through the bedroom door. "The pancakes and sausage are—" Her words trailed off as she saw the quizzical smile take his mouth. "You don't know the old joke, about when Cecil B. DeMille was filming the parting of the Red Sea for one of his biblical epics?" she asked. "How, after it was all over, DeMille called up to his cameraman, way up on a bluff overlooking the scene, and the cameraman called back—"

"Yeah, yeah, I know." He laughed as he extended one arm in invitation. "I was only wondering how come you knew my middle initial, until I remembered that you looked me up. What else do you know about me I don't know?" he asked, his lips moving against her hair. He had to remind himself not to feel puffed up about the fact that she'd "researched" him, since he knew she'd do the same with anyone she was going to interview.

"All your deep, dark secrets," she answered, then rattled off a whole string of "vital" statistics on Charles Butler Merrill.

He laughed and nodded, then purposefully baited her. "Nothing personal?"

"No, I guess you were being pretty cagey about that. No wife or children mentioned, though I suppose that doesn't mean—"

"Come on, Mari! You know better than that. How about we fill in all the missing information? Could even do it in time for the next edition if we'd get right to work on it. What do you say?" Mari wasn't sure if he was joking or not, but before she could think how to respond, he spoke again. "Married to Mari McNichols, nineteen eighty . . . when, Mari? You know now that I'm still the handsome prince, right? That this doesn't have a damn thing to do with the magic of al Andalus!" He lightened the moment with a quick smile. "It's just you and me, Mari honey."

"Three weeks, most of it apart, and you think we know each other?" Mari asked, trying to stem the tide of panic tightening her throat. The light banter had changed to something else without any warning whatsoever. "Why the rush?"

"Why wait?" he shot back. "I want you with me, all the time. We're right together, you know that. We fit, and not just in bed, though I'd be the first to admit that's part of it. An important part. And you can't fool me, Mac, not after this morning. You feel the same way." She felt the blood rush to her neck and cheeks, and hoped he would at least have the grace not to tease her about it.

"Aw, Mari honey, don't!" He pulled her close and she hid her face in the curve of his neck. "Let's at least try to be honest with each other. Hell, it even seems like half the lights have gone out when you're not around. I need you, Mari—I love you, everything about you."

"How can you say that?" she protested against his neck. "You don't really know me. I may think I love you, Charles, but I don't really know you, either. You saw what happened last night, and I can't guarantee it won't happen again. Next time you might not feel quite so forgiving. What about my work? And yours? I don't expect you to give up what you have in Austin, try to move your whole laboratory setup to Rice or, God forbid, that other poor excuse for a university. I'm not even sure I want to stay in Houston, but you can't expect me to give up what I can do here and go read the police blotter at some hick TV station in Austin. So I don't see how—"

Charles grabbed her shoulders and shook her a little, at the same time pushing her away to look into her face. "That doesn't sound like you, Mar, willing to throw in the towel at the first little obstacle. So we still have a few things to learn about each other. How about we try to spend more time together, then?" He grinned slightly and waited until she nodded, then added, "We might even try talking about some of those stumbling blocks you just tossed out, see what we can figure out. Okay?" Again he waited for her to nod. "I'll admit I can be pretty impatient sometimes, but I've been trying to give you room." His eyes and mouth were completely serious now. "Because you're too important to me." One hand came up to frame her face for a second, then stroked back over her hair. "Just promise you'll try to remember one thing, no matter what. I've never loved anybody in my whole life the way I love you."

The way he said it caused tears to flood Mari's eyes. She leaned forward to touch his lips with hers, once, twice, three times, four times, whispering a single word between each one. "I . . . love . . . you . . . too." He hugged her to him then, and they just stood there in silence for a minute, holding each other.

When Charles spoke again, it was in a hoarse whisper. "One of the things I guess you should know about me—this prince turns back into a frog when he has to eat cold pancakes." He gave her a pat on the rear and then turned her toward the door, keeping one hand curled around the back of her neck as they started for the kitchen together.

Charles forked the last bite into his mouth and leaned back from the table, stretching his legs out to the side. "How come you know that was my favorite breakfast? I know I didn't tell that to *American Men of Science.*"

Mari shrugged. "Simple deduction, since you're a good ole Texas boy." She liked to tease him about it because she considered Charles about as far from the stereotype as you could get, except for an occasional unexplained lapse into a West Texas twang.

He decided to ignore her flip reply. "So what's on the agenda next? Anything special you have to do today?"

"No. Oh, I need to call Mom, sometime, see how she's doing. She's been staying with Jackie since Dr. Richardson let her out of the hospital, but when I talked with her Thursday night, she said she was going home."

"Yeah, I know. I talked with her, oh, I guess it was Wednesday night." He saw the surprise on her face. "What'sa matter, you think a poor college professor can't afford a long-distance call to Denver once in a while?"

Mari really shouldn't have been surprised. It was just that he was moving into every corner of her life, and it was happening so fast. And that last remark sounded like a challenge, as if he were daring her to inquire into some of the things she didn't know about him. "Rachel and Tony will be here at seven, but I've already done most of the shopping. Just need to pick up the fish this afternoon sometime."

"Sounds like a lot of work for you. Why don't we go out to eat instead?"

"Uh-uh. It won't take long—with you here to help." She tossed him an impish grin as she began stacking the breakfast dishes.

"Okay, but you've heard about the bull in the china shop? Well, that's me in the kitchen, any kitchen."

"S'funny, I would've figured you for a more original excuse than that, C.B."

"Yeah, and just what's that supposed to mean?"

"You forget, I've watched you at work, seen how you handle all kinds of equipment, even my tape recorder. Watched the deliberate, meticulously coordinated movements of your whole body, and your wonderful hands. And in bed—" She laughed, a little embarrassed at what she was revealing, then jumped up to carry the dishes to the sink. "You couldn't be a bull anywhere, C.B., no matter how hard you tried. Unless you're schizo."

He came up behind her, sliding his hands around her waist and then cupping her breasts, pinning her against the edge of the counter with his body. And he just held her like that while searching for some way to tell her how he felt about what she'd just confessed. There were times when she made him feel positively naive, when her words brought home to him just how limited his own awareness could be, like that day at the Alhambra.

"That was about the nicest way to get called a male chauvinist I've ever heard!" he teased, tickling her ear with his lips. "You see the damnedest things, you know that, Mari honey? Things I don't, or didn't—at least not until you show them to me." It didn't come out sounding the way he'd intended, and he wondered if he'd ever be able to explain to her what he really meant. Her uncanny insights always seemed to resonate with something much deeper than the words actually said. "Can't help wondering what else there is I'm missing. So don't stop. I want to learn to see the way you see," he added before straightening and releasing her. "So what's next? Do we have time to run out to the Common Market?"

"You mean the flea market off the Southwest Freeway?"

"Yeah. Sometimes it's all junk, but you never know." He looked at his watch. "It's nearly ten-thirty. Maybe we could take a look at the new Menil collection, too, catch a bite of lunch somewhere in between, if you think there's time before we have to be back here to start slaving over a hot stove." He paused, bemused by the thought that he could be in love without knowing what she liked to do or how she spent her time when she wasn't working. He didn't want her to go just to please him. "But maybe you don't much like museums. I guess they can be kind of dull."

Mari's eyebrows shot up and stayed there. *"You* think museums are dull?"

"Nope. Just giving you an easy out!"

"Dominique de Menil wanted only part of the collection put on display at a time, so the exhibitions can change. I go fairly often, because I don't want to miss anything. Does that answer your question?"

He grabbed her hands, and then a towel to dry them. "I'll finish up in here, then make a couple of phone calls. You go get dressed." He looped the dish towel around her neck and pulled her toward him, gave her a quick kiss and then another pat on the rear before sending her on her way.

They spent an hour wandering among the outdoor stalls at the flea market, hand in hand, making their way slowly through the throng of people, stopping from time to time when one or the other saw something interesting. The offerings were unpredictable, and ranged from chrome hubcaps to potted plants, and from junk jewelry to old cameras, china, and toys. Finally, near an open stand selling popcorn and hot dogs, Mari spotted a young woman standing alone, holding a black felt-lined tray of glass objects that glittered and flashed in the sun. She pulled Charles with her to see what they were, then tugged on his hand until he bent his head down.

"I want one of those," Mari whispered into his ear, her voice almost quivering with urgency. Or was it suppressed excitement? He looked where she pointed, confused more by the flip-flop in her behavior than the request itself. The faceted pieces of glass appeared to be relics from an old cut-glass chandelier, judging by the holes drilled through the tip of each one. About four inches long, each prism-shaped section was pointed at one end. The other end was attached by a wire to a multifaceted lozenge of glass, which had a delicate wire hook threaded through a hole in the top. He bought two, then stood watching Mari watch the woman wrap each one in a piece of old newspaper.

A few minutes later, as they walked back to the car between the blocks of apartment buildings, he couldn't help kidding her a little. "You're a woman of damned expensive tastes, Mar. Don't know how I'm going to manage if you keep on like this." He'd paid all of two dollars for the crystal—a dollar apiece. "What hit you? You know something about those things I don't?"

"Don't you ever act on impulse, C.B.?" Mari chided. "I just wanted one to hang in my window, in the sun. Those prisms of glass brought back memories of when I used to visit an old lady, a friend of my mother's. I was little—about five, I suppose—and her house was the most atmospheric place I've ever been in. Like a museum. And I suppose it was, of her life. She must have been in her nineties. I can still see the brown cut-velvet sofa, and the floor lamp with the tiffany shade. And the curtain of beads hanging in the arched doorway between her living room and study. They whispered when you went through them. She was the only woman in the world, I thought, with a study, just like a man. She wrote a column for the weekly newspaper." Charles watched her face as she spoke, realizing that she was giving him a glimpse of who she was, deep inside someplace, just by telling him about this one prized childhood memory. "I loved the sound of those beads. I even thought they made a different sound when I walked through them, and afterward I'd sit real quiet, listening, trying to figure out what they were saying to me. She also had an étagère with glass shelves that stood in front of a window, and on one of the shelves there was a glass prism. Whenever I got bored with the 'big people' I'd go sit in her padded wing chair and watch the color spectrum dance on the wall and across her desk. I used to spend hours trying to figure out where all those beautiful colors were coming from, but I never did." She turned to smile at him.

"You didn't ask?"

"Oh, sure. Mom said that's just what happens when light hits a prism."

"That's all?" he asked with a grin, doubting that even as a child she would have been satisfied with that kind of answer.

Mari returned his knowing grin and nodded. "Yeah, she wasn't much interested in stuff like that, always said people were more interesting, and more important, than things. But I knew that was no kind of answer, even at that age, didn't you?"

Charles nodded silently, but had to look away. For the first time in his adult life he had to fight back a rush of emotion so intense that his eyelids began to burn and his throat muscles tighten, making it almost impossible to speak. All because he'd recognized the same curiosity that fueled her inquiring mind today in the child she was, combined with the same flights of imagination that made her so unique, and so dear to him. And he felt strangely deprived because he hadn't known her then—hadn't even known she existed!

Charles unlocked his BMW and slid the sunroof back to let the cooler outside air flush through, but Mari got in right away. "I couldn't eat anything yet, Charles—and, well, couldn't we go back to the apartment?" she asked. "Take a swim instead, save the Menil Collection for another time?"

The bucket seats were separated by the transmission console, but Charles leaned across and put an arm around behind her shoulders, forcing her to turn toward him. "It's okay to just say so when you want to make love, you know." He grinned, then barely touched her lips in a light kiss that lasted only a second before he started the motor.

Neither of them spoke as he drove east on Westheimer, past the Galleria and through one of the most exclusive residential neighborhoods in Houston. By the time he turned south onto Main Street, the atmosphere inside the car was almost electric, and growing more tense with each red traffic light. Mari sat motionless, avoiding even the slightest distraction. Her breath was coming fast and her heart felt like it was in her ears, blocking out the sound of the traffic. She hardly noticed Rice University, or the medical center across the street. Her breasts felt sensitive and swollen, and a strange icy-hot sensation was burning somewhere deep inside her, spreading through her limbs until she wasn't even sure where her legs were anymore! By the time they reached the parking lot next to her apartment building, she was almost mindless with need—the need to be touched, all over and all at once! She wrenched open the car door as soon as it came to a stop, digging in her purse for the door key as she hurried toward the stairs. Without even realizing it, she was already unbuttoning her blouse by the time she reached the second-floor landing, with Charles close behind. Her hands shook as she groped for the keyhole, then finally pushed open the door.

Charles closed it behind him, just as she peeled off her blouse and dropped it on the floor, at the same time turning toward him with outstretched arms. "Please love me," she pleaded, just before he pulled her against him, his mouth hungry to cover hers, his hands moving with the same urgency as hers, knowing exactly what she wanted without having to be told in words. He heard her low moan as she pulled away from him slightly, only to draw him down with her onto the soft carpet. Aroused by her eagerness, he'd been fully erect by the time he walked through the door, and now he quickly unbuckled his belt and let his pants drop, while she slipped out of her skirt. Then he was beside her, his lips traveling down her throat, over first one breast and then the other, stopping briefly at each to arouse her still further. Within seconds she was searching for him with her hand, enclosing to guide him. He slid his body over hers and entered her slowly, using all the will he could muster to extend the filling sensation for her as long as possible. She writhed as the tension in her body built to a nearly unbearable pitch, tossing her head from side to side. Neither of them could last long at this rate, he thought, just as he felt Mari stiffen against him for one long suspended second. And then her hands were pulling at him, urging him still deeper, as the tension began to spill out of her in huge rhythmic waves, washing him along with her into his own powerful release. Her body continued to rock against his, triggering a series of inner contractions that slowed gradually, matching the movement of her lips against the curve of his neck, clutching and releasing him until he felt himself beginning to harden again.

Charles lifted away from her a little, so he could see her face. Her eyes fluttered open as if she were still in some twilight state, and she gave him a dreamy smile. He slipped his hands under her shoulders and lifted both her and himself to a sitting position, face to face, carefully maintaining their intimate connection. At the same time, he straightened his legs behind her and looped her thighs over his. A rag doll with a slightly quizzical smile on her face, Mari gave herself into his care, letting him position her as he would. "I know women are supposed to be able to have multiple orgasms, but I've never—" she began lazily.

"Me either," Charles confessed, interrupting her, "at least not since I was about twenty." She could hear the grin creep into his voice. "Maybe we just lacked inspiration—and practice."

And then he wrapped his arms around her, holding her tight to his body, pressed his face into her hair and began rocking her backward and forward to his own inner rhythm. Sliding, stroking and filling her, leaving no place untouched, inside or out. There was no compelling urgency now, no frantic kisses or roving hands, only the sensations emanating from where they were so closely joined.

Rather than a dimming of conscious awareness, as before, Mari's mental acuity seemed to sharpen, as if until now the mirror of her mind had been slightly fogged. She leaned into him, keeping to his pace, but otherwise did nothing that might distract or break his concentration, or her own, knowing instinctively that to do so would dilute the intensity of the sensations they were sharing. Until, like rays from the sun focused and intensified by a magnifying lens, her body burst into a small white-hot flame, as intense and constant as the fantasy in her head.

CHAPTER

11

Sure, because the bites get shorter all the time," Tony agreed, responding to Charles's question, "which makes the whole newscast seem more fragmented. But actually, the stories are running longer, a change that started at the network for economic reasons, because it costs less to do fewer stories per broadcast. But the change has been filtering down to the affiliates. Even the independents."

"I don't know much about what the networks are doing. I'm hardly ever home that time of day," Charles commented, "and I'm too far out of town to get cable. Thought a time or two about getting a dish so I could pull in CNN, but it hardly seems worth it for the time I spend watching anything. I just bought a VCR, though, to tape the evening news, in case the network uses your Basque stuff. Wouldn't want to miss that."

"What do you think about the local news there?"

"Don't ask!" Charles advised with a grimace. "Only one station covers any national news at all, and even that's usually no more than a picture with their own mindless voice-over. Never let viewers hear the source firsthand, let alone long enough to make any sense out of the story. I heard a real dilly the other night. First a teaser for the latest on how to reduce the risk of heart attack, then you wait and wait, and when the story finally does come on, some dippy female who doesn't have her brain engaged says that researchers have just learned that more heart attacks occur in the morning than later in the day—period, end of story! What the hell are we supposed to conclude from that, I ask you?" He paused a moment, then added, "But they'll go all over the state—all over the country, for that matter—to pick up an accident or a murder, and give you all the gory details."

Tony laughed, apparently at ease with Charles. "Didn't think Austin was still that backwater, a market that size—especially with their audience profile, which has a pretty good tilt toward the high end of the demographic scale."

Mari watched and listened to the two of them through the kitchen pass-through. She'd worried needlessly that Tony might feel threatened by Charles. Would consider him "one of those guys who have the world by the balls"—his description of some of the medical doctors she interviewed—not to mention that Charles could talk with Rachel about her work in a way that he couldn't. She'd even halfway expected him to seek refuge in silence, which she'd also seen happen before. But Charles exuded a quiet confidence that seemed entirely free of arrogance, so was surprisingly easy to be around. Deliberate, tolerant, controlled, *coherent*—she tried one word after another, searching until she found the right one—yet he never seemed to take anything for granted, which meant that at times his questions could be kind of unsettling.

"Not to bring up an unpleasant subject," Rachel injected, raising her voice to make herself heard beyond the kitchen, where she was filling four heavy-bottomed glasses with ice cubes. "I know a lot of stuff hit the fan after last night's broadcast, but did you two know the ad for Cardi-Omega-3 was going to run when you decided to do that story on fish oil?"

"No," Mari replied, "not that it would have made any difference."

"Yeah, we stood our ground for a while," Tony added. "Mari reminded Jack that we wouldn't pull a story for any advertiser, but then she caved in, threw him a bone." He could hardly keep a straight face. "Agreed to switch a story to another night if it conflicted with an ad, unless it was too important to put off."

He jumped up from his chair as Rachel came from the kitchen carrying a tray loaded with the glasses and a tall stoneware pitcher, to take it from her. "Okay, gather 'round, guys, while I construct my magic elixir of love," Rachel ordered breezily as Tony set the tray down on the glass-topped coffee table. She knelt beside the table and began by pouring a little orange juice into the pitcher.

The tail of Mari's navy-blue silk shirt hung to mid-thigh over matching trousers, which looked a little like the pants men wore in India—draping around the hips and thighs but tight below the knee—and she pulled at the knees a little as she knelt next to Charles's chair, then sat on the rug, leaning against his leg. She'd brushed the top of her hair straight back tonight, and pinned it with a silver clip at the back of her head. He toyed with the blunt-cut edge of her hair where it fell into the curve at the back of her neck, and also with the beads of her fetish necklace, stroking the baby-soft skin underneath as he immersed himself in the sense of shared experience that was almost palpable. Rachel finished "constructing" the sangria, then poured it into the glasses and handed them around, lifting hers to Tony in a silent salute before she took a quick sip. She glanced around, waiting for other verdicts, and it occurred to Charles that she looked different than he'd ever seen her tonight. Maybe because she was wearing a dusty pink dress that shaped her generous breasts instead of her usual starched-white lab coat. More than that, though, her personality, or sense of humor, or something, seemed different as well—or was that only a visual impression, too, something to do with the flirty flounced skirt that stopped just short of her knees?

"Perfect!" Mari decided. Tony agreed with a nod, then added, "But I knew it would be." All eyes were on Charles next, waiting. "Even better than at El Roqueo," he announced, "if that's possible."

"So when do we get to see the flamenco tape?" Rachel asked, the down-light from one of the chrome floor lamps dancing across her hair, causing it to flare up like a flame as she moved around to sit between Tony's knees. She looked up too late to catch Mari's warning hand signal. "Oops, I just spilled something I wasn't supposed to, didn't I? Sorry, Mari."

"It doesn't matter." Mari laughed and shrugged. "I'm so excited about it, I probably couldn't have kept the secret much longer, anyway." She glanced up at Charles. "You should see the footage Tony shot in Spain after I left, and in Crete. It's, well, it's going to . . ." She paused, groping for the right word.

Charles ruffled her hair playfully. "How about backing up a little?" He looked across the table to Tony. "You're doing a piece on the flamenco? Mari and I went to a performance in Torremolinos, but I suppose you know a lot more about it than we did."

"Uh-uh. It was *mi compañera*'s idea—as usual. She's full of 'em, in case you haven't noticed," he teased. "By the time Rachel and I got there, she had every bite and bridge sketched out, right from the top. I picked up a few takes after she left, but Mari's the producer."

"Co-producer! When are you going to get that through your *cabeza dura?*" She rapped her knuckles against her own head to emphasize exactly how hard she thought his was. "You know there's not another local yokel anywhere in the state of Texas who can do what you can with a camera—and damn few even at the network, or in Hollywood, either, for that matter."

Tony grinned sheepishly, enjoying every word as she scolded and complimented him at the same time. He couldn't even begin to count the times he'd watched her rerun her five-minute news segment, over and over again, analyzing it dispassionately from every possible angle as she took it apart, bit by agonizing bit, searching for better words and clearer explanations, dreaming up questions she should have answered but hadn't. She didn't mince words when it came to his work, either, especially his on-location editing with the Betacam, giving every shot the same analytical appraisal she gave her own performance. He'd learned more from her in eleven months than in all his years in school, because he'd learned how to look critically, to analyze, which was a whole new way of thinking for him. He knew he was more visually aware than he'd ever been before, and, he was beginning to think, maybe in some other ways as well.

As a result, one word of praise from Mari was worth infinitely more to him than a whole rash of compliments from anyone else.

"It's going to be sort of a minidocumentary," Mari explained to Charles. "Only twenty-three minutes. A little historical information combined with a lot of dancing, singing, and playing. We think it's going to be pretty, uh, exciting, I guess, both the sound and the pictures."

"'Arousing' is what she means, Charles. Must be her Puritan forefathers that keeps her from spitting it out," Tony teased, getting back at Mari in kind for her occasional allusions to his cultural heritage, especially what she called his "Latino hang-ups" about women. "Jack almost wet his pants when we showed him the bites we got of Galiana." He laughed a little, then sent an acknowledging nod toward Mari. "Okay, so we are co-producers." He glanced back at Charles. "But she's still the one who digs up all the pieces and builds the bridges to make them work together. And don't try to deny it!" he added quickly, trying to head off any further protest from Mari.

"Oh, lord, they're into it again," Rachel warned Charles, pulling her face into an exaggerated grimace of dismay. "We'll be sitting here all night now, *our* appetites be damned, while they feed theirs on this mutual-admiration thing they have going!"

Tony slid both hands around her neck and tipped up her chin, gently pulling her head back into his lap, then bent forward to whisper something in Spanish that neither Mari nor Charles could understand. But they watched, spellbound, as he held Rachel's upside-down eyes for a moment with his own, then gave her a quick kiss on the tip of the nose as a rush of blood flooded her neck and cheeks as a result of whatever it was he'd said to her.

"Old Jack has already sweet-talked Al Tischler into putting our flamenco minidoc into the May schedule," Tony continued, as if blithely unaware of the effect his words were having on Rachel. But Mari recognized the smug expression on his face and knew better. "He's the station manager," he explained for Charles's benefit. "May's the toughest ratings month of the year, because most of the network programs have already gone into reruns, yet the May figures are used to set ad rates for the fall programs. God only knows what's going to happen this year. Since they switched to people meters, nobody gets the same numbers for the same program. And now Percy—a Seattle outfit that uses an infrared device to detect when people enter or leave a room—is saying that only about half the audience sticks around during the commercials. Anyway, you know how Jack's always talking how his news division can beat the entertainment guys at their own game, Mari. He says the flamenco video's going to have something for everybody. A little travelogue for the old folks, lots of loud singing and dancing for the kids and teenagers, and—his exact words, Mari, I swear it—the guys in the audience are going to get a hard-on like they haven't had in a month of Sundays."

"What's not to believe? Jack's got a dildo for a brain. You know how it is, Tony. You can lead an ass to knowledge, but you can't make him think!"

"Yeah, right. How about boys will be boys, and so are a lot of middle-aged men?"

"Or what do you expect from a pig but a grunt?"

They continued like that for a couple of minutes, each trying to top the other's snide insult, venting their feelings about Jack. The more Charles listened to them, the more he became aware that they shared a deep mutual understanding, at times even anticipating each other as if their brains were operating on the same wavelength. He suspected Tony was usually the less assertive partner, but after the confrontation with Jack last night, it also was evident that Tony had no trouble finding his voice when Mari was under attack. Which was comforting, in spite of the fact that she obviously was capable of defending herself, because he sensed an undercurrent of vulnerability in her that left him with a mild case of uneasiness. He couldn't help remembering that night in Denver when she'd run into Phillip Ashmore at the hospital. Granted she'd been tired and her defenses were down, but the unexpected encounter had, quite literally, made her sick. And that didn't fit the image she usually projected—of a strong, capable, determined, and savvy professional.

Charles looked around the room while he listened, taking

in all the divergent pieces Mari had made "work together," as Tony put it. At the white walls enlivened by two old Persian watercolors of jousting horsemen, and a rectangular mirror framed in glass, painted from the back side in an ornate black, copper, and gilt design—from Peru, she'd told him earlier, and one of her favorite things—"a gift from Mom." And several small color photographs, including one of pink hollihocks against an adobe wall, and a sepia-toned view down a misty country lane lined with tall trees. Tony sat in one of two diamond-shaped Bertoia chairs, similar to one Charles remembered seeing in the Museum of Modern Art, and next to it was a chromed gooseneck floor lamp, exactly like the ones used in doctors' examining rooms. But it was the thick Tabriz carpet that brought everything together, with its jewel-toned reds and blues and creamy white background. The quality of light, both day and night, the colors and textures, the sounds and smells, made him feel so fantastically good that he wondered whether the euphoria of being with her was getting to him—affecting his judgment. And with a sudden flash of insight he understood what Mari had been trying to tell him, in Spain, about how the light and colors, even the air, of Andalusia made her distrust her own judgment, caused her to feel unsure of what was real, or only imagined.

At the table Tony started praising Charles's salad, while Mari made a ceremony of serving the paella and Rachel filled the green-stemmed glasses with a white Spanish wine.

"The first one I've ever constructed," Charles admitted, then went on to describe exactly how he'd done it. Red and green leaf lettuce—torn, not cut—yellow tomatoes, sliced water chestnuts, and a handful of dark green sunflower sprouts. He also had set the table, choosing the place mats, napkins, and candles all on his own. But it was the salad he considered his masterpiece. Tony continued to mumble unintelligible comments around bites, nodding sagely as he listened to Charles. "The secret is in the herbs. Mari grows them in pots out on the balcony, you know. But I'll bet even she's never tried these two together before." He paused for effect. "Mint and cilantro."

"Ummmmm," Tony murmured approvingly, trying to

look both amazed and admiring at the same time. "A beauty to look at—and a really, uh, unusual flavor," he agreed, finally getting his mouth empty enough to speak.

Rachel raised a quizzical brow at Mari and with pretend innocence asked, "Unusual? Is that the same as calling a painting interesting?"

Both Mari and Charles burst out laughing, while Tony ordered Rachel to "Just eat, woman!" trying to sound stern. But he couldn't keep a straight face, either, and in the end reached out to playfully ruffle her hair, a silent admission that she'd called his bluff.

"Culinary wonders aside, Charles, what do you think about all the latest research stuff on low-cholesterol diets?" Rachel asked.

Charles shrugged. "Depends on how you want to read the data, I suppose. In the Southern Cal study, the amount of low-density lipoproteins in the guys on the special diet plus drugs was lower, no doubt about that. But X rays showed more plaque had formed on the arterial walls in about forty percent of the cases. Only something like sixteen percent came out with less blockage. And we still don't know why. Hell, everybody knows that fat globules show up in the blood within twenty or thirty minutes after ingestion of, oh, say a milkshake. But tying the presence of those lipids to plaque formation is something else. I doubt there is any simple answer—or remedy."

"What's the effect of cholesterol on blood visco-elasticity?" Mari asked.

"Not much, though we really haven't focused on that in any of our clinical tests. Nothing like the elevated values we see in premenstrual women, for instance."

"Or in women on the pill, right?" Rachel added, looking to Charles for confirmation.

"Yeah, you noticed that, huh? See any other drug effects you can identify?"

"A few suspicions, but I think I'll write them down and let Mari hold the paper until after you've run the cross-correlations, just to make sure I don't tilt your conclusions." She was teasing him, and Charles knew it. "We should have about a thousand samples run by the end of this week, by the way. You want me to put the floppy disks in the mail, or will you pick them up yourself?"

Mari suspected Rachel was on a fishing trip, but she didn't say anything. She was too busy wondering whether Charles's Vampire was capable of detecting why, or when, Pamezine might cause the thickening of the blood her anonymous caller had described—if it did. But if the pill alone could cause the red cells to harden and the viscoelasticity to increase, was that likely to mask the effect of a second drug?

"Stick 'em in the mail. Mari's coming to Austin next weekend." He looked at her for confirmation. "Right?"

"Yes, maybe," Mari agreed distractedly. "If I can."

"Which reminds me," Rachel added. "Rich Seldon—he's the chief clinical pathologist at the hospital—has been in almost every day, watching us run the samples with the Vampire, asking questions. Says he wants to meet you next time you're in town."

"Sure," Charles responded. "What's his interest, or did he say?"

"Women with glasses," Tony answered before Rachel had a chance to. "You know, so he can see himself in the reflection." Charles laughed and shook his head as it dawned on him that *that* was why Rachel looked different, or at least one reason. He'd never seen her without her glasses before. Rachel eyed Tony appraisingly, a little surprised at the wisecrack. If she didn't take Rich Seldon seriously, why should he?

"So how's your PBS pilot coming?" she asked Mari, changing the subject.

"It isn't," Mari answered. "With that trip to Spain, editing our Basque interviews, and then the flamenco video, I just haven't had time."

"KPOC is doing a program for public broadcasting?" Charles asked, which didn't seem likely to him, but he was discovering that he really didn't know very much about how the stations and networks cooperated with each other, if or when they did.

"No. I plan to freelance it—what you might call moonlighting—I suppose because I have this ridiculous idea in the back of my mind that someday I'm going to produce documentaries full-time," she explained. "Get free of the daily grind and the time constraints, not to mention the airheads." She grinned at Tony because he'd know who she meant. "I was hoping to propose a six-part series on women's health problems to the PBS Station Program Cooperative when they meet to decide what to buy for next year. That means getting one program on tape to show and the others outlined on paper. Thought maybe I could sell at least the pilot, even if they decide against the series. But the program fair is the first week in May, and I doubt we can finish shooting, let alone do final editing by then."

"Is there really enough for a series on just women's health problems alone?" Charles asked. "Seems to me that pretty much means pregnancy and infertility, problems associated with reproduction, which I'd think would be hard to sell, considering how much exposure that's already had in the media."

Mari tossed Rachel a quick glance. "Oh, there's enough for a series, all right. I'm taking a broad look at how the medical profession treats women. The quantity and quality of information they get from physicians and other health practitioners, how health professionals treat the information they get from female patients, how prescribing practices differ for female and male patients, the ratio of surgical procedures to other types of treatment, women to men, for similar problems, stuff like that."

Charles still looked puzzled. "You're saying that men and women are treated differently, outside of sex-related conditions, or you're just researching to see whether they are?"

Rachel let out a whoop of laughter and turned to Mari with an incredulous look. "Amazing, isn't it, when even someone who's had a firsthand, inside look at the profession can't see what's so obvious to us? I suppose it must be like racism—if it doesn't happen to you, it doesn't exist." Mari's smile was one of ironic agreement.

"You're right, I suppose," Charles admitted, not in the least put off by Rachel's comment. "But I'm sure as hell not going to change my sex to find out, so why don't you lay it on me, Rachel," he invited.

Rachel saw he was serious, and quickly sobered, too,

trying to decide how to answer him, in two minutes or less. "Did you know that doctors in this country didn't even understand the ovarian cycle until the 1930s—fifty years ago—or that most medical textbooks still send the message that the sex drive is stronger in males than females?"

There'd been a time—and not too long ago, either, Mari realized—when Tony would have defended the truth of that assertion, but not since Rachel. She saw the smile begin to play at the corners of his mouth as he glanced back and forth from Rachel to Charles, and knew he was looking forward to this.

"Most male physicians still see women as innately neurotic," Rachel continued, "which means that simply being female is a pathological state. That, in turn, means health problems known to be organic are still being diagnosed as psychosomatic, and treated accordingly. Women with symptoms of heart disease, for instance, are considered for bypass surgery far less often than men. Granted that actually might be a lucky misdemeanor, if bypass surgery is becoming the knee-jerk prescription some critics claim, but doctors recommend presurgical tests for men ten times more often than for women with the same symptoms! The truth is, women's symptoms are attributed to noncardiac causes twice as often as men's. Of course, the big drug companies also perpetuate the view of women as psychological weaklings who need to be treated chemically, because it's good for profits. A vast majority of doctors prescribe mood-altering drugs mostly to women, which undoubtedly helps explain why three quarters of all prescriptions are written for women. And women are twice as likely to get prescriptions for psychotropic drugs. Why? Most of the M.D.s in one study said because of their 'psychological weakness,' which I don't find a bit hard to believe, not after overhearing one of the stars in Houston's medical crown say 'that's just the way the good Lord made them.' To add insult to injury, there are precious few drug studies on females, though women are more likely to experience drug side effects than men. They also die faster and are sicker from AIDS, but no one knows why, which suggests to me that we don't know much about the female endocrine system."

Tony leaned closer to Mari and whispered, "She may be

221

committing overkill on poor Charles, but at least you found out she's a source before you finished your research, instead of after. I'll bet she can give you a journal reference for every point she just made."

"Why don't you go to medical school, Rachel?" Charles asked. "Help change the balance of power." Now that he thought about it, he wondered how come she hadn't already. "The profession needs brains like yours, people who are analytical enough to be good at diagnosis, which is three quarters of the battle."

"Because the work is so damned demanding," Rachel answered without hesitation and only a brief glance at Tony. "And I want some other things, too. Personal things, like a family. I'm not sure I could manage both. Anyway, I'm more interested in research."

"Okay, I admit I didn't know any of what you just said, so I suppose a lot of other people wouldn't, either, including women, which is why you want to do the series, right, Mari?" Charles got up to go get the bottle of wine from the refrigerator, then came back and topped up all their glasses. "But if you really want to produce documentaries full-time, why don't you just go ahead and do it now?"

"Because I couldn't make a living at it, at least not yet. Maybe if I could sell this series, it would help build my reputation at the national level, so I'd have a better chance." How simple and easy he made it sound. Was he really that naive?

"Then if this pilot, the first program, is so important, why not take leave from KPOC for a couple of weeks, or as long as it takes to make sure you do get it done in time?"

"I'm not even sure whether I should go ahead at all, because if I did get PBS funding, I'd *have* to ask for leave, which is playing right into Jack's hands, not to mention Tracy's. I think he's looking for some reason, an opportunity, to dump me, get rid of me once and for all." Her blunt answer came as a revelation to both Rachel and Charles, who decided that she'd just revealed the real reason behind what didn't happen in bed last night. But differing opinions and stupid mistakes didn't add up to a conspiracy against her, so surely she was overreacting.

"Where the hell did you get that idea—just because Tracy

is doing the AIDS Watch? I thought you liked the idea, think it's important and ought to be part of the regular newscast." He sounded as if he thought she was being emotional, or something, which sort of irritated Mari, though she tried not to show it.

"Yes, I do. It's, oh, lots of things, I guess. How the AIDS update was presented, asking me what I thought even though the decision obviously had already been made before I walked into Jack's office. Roping me into digging ditches for Tracy—asking me to script her stories, for God's sake—which I suspect was her idea, not Jack's. Or maybe Lou's. A subtle way of letting everyone in the news division know that her position on the totem pole is higher than mine, that I'm there to serve her. And if I mess up, well, all the better, right? Especially after she's shown everyone that she can handle the medical stories as well, or better, than I do. I don't for one minute believe that trumped-up story about the mix-up on the contraceptive sponge story last night. Uh-uh." She moved her head back and forth to reject the idea even more emphatically. "Someone snuck that story into Tracy's lineup at the last moment, maybe even after she went on the air, so neither Podge nor Ted would discover it in time to warn me. I think it was planned to make me look bad, amateurish, force me to have to ad lib on camera to cover the gaping hole that opened up in my script, show me groping for pad copy."

She sat back, suddenly aware that the air of festivity they'd started out on had evaporated. "Oh hell and damnation, this wasn't what I wanted to even think about tonight, let alone talk about. Can we just turn the clock back, pretend the last five minutes never happened? Please? Anyway, I'm probably just being paranoid."

"Uh-uh, Mari, you're not paranoid," Tony muttered quietly, staring at his empty plate.

That was enough to clinch it for Charles. "What a bunch of assholes!" he exclaimed, more than a little indignant now. "The whole damn bunch ought to be walking on eggshells in fear that you'll just up and leave, go somewhere else."

"I think you were smart to let her have the damned AIDS Watch, Mari," Rachel chimed in.

"*Let* her!" The word exploded from Mari's mouth like a cough. "I didn't have any choice."

"That one, she rips at whatever is in her way," Tony agreed. "A barracuda." Rachel recognized the slightly stilted way he was speaking English, and knew he was angry.

"Listen," she said, turning back to Mari, "you need to remember that the messenger catches the blame for unpleasant messages, and AIDS is certainly that. I doubt viewers are going to like constantly being reminded that the whole damn world is homosexual." Tony looked at her, dumbfounded. "If you don't think so, just take a look at the Vatican, and Wall Street, and football, and fashion designers, and—"

"Enough!" Tony decided, clamping a hand over her mouth. "We get the message! But she may be more right than she knows, Mari. Give the three of them a chance to have at each other, Jack and Tracy and Lou." He grinned suddenly, relishing the thought. "Tracy doesn't give a damn who she has to trample to get to the top, or whose bed she has to climb into along the way. She's got poor old Lou so wound up he can't chase his tail fast enough, getting her territory all staked out, pulling dirty tricks if he has to, like last night. But when he wakes up and discovers she's pillow-talking Jack, too, the shit's really going to hit the fan! Lou's a lot older than her, and maybe he should be grateful for whatever she's willing to put out for him." Mari saw Rachel start, as if she'd just been slapped. "But hell," Tony added, "you'd think even he could see there's more than ego massaging going on between her and Jack!"

Mari had to suppress the urge to kick Tony under the table. Rachel stared down at her plate, refusing to look at anyone, and Mari experienced a kind of queasiness in the pit of her stomach, sensing almost instinctively that Rachel had been deeply hurt by his unthinking remark. "Guess it's true about love being blind, huh?" Tony finished, apparently oblivious to Rachel, who immediately got up from the table, then turned toward Tony with a smile that was a shade too bright as she picked up Mari's plate and then her own.

"Not love, my little spic. It's arrogance that makes men blind! Lou sounds like the kind of fool who thinks a woman loves him just because he loves her." She walked toward the kitchen with the dishes. "Guess it's time for your dessert, huh?" she asked breezily over her shoulder, avoiding Tony's eyes. "Antonio makes the best flan in town, Charles. Learned how to carmelize the sugar from his *mamacita.*"

Tony tried to smile, to carry off the derogatory "little spic" as the joke he thought she undoubtedly intended it to be, without success. He probably didn't much like her other remark, either, Mari thought, about the fool who thinks a woman loves him just because he loves her. The sick feeling in her stomach only got worse, and by the end of the evening Tony had retreated into full-blown silence, though his eyes rarely left Rachel's face, no matter what she and Charles and Mari talked about.

Charles headed west on San Felipe, along the edge of River Oaks. They'd slept late, showered together, and then fixed breakfast, also together, then lazed away another hour on the Sunday paper. It was nearing two o'clock when he'd jumped up all of a sudden and announced, "Time to get dressed, Mari honey! I'm taking you out for lunch, brunch, whatever you want to call it. Got someone I want you to meet."

"Who?"

"You'll find out soon enough."

He wouldn't tell her where they were going, either. When she asked what she should wear, his answer had been, "Anything. Except maybe not jeans." So she put on a sleeveless cotton dress, partly because it was opaque enough, thanks to the woven-in brocade pattern, not to require a slip. The temperature was already nearing ninety, and just thinking about the hot summer ahead brought a little shiver of distaste. "Want me to turn down the air-conditioning?" Charles asked.

"No. I was just thinking about how utterly insane it is for women to encase their bodies in plastic—nylon hose—in this heat. Some women's liberation, huh? How come Texas women—men, too, for that matter—have never been style innovators? Instead they ape the New York fashion scene, or Paris, or else get themselves up in country-western costumes, with lots of petticoats and boots, which are hot as Hades. Even the big guys downtown wear western-style suits and boots to the office when it's ninety-eight degrees out and they're tromping over the hot pavement, not clumps of buffalo grass and cow cakes out on the ranch. By the way, C.B., how come I've never seen you in boots?"

Charles shrugged but grinned, enjoying the unexpected twists and turns her mind sometimes took. "I used to wear 'em, when I was a kid."

He slowed just short of Loop 610, turned right onto a heavily wooded street that looked more like park land than a residential area, and then a half block farther along slowed even more, to ease into the curving driveway of the Remington Hotel. Mari took one look at the two canopied entrances, where the name was written in dark green script on creamy canvas, and felt a sudden rush of dismay. She'd been in the Remington only once, for an interview, but once was enough. The whole place exuded an atmosphere of old-world class consciousness that was almost oppressive, at least to her. And she found it hard to fit Charles Merrill into such a setting, though it certainly wouldn't be the first time she'd made an error in judgment about a man. Charles drove past the big, spreading live oak, surrounded by a well-manicured bed filled with green and white caladiums, to the valet-parking entrance.

"I just wish to hell you'd told me, C.B., so I could have dressed more—"

"You look fine. Maybe too good for 'em," he assured her, just as a uniformed attendant opened her door. She stepped out, noting the blue ageratums edging still another manicured flower bed, and behind them more caladiums, this time with pink and green-veined leaves. Charles took her arm and guided her to the door, which another uniformed attendant was holding open.

Inside, they ran smack into a formal arrangement of huge flowers—bromeliads, Mari guessed—set exactly in the middle of a dark walnut table placed exactly in the center of the small entry. Everything in sight was mauve or pink, from the thick plush carpet to the overstuffed furniture. But there was no sign of the usual hotel desk. The silence felt heavy, and Mari had to fight the urge to whisper as Charles led her down a narrow corridor lined with walnut wainscoting, to the open double doors of what looked to be a long, narrow sun room. At least it was different from the bar, which she remembered as very much a man's room—with floor-to-ceiling, dark wood paneling, orangy sconce lights, dueling pistols and livestock lithographs, not to mention the life-size brown leather bull dominating the room from his three-foot-high pedestal. What she remembered most, though, perhaps because she'd gone there to interview a male gynecologist, was the bull's massive testicles. They were in her line of vision the whole time she was talking to the doctor, hanging just below his left ear like a huge dangling earring. By contrast, this room was all light beige, and a wall of windows looked out on water pouring over a low concrete embankment. Another huge flower arrangement centered a table in the middle of the room, this one surrounded by pastries on doilied pedestal plates. A female harpist dressed in a long black skirt sat just to the left of the entrance, playing the theme song from the PBS production of Evelyn Waugh's *Brideshead Revisited.* From the doorway Mari was able to see only one end of the buffet, but it was the steam rising from a big brass urn and the array of cups surrounding it that gave away what was going on here—it was "high tea" time at the Remington.

A middle-aged maître d' accepted Charles's name with a quiet nod, then led them past the spiky flower arrangement and steaming pot, toward a table near the end of the long room where a woman sat alone. She looked to be about forty-five, Mari thought, and had a "California tan" that was notable even in Texas. Apparently the sun had also streaked her dark blond hair, which was swept back from her face in a stylish cut, stopping just short of her shoulders. She glanced up as they walked toward her, smiled in recognition and then rose to accept Charles's quick hug. She was slim and tall, and was wearing a Chanel-style, dove-gray linen suit that matched her eyes. A huge diamond twinkled on her right hand, matching the smaller ones edging her gold watch, and a choker of several twisted strands of pink coral beads was fastened in front with a big matching stone that was banded in gold and carved like a cameo. Charles turned toward Mari and draped an arm around her shoulders to draw her close in a gesture that said a great deal more than his words.

"Mari, this is my mother, Amy Gramling."

Mari stared, her thoughts stumbling over each other, then recovered enough to say hello and put out her hand. Her upper lip beaded with moisture and she felt hot and unkempt all of a sudden, and intensely aware of her bare legs and toes as she tried to put together the fact that this stylish, youthful-looking woman was not only Charles's mother, but also a "household" name in Houston, where Amy Merrill Gramling and Associates real estate signs were scattered all across the landscape, like litter. The local real estate market might be in a slump right now, but Mari doubted that Charles's mother would need to worry even if she never sold another piece of property for the rest of her life. Hardly a week went by that Amy Gramling's name and picture didn't appear in the newspapers, attending a benefit for the symphony or the art museum, or some exclusive dinner party.

"Mother's in the real estate business," Charles said, coming to Mari's rescue. "And you must've caught Mari on television, Mother. 'Health News with Mari McNichols,' on Channel Five. Fearless girl reporter," he teased, giving Mari's shoulder an affectionate squeeze. "She's the one who did that program on artificial hearts I told you about."

"Yes, I remember you mentioning it, but I don't watch television very much, I'm afraid. Don't have time." Amy smiled apologetically. "But now that I've met you, Mari, I'll have to make a special point of it, won't I?"

Mari simply smiled in response to the rhetorical question, but at least now she knew it had been Amy's idea to meet at the Remington, not Charles's. Still, her whole conception of Charles, of who he was and what he was really like as a person, not a scientist, began to subtly change as she tried to imagine how very different his childhood must have been from hers, with a successful businesswoman for a mother. This brought home the realization that she'd been fantasizing about Charles all this time, making him into who she wanted to believe he was. He'd mentioned his stepfather that day they'd gone swimming, but never a word about his mother or that she lived in Houston, which Mari found curious.

"Mari's on every Monday, Wednesday, and Friday, at

about six-fifteen," Charles continued. "And she's also doing a program on the flamenco that's due to air sometime next month, filmed in Spain, so watch for that, too. In fact, she's just back from there, which is where we ran into each other again. Literally." He gave Mari an intimate smile, sharing the joke only with her.

As soon as the waiter had taken their order, Charles changed the subject, taking the spotlight off Mari so she'd feel more at ease.

"I hear the market is beginning to improve at last, Mother. How come? Not much else in Houston is, from what I hear."

"Because we finally managed to get all new construction stopped," Amy replied. "I've even rehired some of my old sales force, people I had to lay off three years ago." She launched into a detailed description of what kind and how much sales were up in her business.

There was a family resemblance, Mari thought as she watched and listened to them talk, but not much. Mostly it was in the skin tone and deepset dark eyes, and, of course, the naturally curly hair. Now that she was closer, Mari could see that Amy's hair had been lightened and streaked artificially, as a lot of older women were doing to help camouflage the gray. It was natural-looking and very flattering, and much more youthful than the way Janet usually wore hers. Amy Gramling had to be at least ten years older than she looked, since Charles was thirty-eight, because even if she'd married young and had him right away, she'd have to be around fifty-six or -seven. What really impressed Mari, though, was the camaraderie between Charles and his mother, a sort of easy give and take. No crackling electricity charged the air, nor was there a hint of heightened color in either of their faces. As she listened to Amy explain what she thought was going to happen to interest rates and why, she also was aware that there were no dusty clichés or homey homilies spilling from Amy's lips. And then it hit her that Charles's mother belonged to an entirely different generation than hers.

A sudden shrill, high-frequency noise broke the hushed silence, and Mari grabbed guiltily for her purse, to get her beeper turned off as fast as possible. "Sorry about that. The station is trying to reach me," Mari explained quickly, in response to the identical raised eyebrows she saw across the table. Rising from her chair she could feel every eye in the room focused on the middle of her back. "Do you know where I can find a phone, Charles?"

He pushed back his chair and mumbled, "Excuse us a minute, Mother," as he grabbed Mari's hand and hurried her out of the tea room, then down the carpeted corridor the way they'd come, toward the restaurant and bar. Mari punched in the KPOC number and waited.

"It's Mari," she said as soon as she heard Sandy's voice. "What's up?"

"Just a sec, let me get Jack," Sandy answered quickly, leaving her waiting again. Charles waited, too, not saying a word.

"Mari!" Jack's voice exploded in her ear. "Get your ass down here as fast as you can. Just came in on the network feed. A couple of minutes ago. Basque terrorists. Bombed a hotel in Paris. Sixteen people killed. Nine Americans. Five from Houston." The words came in staccato bursts, as if he'd been running and was out of breath. "We're going to air a couple of the bites you picked up in Spain, at six. Lead story. Tony's already on the road. Get moving. Now!" There was a loud click and she turned away from the phone, glancing first at her watch, then at Charles.

"I've got to go, right now. Will you make my apologies to your mother, Charles, while I call a cab?" Her mind was already moving ahead. It was nearly five. Ten minutes to get a cab, fifteen to the station, if they didn't run into any stack-ups on the freeway, which meant she'd have nearly forty-five minutes before air time. Enough, but just barely.

"I'll take you," Charles snapped back. "What's up?"

"But your mother—"

He cut her off. "I'll tell her we're leaving while you go ask the valet to get my car. Be right back. You can fill me in on the way."

Charles and the car came at the same time. "Basque terrorists bombed a hotel in Paris," she explained as he gunned the BMW out of the Remington driveway. "Killed several Americans, some of them from Houston. So Jack's going to use some of our stuff. Don't know what yet.

230

Probably depends on what and how much is coming in on the network feed. Tony's on his way in, too."

"Why Paris, d'you know?" he asked, glancing in the rearview mirror before changing lanes to exit Loop 610 and get onto the Southwest Freeway. There was always a slow-down at this exchange, but on Sundays there were fewer cars than usual, so it didn't take him long to make the switch.

"They've done it before, in retaliation for France deporting Basque refugees. But usually they go after French businesses in Spain, so I don't know. Jack didn't say." She sounded sort of preoccupied, so he was surprised when she turned the conversation to his mother.

"Your mother's a beautiful woman, Charles."

"Yeah, I suppose so." He breathed the words, almost like a sigh.

"And so easy to be around."

This time he simply nodded, careful to keep his face neutral because he was curious as to what she might say next. When she didn't, he added, "Especially since she finally gave up trying to get me to go into the business with her."

"You've got to be joking! I doubt you could sell a doughnut to a starving man." She laughed the words, because just the idea of Charles Merrill wasting his very special talent selling real estate was too preposterous to take seriously.

"Maybe," he conceded with a little smile as he pulled off the freeway. "But she's sure a natural, can sell anything to anybody. I remember when I was a kid, how she started out clerking at Sears, then tramped door to door with cosmetics. Had to. My father never sent us a dime after he left." Mari could hear the admiration, and the pride, in his voice. "After she married Roy Gramling, things got a little better. She didn't have to worry whether she'd be able to pay the bills at the end of the month, which was when she discovered her real forte—selling, trading, and leasing real estate. After that nothing could stop her."

"Roy's the one who taught you to swim?"

"Yeah. They didn't stay married but a few years. I liked him. He was kind of, oh, unusual, I suppose you'd say, maybe a little old fashioned, but—well, I guess it just didn't work out for them, maybe because he was younger than her, who knows."

She thought it more likely that Amy's husband couldn't stand the competition, having a successful businesswoman for a wife, one who probably made more than he did. But she sensed that Charles was finding it difficult to express his personal feelings about either his mother or his stepfather, so she didn't ask any questions.

"But she never has been able to understand why I work on what I do, or why I wanted to stay on and go to graduate school, especially since all I could look forward to afterward was a lousy professor's salary, when I could have come back to Houston and gone into the business with her."

"God, what a terrible waste that would have been!" she responded, without even thinking, then realized how it must sound to him—as if she were casting aspersions on the way his mother made her living—and wished she could call the words back.

But before she could say anything, Charles asked, "You think so, huh?" and he was grinning broadly, sounding pleased beyond all reason.

"I'm sure your mother must be proud of what you do, not to mention how well you do it," she mumbled as he slowed and turned right.

Halfway down the block he pulled into the KPOC parking lot and stopped. "Whatever. Doesn't really matter, one way or the other. Want me to wait? I know you don't need me in there, getting in the way. Got any idea how long you'll be? I can come back later, take you home, but I'm due to catch a flight to Albuquerque about nine."

Mari already had the door open and was starting to get out. "Tonight?" He nodded, and she began fumbling in her purse. "Here." She handed him a key. "Tony will take me home, let me in with his key. I wish you could stay to watch the broadcast, but"—she glanced at her watch—"aren't you cutting it awfully close?" She assumed he was flying out of Austin, and knew it would take him close to three hours to get there.

"Nope. I'm leaving out of Houston Intercontinental. And I have no intention of missing the broadcast, so I'm going back to your place to get my stuff and watch. Have to give a talk in Albuquerque at nine tomorrow morning. If it wasn't kind of late to give notice, I'd cancel." He grinned.

She put one foot down on the heat-softened tarmac, then leaned back in to give him a quick kiss. "See you when you get back then, right, C.B.? Whenever."

He had to fight the urge to hold onto her and to smile as she got out of the car. "Call me at the apartment if you get a minute. I won't be leaving before eight." She nodded quickly, then walked away.

Charles sat in the car watching her walk toward the door, sure that her mind had already left him behind. But she surprised him by turning to throw him a smile and an enthusiastic wave just before she disappeared, reminding him again of that day on the beach, in Torremolinos.

CHAPTER

12

⌒⌣⌒

Mari's portable Sony sat on the far end of the low bookcase that ran the entire length of one wall of the living room, angled so it could be seen from the kitchen and dining area as well as in the living room and halfway facing the wooden puppet standing at the opposite end. Charles tried to remember the puppet's name while he waited for the commercials to end and the newscast to begin. Ardjuna, or Arjuna, or something like that, he thought. The puppet's face was painted white, Mari had told him, because he was one of the "good guys" in a centuries-old morality play still being performed today, in Java. He wore a long batik cotton skirt and a smooth black headdress that swept up into an open loop in back above a gracefully curving neck. And an enigmatic sort of half smile—which made Charles think of Mari's wistful, "How did we ever get started thinking we had to be one or the other, male *or* female? That one was mutually exclusive of the other when it comes to thoughts and feelings? Just to look at Arjuna reminds me that we don't have to be." She'd turned to him with an impish grin. "And also that mammal embryos develop structurally in the beginning as female, which means that males are a modification of the female, not the other way around, as *some* would have us believe."

"Good evening." Tracy's curt, sober-faced greeting claimed Charles's full attention. "Five Houstonians are among the ten Americans killed today when a terrorist bomb destroyed part of the Hotel Angleterre in Paris, France, killing seventeen people and wounding thirteen others." She continued voice-over as at-the-scene shots appeared on the screen, of the still-smoking building and the fire-fighting equipment in the streets surrounding it, identifying by name the Houston residents who had died in the bombing. "Another nine people are still missing, though it is not known for certain at this time whether all of the missing were actually in the hotel when the bomb exploded at around eleven P.M., Paris time." Pictures of injured survivors flashed on the screen, being carried from the rubble by rescue workers, to waiting ambulances. "The French news agency Agence France Press is reporting that the Basque separatist organization ETA has claimed responsibility for the bombing, in retaliation for the deportation by France of more than fifty Basque refugees, who the terrorists say have been imprisoned somewhere in Spain. Here to tell us more about that is Channel Five's Mari McNichols, who is just back from Spain, where she talked to leaders of both the ETA and the Basque territorial government. The voice you will hear translating is Channel Five cameraman Tony Zuniga."

Charles could only wonder at how Mari could possibly explain the separatist movement, which had a history reaching back into the Middle Ages, in sixty seconds or less. How frustrating it must be, knowing, before she even began, that it simply couldn't be done! No wonder she wanted to switch to documentaries, instead of this piecemeal, halfway kind of reporting.

"Strange as it may seem at a time when modern technology has helped reveal so much more than we've ever known before about many ancient civilizations, the origins of the Basque people and their language is still lost somewhere in the mists of prehistory," Mari began. "What we do know, though, is that they have a unique language and cultural heritage. And all the two million Spanish Basques are trying to do today is find some way to preserve that heritage. It is about how to do that that they disagree."

Charles shook his head in admiration and smiled, realizing that she'd laid the groundwork for viewers to at least begin to understand what had happened in Paris and why, with just those few words. The camera panned a long view of glistening ocean, taken from a high corniche road overlooking the curving coastline.

"The Basque provinces border the Pyrenees Mountains and the Bay of Biscay, or La Costa Vasca in Spanish, which in turn is a corruption of the Basque word Vizcaya." The camera swung inland then, revealing a marquetry of contrasting green fields, rolling hills, and dark pine woods. "Just a few miles inland from this coast is Guernica, a small town whose name was branded into our memories forever by German warplanes"—she paused—"and a Spanish painter named Picasso." A chaotic landscape of screaming heads and dismembered limbs floating in disarray against a gray void suddenly exploded onto the screen, mimicking the destruction and horror Picasso's painting was intended to convey. "Guernica was devastated, and more than two thousand residents killed, many of them in the open marketplace in the center of town, because they refused to recognize the fascist military dictatorship of General Franco. And for forty years afterward the Basques were forbidden by law to even speak their own language, let alone teach it in their schools. Juan Luis Zuzaeta, a survivor of the aerial attack, today is the mayor of Guernica."

"To prevent what happened in Guernica from happening again, we must put an end to the arms race." Charles recognized Tony's voice, translating the words spoken by the man on the screen. "But true peace in the world can come only when all men have the right of self-determination." The mayor was replaced by pictures of the rebuilt town.

"Eight years ago," Mari continued voice-over, "the Basques were granted home rule, which means they now can elect a territorial parliament, have the power to tax, and limited control of police and schools. José Antonio Ardanza is the president of the territorial government."

"Franco repressed and punished us because we were on the wrong side of the war. But now, since 1980, we can teach Euskara in the schools again, and we try to restore to our children their lost history. Still, there are some among us who believe the only way to restore and to keep our identity is to become a separate nation."

"An organization called ETA—the initials stand for Basque Homeland and Freedom in the Basque language," Mari continued, "has carried on the war for independence for eighteen years, and is responsible for six hundred violent deaths during that time. The Herri Batasuna party, believed to be the political arm of the ETA, now holds thirteen seats in the regional parliament. Juan Carlos Yoldi is the party's candidate for the presidency of the territorial government. He's also under indictment for the 1984 bombing of three French automobile dealerships."

The face of a much younger man appeared on the screen. "We are demanding amnesty for all persons convicted of these so-called terrorist acts before we will talk with the government in Madrid. Because we fight for our freedom," Yoldi claimed in Tony's voice. "It is only Madrid who paints us as villains. We are no different from your colonists, two hundred years ago. We only do what we must to secure our independence."

Mari appeared on camera again, but this time back in the studio for the wrap. "To the majority of Basques today, the ETA represents a steadily dwindling lunatic fringe rather than a practical means for achieving regional autonomy. For most, the war to preserve their language and culture is being fought on a quieter front—in the schools."

Tracy came back on then, and almost immediately bridged to a commercial break. Charles glanced at his watch. Jack had given Mari all of a minute and a half! He stood up and went into the kitchen, got a can of beer out of the refrigerator, popped it open and stood looking through the pass-through for a couple of minutes. Sunday was a thin news day, and it showed, as the newscast limped from one inconsequential local story to another. When the weather and sports came on, Charles headed for the bedroom, leaving the set on, to take a shower and begin collecting his things together.

Thirty minutes later, his overnighter and briefcase stacked near the door, Charles was pacing from one end of the living room to the other. He kept the TV on, in case there were any news updates on the Paris story, but listened with only half an ear. By the time he'd finished his second beer, he couldn't even imagine what could be keeping Mari from at least calling, so he wandered into her study, where the phone was. Maybe he should try calling her, just to see if he could find out anything. Instead he stood looking out the window, at what Mari called "the river walk," a meandering man-made stream edged with small cypress trees, blue iris, and spikes of green that would form cattails later on, in the fall. Earlier in the day he'd seen oversize goldfish moving lazily with the current, a few of them hovering among the honeycomb river rocks stacked to form an island, which probably hid the pumps used to keep the water moving. Why was she living in an apartment, and on the second floor at that, rather than a house where she could have the trees, grass, and garden she craved so much? He grinned, trying to imagine how she was going to respond to his place in Austin, which he was counting on to breach the last of her defenses.

He glanced around at the room, really seeing it for the first time—the white Formica-wrapped slab resting on two wooden horses, and the bright blue flex-arm lamp that also could be pulled over to the IBM computer and laser printer, which sat next to each other on a slightly lower table jutting out at a right angle to the desk, and the floor-to-ceiling shelves framing it left and right. Two stoneware mugs sat within easy reach, one filled with a miscellany of pens and pencils, the other with a pair of orange-handled Fiskar scissors, a couple of highlighters, a short plastic ruler, and one pen. Curious, he reached for it, only to discover it had a transparent barrel that showed front and back views of a man wearing only the briefest of briefs, which disappeared when Charles depressed the button at the top, revealing all his "assets."

He grinned, pulled his wallet out of his pocket and extracted a slip of paper, then sat down at the desk to punch in a phone number and let his eyes continue to roam while he waited for Rachel to answer. A newspaper headline taped to the end of one shelf unit said SOMETHING WENT WRONG IN JET CRASH, EXPERT SAYS. He scanned the titles of a half-dozen cassettes stacked right next to the phone—Tropical

Rain Forest, Ocean Surf, Mountain Stream, Thunderstorm. What the hell did she do with those?

"Hello," Rachel answered.

"Hi. You hear anything from Tony yet?" he asked, then realized he hadn't even identified himself. "Sorry, this is Charles."

"I know. No, I haven't. Where are you? Did you catch the broadcast?"

"Yeah. Not bad, huh, considering they had only a minute and a half. I'm at Mari's. I dropped her at the station about five-fifteen. She said Tony would bring her home. I have to leave to catch a plane in about twenty minutes, but guess I can't help worrying a little after the way that bastard lit into her Friday, plus what she said last night. And, well—"

"Hold on a minute, Charles, I've got another call."

"Call me back," he said quickly, then sat there, poised on the edge of the chair while his eyes roamed the titles lined up on Mari's shelves. One was packed two deep with paperback novels—*Hungry As the Sea, False Witness, Domina, Visions of the Damned, Flair, The Old Flame, A Catskill Eagle, The Hunt for Red October, Dance of the Tiger, The Mirror,* and a whole bunch more. He wasn't much of a fiction reader and didn't recognize any of them. Another shelf held more kinds of dictionaries than he knew existed, including one called *Newspeak,* a dictionary of jargon, and a thin little volume of British English/American English. He pulled *The Devil's Dictionary* off the shelf, out of curiosity and just to kill time, and it fell open to "corporation," which was defined as "an ingenious device for obtaining individual profit without individual responsibility." There were a dozen or more cookbooks, some of them with little pieces of paper sticking out the top, several medical textbooks, a *Physician's Desk Reference* and a couple of handbooks. *Ladies Home Erotica* was a title that caught his eye, but he was disappointed when he pulled it out and discovered it didn't contain any pictures. The "essays" were written by women, and he started to read a short one called "Ode to the Penis": ". . . Since we don't have anything as obvious and as embarrassingly untrustworthy in our lovemaking paraphernalia, we share your concern for its ups and downs, so much so that we have obliterated our own needs for gratification." Not really intended to be racy, it was setting the stage for the others, all of them written by members of the Kensington Ladies Erotica Society. "We are not trying to diminish your appendage, but we want to enlarge upon those parts of you that have been unjustly ignored. These are the parts that are essential to our pleasure: your hair, your eyes, your lips, your *hands.*"

The last word fairly leaped out at him, reminding him of what Mari had said—"your wonderful hands"—and the more he thought about it, the more he wondered what she'd really meant. Maybe he ought to read some of this . . . The shrill sound of the phone startled him and he grabbed for the receiver. "Hello."

"That was Tony. He said he tried to call you but the line was busy. Doesn't know when they'll be able to get away. Mari's been on the phone on and off for the past hour, to New York. She's talking with Sam Downey, the evening news anchor, right now. The network's planning to run some of their stuff, both in the morning and tomorrow evening. Isn't that wonderful?"

"Yeah. Maybe they'll give them more time than old Jack did."

"Maybe," she agreed, laughing a little. "But I wouldn't count on it. Mari wanted you to know, so you could watch if you get a chance, because she probably won't get a chance to call before you leave, so . . ." Rachel let her words trail off. "Where are you off to?"

"Albuquerque." He told her about the meeting at the University of New Mexico Medical School, where he was due to give a talk in the morning. "Think I'll give Mari's mother a call, maybe cut away from the meeting early and go on up to Denver tomorrow afternoon, if I can get in before network news time. Don't want to miss that."

"I was just thinking that someone ought to tell Jan, so she'd know to watch. But if you're going to—"

"I forgot. You stayed with her in Torremolinos, didn't you, while Tony and Mari went on that fishing trip we just watched? They—does the two of them together ever bother you?" It wasn't Charles's habit to ask personal questions of anybody, let alone a woman he hardly knew, but for some reason he thought she'd understand what he was getting at.

"Yes and no, or maybe just not the way I think you mean. I guess I can't help envying the almost intuitive understanding between them, as if they're somehow able to inhabit each other's minds. Together they add up to a bigger whole than simply the sum of two halves, and some of that spills over, outside of their work. Maybe it's just the difference between being friends and lovers, I don't know. Wish I did."

"Yeah, me too," he sighed. "Well, guess I'd better get going, try to forget all the excitement and see if I can figure out what to say tomorrow. Hoped to find a little time this afternoon to work on it, but after she got that call, everything just sort of came apart. Maybe on the plane, or—what the hell, I guess I can try winging it."

"Listen, 'Doctor' Merrill, when it comes to talking about your research, you wouldn't have a bit of trouble winging it all day if you had to. And you'd still be way out ahead of the rest of the field, so don't expect tea and sympathy from me." She'd called his bluff, and they both knew it. "But be careful driving out to the airport, huh?"

"Yes, Mother," he chided, getting back at her in kind. They both laughed. "See you soon."

He picked up Mari's *Ladies Home Erotica,* scribbled a quick note using the ballpoint pen with the nude man in it—"Borrowed one of your books. See you Tuesday night" —and left the pen on top of the note as a clue to which book he'd taken, switched off the light and headed for the front door.

"Scholars believe the ancestral language of the Basques may have been introduced into the region by immigrants from Asia Minor at the beginning of the Bronze Age, four thousand years ago," Mari was saying. "All they know for sure, though, is that Euskara is a continuation of the language of the Acquitani and the Vascones who lived here during the time of Julius Caesar." As the taped segment moved along, Charles recognized the mayor of Guernica, but now he learned that the spreading oak where she'd spoken with him was the Tree of Guernica, where the Lords of Biscay had come to swear to uphold the rights and privileges of the people in the Middle Ages. "Though not the original, this tree has for centuries been a symbol of liberty to every Basque." As the taped segment continued, Charles also discovered what and just how much Mari and Tony had edited out for the KPOC broadcast the previous night.

"Once the whole world knew us as a separate and free people," President Ardanza was saying in Tony's voice. "Until the nineteenth century, when the French took over and choked us. Then in 1936, just as we were about to recapture our autonomy, civil war broke out. You know"—Ardanza leaned close to Mari, as if to share a confidence—"it took more than German tanks and planes to defeat us. As in the time of the Inquisition, the Nationalist Movement had the support of the Church and masqueraded as a holy crusade."

When the tape came to an end, Charles was surprised to hear Sam Downey, the network anchor, bridge back to Mari with a question. "Does anyone know how many Basques actually support the ETA?"

"No, because membership or allegiance to the ETA is illegal," Mari replied, live from Houston. God, but she looked good, Charles thought, wishing like hell she wasn't a thousand miles away. "But just a few months ago about twenty thousand people attended a rally in Bilbao to demand independence for the region. The rally was organized by the Herri Batasuna party, which as I said is thought to be the political arm of the ETA."

"The perception in Washington seems to be that the government in Madrid has been fairly ineffectual in dealing with the terrorists. Do you think that's likely to change as a result of this latest incident?"

"Until recently, Sam," Mari responded, "the ETA has targeted police and military personnel, or French-owned businesses, in Madrid and the Basque provinces. There've been a number of car bombings in Bilbao, San Sebastian, and Vitorio, for instance. But now the ETA seems to be focusing on Barcelona, which as you know is to be the site of the 1992 Olympic Games. And they've hit innocent civilians. Fifteen people, three of them children, were killed recently in the parking garage of a department store in Barcelona. So even before this bombing in Paris, which I suspect will bring a good deal of pressure on Madrid from the French, the government had already announced that it was cracking down, and would no longer show any lenience at all toward the Basque guerrillas. Unfortunately, Spain has an even more serious problem to deal with in its twenty-one-percent unemployment rate, which has left a million young people unable to find jobs. And they've begun protesting in the streets of Madrid."

"Thank you, Mari McNichols, in Houston," Sam Downey said, wrapping up the story, then turned to another camera and bridged to a commercial break.

"Well, that's it, I guess," Charles said, grinning at Janet. "What do you think of your girl now?"

"Well, it may be news to you that she's better than a lot of those people at the network, Charles, but not to me! I have to confess I don't understand how she does it, though. So little time and so many different places and people, but in the end it all fits together, makes sense. Like ballet dancing, I suspect it's not as easy as she makes it look."

"You ever tell her that, Jan?" Charles asked, staring at the distant scene, trying to locate the Flatirons above Boulder, twenty or more miles away. They were sitting out on Janet's glassed-in sun porch, at the back of the house, though the sun had already disappeared behind the mountains. When she didn't respond, he added, "That's Mari's real talent, isn't it? Putting all the pieces together so the rest of us can understand, making sense out of the chaos?"

"Yes, maybe so," Janet agreed. "I never thought of it quite like that before. Marilyn was always wanting to try something new when she was a child. Seemed to thrive on it, in fact. And she could handle almost anything she tried, at least well enough to get by, which I don't mind telling you wasn't exactly easy for Jackie, who was quite the opposite." Her smile was wistful. "Mari liked to discover everything on her own, loved the adventure and challenge of it, I suppose. Maybe that's why she had such a hard time deciding what to study in college."

"She tell you she wants to produce documentaries full-time, is thinking about leaving KPOC?"

"No, but I'm not surprised. She's awfully good, isn't she? Really, I mean, not just because she's my daughter!"

Her not-so-innocent smile made him laugh. He jumped up from his chair and leaned down to help Jan to her feet, in the process pulling her into his arms for a quick hug. "Don't ask me. I'm in the same boat, Jan! You can brag on your little girl or tell me stories about her all night long if you want to. But not until we get our order in at the New York Connection."

"No, I'd rather hear about your research, Charles, what you've been doing since we talked in Spain. And how the trials are going on your instrument. It's so important to get that out, so people can start using it. Because that's when we'll begin to learn even more, isn't it, about what's happening in the blood under all kinds of different disease conditions?"

"You mean you actually expect me to go back on at ten?" Tracy shrieked. "Let that bitch walk all over me again? Well, screw you, Jacko! You can take this two-bit news operation of yours and shove it—" Tracy's outburst stopped Mari and Tony dead in their tracks as they headed for the front door, on their way for a hamburger before the ten o'clock broadcast. And if they could hear every word, loud and clear, so could everyone else not inside one of the soundproofed studios. "Why the hell did I ever let you talk me into coming?"

"Aw, come on now, Trace, cool down. We can work this out." Jack's words were meant to cajole, and sounded slightly muffled, probably because he was trying to mollify Tracy physically, Mari thought, by putting his arms around her. Jack was a man who believed sex was the answer to everything if a female was involved.

"How?" Tracy demanded. "You promised me the big stories, the ones likely to get national attention. Instead, Little Miss Mousy ends up with the network exposure, not me, and you expect me to stand there and hand it to her on a silver platter! Besides that, you let her have the best cameraman in town. Even send him way the hell to Spain when she crooks her little finger!" Her voice seemed to be getting louder, as if she and Jack were coming down the hall.

Tony raised his eyebrows at Mari and grinned. "Little Miss Mousy? We better get the hell out of here. She sets eyes on you and me while she's throwin' that temper tantrum and she'll go straight into convulsions." He held the door open for Mari. "Best cameraman in town! Hear that?"

"Yeah, is that how come your head looks like a balloon? And when are you going to get rid of this rolling time bomb, by the way?" Mari asked as she pulled at her skirt to step up into his Blazer. "Don't you know these things turn over if someone even tosses a halfway nasty look their way? I'm surprised Rachel's willing to ride with you. Thought she had better sense."

"Where I lead, she follows," he mumbled, watching the traffic.

"That's not the way I hear it," she countered. "According to Rachel, any woman who strives to equal a man only lacks ambition."

He didn't say anything until they were on the freeway. "You and Rachel really get off on each other, don'tcha? Both got the same sharp tongue."

Tony was the only one she could bat the ball around with, and the farther they got from the station, the less tense her stomach felt. "If we're so much alike, then how come you never even tried to put the make on me? What's she got I haven't?"

"Inches, babe, inches. I like my women tall."

By the time they returned to the station, both Jack and Tracy were long gone. Ron Bergner sat in for Tracy on the ten o'clock newscast, which carried excerpts from the earlier network report on the Basque incident, with Mari on camera in the studio afterward, to update the casualty count. Tony stuck around until she was finished, and they were both climbing the stairs to her apartment so he could let her in with his key, when she heard her phone ringing. The thought that it might be Charles brought a burst of adrenaline, and she sprinted into the study to answer it.

"Hi. We heard you, saw you." She began smiling as soon as she heard his voice. "Thought you were great, Tony, too. Just wanted to call and say so. Here." And before Mari had a chance to say anything, he was gone.

"Hello?" The familiar voice brought instant disorientation. "Mom? Where are you?" Tony was waving from the door and mouthing, "See you in the morning." She waved back, and a moment later heard the click of her front door.

"At home," her mother replied with a little laugh. "Charles and I watched the news together, and then he took me out to dinner. Weren't your ears burning? How I wish I could have gone to the Basque country with you and Tony. It looked so beautiful."

"Charles is in Denver, and you were talking about me?"

"Yes, but we agreed that we *could* be a little biased, though we don't really think so. You were very good, you know, as usual."

Mari couldn't remember the last time her mother had actually praised anything she did. Not that Janet didn't "discuss" her work. After seeing the heart program, she'd talked on and on about the idea of using artificial hearts and the medical-research findings, but that wasn't the same thing. And it wasn't until Mari heard the short, simple "you were very good, as usual"—words that acted like a soothing balm on an open wound—that she realized how long and how much she'd been wanting to hear that. Not implied, but straight and clear, undisguised as anything else.

"And Tony, too, of course. His pictures were wonderful. Will you tell him for me?" Janet continued.

"Yes, of course. How are you feeling, Mom?" Mari asked.

"I'm a little tired, but I enjoyed the evening so much. And hearing about Charles's research. But I'm heading for my bed. I'll talk to you again soon. Here's Charles."

"Hi again." She could hear the grin in his voice, and knew he was feeling pleased with himself.

"You're pretty sneaky, you know that?" she teased. "That's what I get for not calling you last night, huh?"

"Right." He told her about talking to Rachel and how he'd decided on the spur of the moment to return to Houston by way of Denver. Mari told him about Tracy's flare-up after the broadcast, and repeated Tony's prediction that Jack would be able to soothe Tracy's "ruffled feathers" in bed, so everything would be back to normal tomorrow.

"Good God, Mari, after tonight I can't see why you have to keep on putting up with shit like that!" The way he rushed to her defense, indignant as an angry father, brought an indulgent smile to Mari's lips.

"Like Mom said, don't you think you might be in my corner whether I'm really any good or not? And maybe it's all just relative—how good I look depends on how bad someone else looks."

"Maybe," he returned agreeably, "but I doubt it. What you do and how you do it stands out like a sore thumb." They talked on, until he remembered that it was an hour later in Houston than in Denver. "Hell, I forgot. You've probably been up since the crack of dawn, must be dead tired by now. No use going on like this when I'll see you tomorrow night."

"Yes, okay. Uh, I'm so glad you called, Charles. I feel . . . well, it makes me feel better—"

"You're as bad as Jan, you know that? What's with you two, anyway?" he burst out, mildly exasperated. "What the hell are you afraid's going to happen if you admit it makes you feel good to talk to me? At least I hope to hell it does, 'cause I have to tell you I'm so damned addicted I start to come apart at the seams after twenty-four hours without talking to you. Don't know how I'm going to stand going back to Austin tomorrow night, not seeing you until the weekend. Think about that, will you?"

Mari was scripting a story when Jack buzzed her on the intercom the next morning. She glanced at her watch. Nine-thirty—early for him, so maybe Tony was wrong about where Jack spent the night.

"Can you come down, talk for a minute?" he asked as soon as she answered, rather than ordering her to his office, which was enough to set off all the alarm bells in her head.

"Come in, have a seat, Mari," he invited as soon as she appeared at his door, motioning her into one of the stuffed chairs ranged around his desk. "Listen, I wanna say first off what a great job you and Tony did on that Basque story. Didn't get a chance to tell you last night. None of the other networks came even close. Enough background for viewers to figure out what the hell's going on over there and why, then talking to guys no one's even been able to identify, let alone get close to." He rubbed his hands together, relishing the thought, then jumped up from his chair and began pacing back and forth behind his desk, as if he couldn't sit still another minute.

"Yes, well, at least there aren't any more fatalities being reported this morning," Mari commented, waiting to hear what was on his mind.

"Hell, Mari, you're too much the professional not to understand, so I'm going to spit it right out. What happened last night sort of threw Trace for a loop, made her feel a little put down or something. But she'll do fine if we give her a little time." He stopped pacing suddenly and turned to watch her. "So I want you to take a couple of weeks off, give her a chance to find her stride. I know how tough that trip to Spain was for you, anyway, what with your mother being so sick and all. So you probably could use a little vacation, right? With pay, of course." He smiled at that. "We promise not to call you, even if there's an emergency. Take a trip to the beach, go to Cozumel or someplace like that, get all rested up."

"What about Tony?" Mari asked, keeping her voice as neutral as possible.

"I'm putting him on city hall, with Ron. Wouldn't hurt him to broaden his experience a little, anyway, add to his job credentials."

Mari stared at him wordlessly for a few seconds, allowing the contempt she felt to show. The nicest word she could think of for what Jack was doing was "dissemble," because Tony's "job credentials" already included plenty of experience with the traditional local beats—the police department, city hall, and the courts—and they both knew it. When Jack looked away and began to pace again, she knew he'd gotten the message.

"Well, I'll see you in a couple of weeks, then," she said finally, letting him off the hook. A sigh of relief hissed out of Jack, as if someone had pricked his balloon with a pin. He came around the desk as she got up, to escort her to the door. Magnanimous in victory, she thought as she walked back to her office.

Once there, she flopped down in her chair and swiveled it around to look out the window, something she'd been doing a lot lately. Staring and thinking. Jack didn't know it, but he'd just handed her what she needed and wanted most right now—time—the chance to complete her research and maybe get some of the PBS pilot on tape. And without losing any salary!

She took the time to think through what she might need from her files, called up the ones she wanted and keyboarded in the command to print, then sat down and stared out the window some more. When the printer quit she closed down the computer, gathered up her things, and walked out of the station without another thought for what she was leaving behind.

"Houston Rape Crisis Center. This is Mari," she answered, for at least the tenth time since her shift had begun, four hours earlier. It was midnight, and she was beginning to wonder if this was going to be one of those nights when she wouldn't get any sleep at all.

"Rape Crisis Center?" Charles repeated, taken by surprise. She'd left nothing but the number where she could be reached on her answering machine. "What the hell are you doing there? And when are you coming home?"

"I'm sorry, Charles. Tuesday's my regular night to do phone counseling at the center. I just forgot last night when you called, had so much on my mind, I guess."

"Yeah, well, thanks a lot for leaving the number on your answering machine! Couldn't you have gotten someone to take your place, just this once?" She didn't have to be clairvoyant to know he was angry, and getting more so each second.

"No, because I'm not coming in next week, and I already missed a couple of weeks while I was in Spain. I just didn't feel right about—"

"Here I am, so damn anxious to see you I race like a bat out of hell from the airport, get to your place, and find it all dark. No note, no nothing." His words rang with accusation. "Finally came by Rachel's, that's where I am now, see if something happened to you. She says try calling, maybe you just stepped out for a minute, otherwise I guess I never would have figured out where the hell you were."

"I'm sorry," she repeated, feeling not only contrite now,

but guilty. "You're right, I should have left a note. I wasn't thinking. Guess I expected you'd call from the airport, find out I wouldn't be able to see you, save coming back to town through all that traffic."

"I don't see how the hell you can afford to waste your time on that sort of stuff anyway, when you could be researching your program instead, if it's as important to you as you say. If you really want to get into documentaries full-time."

"I don't happen to believe that what I do here is a 'waste' of time. Where the hell do *you* get off telling me what's important and what isn't?" She came back at him as if he'd struck a raw nerve, her voice flaring up in pitch and volume. "Who appointed you my keeper?"

For a second Charles was at a loss to know what to say. "I didn't mean for it to sound that way," he mumbled finally. "Have you got any idea how worried I was? All the shit that goes down in Houston, reading about it in the paper all the time, hearing it on TV. Guess my imagination was working overtime." It was both a confession and an apology.

"Look, I'm sorry, too, but nothing can change the fact that I failed to leave a note, that you—I don't know what else I can say."

"How about that you missed me?" he ventured. She could hear the tentative beginnings of a smile in his voice.

"I did. And—And I wanted you here so much, earlier. I needed someone to talk to, needed you," she confessed, then everything came pouring out at once, about how Tracy had managed to get what she wanted after all, probably in bed as Tony'd predicted, how Jack had given her vacation with pay for the next two weeks, that she was going to use the time on her program, had already started, in fact, by spending most of the day at the U.T. Medical Branch library in Galveston. And that she also wanted to spend a couple of days with her mother in Denver.

"Jesus! Why the hell didn't you tell me sooner?"

"You didn't give me a chance. Listen Charles, I hate to say it, but this is a hotline, and I really have to go, need to keep the line open for incoming calls."

"Sure, okay. But there's no reason now why you can't come to Austin, is there? Look, the TMA library is in Austin, and you could use my computer, access just about any data base you need from there. Run up my phone bill, swim in my pool, anything you want." He was trying everything he could think of to persuade her to spend the time with him. "I really need to get back, but I could wait if—"

"No," she interrupted, "I can't come until Friday." She paused, then decided she might as well risk telling him. "Though I want to. But I'm committed to be at the Battered Women's Shelter Thursday night. Here at the crisis center on Tuesdays, there at the shelter on Thursdays—it's all part of the same thing, you know. Men assaulting women. It's important to me to try to help the women that happens to. Sometimes it's the hotline, other times I go to the hospital emergency room, or the police station. You may not like it, or understand it, but—"

"But I'm going to try," he finished for her, "when you have time to explain it to me, in Austin. You gonna fly or drive? Faster to fly, Southwest out of Hobby. And I've also got a pickup, so you won't need your car if you don't mind driving mine." She'd teased him about having a BMW 325, called it a yuppie car the first time she saw it. "Call me tomorrow night, let me know which flight you'll be on. I'll be there to meet you, with bells on my toes, rings on my fingers, come hell or high water." He paused, trying to think up a few more clichés, just to tease her.

"You're sure?"

"You still have to ask, after all that?"

CHAPTER
13

$\smile\!\!\wedge\!\!\smile$

Charles hurried toward Mari as she emerged from the passenger gangway, relieving her of the hanging bag she carried over her arm while giving her a brief kiss, then turned to the man standing behind him.

"Here she is, Rafael." Mari recognized him instantly, though she'd never seen Rafael Prados before, perhaps because he looked the way she thought a Spaniard was supposed to!

"This is a nice surprise," she said with a wide smile as she took his offered hand, responding to the flash of white teeth and the lively dark eyes. There was an aura of physical sexuality about him that hinted of adventure tinged with danger, even though he was a little on the short side physically, at least compared to Charles. He looked to be about forty-five, though there was an ageless kind of boyishness or playfulness about him, which probably was heightened by the informality of his clothes—a textured cotton sweater and jeans.

"I would have recognized you in any case, Mari, from Charles's description," he murmured with a conspiratorial grin, then lifted her hand to his lips in the age-old salute of the gallant male to a beautiful female. "At first I think he must speak through the eyes of love, because no woman could be so beautiful. But now I see that he was being quite conservative—as usual." He gave the "as usual" a droll twist.

"You have to watch him, Mari. Rafe's partial to blondes. He believes he's Don Juan reincarnated," Charles chided, letting Mari know that they were much more than professional colleagues, "in spite of the fact that he's married to Helen of Troy and has four little *niñas* at home."

Rafael gave Mari a rueful, slightly apologetic smile. "Because my wife insist we try for a boy. But no more. Four is enough, yes?"

"I'm glad to have the chance to thank you personally, Rafael, for your help with my mother. I doubt she would have made it if you two hadn't come to her rescue." This time she included Charles in her smile.

"Perhaps. But who can really know what makes the crucial difference in such cases?" Rafael beamed a bright smile back at her while his shrewd eyes assessed her pale face and tired eyes, which even the extra color she'd applied so carefully didn't hide. "Cisco was right about love, you know. Charles told me what he said. But Charles also says your mother is a woman of strong will. It is impossible to measure the effect of such things, you know"—she saw him glance at Charles—"yet we know they can make a big difference in the outcome."

Rafael wasn't the only one to notice her eyes, and Charles couldn't hide his concern any longer. She looked nifty enough in her crispy-creased linen trousers and white silk blazer, but there definitely was something wrong, and he intended to find out what. "You sure you're feeling okay, Mari honey? You don't look too—"

"I know," Mari agreed, cutting him short. "Had kind of a rough night, that's all. Didn't get much sleep." Even her smile looked wan now.

"But I thought you were only supposed to be at the shelter till midnight."

"Yes, but . . . well, that's not how it turned out. And then when I did finally get home, I couldn't sleep." She raised her chin a little and turned to Rafael, hoping Charles would get the message that she didn't want to talk about it. "Did you just arrive?"

"Last night, but I leave in the morning, for New York, so

not to worry." He beamed at Charles. "I surprise him at the last minute, because I think, 'Why not go to New York by way of Texas, see what new tricks Charles is doing with his Vampire, eat a little barbecue?'"

"Yeah, we've been taking measurements all day, on blood samples Rafael brought. He did his usual tests in Madrid, then packed 'em in dry ice and toted 'em along on the plane," Charles explained as they walked down the long corridor toward the luggage return. He slipped an arm around Mari's waist, mostly because he felt the need to make some kind of protective or supportive gesture. "Thought we'd go out to the house first, dump your stuff and give you a chance to wash up, relax, have a drink, then go eat at San Miguel, have some real Mexican food, not TexMex."

Driving through town between the familiar capitol dome and the needlelike university tower felt a little like returning home to Mari, because Austin was different from other Texas cities she'd seen. Perhaps "genteel" was the word that best described it. Explosive growth in recent years had given it more of a big-city skyline, but even with nearly a half-million people, Austin was still a state government–university town, because its character had been set early by those two institutions. In contrast with Houston, which was famous—or infamous—for having no zoning ordinances, quite a few Austin residents weren't yet ready to trade the natural beauty and quiet dignity of their city for the chance to make a quick buck on a real estate deal. Mari remembered hearing news reports back when she'd first gone to Houston, about neighborhood groups in Austin distributing bumper stickers that read, "Sentence the City Council to Houston" and "Say No to the Houstonization of Austin." It was a sentiment she could empathize with since there was something blowzy and temporary about Houston, perhaps because everyone there seemed to embrace anything that was big and new, even if it was cheap and crass. Of course, now that the economy was floundering, advocates of relaxed controls on development were gaining ground again. Like snake-oil salesmen, they claimed that development of any kind was needed to broaden the tax base, thereby relieving the unbearable burden on citizens. There was never any mention of the cost of roads, sewers, water and electricity, or police and fire protection, not to mention the cost to the environment.

Leaving the city behind, Charles drove out Enfield Road to the lake, crossed the low-water bridge below the dam on the Colorado River, and then up the steep hill on the opposite bank. The Colorado followed the line of the Balcones Fault and marked the edge of the Texas hill country, which had become famous when Lyndon Johnson and a trailing horde of journalists made weekend forays to "the ranch" near Johnson City. Here, where there was more water, the hills were velvety with dark green cedars and live oaks, mottled and sculpted at this time of year by the brash new yellow-green foliage of Spanish oaks. Bluebonnets and Indian paintbrush were at their peak, Mari noticed, though they were already over the hill in Houston.

Then they were winding their way through a long valley, and all she knew for sure was that they were going more or less west, because the sun was setting behind the hills looming ahead. Suddenly Charles veered left and began climbing a rough, narrow, curving black-topped road, which slowly turned back on itself. And then he turned into a driveway that dropped down the hill toward a two-story yellow-brick house. From what little she could see, it was a simple two-story rectangle perched on the side of the hill. Natural cedar decks weathered to a silvery gray projected out on either side at the second level, but like children's treehouses, were partially hidden by the branches of surrounding trees.

Rafael climbed out and opened the car door for Mari while Charles retrieved her luggage from the trunk, and then they started across the wood bridge connecting the drive to the double front doors. It reminded Mari of a drawbridge, the kind that spanned a castle moat, and she leaned over the railing to see the hill falling away below. Charles turned to her with a smile, then motioned her through the door ahead of him. They were entering at the second level, so, unlike most houses, the bedrooms must be down and the living room up. "Can you pull up the bridge when you're under siege?" she inquired, relishing the idea.

Natural light flooded the big space opening out in front of

her, and Mari moved toward the floor-to-ceiling glass wall, which the floor appeared to pass through uninterrupted to become the broad wood deck beyond, where the leaves of trees filtered and diffused the light, and also framed the distant view of hills and the long valley they'd just driven through. She turned around, taking in the details of the interior space for the first time. The most powerful effect of the almost spartan-looking room was one of openness and light, a feeling that was enhanced by the high ceiling and undraped glass, but also by the lack of interior walls, at least none that completely closed off any rooms she could see. The floor was all one material and color—big, square, terra-cotta Mexican tiles, with a softly burnished shine that reminded her of Charles's shoes. The big living/dining area contained two islands of furniture—one a teak dining table surrounded by six chairs, and the other twin couches covered in corduroy the color of wild honey, which faced each other across a low, white Parson's table. An ancient-looking Bokhara rug, faded blue and red, both warmed and contained the intimate arrangement. One wall was all shelves, filled with books and a couple of speakers, except for the slate-faced fireplace recessed into the middle of it, while the others were a veritable museum, of paintings and woven tapestries, one of which she suspected was a Moroc-can rug. Mari turned around and around, lost in the luxurious space and light, trees, sky, and distant view, like a cat rubbing her fur against the feel of the place, until Charles pulled open the sliding glass door, inviting her out onto the deck.

"Why didn't you tell me?" she asked wonderingly as she breathed in the fresh air, faintly scented with cedar and a mix of spring blooms.

"Because I wanted you to see it through your eyes, not mine." His answer said he understood her better than she imagined, even in her fantasies. He gave her a quick hug and kiss, then muttered, "I'll go fix drinks while you look around. Or just sit out here and relax, if you want." Rafael left with him, perhaps because he sensed that Charles wanted to give her a few minutes alone.

In the distance the spike of the university tower jutted up into the triangle of sky formed by the hills on either side of the valley. That Charles's home was uncluttered and functional in appearance didn't surprise her, not after seeing the way he kept his lab, but his desire to live where he could immerse himself in the natural environment did. Because to live here and not be on intimate terms with the march of the sun across the sky, or the rise and fall of the sap in the spring and fall, simply didn't seem possible. And it was going to take more than a few minutes to digest it all, especially this side of Charles she hadn't realized even existed. She stepped back inside and followed their voices to the kitchen, which opened at least partially to the dining area.

"With some materials the molecular relaxation times can be so slow you get a more accurate picture of what's going on by taking data over a fairly long period of time," Charles was explaining to Rafael when she joined them. He tossed her a quick smile of greeting and handed her a glass of white wine. She only halfway listened to what Charles was saying, thinking instead about how different they looked, standing there together. Rafael seemed so compact, his yellow sweater defining a well-developed chest and shoulders, in contrast to Charles's stretched-out height. She looked at Charles, taking in his red-navy checked shirt and navy trousers, simultaneously admiring and envying him, because he looked so damn good, no matter what color he wore!

"The software we use to run the Vampire instructs the computer to take a reading at specified intervals, from seconds to every hour, whatever space of time you want." He slipped an arm around her waist while he continued talking, and pulled her against him, only vaguely conscious of the fact that he needed the physical confirmation that she was finally here, in his house. Rafael tipped his glass at Mari and Charles in silent salute, then took a sip before changing the subject to include her.

"I suspect you found our hospitals a bit rustic, compared to what you're used to in Houston."

"A little," she agreed, "but some things are the same everywhere. The nurses came breezing into Mom's room with *Buenas tardes, como estamos?*—How are we this afternoon?—just like they do here. They also refuse to give out any information to patients or their relatives, even blood-pressure readings, same as here. Which I assume means the medical establishment wields the same iron hand in Spain as it does here, relegating other professionals to underlings who only are allowed to carry out their orders." Rafael raised a brow at Charles, intrigued by this unexpected response to his comment.

"Cisco told me he took his residency in Boston. Is that unusual?" she asked.

"Yes, because it is not so easy to obtain a place here. We must be very good and be able to prove it, since there is some suspicion about the quality of our medical education. Perhaps with good reason."

"Yes, but Americans are always so sure that our way is best, I suppose partly out of isolation and ignorance."

"Our medical profession is so damned entrenched and conservative it's a wonder we ever see any new treatment concepts, or drugs, let alone new technology," Charles added. "And the AMA works full-time at keeping it that way."

"Reactionary and backward, I'd call it," Mari amended with considerable heat, "especially when it has to do with women. I ran across a textbook, just the other day in the library at Galveston, which pointed out that—and I quote —'Men don't indulge in menopause.' Granted it was ten years old, but—'indulge'?" she asked, sounding so incredulous that both Charles and Rafael had to laugh.

"But you have perhaps the best health care in the world today," Rafael protested, still laughing around the words.

"Maybe in some fields," Charles agreed, "but it's getting less and less available all the time, because it costs too much. And the profession still focuses on treating symptoms rather than causes, and on disease while mostly ignoring how to keep the healthy well."

"Gimme a for-instance," Rafael suggested, bouncing his body against the edge of the kitchen counter.

"Nutrition," Mari replied. "A patient on a diuretic, a heart patient like my mother, needs nutritional supplements to replace the water-soluble vitamins and minerals being leached out of the system along with the excess fluid. Don't you agree? And I don't mean just potassium for her heart, but calcium, fluoride, and vitamin D for her bones, A and C for her immune system. Yet in Denver just as in Torremolinos, her doctor never even suggested it. She wasn't only in heart failure in Torremolinos, Rafael, she was starving to death!"

"You just tangled with a woman who knows whereof she speaks!" Charles laughed, enjoying the look on Rafael's face. "If you heard some of the horror stories she runs into, you'd understand what I've been trying to tell you for a long time. Guys like you are scarce as hen's teeth in this business!"

He straightened away from the kitchen counter, pulling Mari with him. "Come on, Marilyn. Time to show you where I put your stuff, so you can go powder your nose, or whatever, before we go eat."

Huge, pierced brass lamps hung from massive wood beams overhead, projecting lacy patterns onto the dusty pink walls and tiled floor. An orange glow radiated from the fat flickering candle set in amber glass, in the center of their table. They started with frozen margaritas and *chile con queso* Chihuahua style, a thick melted white cheese full of chunks of soft onion and poblano pepper. Charles played host, spooning a line of the gooey stuff across the middle of a flour tortilla, then rolling it up and handing one first to Mari, then to Rafael. While they ate they watched "the tortilla lady" through a window in the nearby corner alcove, rolling a pinch of dough into a ball between her palms, then flattening it in a tortilla press. From time to time she layered the hot bread onto plates, to be picked up by the waiters as they rushed past with their arms stacked high with plates.

"Charles showed me your TV program last night. 'Have a Heart'—I like that." Rafael smiled across the table at Mari. "You are an artist with film, Mari, I liked it very much."

"Thank you," she mumbled, a little embarrassed, "but the artist with the camera is Tony Zuniga, my partner, not me."

"Perhaps. The pictures in this film are important, yes. I'm sorry if I do not explain myself well, but I think they are not so important as what you make us understand. Charles and I, we talked about this, late into the night. You not only answer, but raise questions as well, show us how life is not so easy or simple as we might like. It is the same with Charles, you know."

"No, I'm not sure that I do," she replied, suddenly much more interested in what he was saying.

"Always before we think of the red cell as a single cell, suspended in plasma, moving freely, uncomplicated, even though we know it is not really so in life. But now Charles forces us to think not of cells, but of cell *interactions*. He has shown that what happens between the cells depends on the rate of flow, which is still more complex, so he makes life more difficult for us. Yet we know more, and understand more, which is also a kind of simplicity, no?"

Rafael sent a devilish grin across the table. "This is not a man who accepts approximations or generalities. For him, there is a specific reason or explanation for everything. And a way to measure it." Mari suspected that Rafael was referring to some discussion between them she hadn't heard, perhaps even a difference of opinion.

The waiter came with their *enchiladas verdes* and *calabaza rellena*—chicken-filled tortillas with tomatillo sauce, and zucchini stuffed with corn and white cheese—along with side dishes of soft black beans and delicately seasoned rice. They were busy tasting and exchanging comments about the food for several minutes, and then Rafael took the conversation in a completely different direction.

"Charles tells me you were much taken with al Andalus, Mari, and also the flamenco."

"Yes, though I guess I'll always wonder what might have been, if the Moors hadn't been defeated and then persecuted. Would your country now be a force to be reckoned with, leading the rest of us toward a more humane kind of enlightenment and justice—or not?"

"But Spain did become a power to be reckoned with, under Ferdinand and Isabella, so unification was the right thing, no? Even your Abraham Lincoln said, 'United we stand, divided we fall.' He, too, was willing to go to war for something he believed in—the union."

"Yes, I know. But I didn't mean a world power in the military sense. Spain under Isabella suffered delusions of grandeur. Financial overextension ended in the defeat of the Spanish Armada by the English, and finally the loss of Holland under Charles, when the Dutch opened their dikes and flooded Leiden." Rafael threw a quick glance at Charles, saw the little smile and knew he was really enjoying this. "That's the real reason for the difference between Belgium and Holland today—one got out from under the domination of Spain and the other didn't. Because with Isabella came the Inquisition, a holy war as vicious and bloody as any we've ever known—first against the Moors and Jews, later the Protestants." Like an avalanche, she picked up momentum as she went along. "Power politics costumed in the name of God and the Church. Four hundred years of Church-sanctioned torture and killing, not to mention oppression of the human spirit, all in the name of a peaceful, forgiving, and loving God!"

"Come on, Mari!" Charles admonished, surprised at how intense she'd become, but Rafael waved a forestalling hand.

"No, she is right, Charles. Man is never so fanatical as when he believes his cause is the cause of God."

"Well, it's all history now." Charles sighed, hoping that would put an end to the whole conversation.

"Not really," Mari returned, refusing to let it go. "Look at Northern Ireland today, and Iran. Even in this country the Righteous Right, or whatever they're called this year, are trying to impose what they believe is moral and what isn't on all the rest of us, attacking everything from judges who believe in equality to textbooks. And if you don't agree with them, you're one of the ungodly, a 'secular humanist.' The Moral Majority indicted *Our Bodies, Ourselves* as 'secular humanist garbage,' a book that told women what they needed to know about their own bodies, probably because the 'old-time' religions were the first to recognize the women's health movement for exactly what it was—part of the broad attack on male power and domination. The fundamentalist/fascist-right coalition will do away with our rights and freedoms if we let them, dehumanize us all—not just women—and change this country forever." She let the words trail off, to stare with unseeing eyes at her half-eaten enchiladas.

"Well, I don't see why you're getting so heated up over it,"

Charles mumbled. "I bet you don't even let them slap a pressure cuff around your arm without getting your written permission first!" Though he'd meant it to be a joke, he knew it was a mistake the instant he said it, even before he saw the heat of anger flare in her face and the cold contempt in her eyes.

"Because I'm a woman, that's why." She started to say more, then gave up, overwhelmed by the futility of trying to explain. It took all the control she could muster not to strike out at something, anything, and not just verbally. And not to get up and run, anywhere, to escape the demon in her head. Because it had taken her years to climb out of the pit of black depression, and only twenty-four hours to slide back in. Even the guilt, for having cast a pall of doom and gloom over the evening, felt like an old shoe, so familiar it was almost comfortable.

"Sleepy?" Charles asked as he turned into the driveway. He'd made no attempt to make conversation on the drive back to his house, after dropping Rafael at his hotel.

"A little," Mari admitted.

"How about if I fix you a nightcap while you go soak in a hot tub," he suggested, putting his arm around her shoulders as they walked across the bridge to the door, "then come tuck you into bed?"

"Alone?"

He glanced at her face, saw the tiny smile twitching at the corner of her mouth, and just laughed, as if the question didn't deserve an answer. "Go on," he urged, giving her a little push toward the stairs, "I'll be down in a minute."

Mari slipped off her shoes so she could feel the plush carpet with her toes as she walked across his big bedroom to the bath. She turned the faucets on full blast, to fill the room with steam, then went back out and stood looking around, taking more time now than she had before dinner. A Sony TV sat on one of three matching chests of drawers, facing the king-size bed from the opposite wall, while a shortwave radio and stack of scientific journals almost hid the table on the other side of the bed. A half-dozen pillows were thrown helter-skelter across the dark brown corduroy spread, more or less at the head of the bed, all different colors and patterns, apparently for arranging however the reader/viewer/sleeper wanted. Charles's bedroom was as lean and clean as the rest of the house, yet it, too, was overlaid with the same aura of lush sensuality she'd noticed upstairs. She smiled at the leather slippers set neatly together under the straight-backed chair, and pictured him sitting there to put on his shoes, his richly polished shoes, which started a warm glow in the pit of her stomach.

Consciously trying to release the tension by immersing herself in the hot water, Mari leaned back in the tub to submerge her torso, and touched the foot of the tub with her toes. A perfect fit. She sighed, finally letting go, freeing her conscious mind to wander, losing all sense of time and place.

Charles came in quietly with a short, round glass in each hand—she never knew how much later—and stood next to the tub, looking down at her, then bent to his knees and put one hand behind her neck to lift her head enough to put the glass to her lips and tilt it, without spilling the drink down her chin.

"What is it?" She struggled to sit up, feeling no shyness whatsoever with him.

"Stay where you are," he ordered, and held the glass to her lips for another taste. "Cognac with a little water." He grinned suddenly, as if he'd just had a bright idea. "Can I wash your back?"

Her back was underwater, but before she could respond or move, he had the soap between his hands and was rubbing suds over her shoulders and chest, slowly making his way down to the swell of her breasts. He drew slippery circles around her nipples, watched them pucker, then slid down to her navel and teased it the same way. Mari peered up at him through slitted lids, watching him watch her body respond to what he was doing. Let him play the scientist, if that's what he wants to do! She could play that game, too, and see how long he managed to maintain his objectivity as an experimenter and observer.

His hand slid down over and around her thigh, then down lower to gently massage her calf before finally circling her ankle. Then, taking what seemed like endless long minutes, he began the same treatment in reverse, this time on the other leg, until he was stroking up the soft inside of her thigh again. Without even realizing it, she waited, holding her breath in anticipation of what surely was coming next, until she couldn't hold it any longer. Disappointment took her breath again when his fingers detoured around where she really wanted them, sliding away and then back, only to circle their target, which of course firmly fixed her attention there, until her body began to move of its own volition, in a rhythm intended to catch the hand that tormented her, seeking even the slightest intensification of sensation.

"Charles, please," she breathed at last, in an agony of arousal, the words fluttering between barely parted lips. His big hand cupped the mound between her legs, covering it completely, and then one long finger stole away from the rest to curve inward in a soft, slippery exploration that sent her soaring with exquisite pleasure. She couldn't help crying out, though in her experience this most intimate of acts had always been enveloped in complete silence from beginning to end, no matter what happened in between. Then Charles was splashing warm water up to rinse the suds off her body, and lifting her, holding her upright while he wrapped her in a big fluffy towel. Her lids were too heavy to hold open, but fluttered from time to time as he ran his hands up and down, leaving no part of her untouched by the plush towel in his attempt to dry her. Finished to his satisfaction at last, he lifted her out of the tub, bent down to dry her feet, then turned her toward the door and gave her a little shove.

"I'm gonna get you for this, C.B.," she murmured dreamily, but did exactly as she was told, meekly and willingly, unable for the moment to concentrate on anything beyond the aching need between her thighs. It was almost more than she could manage just to pull back the spread, climb between the sheets and lie there quietly, with her eyes closed, trying to stop the free fall of her aroused body with her mind, while waiting for him to strip off his shirt and pants. His hand sought to arrest her descent as soon as he stretched out beside her, driving her back toward the peak where he'd left her only seconds before. She reached for him, more out of instinct than conscious intent, for one brief instant knowing panic at the thought that he might not be ready for her, then moaned in relief as her hand closed around him. She lifted herself in order to enclose him swiftly and completely, letting the onslaught of sensation rage completely out of control, sweeping everything else before it like a giant cresting wave—until a vibrant burst of energy flashed through her brain and body at the same instant in one single, wondrous moment out of all eternity —and then began to reverse direction, ebbing back to sea, only to return again and again, and again.

Charles was nowhere in sight when Mari woke Saturday morning. She squinted an eye at the electric clock on the chest of drawers across from the bed, then stretched like a cat, relishing the luxury of time. Time to do or not to do, time to let herself feel as well as to know, time to saturate herself in Charles and this place. She grinned, suddenly impatient to find him, and touch him, and bounded out of the bed to hurry into the bathroom.

Fifteen minutes later she found him in his study, a room perched like an eagle's aerie among the branches of oaks and yaupons, which she hadn't even noticed last night. He heard her come up the stairs, pushed back from his desk a little and motioned her to his lap. There were at least a thousand things she wanted to say to him this morning, yet couldn't quite make up her mind how to begin. So instead she circled his neck with her arm as he wrapped both of his around her and silently pressed her cheek against his hair. She looked around at the room where she knew he spent so much time, trying to fix it firmly in her memory so she could picture him here later, relaxing in the rice planter's chair, reading a journal article with a leg looped carelessly over the oddly extended paddle arm. She took in the computer and printer, and more speakers, and wondered what was behind the wall of accordion doors adjacent to his desk.

"Feel better?" he mumbled into the soft skin under her jaw, sending a shiver skittering along the surface of her arms.

She rubbed her cheek against his hair. "Heap powerful medicine, your lovemaking, and addictive, I'm afraid."

"No problem. Speaking of which, you want your book back yet? I haven't quite finished it, but—"

"Which book? I never did know."

"And you still don't, even after last night?" He was teasing her, but she didn't have the slightest idea what about. "I even left you a clue. Your ballpoint with the male stripper in the barrel." Holding her away from him so he could watch her face, he said, "The Kensington Ladies?" then began to laugh when he saw the rush of color, and lifted her off his lap. "Come on. I'll fix your breakfast, unless you'd rather have lunch. It's already past noon."

They compromised on egg-salad sandwiches, which Mari helped him make, then while Charles stacked the dishwasher, she picked up the paperback novel she'd started reading on the plane and wandered out onto the deck, the one that looked down on the swimming pool, at least a floor below, and over the valley toward town and the university.

"Anything special you want to do?" Charles asked as he came out to join her.

What she wanted most to do right now was to simply be with him, to saturate herself in him, but she couldn't quite bring herself to say so. "Would you mind too much if we just sat out here for a while? Soak up the trees and the sky, listen to the birds sing and the squirrels chatter, and to the quiet? Unless you need to work." She rushed on as if he'd said he did. "That's okay. I don't mind being alone. Really. I even go a little crazy sometimes when I don't get to be alone enough, like this past week."

"Exactly what I had in mind! And I promise not to make any noise, so you can hear the quiet." He disappeared for a few minutes, then returned with a journal in his hand and moved the other deck chair so he could put his feet up on the low square table between them. "Here." He tossed her a small plastic bottle of sunscreen lotion. "Better put some on, at least on your face." The bright sunlight was filtered by closely spaced two-by-fours overhead, but even diffuse light could cause a burn. She glanced at the number on the side of the bottle, then up at Charles, and knew he'd bought it especially for her.

Charles was anything but disappointed that she wanted to stay at the house, since that probably meant the place was having the effect he'd hoped it would on her. But he was still worried about the way she'd looked last night, and the despair he could hear in her voice during dinner, when she was talking about history repeating itself. If the old adage were true—that the eyes are the windows of the soul—then something was hurting her pretty bad. Even Rafael had noticed. But he still didn't know what was going on, because she was still talking all around, not about, whatever it was that was bothering her.

The shadows broadened as they sat together in companionable silence. Charles pretended to read, but in fact was pondering how to persuade her to move here, right now, or tomorrow, or the next day. And get married as soon as it was legally possible. How long was that? Two or three days? He felt a compelling urge to get everything settled between them once and for all, to get their relationship on a more definite footing, which surprised even him since he considered himself anything but a traditionalist. But he was beset by a nagging worry, as nameless and constant as background music, that hovered at the edge of his consciousness, a worry that had grown in direct proportion to his awareness of how much he loved and needed her—until it was a distraction that interfered with his ability to concentrate, on anything and everything. She was *always* on his mind, no matter what he was doing or where he was.

"Damn!" He dropped his feet to the wood deck with a clunk that startled Mari, then mumbled "Sorry" as he jumped up and disappeared through the open glass door. Mari hadn't really been concentrating on her book, perhaps because Robin Cook's latest medical thriller was, as usual, peopled by bloodless robots masquerading as normal human beings, so she really didn't much care what happened to them or didn't. So her eyes kept straying to the view across the valley, which seemed a far more enticing fantasy.

Charles came back through the open door and scooted his chair closer to hers. "Just remembered that I brought you something from Albuquerque." He dropped a small white cardboard box into her lap, then perched on the edge of his seat to watch her open it. She stared at the box for a second, remembering that she'd brought him something, too—a copy of the flamenco videotape—and that it was still downstairs in her suitcase.

"It doesn't look like much on the outside, but the guy I got it from isn't into fancy wrappings," he mumbled. "Go on, open it." She lifted the lid and began to unfold the white tissue, keeping her eyes on Charles's face to prolong the suspense, until she simply couldn't put off knowing any longer. She looked down to find a Zuni inlay bracelet with black and turquoise stones set into a band of thick silver, all geometrical and smooth and simple.

She looked up at Charles, then back at the bracelet, and then the tears welled in her eyes as a hundred thoughts collided in her head, all of them finally coming together as her eyes met his again.

"Have I no secrets from you?"

He grinned, understanding her question for the metaphor it was, knowing that to her there was a deeper meaning in the alternating triangles of turquoise and jet fitted together so perfectly between narrow lines of silver, something that went far beyond material value alone. "Put it on," he urged, wanting to see it on her and to run his fingers over the stones and silver, all polished to one smooth, uninterrupted surface.

Mari cupped her hand over the C-shaped band to place it properly, still struggling to find the words to say what she was feeling. "Beautiful" sounded so trite, but that's all she could think of.

"It was made by a man named Paquin, a Zuni from Isleta, near Albuquerque. He trained all his sons to be silversmiths, too, including the one who's now a doctor. I met him at the meeting, got to talking, and he told me about his father. Even the son I met still works at it when he has time, takes off a week every summer, goes up to Santa Fe and sits with the other Indians in front of the Governor's Palace, to sell his stuff to the white man. Says it helps him stay in touch with his history."

Mari slipped across the short distance between them and onto Charles's lap, unable to resist any longer. "I love it," she whispered as she slid her arm around his neck and put her cheek against his, "and I love you. I think I forgot to tell you that last night." She touched his face with her fingers, then his lips with her own.

"Mari honey?" he began softly, but paused when he felt her lips butterfly to the corner of his eye. "You're sure now, aren't you? That this isn't some casual thing, or whatever you were talking about in Torremolinos? You know I love you. I want you with me, here, all the time." She pulled away to look at his face, and again he saw tears glittering along the edges of her eyelashes, but they looked like tears of happiness this time. "Let's get married. Tomorrow. No, I forgot, tomorrow's Sunday. Monday, then."

"Ah God, Charles, stop!" she objected, laughing, yet halfway serious. "Do you have any idea how you tempt me? Or how much I love this place already? It's medicine for the soul. You don't need to pull up the drawbridge of your castle, because all this"—she waved an arm at the trees and view and house—"wipes away the dirt and the meanness, makes me feel brave enough to dare anything, even believe that the world will beat a path to my door. And that I can have everything I want after all—my documentaries, a child or two, and you."

"Sure you can, only I think you've got things in the wrong order. The way I hear it, I come before the kids," he teased, then quickly sobered. "You're serious? You want to have kids? Soon?" He was still only half willing to admit, even to himself, that he'd been thinking about that a lot lately, and for the first time in his life found the idea strangely appealing.

"Well, maybe not tomorrow," she teased, "but I'm not getting any younger. I'm not over the hill, either, but my chances of getting pregnant are dropping drastically with every passing year."

"So let's not waste any more time. Like I said, Monday morning . . ." Always before, he'd shied away from getting in too deep, fearing the kind of relationship that would commit him in a way that might interfere with his work. But now the tables were turned, and not having a no-holds-barred commitment from Mari was a devil riding his back.

"Not yet, Charles, I can't." She put her cheek against his hair, trying to hide her face. "I'm right in the middle of this women's health series. But besides that, I can't just quit and walk away, let Tracy and Jack tear my reputation to shreds, throw all the years of work away as if they'd never been. Please don't ask me to do that!"

"I'm not!" he protested, stung by what sounded like an

accusation, whether she meant it to be or not. "You want to do documentaries full-time, then do it, right here! You could even go back to writing, do a book or two. You're too damned good not to make it nationally, especially if you concentrate on developing your expertise in one area, like women's health." He pushed her away, needing to be able to read her face. "How about letting me be your angel, at least until you get going, be your first investor?"

"No!" It was abrupt, and sounded final. "Anyway, I've already got one." She got up from his lap and went back to her own chair.

"Who?" Charles demanded, but Mari just stared at the ridge of hills across the valley. He waited a few seconds. "You're not going to tell me?" Mari shook her head, refusing to look at him. "Why not?"

She wasn't sure what he was asking—why wouldn't she tell him, or why she wouldn't let him invest in her TV pilot? Maybe even why she was saying no to getting married and having babies right away, to giving up her job in Houston. And the more she thought about it, the more it was that last question that she felt compelled to try to answer.

"Because you see the world as a place where all problems are solvable, and they aren't. I'm not sure . . . I don't have—"

"Okay, I agree to some extent. I know you probably have to work twice as hard as me for the same financial reward, and maybe even then, sometimes, not get it. I'm not exactly Malcolm Forbes, but money's not a problem, either."

"I wasn't talking about money," she mumbled.

"Then what the hell were you talking about?"

"Do you have the slightest idea what it's like to be constantly reminded, every minute of every day of your life, in your own home, out walking the city streets or in a parking lot, that someone stronger than you might decide to rape you? Because angry, powerless men assault women in order to gain a sense of power and control over *something* in their lives."

"You're talking in riddles! For God's sake, Mari, tell me what in the holy hell happened Thursday night, at the shelter, or whatever you call it." He raised his voice to try to get through to her, then leaned forward and grabbed both her hands in his as he watched her try to mentally turn back the clock.

"Not at the shelter. Hermann Hospital." She paused so long, he thought that was all she was going to say. "And then the police station." She was still avoiding his eyes, but it really didn't matter now, because hers were turned inward, to another place and time.

"Why?"

"I tried . . . thought she was beginning to . . . I was getting . . . would get her . . . out."

"Who?" Charles held tight to her hands, giving her something to hold onto.

"Ruthie. She . . . a women I starting working with when I first came to Houston. Three kids . . . one, two, three . . . every year. Thought . . ." Articulate as she usually was, he could hardly make sense of her fragmented words and phrases, and a twinge of anguish tightened his gut at the realization of how hard this must be for her.

"Thought you would get her out of what?" he prompted, still trying to help.

"The house. Away from her husband. The fear. And the guilt." She straightened, as if physically rejecting whatever it was, pushing her shoulders back against the chair. Then she looked straight into Charles's eyes. "You've probably heard the joke where the guy says, 'Hey, did ya hear the one about the guy who was stabbed to death by a woman? Gave him the surprise of his life!' Then the feminists came along and added a new line. 'Yeah, and I knew a woman who was beaten to death by a man. It didn't surprise her in the least!' Only it isn't a joke. Not for Ruthie, not for—" Her eyes flooded and began to run over. Charles whipped the handkerchief out of his back pocket and handed it to her.

"Come on, Mari, tell me. What happened? Get it out, it'll make you feel better."

She shook her head, back and forth, slowly, denying it over and over again as the tears ran down her cheeks unheeded, until at last she crossed her arms over her breasts, as if needing to hold herself together. "No. I won't. Feel better. Ever. And neither will she. Three times he beat and . . . raped her. Broke her face, her eardrum. Pulled her arm out of the socket. Threw her down the stairs." She filled in the gaps between words with her body, rocking herself back and forth, keeping time to the cadence of an agony only she could feel. "I almost got her out. Last time. But he convinced her . . . again . . . she couldn't make it alone."

Charles could hardly believe what she was telling him. Not that it didn't happen, but that she would voluntarily put herself in the position of having to associate with, or deal with, the kind of people who were on the fringes of society, most of them the dregs of humanity who were probably beyond help. "I suppose it usually starts over money, or a bad temper triggered by alcohol. What was it this time—or do you know?" he asked, trying to keep his voice as neutral as possible, to hide how he felt about the whole distasteful business.

"Oh yes, I know." No longer on a slow boil, Mari's anger flared out of control, shooting adrenaline through her veins. Her words began to come like bullets from a gun now, fast, clean, and sharp. "I also know that you and I live in two different worlds. That you still don't see the one I live in at all, don't even believe my world actually exists. Or that men assault women because society teaches them to use physical force, violence, to resolve problems. To act out their impotence on those who are weaker. Vulnerable.

"Ruthie's husband is a stockbroker, one of those guys you see driving around town in his Mercedes wearing a three-piece suit, blow-dried hair, and a Rolex. Lives in a fancy house with a pool, works out three times a week at his health club, belongs to a private tennis club, the whole bit. Or he did." She paused and let her eyes drill into his, hot as a laser.

"Thursday night he went on another power trip, did it to her again. For the last time. She . . . he killed her."

CHAPTER

14

The next few days were idyllic, or almost. On Sunday
Charles took Mari to Fiesta, an annual two-day arts and
crafts fair held on the spacious grounds of the local art
museum, which once had been a private home on the shores
of Lake Austin. Just inside the gate they encountered a
couple of women selling wide-brimmed straw hats adorned
with artificial flower wreaths, and Charles grabbed Mari's
arm to pull her toward the display, insisting that she have
one to protect her face from the hot Texas sun. He surprised
her by picking out a bright red one with a wide floppy brim
that dipped down a little, front and back. Then she surprised him by chosing the splashiest big blooms she could
find to go around the crown, big white magnolia blossoms
with deep green leaves, intertwined with some nondescript
apricot-colored blooms. He eyed her appraisingly, nodding
the whole time. "Gives you a certain savoir faire, or
something."

She laughed. "Something is probably right."

"Looks great. I like it, like you in red, like you, love
you—"

"Help, police, he's going to eat me," she yelled, a frantic
look on her face.

They both started laughing at the same time, and he

273

pulled her over for a quick kiss, ducking his head under the brim of her hat before they walked on, hand in hand. They browsed the booths, stopping from time to time to take a closer look, sipped cold beer and snacked on nachos, then watched a man throw pots on a wheel, sipped more cold beer and nibbled on flautas. Of all the pots, paintings, prints, jewelry, and other articles scattered over the two or three acres of grounds, though, only one display really caught Mari's eye and imagination. All of the oakwood baskets were functional and a good size, with wood handles carved to suit the particular shape they served. Charles listened without saying a word while she talked to the young man and woman who'd made them, getting not only their names but a detailed explanation of how David Blaisus used a double-handled knife he'd developed himself to cut the thin, narrow strips of oak from specially prepared logs, which the woman, Rain Mako, wove into baskets.

Charles wanted to buy one for her, but Mari demurred, insisting they were "too expensive." Her right hand curved over the Zuni bracelet on her left wrist, and he knew exactly what was running through her mind. But she couldn't stop talking about the baskets or the couple. "Rain Mako," she mused as they walked on. "Don't you love the sound of her name? Makes me think of the forest primeval, secret ceremonies and incantations to the gods." Later, while they were sitting on a low wall nibbling big ears of buttered corn, she remembered something else, and asked, "Did you hear Rain say that they live on Cave Mountain, near Pettigrew, Arkansas?" He steered her through the grounds, snaking in and out between booths they hadn't explored yet, letting her talk on. "That sort of medium-sized, oval shape, the one that was all natural—didn't you think it was the most unusual one of all, especially the way the handle was connected to the basket?" When he pulled her to a stop only a few feet from the basketmakers' booth, having approached it from the opposite direction, he stopped her protest with a warning hand, then bent toward her ear to make sure she could hear him.

"Consider how much time and work and love they put into one of those baskets," he whispered in her ear, "and then tell me again that eighty dollars, a hundred, or whatever it is, is too much!" He nibbled at her ear, sending shivers down her spine. "I know you want that basket so bad you can taste it. I never heard of Pettigrew, Arkansas, but I have heard of a bird in the hand."

"I confess, I do want it!" Mari admitted, clapping both hands over her ears. "And I know my expensive tastes are going to drive us straight to the poorhouse. It's a sickness." She hopped around from one foot to the other, all eager impatience, so happy she couldn't stand still.

Charles bought the basket he knew she'd had her eye on all along, and shortly afterward they left for home, sated with the pleasure of owning an objet d'art extraordinaire, as Charles called it, straight from the Ozarks, not to mention the beer, food, and sun.

It took no such lengthy deliberation or persuasion to decide what to do next. As if by mutual agreement they both headed straight for the pool as soon as they got inside the house, detouring only to change into their suits.

"Why?" Charles wanted to know. "Nobody can see the pool, from the road or even from across the valley. And I don't think West Lake Hills has a decency brigade out peering through the bushes, though that may not be too far off, considering the Neanderthals sitting on the city council right now."

"Oh, because I need my crutches and props, I suppose, things I'm used to. I'm uncomfortable enough as it is."

"Uncomfortable? With what?"

"I'm not a very good swimmer, never spent much time in pools when I was a kid. Season was too short. How are you on snow skis?"

"Gotcha," he popped back, getting her point instantly.

Mari walked to the edge of the rectangular pool and balanced on one foot, so she could dunk her toes in to test the temperature, but Charles went to the deep end and dove right in. She sat down on the edge and dangled her legs in the water, watching him stretch out into a crawl. The joints of his arms and shoulders moved as if they were loose, and his arms rose out of the water just enough to drop back down, reaching ahead, while his long legs and feet moved in a powerful flutter kick, as smooth and constant as a turning propeller. He was at her end of the pool in no time, flipped into a turn and came out of it on his back, stroking up and over his head in the opposite direction, but with the same flutter kick. She'd never seen anyone swim with so little splash, or such ease, lap after lap, alternating between the crawl and the backstroke, the crawl and the breaststroke. But the stroke she liked best was a kind of reverse butterfly, only much less strenuous. He seemed to just relax back, letting his body sink until his face was underwater, while pulling up his legs and raising both arms in a kind of lazy stretch, then with hands together dropped them into the water over his head and straight down to his thighs in one powerful pull, while pushing his legs out straight. It looked so easy.

Mari slipped off the edge of the pool and into the water, to cool off and try to swim along with him, but he was stroking at least two lengths to every one of hers, so they were side by side only in passing. After a couple of laps she climbed back out.

"Too cold?" he called as he pulled himself out of the pool a few minutes later.

She watched his chest, amazed that after all that exertion his respiration rate seemed only slightly elevated. "No. You're too good for me."

He stopped rubbing his arms with the towel and just looked at her. "I didn't know we were in competition."

"Noooo?" She drawled the word, letting her skepticism show. "Maybe that's because you're so far out front."

"What the hell does that mean?" he asked, expelling the words as he dropped down into the chair beside her.

"Just that you're so good in the water, it's no fun for me, though watching the way your body moves is . . . uh, pleasurable, I have to admit." She flipped him a mischievous little smile. "It's also demoralizing. Makes me feel inferior, disadvantaged, aware that I have such a long way to go and so little chance of ever catching up. That's what I meant."

"You could—catch up—if you'd let me give you a few lessons," he offered. "Free of charge, of course, more or less, uh, since I'd get to put my hands on that luscious body whenever you need a little assist. You know what I mean." He let his eyes roam over her breasts and then down to her thighs while a teasing grin curled his lips, slowly turning into an exaggerated leer as he wiggled his eyebrows. "A few minutes of instruction every day. And you could practice however much you want, every day for the rest of your life if you want, right here in this pool. Don't see how you can pass up an offer like that!"

"You think I could learn to do that stroke you were just doing, that lazy thing where you just lie back and let yourself sink?" she asked, ignoring his last remark.

He looked first, to see if she was serious. "Sure, but I think we ought to start with the crawl, get your confidence up, because you'll feel more in control if you're facedown in the water. Then you won't panic when you start to sink, as you call it."

"Okay. I'm game." She jumped up from her chair and stood ready and waiting, like an overeager kid. "Can we begin right now?"

He shook his head but smiled as he pulled himself out of the chair, then threw an arm around her shoulder and walked with her to the shallow end of the pool. They sat down together, dangling their legs in the water while Charles described what he wanted her to do and then showed her exactly how to do it. Mari practiced arm movements and breathing, until she could synchronize them the way he said to, and then they slid into the water together, so she could try out what she'd learned there. She noticed every touch of his firm, reassuring hands, and had to consciously try to ignore it, in order to concentrate on his instructions. He never corrected her with words, or passed judgment on her performance, which only would have pointed up her failings and made her even more self-conscious. Instead, he repeated and demonstrated, again and again, as many times as necessary, never sounding impatient, no matter how many times it took before she got something right. As a result she learned quickly, and the more she learned, the more she was able to relax in the water, which came as a revelation, because now she knew for sure that her former timidness in the water had been nothing less than fear. She bubbled over, laughing with the pure pleasure and excitement of accomplishment. Charles grinned, too, watching her antics in the water and her uninhibited enjoyment. He couldn't remember when he'd had so much fun, or felt so much satisfaction in teaching anyone anything.

It was with reluctance that he finally called a halt thirty minutes later, knowing she'd be sorry later tonight, and tomorrow, if he didn't. "No more for you today." He grabbed her around the waist, holding her under his arm like a bundle of sticks, and hauled her toward the steps at the corner of the pool.

"Put me down, you brute! Don't you dare pull the caveman act with me," she yelled, trying to break the band of steel that was threatening to crack her ribs. "I'm not finished yet!"

"You're turning into a lobster, little girl, in case you haven't noticed. And listening to you cuss me in bed tonight is not what I had in mind." He climbed out of the pool and set her on her feet, but kept his arms around her, until cool skin began to feel warm wherever their torsos touched. Mari snuggled her face into his neck.

"Thank you," she whispered, then let her tongue snake out to lick his skin, sending an involuntary shiver down his spine. "I've got all kinds of memories of you to take to bed with me tonight, and tomorrow night, and the next," she murmured against the undercurve of his jaw, pressing soft kisses between words, "of your hands on my body. Underwater. In the pool. Slippery with soap, and—"

"Sure, you're welcome, any time," he interrupted, knowing that his control was fast coming to an end. "But we still need to get you out of the sun."

The next few days were a revelation to Mari, as she learned to mix work with play in a way she'd never known was possible before. Charles got up and left each morning as usual—to "teach my class" or "check with my graduate students, see if everything's going okay in the lab"—but called her every couple of hours, just for the pure pleasure of it. Not that he ever admitted that to her. Instead, he always found some excuse, like "what do you want to do for supper tonight?" or "I've got a budget-council meeting at three, so I may be late getting home." But no matter what came up, he always managed to be home by four o'clock at the latest, more often by three, for her swimming lesson. And she knew without needing to be told that that was not his usual routine.

Mari spent most of Monday and Tuesday on the phone, doing preliminary interviews with several people she wanted to get on camera for her program, trying to schedule the tapings at the same time, for sometime during the next couple of weeks, groaning inwardly at the thought of what the plane fare/hotel bill for her and Tony was going to cost her, because she didn't have any "angel," as Charles put it. In the process she ran across other stories as well, only tangential to what she was inquiring into now, which beckoned and tempted her attention to stray. Like the drug monopolies being set up under the guise of computerized marketing-ordering networks. McKesson, for instance, already had a network of fifteen thousand independent druggists linked to the company by computer, which allowed them to match or better the drug chains on prices and availability. It also made them dependent on McKesson, with the result that the company now had nearly thirty percent of the wholesale drug business in the U.S. And now they were going after the M.D.s, too, since physicians were beginning to sell the drugs they prescribed, which raised lots of questions in Mari's fertile mind. Would a doctor prescribe a drug other than the one that was preferred, simply because his supplier manufactured it? Another story she had a hard time ignoring was the expanding cross-ownership of pharmaceuticals and some of the biggest health-care providers, such as Johnson and Johnson with National Medical Enterprises, and Bristol-Myers with Hospital Corporation of America.

She continued to follow up leads from sources she'd contacted earlier, the most time-consuming aspect of digging below the surface of a story, prying a piece of information out of A that led to B, and from B that led to C, one step at a time. Often that meant one or more calls to find out who would best be able to answer her question, and still another to reach the source, which could run up the telephone bill like crazy—which she also was very conscious of, since KPOC wasn't footing the bills. She scribbled a note, to remind herself to get the charges from the phone company before she left Austin, because she had no intention of saddling Charles with the bill.

She called Hoffman-LaRoche, the company that had developed three of the most popular tranquilizers on the market, and talked to a woman who said Valium worked equally well "for people with pulled muscles or people who are worried about pulled muscles," and Ciba Geigy, to ask similar questions about Elavil and Tofranil. She also called Pharmacol, the company that manufactured Pamezine, the drug she'd received the phone call about way back before she'd gone to Spain, and got more of the same. She was connected with a man in the public relations department, who admitted that close to eighty percent of prescriptions for their drug were for "nonspecific nervous complaints." When she asked him what that meant, he didn't hesitate for even a second. "Oh, you know, loneliness, fear, worry, marital anxiety, whatever the doctor imagines is bothering her."

"Her?" she shot back, furious at what he was implying. "Doctors are prescribing drugs now for what they *imagine* is wrong with a patient?" She was instantly sorry, knowing that her sarcasm would only serve to put a guard on his tongue. Or worse, that he would claim she'd misunderstood him. And she was right.

"No, that's not what I said at all, lady. Many physicians find it in the best interest of their female patients to attempt to relieve their anxieties, which often are only imaginary, but nevertheless can have deleterious effects on their health."

He became even more evasive when she began asking questions about the scattered reports of side effects associated with the use of Pamezine, not only drowsiness, vomiting, "confusion," and abnormal drops in blood pressure—as was the case with most tranquilizers—but also irregular menstrual periods and tingling in the hands or feet, especially in young women. He hemmed and hawed about giving her the name of someone she could talk to in the company's research lab, claiming that his office was able, and willing, to answer any legitimate questions she might have. He even questioned her identity as a member of "the press," since some of her questions were too technical to be of even remote interest to the general public. She was, in addition— or so he claimed—inquiring into what amounted to proprietary information, or the company's "trade secrets." Mari recognized the tactic for just what it was, an attempt to put her on the defensive by hinting that she might be a spy for one of the company's competitors. In the end she simply called back and asked the receptionist for the name of the person in charge of clinical testing, who, it turned out, was out of town for the rest of the week. She also talked briefly with the company's director of research, who was much smoother at stonewalling than the PR man, and decided she might as well let it ride for now.

She contacted a doctor at the Addiction Research Foundation in Toronto, who'd just completed a study of Valium, Dalmane, Librium, and Ativan, and found out that patients who'd taken those drugs for a long period of time could expect to experience "mild" withdrawal symptoms for at least five weeks after they stopped—blurred vision, stiff necks, numb hands, and ringing ears. And Dr. Sidney Wolfe, the director of the Public Citizen Health Research Group in Washington, told her that long-term use of Valium, or any of a whole class of related drugs called benzodiazepines, also impaired judgment and thinking. "They're generally not lethal unless taken with alcohol, but they're dangerous nonetheless. I certainly wouldn't want to be on an airplane with a pilot who has taken a benzodiazepine." His comments reminded her that a number of highly placed people in government, from Betty Ford to Michael Deaver, were known to have been hooked on Valium *and* alcohol. A Washington psychiatrist she contacted even commented that, "Valium is probably the most abused drug in town."

She called the Food and Drug Administration a couple of times, and also tried to reach Tony in Houston, to no avail, so called Rachel instead, just to touch base. But when she asked if anything special was going on at the station, Rachel sounded evasive.

"Not that I know of, or can tell from watching the news. But I'm not the one to ask. Tony hasn't been around much, uh, for the past few days."

"Why?" Mari asked with a sinking feeling in the pit of her stomach. She couldn't help remembering how he'd gone silent that night after dinner. She'd sensed that something had gone awry, but the blowup at the station a couple of days later had pushed everything else out of her mind. "What happened?"

"I'm not sure. Perhaps he just feels the need for a . . . a breather. Or has found someone more to his liking, more his type, you might say. Sweet, young—and short." She laughed, trying to make a joke of it, but failed miserably. Hearing the near-tears in her voice made Mari want to cry, too.

"Listen, I'll be back Sunday night. Let's have lunch, uh, let's see—Monday's going to be terrible. How about Tuesday? I won't be doing a broadcast that night. Would that work for you?"

"Sure. Any time, any day. How about Butera's, around twelve-thirty?"

The next morning after breakfast, while she and Charles were having a second cup of coffee out on the deck, Mari ran across a story in the business pages of the *New York Times* about Volvo upping its stock in Pharmacia, the Swedish pharmaceutical, to forty-three percent. A few pages later on she noticed a full-page ad for Hoechst Celanese, with white letters dropped out of the blackened page to make it look like a school kid had printed the words on a blackboard, with "(Herkst Sel-a-neez)" underneath. She nudged Charles, and he read the rest of it out loud. "Our name may be hard to say, but the billion dollars we spend on research and development speaks for itself. It's a name worth remembering. Why? Because it's the name of a newly merged corporation that's already one of the most exciting science- and market-driven chemicals, pharmaceuticals, fibers, and advanced-materials companies in the United States." She also ran across a piece in the business pages reporting that "industry experts" were expecting Universal Broadcasting Corporation, "the number-two network," to sell several of its television stations as a result of the continuing drop in ad revenues reported for the first quarter. But she'd heard similar predictions on and off since she'd been in Houston, and even if they were true, it was unlikely that KPOC-TV would be among the stations UBC would get rid of, since it was such a consistent profit-maker for the network.

Wednesday after their late-afternoon swim, Charles called Zippy's Pizza and ordered a large pepperoni and onion delivered to the house, opened a bottle of cabernet sauvignon and stood in the kitchen telling her about his day while Mari made a salad. He'd recently received some samples of synovial fluid from an orthopedic surgeon at the med school in San Antonio, taken from both "normal" joints as well as from patients with various forms of arthritis. Using a variety of test procedures, they were trying to characterize both the physical and chemical properties of the body's natural joint lubricant, so it would then be possible to create an artificial substitute to replace the defective fluid in diseased joints. She gave him a blow-by-blow description of the trials and tribulations she'd encountered in her effort to obtain information about Pamezine. "I may end up having to go to Washington, maybe even file formally under the Freedom of Information Act, if the FDA drags its feet too much."

"Why bother? Just because those guys at Pharmacol refused to spill their guts to you, and you can't refuse a challenge?" Charles asked. "What's so special about this particular drug?"

Mari shook her head, then told him about her anonymous telephone caller. "He was probably just a crank or something, but I can't just ignore it, not even try to check it out. And after today . . . well, the guys I talked to sure were quick to clam up, as if they had their speeches all prepared. One even hinted that I must have an ulterior motive, was an industrial spy or something! Maybe they have reason to be paranoid, with competition what it is, but it does sort of make you wonder whether they have something to hide."

"Yeah, but a lot of that stuff is a matter of public record, isn't it, like the results of the clinical trials they had to file with the FDA?"

"Oh sure, but it could take the FDA two or three months, maybe even longer, to 'locate' it. There's more than one way to skin a cat, you know, especially if there's anything in those records the FDA isn't anxious to have get out. They've been taking a lot of flak lately, especially after turning down the Genentech heart-attack drug, and you saw how quick they were to change their decision on that one! At least the FOI puts a limit on how long they can fudge around, putting you off with one excuse after another."

After supper Mari went to the university with Charles, because he'd left some equipment running in order to complete the final data run on a sample of synovial fluid.

"Have you been banished to Siberia?" Mari joked as they walked down the long corridor to his lab on the top floor of the engineering building.

"Not yet, though it could happen any day, I suppose. Some of my opinions aren't exactly popular around here. No, I chose this corner for quiet. Need to isolate the equipment from building noise, vibration, as it is."

Almost every bench and shelf was filled with equipment —oscilloscopes, lasers, two or three frequency-response analyzers—most of them connected to shop-built, one-of-a-kind instruments Charles had designed. "Come over here," he ordered. "Want to show you how I've changed the Vampire since you last saw it." He walked straight to the two tables pushed together in the center of the room, eased down onto a tall stool in front of the Tektronix computer and keyboarded in a couple of commands, then waved a hand at the instrument sitting next to it. The first thing she noticed was that the glass syringes mounted across the top were gone.

"I automated the filling and emptying," he explained, pointing to three switches lined up together on the front panel. "And added a couple of visual indicators, here, to jazz it up a little." He gave her a boyish grin. "Just to psych up the operator, reinforce what you know the instrument's doing, even though you can't actually see it." He pointed to the narrow strip of green light moving on the control panel. "Mounted it vertically, just like the tube that sucks up the blood or whatever. Actually, all it does is reflect the amplitude of motion in the tube. See what happens when I turn it up?" He changed the setting of one of the controls and the green light jumped higher, like mercury rising in a thermometer, except that it continued to bounce up and down, just like the fluid inside the tube was pulsing in imitation of blood flowing through the vessels. He flipped another switch, waited a second, then removed the little plastic cup from the sample-holding stage and carried it into another room.

Mari followed along behind, watching how carefully he sealed it inside a Ziploc plastic bag before disposing of the fluid in a covered waste container. This was the "kitchen" of the lab, where he stored, handled, and prepared the biological materials he tested, and it was as elaborately equipped as any gourmet chef's kitchen, perhaps more so, with not only hot and cold water at the stainless-steel sink, but also distilled water and air. A full-size refrigerator stood in one corner, and next to that was a small oven and a digital scale capable of extremely sensitive readings. Blenders and centrifuges lined another countertop, and boxed lab tissues and rubber gloves were scattered everywhere, within easy reach of every work space, both here and in the larger room.

"Want to see what the synovial fluid looks like?" Charles asked as he slid a sheet of paper into the graphics plotter sitting next to the Tektronix, knowing just from the look on her face that she was already hooked. He stabbed at the keyboard with two fingers, watching the monitor from time to time, then waited until the plotter went into action. Within seconds it had the vertical and horizontal axes drawn, and then the data points began to appear as tiny black triangles.

"Fantastic," Mari whispered, mesmerized by the bodyless arm taking direction from the brain in a box, as a continuous line began to connect up all the triangles, revealing the shape of this particular "curve."

"More?" Charles asked. When she nodded, he reached for a different pen, to replace the one that had drawn the first curve, then instructed the computer again. This time the data points were little green squares, and a smooth green line connected them together. When the plotter arm returned to the starting position, he jumped up from his stool, pulled the sheet of paper loose and handed it to her, then moved to stand behind her and peer over her shoulder. "The black line is the viscosity, and the green is the elasticity," he explained. "See what's happening here?" He reached an arm around her to point to where the two curves crossed, one dropping just about where the other started to rise. When his other arm came around her, too, she twisted around and hooked her hands behind his neck. She was wearing low-heeled sandals, so had to tiptoe up to reach him, which also bared her midriff, because her blouse was short to begin with, coming only to the waistband of her full denim skirt.

"Was all this just a macho ploy, getting me up here to see your 'etchings,' so you could seduce me?" she murmured against his lips.

"You wanna be seduced?" he asked, imitating her but adding a little something extra by way of persuasion as his mouth moved across hers to flick his tongue into one corner.

"Too late to ask, I'm afraid," she mumbled, then felt his lips stretch into a smile. One of his thighs pushed against hers, and then the other, as he walked her backward until she came up against the lab bench behind her. Then his hands were at her waist and he was lifting her onto it, keeping her lips covered with his. Next thing she knew he was pushing her knees apart, insinuating his body between them, and his hands were sliding up to shape the sides of her rib cage, then over her breasts, and finally up either side of her neck and into her hair. When he clasped her head between his hands and moved her face away a little, their eyes were at the same level. And she saw that all the teasing was gone from his face.

"I've been thinking about this, you . . . here . . . like this . . . all week." His hands grew more insistent and his mouth was urgent. Mari felt the familiar warmth rising as his tongue danced with hers, stroking, stabbing, circling, and caressing, the arrangement of their bodies too suggestive to resist. With her knees spread and her feet swinging free of the floor, he had easy access to the place he wanted and needed. He pulled up her skirt as he nuzzled her face, butterflying kisses across her cheeks and into her hair, to the corner of her eye, and her lips, eager to cover every inch of her with his mouth, blindly searching for the band of her panties, wanting this last barrier out of the way.

It took a second or two to hit him, but then he jerked back, disbelieving the message his groping fingers were sending to his brain. He felt again, just to make sure. *"Me* seduce *you!*" he blurted, then threw back his head and started laughing.

"I, uh, thought maybe I'd be ready to offer, uh, special inducements, just in case—" Her face was already flushed with arousal.

"You mean you—all that time, in the kitchen, when you were making the salad, and I was talking—while we were eating, and—" He started to laugh again.

"I knew you were going to be working in the lab all day, thought you might come home preoccupied. I know how it is with you science types, how hard it is to get your mind off your work," she explained, struggling to carry it through without even cracking a smile.

"You can still say that after the last few days! I thought it was going to be easier having you here—but it's not. Worse, if anything." His mouth came back to hers, wet and hot, and urgent, while his hands lifted her legs and wrapped them around his hips. "Talk about single-minded—hell, I can hardly think about anything but this, with you out there, just across the lake, ready and waitin'." He grasped her buttocks and breathed, "Scoot forward a little," triggering a mental picture that caused her to giggle into his mouth—of herself lying with her knees spread, her feet in the stirrups, and her gynecologist ordering her to "scoot down a little."

She heard his zipper, and then he was pulling her to meet his thrust, stilling for a second so both of them could savor the sensation of completion, of perfect fit. But when he began to move again, she discovered she was a prisoner, had as little control as on the examining table she'd just visualized. Except internally. So she tried contracting and relaxing her inner muscles around him, timing herself to his thrusts, which only divided her attention, stealing it away from her own response, such as it was.

With Charles she was becoming much more aware of the monthly changes in her body—aware in a way that had very little to do with reading clinical descriptions of the same thing, in medical journals—and knew that she would never reach orgasm unless she could relax enough to concentrate. Because that's what it usually took during the second half of her cycle, in contrast to the more spontaneous, and quicker, response of her body in the week or so immediately after her monthly period. Perched precariously on the edge of a lab bench—unable to do anything to control the angle of his thrust, his hands occupied primarily with holding her in place—was a losing proposition for her, if not for him, so she quit even trying. Instead, she concentrated on heightening his sensations, and when she heard his breath coming in gasps, whispered, "Go ahead." He thrust deeply, holding onto to her like a drowning man grabbing at a life preserver.

She waited until his breathing slowed, then whispered, "What do we do now?"

He pulled away, straightening his pants at the same time. "Looked like it ought to work," he commented, a half-apologetic, half-puzzled smile curling up the corners of his mouth. "But it didn't, did it?"

She shook her head and slid off the bench, letting her skirt fall and straighten itself. "Not for me." She started toward the door.

Charles caught her arm. "I'll make it up to you at home."

"Are you confessing—or bragging?" she drawled, unable to hide the fact that she was actually kind of put off by the failure of his little "experiment," because he'd left her halfway up the mountain, so to speak, which made her feel taut as a tightly drawn bow string, with the adrenaline still pumping through her blood, preparing her body for something that wasn't going to happen. "Don't worry about it, I'll probably live," she tossed back at him over her shoulder as she started for the door again. "You *do* have a 'ladies' hidden somewhere in this state-supported bordello, don't you?"

"Sure," he sighed. "Two doors down the hall, on your right. I'll close up here, be ready to go whenever you are." Charles felt an irrational flash of anger at her implication that he'd done something wrong, when *she* was the one who hadn't been able to keep up, followed immediately by a sort of guilty chagrin because he'd gone ahead without her.

Mari spent Thursday morning at Charles's computer, querying one of the data bases at the National Library of Medicine in Washington, the largest medical research library in the world—with four million books, technical reports, and manuscripts in seventy languages, including the handwritten notes of Florence Nightingale and Louis Pasteur, and medical texts dating back to the eleventh century—and most of the afternoon in the swimming pool, perfecting her breathing and practicing her flutter kick. Charles thought she was working on the reverse butterfly, but whenever he wasn't around, she spent most of her pool time on the crawl, trying to get it as clean and easy, and as powerful, as his, in spite of the fact that her feet were only about half as long. She would be leaving for Denver tomorrow to spend the weekend with her mother, so it was her last chance to prove to herself and him that she could keep up with him for at least one length of the pool. Which she did, but for two laps instead of one, which surprised her as much as him.

Charles took her to Kate's for dinner that night, an unprepossessing-looking little restaurant located in an old house in one of Austin's declining neighborhoods, near the university married-student housing.

"They're positively indecent!" Mari complained as they drove past the rows of buff-painted plaster clones. "Look nude, exposed, all laid out like a bunch of cadavers. You'd think one of the richest universities in the country could afford a few shrubs to hide their ugliness, wouldn't you?"

"You're so old-fashioned, Mari, talking beauty, character, stuff like that. Who needs it if you can't make money off of it? Ever notice the motto carved on the front of main building, which used to be the library—'Ye shall know the truth and the truth shall make you free'? A few years back a bunch of students got up there one night, covered it over with a banner that read, 'Money talks!'"

Mari laughed, remembering a similar incident at the University of Colorado. "Same thing happened in Boulder. Same place, the library, which I guess is where all the profound homilies get carved in stone. 'Who knows only his own generation remains always a child.' Some women students climbed up there one night, and the next morning it read, 'Who knows only *her* own generation remains always a child.'"

The minute they walked in the door of Kate's, Mari knew

the evening was going to be special. There was nothing particularly notable about the decor, except for the dark polished-wood floor, but the place felt warm, perhaps because it had once been a home. The woman who met them at the door led them to a table in a small room— formerly a sun porch, Mari guessed—opening off the larger main room. She accepted the menu the woman offered, noting the small vase of flowers and the squat little candles on each table. When she glanced back at Charles, he was watching her. She smiled and reached out a caressing hand, unable to resist touching the soft cashmere lapel of his camel sport coat. He was wearing the dark brown suede tie he'd bought in Madrid, and the combination, especially next to his tanned face, was stunning.

"I like it. Does the food live up to the way it feels?"

"We'll see," he answered, opening his menu with one hand. They spent the next couple of minutes reading the short list of entrées—one chicken, one beef, and one lamb dish, and several kinds of fish.

"I'm going to do fish, but I don't know which one," Mari decided.

"Me too. Fresh salmon with horseradish and dill sauce. Salad comes with everything, and some other stuff, too, a vegetable, rice, whatever. Have you looked at the appetizers? Maybe that'll help you decide." In the end she chose the redfish with an avocado, mushroom, cilantro and lime sauce, but no appetizer. "If I have any room left, I'm going to have dessert instead, because this looks like the kind of place that makes wonderful coffee, where you'd like to sit around after, talking and savoring it, don't you think?"

"Depends on the company. Tonight yes." He squeezed her hand, hardly able to keep his eyes or his hands off her shiny, undulating hair, or her slightly sunburned face. Even in the candlelight her eyes were blue-green tonight, though he wasn't sure why, since she was wearing white—a simple vee-necked, cotton-knit chemise that draped her body, moving like fluid over her hips and breasts as she moved, teasing the imagination with subtle hints of what he knew was underneath. And what wasn't. She also had on the Zuni bracelet he'd given her, and silver earrings dangled from her ears, reflecting light from the candle on the table whenever she moved her head—like the flashes of light from a lighthouse, beckoning and calling him to her.

The waiter set a bucket of ice on the corner of their table, pulled the cork from the bottle of Fall Creek White Zinfandel, one of the first Texas wines to win national recognition, and poured a little into two glasses. Mari looked at him with a pleased smile while he waited for each of them to taste it, relishing being included in this traditional male ritual, sure now that this was a place like no other—existing only to indulge her fantasies.

"It's perfect!" she announced, not sure whether she meant the wine, the place, or Charles.

After the waiter filled their glasses and then left, Charles reached over to smooth a strand of hair back from her cheek, then cupped the back of her neck with his hand and pulled her to him for a quick kiss. "It's been good for you here, hasn't it, Mari? What happened at the shelter the other night is fading, isn't it?" He'd been watching her closely for signs that the events of that night still haunted her. But telling him about it seemed to have served to help relieve her of the visions and memories that had driven her to the brink of utter despair. Almost overnight, or so it seemed to him, she'd become her usual self again, consumed with curiosity, avidly adventuresome, ready to try anything, flip-flopping from serious to laughing on the turn of a word or a look.

"Yes," she agreed with a little smile. "It's a place out of my most cherished fantasies. But you knew, didn't you, how I'd feel about your wonderful house—the light and the trees, and all the animals?"

"Since the Alhambra," he agreed with a crooked smile. "But I was keeping my fingers crossed all the same, 'cause I'm not too sure of a helluva whole lot where you're concerned. Only that I love you, need you, want you—all the time."

"I know, me too. Though I'm still afraid I may wake up any time and find that it's all a dream, which probably sounds silly and adolescent. You seem able to take everything in stride, as if it's the most natural thing in the world to have the outrageous good luck to find someone to love, at least the way I love you." She straightened and looked around, suddenly self-conscious. "Maybe I—I'm probably saying too much."

"You can never say too much to suit me." He was perfectly serious. "Why would you think that, Mari?"

"Well, for one thing, it'll just go straight to your head, or your ego, or something, and then you'll be absolutely impossible to live with." She was trying to lighten up, to shake off the rush of emotion, knowing she would probably dissolve in tears if she didn't.

Charles smoothed a hand over her hair, indulging himself. "I haven't taken *you* in stride at all. Nothing is the same. You've upset what I realize now was a very tranquil existence—satisfying, probably even good—but now, well, the house feels empty since I came back from Spain. And I have a new pair of eyes and ears, see things I've never noticed before, hear things in music I've listened to all my life that I never heard before. I have these wild ideas I can't wait to try out with you—some better than others, right?— because I want us to experience everything, wring every pleasure there is from our bodies and hearts and minds. You belong here, with me."

"Maybe, but that doesn't mean it's going to be easy to make happen, at least not any time soon."

"I don't see why the hell not, especially now!" He started to tell her about the licensing agreement, then changed his mind.

"What's so different about now? I still have to go back to work Monday, with sword in hand. And somehow manage to get all the cuts I need for the PBS program, between broadcasts, without Jack catching on, which means I'm probably going to be on the road every minute I can spare for the next month. Tony, too."

"The difference is that we're going to start working on whatever the problems are together. I want you to level with me, explain what I don't know or understand, let me help where I can, because I want you to be able to do what you want, too, Mari honey," he said softly, seductively, pulling her hand up to his lips, "whether it's producing television documentaries or babies. Or both. And the sooner the better, as far as I'm concerned."

CHAPTER

15

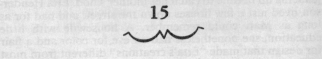

Mari stabbed the top of the lemon pudding cake with her mother's two-tined kitchen fork, then began dribbling icing over the top, a little at a time, letting some soak in and some run down the sides. Every time she tried doing this in Houston, the icing kept right on running until it pooled on the plate, which said more about Denver's mile-high, dry atmosphere than it did about her expertise. "The girls" were coming this afternoon, friends of Janet's who'd been meeting together for years to "piece and quilt," which Mari considered quaintly old-fashioned, like the women themselves. Their number varied from year to year, but they all had two things in common—a talent for meticulous stitching, and a willingness to work communally, which meant contributing to a product they'd never be able to call entirely their own.

"Whose design are you working on this time?" Mari asked, more to make conversation than out of real curiosity.

"You'll know, soon as you see it. Could you reach the decaf for me?" Janet asked, pouring water into the top of the coffee maker. "It's in the cabinet right there in front of you." Even the refreshments she always offered were traditional— a homemade dessert with either coffee or tea, served on her best china—though in recent years she'd added apple juice

293

because several of the women had experienced digestive problems as they grew older. Janet believed in apples as a curative for all kinds of stomach ills, and Mari remembered that as a child she'd always been given small pieces of carefully peeled apple for an upset tummy, instead of Pepto-Bismol or one of the other drugstore medications her friends got.

"Mrs. Henderson?" Mari asked, more interested now, glancing up in time to catch her mother's nod. Etta Henderson lived just a few houses down the street, and had for as long as Mari could remember. A housewife with little education, she nonetheless had an eye for color and a flair for design that made "Etta's creations" different from most of the others. "Have any of the local museums ever shown Mrs. Henderson's quilts, Mom? Not that the others aren't—"

"Don't apologize. We all realize that hers are exceptional." Mari guessed Etta Henderson to be about ten years older than Janet, which put her somewhere in her late seventies. The Henderson children were several years older than both Mari and Jackie, so they'd never played together. Mari's most vivid memory about the family, in fact, was the night she'd been awakened by the ambulance siren, because, as it turned out, Mr. Henderson had accidentally shot himself while cleaning his gun. He'd died two days later, in the hospital.

"I don't care what anyone says, divorce isn't always such a bad thing, you know," Janet muttered, taking a conversational leap that threw Mari for a mental loop.

"What—Who are you talking about, Mom?"

"Why, Etta Henderson, of course! In her day, you know, you were supposed to stay married no matter what—for the children's sake! Of course other things were different then, too. A man's home was his castle, everyone said. And so did the law. A man had the right to do whatever he wanted to in the privacy of his own home. But that man of hers had a streak of meanness in him a mile wide. And if that wasn't enough, he was also an alcoholic! She should've left him, but then she would've had nothing, not even a home—and her with three children to support. So she put up with him. As long as she could. Maybe if she'd been able to divorce him, it might never have come to that."

"I'm afraid you lost me somewhere, Mom. Come to what?" The teakettle whistled a shrill warning, and Mari reached for the control, to turn down the burner.

"Why, I thought you knew," Janet said, turning toward her with a surprised look. "She shot him!"

Mari's legs went suddenly weak and she had to sit down at the little breakfast table. "No, I didn't," she breathed, but was saved from having to explain further by the peal of the door-bell chimes. She just sat there, stunned, while Janet hurried into the other room to answer it. What else did she remember "wrong" as a result of her childish naiveté? Mari wondered.

When Mari finished with the cake a few minutes later and went into the living room to greet her mother's friends, she found it hard not to stare at Etta Henderson. She'd planned to stay only long enough to help Janet serve the cake and coffee, then leave the women to themselves, but got caught up in watching them place the backing fabric, then the layer of stuffing, and finally the pieced top of the quilt over the stretchers, constantly adjusting until they got everything exactly the way they wanted it. When they settled down to actually start quilting, the talk began in earnest, and her presence in no way inhibited what anyone had to say, beginning with the subject of yesterday's Oprah Winfrey show—lesbians.

"Have you girls ever stopped to wonder why it is that lesbian women don't engage in violent sexual practices the way gay men do?" Hetty Schuler asked, without preamble or embarrassment, bringing up a subject that most women her age avoided like the plague. Or so Mari had believed till now. "And why most lesbians form monogamous relationships, while so many male homosexuals go in for one-night stands? Which I understand has a lot to do with why they're the ones who are getting AIDS!"

"Perhaps because women are more advanced than men in the evolutionary sense," Etta Henderson suggested. "I read an article the other day—in *Psychology Today,* I think it was—about how natural selection favored human females who developed the ability to maintain the sex drive beyond when they were in heat—they were like other animals back then, in prehistoric times—so they could attract males to help care for their young. To do that they had to evolve brains that could be activated by some hormone, even when they weren't ovulating, which means that the brain is more involved in sexual arousal in females than it is in males. With men it's more mindless. So what else is new, huh, girls?" She laughed.

"Everyone knows that women are much more civilized than men," Maggie Doyle injected, "and have been for centuries, which I suppose is just another way of saying the same thing."

"I wouldn't be too sure of that," Eleanor Manning objected. "From what my daughter tells me, some of the women she works with are vicious bitches. Do any of you remember that book by Dr. Seuss— *Yertle the Turtle*, I think it was called—about a turtle who wanted to get ahead so bad he didn't care whose back he had to climb on, or how he got up there?"

The women left around four-thirty, and Mari sent Janet off to her bedroom to rest while she cleaned up the dishes. After that she got her sweater, poured herself a glass of wine, and went out to the sun porch, to sit quietly and relax—and to get some of her shattered assumptions sorted out in her head. She sipped and stared, mostly at the backbone of the Rocky Mountains, gone hazy now under the dying sun, and let her thoughts go back to a time when her whole world had been this house, yard, and street. A time when she'd believed that all the other streets and houses, and the people in them, were just like hers. Full of warm, friendly people who loved and took care of each other, who were always there when you needed them. She knew better now, so why should she find it so disturbing to discover that even then—here on this ordinary, quiet middle-class street— there had been people living in the hell of degradation and violence behind the facade of their lovely houses?

Why had it been such a revelation, listening to those women today? Certainly a lot more than quilting held "the girls" together, for their meetings also were a chance to bounce ideas off each other, to get a feel for what other women, or their children, were thinking about and doing. She'd drifted into a sort of fantasy as she listened to them, imagining that the thread they wove in and out of the fabric was being transformed into a common bond, connecting them to both the past and a present experienced largely through their husbands and children. Had she really thought, up to now, that *she* was the only one who'd changed with the years? If so, perhaps it was because she hadn't really bothered to notice, because her eyes and ears were turned inward, concerned only with her own life. But truth be told, she knew damned well it was more than that, that in fact she'd tried to tune Janet out of her life as much as possible. And for the first time it dawned on her that what "growing up" really meant was being able to see her parents as fallible and vulnerable rather than superhuman, with neither the power to make everything right nor to say no.

Janet was clearly a very different person now from the woman who'd been so uptight and compulsively perfectionist where her two daughters were concerned, so paradoxically sure of herself yet indecisive about little things. Not that Mari understood everything about her mother, even now. She remembered the time Janet had gone to the school principal's office, to insist that he remove some silly test score from her permanent school record, and had created an embarrassing scene. Why could Janet never bring herself to call the plumber, instead of dithering around about it, wondering whether she should, in the end always waiting until her husband came home from work? Yet after he'd died, she bought new furniture for the living room, traveled all over the globe, and managed her stock portfolio with a kind of devil-may-care worldliness, nearly doubling the value of his estate in less than six years.

Mari lost track of time, sitting there lost in the mysteries of childhood, wondering at the myths she'd constructed and lived by for so long.

"Oh, you already have some," Janet said from the doorway. She was carrying two small glasses of wine. "I know I shouldn't, but just a little bit won't hurt, do you think, on special occasions?" She set one glass on the table next to Mari, then sat down in her usual chair, which faced west and had a full view of the mountains. "I know you're worried about what happened at the station, Mari, but I'm glad of it, in a way. It's given you and Charles a chance to spend a little time together. And you and me, too." Mari nodded, but otherwise didn't acknowledge the mention of Charles.

They were due at Jackie's in about an hour, but there was time, so they watched the sun drop behind the mountains, and let the minutes spin out in silence. "A few more days like this and the iris will be showing buds," Janet commented, seeking neutral ground, then let the silence descend again.

"Do you remember my little green and white tricycle, the one with the balloon tires?" Mari's voice sounded as if it came from a long long way off.

"Oh yes, of course."

"Did you know that I've always wondered what happened to it? Dad said he was taking it to Winky's to get it fixed." She could picture the front of Winkleman's auto and bicycle repair shop. "I kept asking him, week after week, month after month, when it was going to be ready, when he was going to bring it back. Until I finally figured out that he never was, and quit asking." She stared out the windows. "He never intended to bring it back, right from the first, did he?"

"You'd outgrown it, Mari. Your knees were bumping the handlebars, and he thought it would be easier for you, because you were so attached—"

"It's the one thing I've never really forgiven him for, you know. Taking it, and lying to me." Remembered hurt and disappointment still had the power to fan the embers of old fires.

"You can try to always do what you think is best for a child, Mari, but that doesn't mean you don't make mistakes. If that's the only time he lied to you, I'd say that's an enviable record, for any parent, one you may want to keep in mind when you become one yourself."

"If I ever do," Mari muttered, holding tight to remembered resentment. A few more minutes slipped by in silence. "What was that scene all about, anyway? The one you made in Mr. Whitmore's office when I was in sixth grade? Were my scores so terrible as all that?" Might as well get that straight, too, while the opportunity presented itself.

Janet laughed, a little taken back. "No, of course not!

They were quite good, in fact. Too good." Her answer brought Mari up straight in her chair.

"Good? And you wait till now to tell me that? My God, I didn't think any grade, any score, could be too high! You threw such a fit, I thought I'd bombed and embarrassed you and Dad!"

"All this time . . ." Janet let the words trail off, shaking her head in dismay, then turned toward Mari. "I learned a lesson, with Jackie, which happens a lot to the first child. She wasn't quick, like you, or very good at taking tests. And she had to live with having those scores being thrown up to her, one way or another, just because they were there on her permanent record for all her teachers to see. Things like that always have a way of getting out, you know. I remember when she came home one time, asking what I.Q. meant, because her teacher had reprimanded a couple of the kids for chiding her about a grade she made on some paper. Seems Mrs. Flatello—you remember her, in fifth grade?— took it as an opportunity to give the whole class a lecture on tolerance, on how there were innate differences between people, like skin color and I.Q. Then, as if that weren't enough, when she was in high school the counselor advised Jackie not to set her sights too high, warned her that she shouldn't expect to get into any of the really good colleges." She looked away, but not before Mari saw the glitter of tears in her eyes, which shocked Mari more than anything, because she'd seen her mother cry only once before in her entire life, and that had been about a week after her father died. She'd rationalized it as probably due more to a shortage of prolactin than any lack of emotion, since she knew her mother had never been able to nurse her babies, and the same hormone that stimulated lactation also stimulated tears.

"I had to live with— I tried. But once it was done, what could I do?" Mari could tell the question still haunted Janet, that she still wondered whether there was something she could have done for Jackie and hadn't. "So I was determined that you weren't going to carry the same burden. It doesn't really matter whether the scores are high or low. Children shouldn't have labels put on them. I didn't want your teachers nagging you, making you feel bad about yourself whenever you didn't come up to *their* expectations. And I didn't want you getting any self-important ideas, either!" She laughed a little at that.

No, Mari wanted to scream, you've got it all wrong! *You're the one I could never satisfy, the one who always expected too much of me!* Was she losing her mind? It seemed that nobody was who, or what, she thought they were. Not her mother, and not Etta Henderson. Not even her own sister, who'd always seemed lacking in ambition, at least until recently. Certainly Mari had been as wrong as wrong could be about Phillip Ashmore, to her everlasting sorrow. And what about Charles Merrill? Was he not as he seemed, either? The question came like a streak of lightning, illuminating the dark crannies of her mind for one brief instant before she pushed it back into hiding again.

"Your father and I were so worried when Jackie married Nick, started having babies right away," Janet continued, completely unaware of the havoc she'd created in her daughter's head. "A skinny boy of nineteen, working as a carpenter's helper. Hardly able to feed himself, let alone a wife and child. Still wet behind the ears, your father said. But Jackie loved him, had faith in him, and he bloomed like a desert cactus after a rain." Mari had to grin at her mother's simile—trite, but so true. "Who would've thought then that he'd end up one of the most successful building contractors in the state? But more important, he's given Jackie faith in herself, as a woman. And the rest will follow." She paused and turned to Mari with a slow smile. "I worried about you, too, you know, but for different reasons. You were always into something. I never knew what it would be next. Kept me on pins and needles."

Maybe that was the problem between them, and always had been, Mari thought. Janet worried too much about her, because she cared too much. Maybe caring too much was the inescapable "sin" of all mothers. Or was it only women like her mother, whose every waking thought centered on their husbands and children? Women who never knew any identity beyond that of daughter, wife, mother, and finally grandmother, whose sense of worth came from their relation to others.

Mari knew she could never be that kind of woman, loving

and considerate as her father had been, because the scales in a relationship like that were too far out of balance, exacting too much from one partner at the expense of the other—far more than was fair, or *right*. She also suspected that her mother had "visited" upon her daughters the anger and resentment generated by the war she'd waged within herself —anger at herself for sacrificing her own aspirations, albeit voluntarily, and resentment of the society that had conditioned her to believe that self-sacrifice was the only proper thing for a "good" woman, especially a mother, to do. But it didn't have to be that way. Charles's mother was proof of that! Forced out on her own in order to support herself and a child, Amy Merrill Gramling obviously had developed a sense of identity and autonomy. And that must have been good for both her *and* her son, because it not only gave free rein to her own aspirations, but to Charles's as well, allowing him to find and develop confidence in himself at an early age, unencumbered by his mother's overweening love. Mari pictured Charles's mother as she'd looked that day at the Remington, with her sun-streaked hair and designer suit, but she knew it was far more than appearance or age that separated Amy from her mother.

"Charles and I sat here, just like this, watching the sun go down," Janet murmured. "Talking. Or did I already tell you that? Sometimes I can't remember whether I've said something or just thought it."

"What about?" Mari asked, reaching for the glass of wine her mother had brought out.

"You, of course! What else? I bragged on you shamefully, couldn't seem to help myself, especially right after seeing you on TV. But we both got a little carried away." She chuckled, remembering, then sobered. "He asked me, asked if—" Old habits were slow to die, and she was having trouble getting it out.

"Asked what?" Mari urged, curious.

"As soon as the broadcast ended he turned and asked, 'Now what do you think of your little girl?' I said you were much better than most of the network reporters, which I've known for a long time. And he asked if I'd ever told you, which made me realize that I shouldn't just assume that you know things like that. I always knew you could do whatever you set your mind on, of course, and better than most anyone else. You're my best performance, Mari. I know it hasn't been easy, that it was so hard for you, after Phillip, and, well, what I'm trying to say is, I just wish—"

Now the tears were in Mari's eyes, and choking her throat so she could hardly speak. "Wish what?"

Janet didn't answer for a few seconds. "Did I tell you that he came to see me while I was in the hospital?"

"Phillip?"

"Yes. Please don't think that I'm trying to interfere, Mari, but I hope you won't let—" She broke off and then started over. "Charles is so excited about loving you, he's like a little boy. Almost breaks my heart, just listening to him, seeing how his eyes light up when he talks about you. Don't throw that away, Mari, because of what happened with Phillip. Can't you put him behind you at last, and have the kind of life you want with Charles?"

"Maybe. I just don't know whether to trust my feelings or not, Mom. I did once, and—"

"So you're going to let one mistake override all the other good decisions you've made in your life? You've come so far since then."

"Yes, I know, but Phillip was the kind of mistake I just can't afford to make again, Mom."

"But you're not the same person now, Mari."

"Older and wiser, huh? God, I hope so, but there are so damn many problems, so many questions. And there don't seem to be any good answers. Like where would I work? Doing what? What would I do if I—if we decided to have a child? Charles insists that he makes enough money for both of us, and thinks that takes care of everything. Doesn't seem to have even an inkling of why I simply can't live like that."

"Give it a little time. Think of it like a good soup, Mari. You'll just have to let everything simmer together until it's ready. And depending on what ingredients you throw into the pot, it can sometimes be pretty difficult to predict exactly how long that might take."

There she goes again, Mari thought, with another one of those blasted truisms of hers, just when I was beginning to think we actually could learn to talk to each other without my blood pressure going through the roof. She couldn't decide whether to laugh or cry, because she felt like doing both, and instead reached up and switched on the table lamp, then glanced at her watch.

"I suppose we ought to get our stuff together and go. Jackie's expecting us about six-thirty." They were not only going to have supper at Jackie's, but also spend the night, so Mari would have some time with the whole family. "Is there anything else I should know, I mean about what you two said about me when I wasn't here to defend myself?" She tried to make a joke out of it, but in fact she was more than a little curious.

"Well, later, when we were at dinner, he asked me to tell him what you were like when you were little. I told you you were a regular daredevil," Janet confessed, "racing all over the neighborhood on your little green and white tricycle. Kind of a funny coincidence, isn't it?"

Mari's flight to Houston was late loading and then sat at the end of the runway for an hour, which was standard operating procedure at Stapleton. As a result, it was nearly midnight by the time she pulled into the parking lot behind her apartment. She was fumbling in the dark, trying to get her key into the door, when she heard her phone. "Open, dammit!" she muttered out loud. Any other time she would have let the answering machine take it, but she hadn't thought to even turn it on before she left. And it must be Charles—who else would call at this hour?—wondering why she wasn't home yet, worried about her. She flicked the light on and raced for the phone, leaving her suitcase outside.

"You sure are hard to get a hold of."

She recognized the unisex voice immediately. "I . . . I've been out of town. Sorry," she mumbled, without knowing why. It wasn't her fault, after all, that he'd called while she was gone.

"Haven't seen anything on the tube, thought maybe I better give you a call, find out why not."

She twisted the switch on her desk lamp and reached for a pad of paper and pencil. "I think I'm finally on the right track," she began, forgetting all about her suitcase or that the front door to her apartment was still standing wide open. "I talked with a doctor in New York, just last week, who's been treating cocaine abusers. The one who prescribed imipramine for cocaine-related depression and discovered it blocks the dopamine receptors in the brain. Found out by accident that most of his addicts who were on Tofranil couldn't get high on coke. Because it binds to the same receptors in the brain, blocks both the euphoria and the craving for more." She mentally reviewed the effects of cocaine—chronic cough, chest congestion, impotence, infertility, lactation in women and enlarged breasts in men, brain seizures and cardiac arrest.

"Yeah, I know about that."

How could he be so damned noncommittal? "Well, there has to be some connection—between lactation, menstrual abnormalities, psychotropic drugs that block dopamine receptors, and the fact that women in particular are at risk with Pamezine—if I could just find it!" She was tired and frustrated, and she didn't care if he knew it. Unlike Bob Woodward and *his* Deepthroat, they didn't have any prearranged signal she could use to let him know when she needed help, or at least a little guidance.

"Maybe, maybe not. Sounds to me like you're letting someone lead you down the garden path, or the long way around."

If I am, it's your own damn fault! she wanted to yell at him, to somehow shake him loose from his detachment.

"What'd you get from the FDA?"

"The Office of Drug Research and Review has received about three thousand reports of adverse effects associated with the use of Pamezine over the past three years, nearly two hundred of them fatalities. Spontaneous reports, which must be only a fraction of the total number of adverse reactions. I also got through to Pharmacol's CEO, though it took a while. He couldn't say enough good about Pamezine, which I guess isn't surprising in view of the fact that it's the company's most lucrative product ever, with four hundred million in sales last year alone. But when I started to question him about adverse effects, he clammed up. Said, and I quote, 'We've seen no unexpected results from the launching of the product.' Period."

"Jesus, lady! I thought you were smarter than that. You're

not going to get to first base digging around at Pharmacol. All you'll do is warn them off—if you haven't already, screwing around with the president like that. Scare 'em into covering everything in shit so thick nobody'd ever be able to dig out. And believe me, they're experts at doing that! I told you, what you're looking for's at the FDA."

"Well, maybe if you'd been more help, or gotten back in touch sooner—"

He cut her off again. "Adverse reports have begun pouring in, faster than anybody ever thought they would. The company's just decided to start easing Pamezine off the market, a little at a time, so no one catches on. Can't afford to admit anything, because the cost of litigation and compensation would kill us, or so the word goes around here. I suspect there's more to it than that. Maybe even criminal liability for the top guys."

"But I don't even know what I'm looking for!" She was really exasperated by now, and on the verge of throwing in the towel. Her caller was probably just a crazy, anyway, a guy who got his kicks out of guessing games—games where he held all the cards. She'd been a fool for wasting any of her time chasing his miserly clues.

"You ever hear of Feldene, the anti-inflammatory drug put out by Pfizer? For rheumatoid and osteo arthritis. A damned wonder drug, except that it also causes massive gastrointestinal bleeding. Company knew patients in Europe were dying from the stuff. Ireland, Switzerland, Germany, even Canada. But did they inform the FDA? No, even though the law requires them to. The FDA found out six months after they approved the damned drug. Politics, honey! Take a look at the Feldene case, you'll see what I mean."

And then he was gone, and she was left sitting there with her mouth open, her brain still running amok with unanswered questions.

After a while she went back out to retrieve her suitcase and the little bag of groceries she'd picked up at a 7-Eleven on the way in from Houston Intercontinental—milk, bread, and eggs for breakfast—moving like a robot, hardly aware of what she was doing. Because her mind was working on something else, trying to recall everything she'd ever heard about Feldene. Going over every detail she could remember, piece by piece, again and again. She unpacked and hung clothes in the closet, washed out two pair of panty hose, shampooed her hair, and even took a hot bath, hoping it would help her relax enough to go to sleep, all to no avail. She tossed and turned in the bed, finally gave up and turned on the lamp, searched through the paperbacks stacked on the floor beside her bed, looking for something really boring. She read awhile, then went to the kitchen to scramble an egg, make a piece of toast, and drink a glass of milk. She wasn't really hungry, but sometimes eating helped. Still, the night marched endlessly on, and she was aware of every minute of it, until the first cold light of dawn began to filter through the drapes.

Like Pavlov's dog, the sound of a telephone always brought a conditioned response from Mari, and the next thing she knew she was sitting upright in bed, trying to fight clear of the covers. She glanced around the room, disoriented, feeling the breathless rush of adrenaline, and then, for one brief second, panic. The familiar room was already bright with filtered sunlight. She glanced hastily at the clock next to her bed, her eyes still clouded by deep sleep, and then her bare feet hit the cold floor.

"Hello?"

"Are you okay? Anything wrong?" Tony asked, sensing immediately that something was. "Did I wake you? What'sa matter, are you sick?"

"No, uh, yes. I mean yes you did wake me, and good thing, too. I don't know wha—my plane was late, and then I couldn't sleep. Guess I forgot to set my alarm. Overslept. Sorry."

"It's okay. We were just getting a little worried when you didn't come in and didn't call. You planning on coming in today?"

"Of course! Just give me time to throw on some clothes. Something breaking we need to get going on?"

"I suppose you could say that. Jack's waiting, wants to see you. Beginning to get kind of impatient, in fact."

"Oh God, what is it now?" she groaned. "Did he discover I'm indispensable, or never even knew I was gone? I suppose he's waiting for me to come in so he can fire me!"

Tony laughed out loud at that. "Not today, bebé, not today. How long before you'll be here?"

"Twenty minutes to get dressed, fifteen to get there—about thirty-five or forty minutes."

"Okay, see you then. I'll tell Jack."

Good as her word, and because she skipped breakfast—who needed it after scrambled eggs and toast at three-thirty in the morning?—Mari pulled into the KPOC lot thirty-five minutes later.

The minute she opened the front door, all hell broke loose. The entire reception area was crowded with people—cameramen, reporters, editors, and control-room engineers—who parted to let her through, yelling, grinning, whistling, and clapping. Balloons bounced against the ceiling, trailing colorful streamers, and straight ahead, above a table loaded with food, was a paper banner with KPOC'S GOT HEART painted across it in bright red letters. Sandy Pittman and Podge Pearsall were opening bottles of champagne as fast as they could at another table, grinning like a couple of fools.

"Well, here she is at last, folks," Jack called out when he spotted her. Then every eye in the room seemed to turn toward Mari, and the clapping got even louder. Even more disoriented than when Tony had called, she looked around for him, trying to get some clue as to what was going on, and finally spotted him standing with Ron Bergner, a big grin on his face, watching her. Jack motioned her closer, then held up his hands to the crowd, calling for quiet before turning back to Mari.

"My cup runneth over! Any of you ever see Mari McNichols speechless before?" Everyone laughed at his little joke, then followed it with a new scattering of applause. "Guess it's time to let her in on why we're celebrating, huh, since she's the star of this show." He draped one arm around her shoulder and shoved a slightly worn, crumpled-looking telegram into her hand. But before she could read it, a glass of champagne was shoved into her other hand and Jack was lifting his. "To Mari McNichols, and 'Have a Heart,' for handing the gold baton to KPOC!"

There was one brief moment of quiet, while everyone sipped a champagne salute to Mari, followed by shouts of "Mari, Mari, quite contrary!" and "Bravo, Mari," and

"Speech!" But Mari still didn't have the slightest idea what was going on, or why, and it showed. It was Al Tischler, KPOC's general manager, who finally took pity on her. And the instant he started to speak, everyone quieted again.

"It is my very great pleasure to announce that KPOC-TV and 'Have a Heart' have just been awarded a gold baton in the Alfred I. DuPont–Columbia University competition. As most of you know, the DuPont–Columbia Awards are given annually for excellence in broadcast journalism. They are, in fact, the Pulitzers of broadcast journalism. There were eleven silver batons awarded this year, and certainly to be selected for any award in this national competition is quite an honor. But to receive the gold baton—for the program judged to have made the greatest contribution to the public's understanding of important issues or news events, is—well, the highest accolade." After that Mari heard only bits and pieces, as Al read the jury's citation.

"Exquisitely edited, masterfully executed." She turned to look at Tony, nodding her head to let him know that she very much agreed. "Raises unflinching questions—technological, moral, economic, and political—that we must deal with both as a society and as individuals, and demands equally unflinching answers." But it was the last part that brought tears to her eyes, and she had to look down, blinking them back in order not to embarrass herself, and everyone else. "Renders the complex world of physiology and medical technology understandable, while never letting us forget or ignore that it is the quality of life that must be our ultimate concern. 'Have a Heart' is, first and last, a moving testimony to the human spirit."

As soon as Al finished, Mari looked for Tony again, determined that if he wouldn't come to her, she would go to him. "You did it, bebé," he whispered in her ear when she threw her arms around his neck to give him a big hug.

But she shook her head against his cheek and whispered back, "Uh-uh, *we* did it, you turkey."

The next hour passed in a blur of murmured congratulations, hugs and kisses, questions from newspaper reporters, one of them a stringer for the *New York Times,* and still more champagne—not to mention chips and dips, barbecue, cole slaw and beans. At one point Mari glanced up to see Lou Slocum standing off by himself, tight-lipped and unsmiling, but she never did see Tracy Sadler.

"Not to worry about the broadcast tonight," Tony advised when he noticed that she kept glancing down at her watch. "Orders from headquarters. I pulled some stuff from the wire this morning, while we were waiting for you to get here, and Jack plans to air a few clips from 'Heart' during your segment, with Ron doing the voice-over about it winning the gold baton." He glanced around at the thinning crowd. "No need for you to stick around any longer, if you want to go call him, let him know."

"Him? Who do you mean?" She tried for an innocent look but couldn't carry it off, could hardly keep from laughing with excitement, in fact, still hardly able to believe it had actually happened—not just any award, but the gold baton!—that it wasn't just one of her wish-fulfillment daydreams. "Think I'll go call my mom first, read her the citation. Then maybe after that, see if I can get 'him,' which reminds me, does Rachel know?"

Tony shook his head, refusing to look her in the eye, but before she could question him further, Jack was interrupting them.

"Listen, Mari, the station is planning a really big celebration a week from Friday night—black tie, the works, at the Hyatt-Regency—to formally announce the award here, the night before the awards ceremony in New York, on the first. Gonna invite all the big guys from the medical center, DeBakey, Cooley," he raised a brow at Mari, "maybe even Red Duke," then laughed at his little joke. "Also a bunch of the biggies in Houston society. You know anybody you think should go on the invite list, get their names to Sandy soon as possible." Mari was already mentally listing who she wanted to invite, and topping the list was Charles, and his mother. Certainly Amy Gramling was one of the "biggies" of Houston society. And Rachel— Her mind came to a screeching halt, then began to back up.

"Am I expected to be there, too—in New York, I mean? On the first?"

"You bet. You, me, and Al are all going to be there with bells on."

"And Tony. The award is as much his as mine."

Tony's eyes darted back and forth from Jack to Mari, then back to Jack, but he didn't say a word.

"Well, sure, but—"

She cut him off. "Tony doesn't go, I don't go." The way she said it, both Tony and Jack knew she wasn't bluffing.

Jack didn't hesitate, she had to give him credit for that. "You got it." He started to move away, then turned back, as if he sensed she wasn't quite finished. "Anything else?"

"The rest of the week off, starting Wednesday, both of us." She paused, gathering her nerve. "And final edit on the script for tonight, about winning the award."

Jack's brows leaped, widening his eyes momentarily, and he stared at her as if he couldn't believe what he'd just heard. Mari saw his Adam's apple jump up and down when he swallowed. He nodded once, then walked away from them without another word. She looked at Tony with a wide, satisfied smile.

"You're some kinda daredevil, you know that?"

"Strike while the iron's hot—I learned that at my mother's knee. Anyway, he can't possibly fire me now, at least not for a couple of weeks. And something else, which I learned from you—you don't ask, you don't get!" She laughed happily. "Which reminds me. Rachel. Don't you think it's time to spread a little of this glory around?"

CHAPTER

16

I'm still trying to recover from yesterday," Mari explained to Rachel as she unloaded her tray, which didn't take long, since she'd ordered only a mug of cream of mushroom soup, then picked up a fat little bottle of Martinelli apple juice from the self-serve line. "Guess I overindulged, on everything."

"Yeah, even on Jack, from what I heard. Tony gave me a blow-by-blow last night. But what better reason, to overindulge, I mean? What a coup, girl!" She took a bite of eggplant quiche. "I think the whole thing is just beginning to sink in with Tony. Funny how cautious he can be at times, even about believing in himself. Not much like the guys I used to know, ten years ago, when I was twenty-five."

"Not like most of them today, either, I'd say, not that I spend much time with twenty-odd-year-old males. But most of the ones I do run into are insufferably arrogant, and juvenile, always smiling or laughing at the wrong time." Mari tossed Rachel an assessing look while she sipped at her apple juice. "What's been going on with you two, anyway? My partner goes silent as the grave every time I mention your name. I hate to pry, but—is he being an ass, or are you?"

Rachel burst out laughing, then began shaking her head.

"Maybe both of us, I don't know anymore. One minute he's the sweetest guy in the world, wants to talk, 'reason everything out,' as he calls it. And the next he's strutting around like a banty rooster, with his brains between his legs! I finally told him I was beginning to feel like a puppet, and I didn't much like being jerked around on the end of somebody else's string."

"What'd he say?"

"Jumped up, said he could fix that in a hurry, and just walked out. I haven't seen much of him since. I think it's called self-denial. He's denying me his precious self."

"But you saw him last night. He told me he was taking you to dinner, to celebrate."

Rachel nodded, then looked down at her plate. "Yeah, I don't blame him for wanting to strut his stuff, though I don't think it turned out exactly the way he planned it. He was trying to be so damn 'adult,' said he wanted to talk things out. So I said, 'Okay, talk.' He started off telling me I was the most sensitive woman he'd ever met, about people's feelings, that I never said anything that might hurt someone. So how come I could be so insensitive as to call him a little spic, since that wasn't like me at all."

"And what'd you say?" Mari urged, eager to know.

"I pointed out that he also believed I couldn't *really* love a man whose body is shorter than mine, or who's younger than me, or whatever, and I'm not like that, either. So I figured if he was so big on stereotypes, I'd try to be exactly what he thought I was—a bitch in heat out doing a little ethnic slumming."

"Wow! You do believe in shock treatment, don't you?" Mari could imagine Tony's response to that. "And that's when he got in a huff and walked out on you again?"

"No. He just grinned and said he'd have to give that a little thought. Can you believe it?"

"Sometimes I think all men are born kinky! Mom and I were at my sister's the other night, and my brother-in-law, who normally is one of the great guys in this world, flies into a tizzy because Jackie chopped the lettuce for the salad instead of tearing it! I asked him, later, when we were alone, 'What's with the little-boy routine, Nick? Didn't get your quota of attention today or what?' You know what he said?"

Rachel shook her head, even though she knew Mari's question was only rhetorical. "'Jackie complains that I love her too much, says she has a tough enough time handling her guilt about going back to school, making the kids share her time and attention, without having the responsibility for my feelings dumped on her, too. Guess I act up like that to show her I don't love her too much.' I told him I thought he was confused, that if he really wanted to relieve the burden on Jackie, he could pick up some of the responsibility around the house. Tried to explain the difference between helping out and taking responsibility, pointed out that it was one thing to run to the store for milk and bread when she asked him to, and something else for him to keep track and know when to buy more. Guess what his response was to that?" Rachel shook her head again. "Asked if I thought Jackie would feel he was invading her territory if he tried to do that!"

"There are plenty of women who would, you know," Rachel commented, then took another bite of her quiche. Neither one of them spoke again for a couple of minutes.

"But I probably did overplay my hand last night," Rachel said at last, completely serious again. Mari was just lifting a spoonful of soup to her mouth, but when she saw the almost sad expression in Rachel's eyes, she let it spill back into the mug and pushed it away. "Remember that segment Tracy did on single-mothers-by-choice? That's what I was going to do, when I first met Tony. And then, after he waged that silly campaign, went through all those blood tests to convince me it was safe to go to bed with him, guess what? I was hooked, knew I couldn't do it to him, even if I'd had a chance. Which I didn't, because even after all that, he still insisted on using a condom. Still does, because they've discovered it can take a year or more for antibodies to the immunodeficiency virus to show up in the blood, if it's been passed through sexual intercourse. Doesn't want me taking any chances." She laughed again, but mirthlessly.

Rachel's confession was like a blow to the solar plexus, hitting so close to home that it rendered Mari speechless for a moment. "You, too?" She shook her head and sighed. "I don't know why I should be surprised. It's just that, well, I thought about doing the same thing. In Spain." Rachel didn't seem particularly surprised. "So what else happened last night?"

"Oh! Well, I told him straight out in plain English that I wanted to have a baby, that I'm going to be thirty-six in a couple of months, and chromosomal abnormalities—Down syndrome, stuff like that—increase dramatically in women between the ages of thirty and thirty-five. And at forty, it happens in about one out of every hundred births."

"Yes, but with the monitoring available now," Mari argued, "amniocentesis, and chorionic villus sampling—"

"That's what he said, and also that more women are having babies after forty all the time. Sally Field, Mia Farrow, and Diana Ross, to name a few." She drew circles in the water pooled around her glass of iced tea with one finger, rather than meet Mari's eyes. "I admitted that for some reason even I don't quite understand, it's important to me to have a child. So important that I'll probably never go back to graduate school, or do some of the other things I've been considering. Told him I had no intention of trying to trick him, to get pregnant without him knowing, but that I wasn't willing to wait around forever, either, that I'd like for him to decide whether he could consider fathering my child, and that I wouldn't ask for anything else, no money or legal admission that the child is his." She straightened against the back of her chair and looked up, wearing a self-deprecating smile. "I think I blew it."

"Why! What did he say?"

"You're not going to believe this either! God, you'd have thought I was asking if he wanted to rent my apartment or something! He just sits there on the couch, cool as a cucumber, says he's glad to finally find out what's going on inside my head, what it is that's been bothering me, that he now has some serious thinking to do, especially after yesterday. And if I can wait that long, he'd like to get back to me in a couple of weeks!"

Mari was already laughing and nodding her head by the time Rachel finished. "Always expect the unexpected with Tony, haven't you learned that yet?"

"He's been expecting you to leave kapok for some time now." Rachel pronounced the station's call letters phonetically. "Says he won't stay there if you leave. And now, with the award, he probably can go wherever he wants. But maybe you're right. It didn't seem to put him off—at least he didn't rush off right afterward." She let the words trail off with a rueful smile.

"Good thing, since you're not going to see much of him for the next week or so. You know we're leaving for Washington tomorrow, to get some of the PBS interviews on tape?"

Rachel nodded. "Yeah, he told me. And after that I suppose you'll be buried with his editing equipment every free minute you can manage?"

"Have to if we're going to make the Annual Program Fair, which is the first week in May. One of the PBS stations in Denver is going to co-submit the proposal, and co-produce if the series gets funding. Which reminds me. Tell me what you know about getting FDA approval of a new drug. What does it take?"

"About a hundred million bucks, and maybe ten years. Why?"

All the hoopla yesterday had driven the phone call right out of her mind, but now she could hardly think about anything else. She told Rachel everything, starting with the first phone call, what she'd found out about Pamezine, the reports of adverse effects, and then about the second phone call, late Sunday night.

"Certainly sounds like someone who works at Pharmacol to me," Rachel concluded as soon as she finished, "trying to play it close to the chest, so whatever comes out can't be traced back to him. But if he thinks there's something off color about what they submitted to the FDA, I don't see how you can possibly ignore him, do you?"

Mari shook her head. It was a relief, and reassuring, to hear it from Rachel. "Tell me what you know about that."

"Well, all the preclinical stuff—chemical screening for toxic effects and animals tests—gets done before they ever make formal application to the FDA to get it classified as an investigational new drug, which permits the company to carry out the first limited tests on humans. After that, the agency requires tests that show the drug is both safe and effective, that it works for what they say it does. Phase-one testing determines the dosage and toxicity levels, phase two, the effectiveness—and usually requires a double blind kind of protocol, where neither the patient nor prescribing physician knows who's getting the drug or a placebo. And then phase three is more of the same. Dosage, safety, and effectiveness, but on a much larger number of patients, often several thousand."

"What could be political about phase two and three? Any ideas?"

"I may be wrong, but I think I remember hearing that Feldene was turned down the first time around. If so, it must have been reported in industry journals, maybe even the *New York Times*. See if you can find out why."

"Think I'll go straight to the horse's mouth, stop at the FDA while I'm in Washington." She reached across the table for Rachel's check. "My treat—I'm feeling expansive, as the saying goes. Still riding the cloud."

They got up and walked together toward the cash register, then retraced their steps in order to leave through the front door, which emptied out onto the corner of Alabama and Shepherd Drive. "I need to stop off at the Bookstop, next door, before I go back to the station," Mari explained, indicating the old Alabama theater, just to the north of Butera's in the small strip shopping center. Dating from the 1930s, the opulent old movie house had been converted into a discount bookstore, with rows of shelves instead of seats marching down its sloping aisles.

"Charles is coming to the big shindig next week, isn't he?" Rachel asked as they were about to part.

Mari nodded. "I talked to him yesterday."

"Great about his licensing deal, isn't it?"

"What?" Mari asked, bewildered.

"The deal he just signed with Biomed, to market the Vampire?" She took in Mari's look of complete surprise. "You mean you don't know? Oh God, I bet I let out something he was keeping to surprise you. I'm sorry, Mari. When am I ever going to learn to keep my big mouth shut?"

"No, it's all right. He probably didn't tell me because he couldn't get a word in edgewise. When did all this happen?"

Rachel dug around in her purse for her sunglasses. "I'm not sure. Couple of weeks ago, maybe. Biomed's going to market it as a research instrument while they're waiting to get final approval from the FDA for clinical use. My guess is it won't be long before Charles is rolling in the green. Talking about drug approval is what reminded me, I guess." Mari nodded, wondering why he hadn't mentioned it when she was in Austin. "Well, see you, next week if not before, huh?" Rachel started toward her car, then turned back. "Mari?"

Mari turned around. "Yeah?"

"I just wanted to say thanks . . . for what you've done with Tony," Rachel stammered, struggling to get the words out.

"Why? You know he deserves every word of praise he gets, from me or anyone else. He's good technically, but he also has a special way of seeing with a camera, and the awards jury recognized that. We just happen to complement each other."

"Sure, I know. But I also know there are plenty of Tracys running around loose. I doubt there's another reporter or producer in the business who would've worked with him the way you have, given him the opportunity to grow and to show what he can do. Shared the limelight with him. First the Basque thing, and now this. Lately, more and more, he's begun to say 'we,' instead of 'she,' especially since Spain. What I meant was, well, if Tony and I have any chance at all, Mari, it's because of you."

"Nothing to do with that red hair of yours?" Mari grinned and shook her head. "He may be a banty rooster, and even a little conservative at times, but he's no fool, Rachel."

Little else had changed while Mari was in Washington, but at least Jack had finally seen the light about asking an award-winning reporter/producer to write script for his evening news anchor. On the following Friday, the night of the big party, he canceled her regular broadcast and sent her home early, to "Go get beautiful. Trace is doing the story on Methodist Hospital's decision to test all entering patients for the AIDS virus, which ought to be enough to keep your fans pacified for one night."

She drove home with all the freewheeling abandon of a native Houstonian, hoping that Charles might even be there already, waiting, because he said he'd try to get away early.

It seemed longer than two weeks since she'd seen him, especially with Denver, Washington, and several other short trips in between, so she'd been looking forward to tonight all week. And now that it was almost here, she felt a panicky sort of urgency to get home, to be with him, to— She had to force her mind away from the steamy pictures her mind was painting and to concentrate on the traffic.

But he wasn't there, and when she checked her answering machine, she found he'd left a message, instructing her to go on because he was going to be late and would come directly to the hotel. Disappointed, and then a little worried that he might forget about Jack's "black-tie" decree, she called Austin. But he didn't answer, which she hoped meant he was already on his way.

Charles stopped just inside the door of the big room at the Hyatt-Regency, taking in the crowd of Houston's finest, which looked to him like a milling herd of purebred cattle. Especially the men, all decked out in the same slick black coats, ruffled or pleated white chests, shiny hoofs and carefully curried, razor-cut fur. Though more colorful, their mates had a sameness about them, too, in their short bubbles and poufs which made them look leggy as little girls, contradicting their painted faces and artful smiles. Showcasing their husbands' bank accounts, they glittered and sparkled as they moved, preening themselves in the light of a dozen huge crystal chandeliers. The sight brought fresh awareness of the game of oneupsmanship played by the "idle" rich, reminding Charles of just how different his own existence was—informal, without regimentation, free from such superficial and mindless ostentation.

He felt miserable already, whether because of the clothes or the company, he wasn't sure. A rented suit, for God's sake! Just the thought of it made him squirm, mentally as well as physically, and he snagged a glass of champagne off the tray of a passing waiter, hoping it might help quiet his somewhat queasy stomach. He sure as hell hoped Mari appreciated the fact that he'd never done this before for any woman. Finally he began sauntering around, searching for Mari, or at least someone he could stand talking to until he could find her.

The place was catered to the teeth, with food and drink everywhere, passed among the guests on trays and displayed on white-clothed tables scattered all around the edge of the large open floor. The one closest to where he was standing offered little pastry cups filled with shredded crab topped with sun-dried tomatoes, truffle paté on rounds of toast, and a huge bowl of cold shrimp on a bed of ice. About dead center of the room a six-foot-tall, tiered fountain was bubbling like a witch's caldron, with pink champagne waterfalling over the rim of the smallest silver bowl, only to be caught by a slightly larger one below, and then ever larger ones, all the way down to the floor. And the first person Charles recognized was the woman standing with a group of five or six men, just to the left of the fountain. She stood out, in fact, even in this crowd, with her sun-streaked hair and throaty laugh, and her consummate flair for always looking right, no matter the place or occasion.

He stared at her dispassionately, trying to see her as everyone here probably did—attractive, even a little mysterious, perhaps, with that strange, intangible hint of sexuality that even he was able to detect at times, in spite of her calm, dignified, even sedate demeanor. Probably something to do with her hair, which was so curly it always looked just a little bit mussed. Amy Merrill Gramling. A consummately handsome woman, generous with her time and money, a pillar of society, admired by everyone. But then, not everyone really knew her as he did.

He felt someone touch his arm and looked down into Rachel's glowing face. A smile broke over his own, and then widened when he saw Tony standing just behind her. "Hey, you guys are a sight for sore eyes." He shifted his glass, circled Rachel's shoulder with his free arm and pulled her to him for a hug and kiss, then straightened and shook Tony's hand. "If you can stand to hear the word one more time, congratulations! Hate to go on about it too much, since I'm in it, but I told her, way back—on the way to Madrid, I think it was—that that program was the best damn thing I've ever seen on TV! I suppose she's here, but I haven't seen her yet. Got in a little later than I planned."

"Yeah, that's what she said, that you were going to be late," Tony confirmed. "I'm surprised she hasn't spied you and come running, though. Her eye's been on the door all night." He laughed just as Rachel pulled on his arm and dipped her head toward the corner of the room, behind Charles's right shoulder. "Oh yeah, there she is."

Charles turned and saw her—then wished he hadn't. *What the hell did you do to your hair?* The words careened around inside his head like a caged tennis ball, and he had to clamp his jaw shut to keep from saying what he thought. His stomach tightened painfully, cringing with a sense of deprivation that came without warning.

As if she could feel his eyes on her, Mari turned and looked right at him, and her face lightened with a happy smile. She hastily excused herself to the people around her and hurried toward him. "Hi," she said, almost shyly. "Everything okay?"

Charles knew she was referring to the fact that he'd been delayed, so he simply nodded. "Almost didn't recognize you," he mumbled, looking her up and down rather obviously, to the amusement of both Rachel and Tony, who stood watching them. She was wearing jade green tonight, a satiny silk thing that looked more like a slip than a dress. Held by fragile spaghetti straps, it bared every inch of skin from her shoulders to the tops of her breasts, then seemed to ripple like a fluid over the curves of her body. She also seemed taller, perhaps because of her high-heeled sandals, which were the same jade green and the same skimpy-looking straps. A long chain of gold interwoven with tiny seed pearls wrapped her neck like a choker, but fell almost to her waist in the back, from just below the nape of her neck where it was clasped by a big square-cut emerald. Everything about her was smooth, shiny, and sleek. Except her hair!

No longer straight, it wasn't exactly curly either. Kinky was more like it. He remembered seeing pictures in the paper of fashion models with the same "spontaneous" and "free" look, but to Charles it looked unkempt, as if she'd run her fingers through it rather than a brush. Maybe it was just a temporary thing, done specially for tonight's big bash, and tomorrow could be smoothed away with a little shampoo and a brush. He smiled, encouraged by the thought.

"You look like a regular celebrity, which I guess you are. How's it going?"

"Fine, now that you're here. What happened?"

"An equipment problem. Lupe's working against a deadline, needs to get some data for a paper she's giving in San Francisco next week." He turned to Rachel and Tony. "One of my graduate students, Lupe Gonzalez." He looked back at Mari. "Didn't have much choice. Sorry."

In fact the equipment breakdown that delayed him was only the last of a string of disasters stretching back over the past two weeks. Earlier in the week the dean had announced at a faculty meeting that he was closing the department's machine shop because it wasn't "cost-effective," a decision that came right on top of a similar one by the chemistry department to close the glass shop. Little enough research was being done that required custom-designed and -built equipment, which meant that if there wasn't an instrument already on the market to do a particular job, some questions simply wouldn't be investigated. As if that wasn't enough, he'd also received a memo from the dean stating that every member of the engineering faculty was expected to bring in at least twice his own salary in research grants each year— which meant less time actually doing research and more time trying to get grants, half of which went to the university for "overhead." Unfortunately, overhead not only paid the utility bills, but also fed a constantly expanding bureaucracy, which in turn created more regulations and paperwork to hamstring the progress of research, not to mention the process of education, which in any case was the last concern of the administration. To Charles it was just another symptom of the sickness creeping through the nation's universities. With the positions and money going to faculty who could and would develop direct ties to industry—the idea being that "high tech" would form a new economic base for the state and the country—the "basic" research that once had fueled the nation's technological prowess was drying up. Indeed, much of it had already disappeared.

"Is anything wrong?" Mari asked, concerned about the faraway look in his eyes, as if his body had arrived but his mind were still somewhere else.

"Nope," he assured her as he leaned over to give her a quick kiss on the cheek, also taking the opportunity to whisper in her ear. "Missed you."

Her face lightened noticeably at that. "Your mother's here," she told him, expecting to surprise him with the news.

"Yeah, I noticed," he acknowledged, then turned to Tony. "You going with her tomorrow, to New York?"

"She twisted my arm, said she wouldn't go without me." Tony gave Mari an affectionate look, with eyes that were suspiciously wet. "Is getting kinda bad about that, in fact," he added softly, "just another one of the crazy things I have to put up with from her."

Mari returned his smile, and then, after a quick glance around to make sure no one was watching, snaked her tongue out and made a childish face at him.

Rachel looked at Charles. "You know how it is when two naughty kids get together?" she asked innocently. "I hear stories about them, all the time, down at the hospital. 'Double trouble' everyone calls 'em."

Tony grabbed Rachel around the waist and planted a loud smack on the nearest cheek. "Not to worry, Charles, I will look after her, see to it that your woman doesn't get into trouble in the big city."

Now it was Mari's turn to look chagrined. She turned to Rachel. "Your woman?" she asked, her voice dripping with disbelief.

Rachel nodded. "Banty rooster, just like I said."

"Okay, that's enough of that," Mari decided suddenly, grabbing Charles's arm. "Got to be serious for a few minutes. I have several people who've been waiting all night to meet you, so let's—"

"Who?" Charles asked suspiciously, refusing to budge.

"Well, one is from Rice, the engineer who worked with DeBakey to develop the first assist pump, several years ago. And another is a surgeon I interviewed for 'Have a Heart,' who—"

"Okay," he agreed readily, then added, "but none of the leeches."

She stared at him, puzzled, but before she could ask who he meant, Rachel interrupted. "And after she's through with you, Charles, maybe I can borrow you for a few minutes, to

322

meet a couple of guys who are interested in talking to you about the Vampire. Told them you were going to be here tonight."

"You bet," he assured her, then followed Mari through the crowd.

The evening passed swiftly after that, as Charles moved with Mari from one group of people to another, most of them names and faces he'd never be able to put together, or remember, in the morning—except for Ron Bergner and his wife, and Podge Pearsall, and Sandy Pittman, whom he felt he already knew, just from talking with her so often on the phone. And, of course, Jack Lunsford, who was working the crowd with one arm draped around Tracy Sadler's shoulder, or waist, or neck, as if he couldn't keep his hands off her, even here.

"Just Jack's way of indicating ownership, showing off his bedtime toy," Mari commented when she saw Charles watching them, "making sure everyone knows."

He had to push himself to be civil, for Mari's sake, when Jack approached them, greeting Charles with the bonhomie generally reserved for old friends. Even for Mari, though, he couldn't bring himself to do anything but ignore Tracy, and hope that the bitch wasn't too obtuse to get the point—that he neither liked nor found her of any interest whatsoever, either personally or professionally.

They spoke briefly with Charles's mother, who was much more effusive about Mari's talents than she'd been the day they'd met at the Remington, teasing her about "making a TV star out of my reclusive son." Amy didn't even try to hide the fact that she'd never seen "Have a Heart," even though it had been aired twice in Houston, protesting that "I'm just too busy to watch television."

It was at about that moment that Tony slipped up behind Mari and whispered, "Ready whenever you are. Be waiting outside." Charles quirked a puzzled brow at her, but she simply shook her head and took his hand, excused them from the group and slowly led him toward the door, telling a few of her friends good night as they went.

Once outside they followed Tony and Rachel, in Charles's car. Mari claimed ignorance about where they were going, so Charles stayed close, to make sure he didn't lose Tony's

Blazer as they cruised down one narrow, cracked-up street after another, through a part of town even Charles didn't know. Finally he saw Tony brake and then swing into an empty spot in front of a little neighborhood restaurant, where a red and green neon sign spelled out the invitation, *Mi casa es su casa*. Little different than a hundred others scattered throughout Houston's barrios, Charles couldn't help wondering why they'd come here, and at eleven o'clock at night.

Tony didn't keep them wondering for long. "All is arranged. Now it is my turn, my party," he explained with a satisfied little smile as he turned the knob and pushed the door open for them.

Loud music and voices, laughing and calling to each other, and the clinking of glasses and dishes, all came pouring through the door, borne on the wavery strains of a mariachi band. A small black-haired woman with shining dark eyes hurried to greet them, and Tony threw his arms around her, lifted her off her feet and twirled her around, then set her back down and turned to Rachel, including Mari and Charles when he spoke.

"My mother doesn't think her English is very good, so she asked me to welcome you to her house."

Rachel was first to stretch out her hand, but the woman took her into her arms instead, kissed her first on one cheek and then the other, murmuring softly all the while. When she released her, Rachel looked over at Tony, wondering if she'd understood his mother's few hesitant words of English correctly, only to find him grinning and nodding. And then he was introducing them all to his Tejano friends, who started shouting and clapping. At last, holding Rachel's hand tightly in his own, he directed Charles and Mari to seats reserved especially for them, then took Rachel with him to the head of the table, to share the place of honor.

Three teenage girls appeared with trays of frozen margaritas, while bottles of Corona and Dos Equis started down the table like a moving mass-production line. Before long the entire table was inundated with talk and music and food—chips and salsa, bowls of guacamole and plates hot from the oven filled with tacos al carbon, cabrito flautas, chalupas, and chiles rellenos. The noise level dropped noticeably when the eating turned serious, and a single guitarist took the place of the band, plucking plaintive love songs.

As the evening began to turn mellow, Tony rose and raised his glass, silently asking for quiet so he could speak. "No speeches, so not to worry. Only a toast to my women." He darted a quick grin at Mari, and then Charles, waiting for the laughter to die down. "The three women who make this night happen for me—my holy trinity."

He dipped his glass first toward his mother, who was standing near the door to the restaurant kitchen. She'd refused to join them at the table, insisting instead on supervising the serving of the meal. "The one who loved me enough to point her finger at the door every morning and order me to *escuela.*" His tongue curled around the Spanish word for school, trying to give it the same inflection he'd heard so often in her voice.

Then he turned toward Rachel, mischief dancing in his eyes. "And the woman who will be the mother of my children." There was a moment of stunned silence, and then everyone broke into loud applause and laughter. Shouts of "When?" and "How many?" rose around the table, causing Rachel's face to flame. Tony leaned down and gave her a long, loving kiss, on the mouth, to the delight of everyone. Then he straightened, still holding her eyes with his. "But first she will be my wife." Applause erupted again, but he wasn't finished yet, so he held up one hand and glanced around at his friends. "Always I go for the tall woman—as most of you know. But only this one make me believe I am as tall as her."

It was funny how Tony's speech resonated with the harmonics of his other "native" language whenever he tried to express his personal feelings, Mari thought, listening to him, yet was completely unaffected when he was talking a cold open, tight shot, or squeeze zoom. How did he manage to live in two cultures at the same time, she wondered, without becoming schizo? And what language did he speak inside his head when he was making love, when his brain was on automatic pilot?

Next, he looked at Mari, sending her a kind of conspiratorial grin. "And my partner, the little witch in green who uses words to weave her magic spell. For this woman I think maybe two languages are not enough. From her I learn to see in a new way—not just what is, but what can be. More than that, I begin to understand that to be a man is to love a woman not only with this"—he let one hand fall to cup his genitals, bringing a new burst of laughter from his friends, then moved it up to cover his heart—"but also with this"—then to his head—"and this." Everyone laughed at that, turning toward Mari, and began applauding again. But Tony didn't laugh with them, and when his eyes sought Mari's, there was no mistaking the message she saw there.

Mari leaned her head back and closed her eyes when she realized they were almost home. "Tired?" Charles asked.

"Coming down off the ceiling, I guess," she admitted.

"What time are you leaving tomorrow?"

"Tony's picking me up at ten. Plane leaves a little after eleven. Why don't you stay here, visit with your mother?"

"Too much to do, need to get back to work," he mumbled as he turned into the apartment parking lot.

Just inside the door of her apartment Mari kicked off her sandals and moaned with relief. "God, but that feels good," she sighed as she turned and put her arms around Charles's neck. "And so does this. I've been waiting all night," she murmured against his lips. They were the last words spoken by either one of them for several minutes.

"Aren't you going to invite me in, or do you want me standing here by the door all night?" Charles asked finally, speaking around a smiling kiss as he let his hands slide from her neck down over her back to the sloping curve at her waist, down over her buttocks, getting high on the feel of her body through the slippery fabric. He cupped both his hands to lift and pull her more tightly against him. "Have to admit this thing does have its merits, in spite of what I thought when I first saw you tonight."

Mari drew away from him in surprise. "You didn't like my dress? That's what all the frowning was about?"

"Never frown, you gotta be thinking of someone else," he murmured, nuzzling his face into her neck, butterflying light kisses down across her chest to the swell of her left breast, while his fingers worked at the thin little straps, trying to slide them off her shoulders, one at a time. "How the hell do you get this damn thing off?" he exploded finally, exasperated. "Or I should just rip it off, have done with it?" Mari spun away from him, leaving him standing there with his empty arms still extended.

"What'sa matter? I was just joking."

Well, I don't think it's funny! She wanted to shout the words at him, feeling the sudden flash of alarm followed by a hot spurt of adrenaline. It was the same reflexive response her body had learned long ago and, apparently, could never forget. Instead she only nodded. "I know." Then tried harder, to make amends. "Come with me and I'll show you how, show you all my secrets, or most of them." She draped herself around the edge of the doorway into her bedroom, disappearing from view a little at a time, leaving one arm beckoning him to her, watching his face as she gradually revealed the entire length of one nylon-clad leg, just before she disappeared from sight entirely.

Charles grinned and bounded after her, peeling his jacket off as he went, catching up with her just as the green satin slip slithered down over her hips and thighs to pool around her ankles like honey dripping from a spoon. From the waist down she was transparent panty hose, from the waist up nothing but creamy skin. And pink nipples. He fed his eyes and his brain and his genitals on her, then covered the distance between them in two long steps, taking her back into his arms, holding her so tight she could hardly breathe.

"I . . . I knew, kept seeing you like this, the whole damn night," he whispered against her temple. "Tony's right— you're a witch." She laughed as he feathered kisses from her forehead to her chin, stopping to tease the corner of her mouth with his tongue. Her hands worked at his belt buckle, then his shirt buttons, and then he was pushing her away a little, so he could finish what she'd begun. She peeled the panty hose from her legs, laughing the entire time at both herself and him—racing to get free of their clothes like two hot, turned-on teenagers.

And then his warm skin was drawing fiery shivers from hers, from breast to thigh. He bent to pull back the spread covering the bed, just before she fell across it, pulling him down with her, almost on top of her, though he tried to break his fall with one arm. She felt his erection push against her as she turned her mouth into his, beginning a kiss of avid exploration, while his long fingers stroked the inside of her thigh, sending a ripple of anticipation skimming across the surface of her skin, before inching higher and higher.

Her hands explored, too, painting pictures in her head as they went, combing through the tight curls to shape his head, massaging the muscles in his neck before smoothing over his shoulders and back and his firm buttocks. Her knees parted to give him access, letting him know her body was almost ready for him. Then she smoothed out the crinkles at the corner of his eye with her fingers, before drawing a line down the edge of his cheek, stopping momentarily to tease the tip of her forefinger into the corner of his mouth, still joined with her own. "Ah, Mari honey," he breathed around her finger, catching it between his teeth. She'd intended to leave no part of him untouched, but when she felt his tongue stroking her finger, her hand moved unerringly to his penis, to both reciprocate and then to guide him. As she closed around him, Charles reached his free hand up to slide it over her hair, seeking to intensify the exquisite sensations touching her always brought. But the instant his fingers came in contact with the rough-textured strands, a bizarre picture exploded inside his brain—and he jerked his hand back as if from a raging fire!

Mari felt him go flaccid in her hand, with a suddenness she hadn't known was possible. "Charles?" she ventured softly.

He let his forehead drop to the pillow next to her and moved his head back and forth a couple of times in silent negation. Of what, she wasn't sure. His breath still pumped loudly in her ear, and his heart shook his body with every beat. So she just continued to hold him in her hand, wondering, guessing, speculating.

"Are you okay?" she asked finally, as seconds became minutes and he still didn't move, or say anything.

"Yeah, sure," he breathed, and without further explanation simply rolled from the bed and went into the bathroom, leaving her still guessing. She sat up but didn't turn on a light, then slid under the covers on one side of the bed and just lay there, her heart still pounding, listening to the water run in the sink, and then the toilet flush. When he returned, he climbed into the bed from the other side and pulled her into his arms again. His skin felt cool to the touch.

"Sorry," he mumbled apologetically. "Guess the day's been too much for me." He lay still, all passion gone, making no move to pick up where they'd left off. Mari's mind gaped with shock, first at the idea that any day could be too much for Charles Merrill, and then at what he was really saying—that he had no interest in continuing, or even trying to, that he was finished whether she was or not!

Suddenly she could feel Phillip's body again, pushing her down into the mattress, once, twice, three times, finishing quickly, then leaving her to lie there alone, suspended halfway between arousal and completion—never uttering a word, because he'd taught her so well to never complain. Something deep inside rose up in furious rebellion at the memory, and Mari sat up, threw back the covers and reached over to switch on the lamp beside the bed, wanting to see his face. Then she twisted around to peer at him.

"You're sorry? That's it?" She leaped from the bed and swept her short robe off the chair all in one fell swoop, wrapped it around her and tied the sash in a knot, pulling on the two ends until it was so tight she'd probably have to cut the damn thing off!

"I don't—what do you mean?" he stuttered, confused by her sudden angry response.

"What do I mean, he says!" she asked the ceiling, as if there were someone up there. Then she drilled him with a heated stare. "You ever hear of orgasmic urgency, Doctor Merrill—or if you prefer, blue balls?"

He started to laugh, then thought better of it when he saw that she didn't intend it to be funny. "Blue balls, yeah, orgasmic urgency, no. So?"

"So blue balls is the painful condition men claim they get—if a woman gets 'em all turned on and then reneges, refuses to 'go all the way,' right?"

"Yeah, it can be pretty uncomfortable." The corners of his mouth twitched a little, whether because he disliked talking about this or simply thought it was funny, she couldn't tell.

"I'll bet, though, that you've never heard of 'blue clit,'

right? Even though Taylor's syndrome is a real, medically recognized condition in females—vasocongestion from a high level of excitement that can cause pain and other physical complications if orgasm doesn't occur."

"Okay, okay, I get the message. Come back to bed and I'll see what I can do."

"Aren't you the magnanimous one, though?" she hissed scornfully. "Playing the martyred saint, huh? No thanks! I wouldn't let you touch me now for all the rice in China. Anyway, what makes you think I really need *you,* if it comes to that?" Wound as tight as a spring, she began pacing back and forth at the foot of the bed. Mind racing as fast as her heart, she finally let the thought she'd been pushing away all evening come bursting forth. "What's with you tonight? Can't stand the competition? Was I getting too much attention for your ego to take, limelight was on me, instead of you?"

"Dammit, there you go again! Why do you keep on about us being in competition with each other?" He was feeling a surge of heat now himself, even though he suspected there was more bothering her than she was admitting. It wasn't like her to be so unreasonable. "What the hell is wrong with you tonight?"

"Me?" She shouted indignantly, venting her anger. "I just won an award that most people in the news business would sell their souls for. Yet you can't even bring yourself to gracefully share in my success, be happy for me. You not only arrive late, but then stand around pouting like a jealous little boy. And now you're holding out on me."

"You're crazy. I'm just tired. And I *am* proud of you. But I guess I am a little surprised that you need the kind of phony stuff that was being passed around down there tonight. You tell me what's so important about hearing accolades from a real estate broker who doesn't even watch television and doesn't give a shit about artificial hearts or anything else you pour your heart and soul into?"

"Maybe because she's your mother! Did you ever consider that?"

"Rubbish!"

She gaped at him, too angry even to speak.

"Come on back to bed and let's get some sleep. We can

330

talk about it in the morning—if we have to. I wish to hell you wouldn't let every little thing set you off like this."

"Little thing?" she shot back.

"Yeah, even the Spanish Inquisition can get you going."

"Well, I certainly am glad to find out how you feel about that! Explains a lot, like how you can bury yourself in your lab and just conveniently ignore what's going on in the real world."

"I only meant, well, why the hell do you have to take everything personally?"

"Who will, if I don't? I dare you to come with me just one night—see the women I see, with their faces swollen beyond recognition, eyes black and blue, teeth broken and missing, lips cut and bleeding—and then ask me again why I take it personally. What do you think is going to happen when all of us stop caring enough to get personally involved? Who do you think is going to help the women men rape feel human again?" She answered her own question with another, her voice turning sarcastic. "Men like you, who are so damned good at keeping their distance?"

He resented the broad indictment, but tried not to show it. If she wanted a fight, she was going to have to go somewhere else to get it. He'd heard enough angry accusations and acrimonious epithets flung back and forth between two people who supposedly loved each other to last him a lifetime. Now, as then, he knew only one way to deal with what was happening—to simply go to sleep. "Please come to bed, Mari, for God's sake, so we can get some sleep! You're getting irrational, losing all your objectivity." That only seemed to set her off again, or else she still just wasn't ready to quit.

"Who said I ever had any? Call what I do advocacy journalism if you want—I'd be the first to admit it. Did Bill Moyers take a neutral stance in his program about black America, or the one he did on threats to the American Constitution? Do you think I'm standing in a neutral corner when I tell viewers that half the hysterectomies and caesarean sections being performed are unnecessary, not to mention what Nancy Reagan let them do to her breast? I think it's time to stand up and take sides when you see people being treated like trash, or being hurt. Call it old-fashioned morality if you want. It's mine, and it's the only way I know. And if that makes you uncomfortable, so be it."

She was bouncing from one subject to another so fast now that he was just beginning to figure out what she was saying when off she'd go on a different tangent. "I refuse to even try to talk to you while you're behaving like this."

"Oh, so you're the one who's calling all the shots, huh?" she asked derisively, knowing she had to keep on now, if only to let him know that she wasn't about to knuckle under. "Objectivity!" She pronounced the word with all the scorn she could muster. "Did you think you were standing in a neutral corner when you decided to work on blood instead of missile guidance systems?" She couldn't stop herself from taking one more parting shot. "And after what you just pulled, you've got one helluva lot of nerve accusing me of being irrational!"

CHAPTER

17

~~~~~~~~

Mari was fixing breakfast when Charles came into the kitchen the next morning. Judging from the way the other side of the bed looked, and the rumpled blanket and pillow on the couch in the living room, she'd never come back to bed last night. He stood in the doorway watching her, trying to read her mood. Then, still feeling slightly guilty and more than a little bewildered by her behavior, he decided there was only one way to make amends.

Mari felt his presence just before his arms came around her from behind, and then his face and lips were nuzzling into her hair and neck. "Come back to bed," he mumbled, his voice still hoarse with sleep. She stilled, but didn't respond. "Please?" he pleaded. "Let me make up to you for last night. Don't let's part like this, Mari, leaving it unfinished between us."

He knew damned well that what happened last night wasn't entirely his fault by any means, just from the wildly disconnected statements she'd thrown at him. No matter how he tried to mollify her, she'd responded like a rogue tennis ball, bouncing off the wall to come at him when and where he least expected it, answering questions he'd never asked, accusing him of ulterior motives he didn't have.

"I don't have time," she said quietly, moving out of his

arms on the pretext of tending to something cooking on the stove. "You didn't mind leaving it unfinished last night. What's different about now? You'd better go on and get dressed. Breakfast will be ready in a few minutes."

So she was still hung up about the same thing, even this morning, which meant he was going to have to try some other tack. He glanced at his watch. It was already a little after eight. "Okay."

Five minutes later he was back, dressed and with his teeth brushed, but his face still unshaven. "What can I do to help?" Mari cast a quick glance in his direction, taking in his bare feet, jeans, and T-shirt.

"You might set the table, pour the coffee. I'll have these out in a minute." She flipped the eggs over, got a platter out of the cabinet overhead and dumped the bacon onto it by upending the paper towel she'd placed it on to absorb the grease.

"Think anybody's going to televise the awards ceremony tonight?"

"I doubt it," she answered coolly, "unless maybe CNN, if it happens to be a slow news night."

"Think I'll call Cablevision in Austin when I get back, see if they know anything." He stayed right on her heels, like a puppy, when she took the platter of eggs and bacon to the table in the dining alcove.

"Why?" she asked over her shoulder. "Since you can't get cable."

"No, but I know people who can." He waited for her to slide an egg and a couple of slices of bacon onto her plate, then accepted the platter when she handed it to him. They both ate in silence for a few minutes.

"What did you think of the flamenco tape, by the way?" she asked, looking directly at him for the first time.

He finished chewing, taking his time, trying to decide whether to admit that he hadn't looked at it yet. "I'm waiting until we can do it together. Doesn't seem right, somehow, to watch it without you." She looked at him a second longer, then just went back to eating, and not looking at him.

"Mari honey," he began, then set his fork down and took her hand in his. "Whatever you may have thought last night,

334

and I know I'm not very good at expressing myself, I *am* happy for you, about the award. I know it's important recognition, for . . . for everything you bring to your work, that's so uniquely you. Please believe me. There's no jealousy, no feeling of competition. And I'm sorry as hell if I did anything to spoil the celebration for you."

She looked at him, swallowed and nodded, seeming to accept his apology, then picked up her coffee and sipped at it in silence.

"It's the national recognition you've been waiting for, isn't it? What you need to be able to make it on your own as an independent producer?" He grinned, suddenly remembering something, then jumped up from the table and hurried into the bedroom. Back a few seconds later, he pushed his plate aside and began to unroll a big piece of paper. "Take at least a quick look at this, tell me what you think of it."

Startled by the sudden switch of subject and the architect's drawing he was spreading out before her, Mari could only stare, completely dumbfounded by what he was asking her to do. She didn't have time for this, whatever it was, with little more than an hour until she had to leave for the airport. She still hadn't dressed or packed, hadn't even decided what to take to wear tonight. "What is it?"

"Preliminary plans for an addition to the house. I was saving it as a surprise for you, but—well, I thought we could come out right here," he explained eagerly, pointing to the glass door of his bedroom on the plan, "add a dressing room and walk-in closet for you. And then, coming farther this way, a study or studio, whatever you want to call it. Maybe just leave the brick wall as it is. It would look pretty good as an interior wall, don't you think?"

Mari's mind was a battleground of angry voices, some arguing, others trying to placate, all talking at once, bumping and stumbling into each other. "Looks big, expensive," she commented finally. The area he referred to as a studio was twenty-five feet by twenty, with a silent cork floor, special sound insulation, a high ceiling to accommodate changing sets, its own cooling and heating unit, and continuous electrical outlet tracks for both 110 and 220.

"Money's not a problem, I told you that. I just need for

you to tell me if you think this is in the ballpark of what you're going to need, so I can get the architect moving on more drawings. You can always talk with him about the interior layout later."

"Why didn't you tell me about your deal with Biomed?"

Charles looked up, surprised that she knew about that. "I didn't want you to think I was trying to push you," he said, being as straightforward as he knew how.

"But this is not . . . pushing me?" She pointed to the drawing. He noticed that her face was beginning to flush.

"I just thought, well, that now, with this award, you'd be free to work independently, in Austin, if you had the facilities. That we could go ahead and get married, produce kids and documentaries, full-time, like you want." He smiled, confident that she'd understand that he was trying to help, not push or compete with her—that he was trying to show her how much he loved her.

Trying to coax me like a child, are you, with a piece of candy? Sweetening the deal with a production studio that only you can afford!

"I know you could do it, Mari, especially if you'd stick with one area of expertise instead of jumping around all over the place, from flamenco to artificial hearts to who the hell knows what next? Go with your women's health idea, for instance, build up your reputation there, do some writing as well as film and video, maybe even a syndicated column."

"You and my mother have it all figured out, don't you?" she shouted suddenly. "Where I'm going to work, what I'm to work on! I'll bet you even decided how many children I should have, didn't you, and when I should have them! As soon as possible, right? Did you also decide how many hours a week I should spend changing diapers, how many I'd be allowed in the studio *you* built for me?" She could just hear them, Charles and her mother, talking about her when she wasn't there, deciding between themselves what was best for her! Without even consulting her!

She jumped up from the table, her face livid, and grabbed the blueprint, grasped it along the top edge and ripped it right down the middle.

"You wanted to know what I think—that's what I think!"

she yelled, threw the pieces down on top of his congealing egg yolks and marched into the bedroom without another word, leaving him sitting there, stunned speechless. Charles could hear her dragging her suitcase out of the bedroom closet, bumping it against the doorjamb in the process, and then the snap of the catches as she opened it. More thumps and bumps followed, as she stomped across the floor, gathering her hair dryer from the bathroom and her shoes from the closet, and threw them into her suitcase.

"I want to know what the hell is going on with you!" he shouted as he came through the door of the bedroom, looking like Zeus with a bundle of thunderbolts in his hand. Mari froze right where she was, waiting, trying to prepare herself for what surely was coming next. "You just can't let go, can you?" he continued in the same angry tone. "You're still hung up about last night! What the hell do you think I am—some damned superstud?"

"What did you think was going to happen?" she returned hotly. "That everything would magically go away as if it never happened, if you just refused to talk about it? It doesn't, you know. In fact, that only makes it worse. How did you expect me to feel this morning, after you take control, deny me the chance to get what was bothering me out of my system, clear the air, try to figure out what the hell was going on with you? Instead, you clam up, then turn over and go to sleep. Boy, did I ever get the message! Sorry I've been so obtuse. Until last night I actually thought you cared about me! Isn't that a crock?"

"You were getting irrational—which is no damned time to talk about anything," he growled.

She turned on him. "And who the hell appointed you the judge and jury to decide when or whether I'm rational?"

He started, then ducked as a shoe flew toward his head. It hit the wall behind him and fell to the floor with a dull thud.

"I don't believe this," he muttered darkly, between tightly clenched teeth. "Will you get a hold of yourself, for God's sake! I was only trying to help, to do something I thought would please you. But all you wanna do is play 'gotcha'! I'm damned if I do and damned if I don't. Either way I jump you've got me, right?"

She strode to the chest of drawers, refusing to dignify his

accusation with a response, pulled the top drawer open and rummaged around until she found a couple of unopened packages of panty hose, tossed them into her suitcase and then disappeared into the walk-in closet.

Charles took a deep breath, determined not to lose control. When she came back he tried again. "Look, Mari honey, all I was trying to do was fix it so we can both work in peace. Put an end to all this tear-up, traveling back and forth all the time, never knowing where you are, when I'm going to see you next. I want you with me all the time, not just a weekend now and then."

"Sure," she tossed back sarcastically. "Only I'm the one who does all the compromising, beginning with moving to where you want to live, making your life smoother, making my work fit the demands of yours."

"But my work is important to me!"

"And mine's not? I know I can't compete with what you're probably going to make off the Vampire, but—"

"Not to mention several other instruments I've got coming, in different stages of development," he injected, really riled now and ready to let her know it.

"Okay, but I'll bet you I make pretty damn close to the same salary you do at the university, big professorship and all! You wanted to know who's putting up the money for my PBS pilot, I'll tell you. Me, that's who!"

"I didn't mean money, for christsake! If I did, I sure as hell wouldn't be where I am."

"Yeah, I'm glad you brought that up. Remember way back, months ago, when I asked why a talented research scientist like you was wasting his time teaching, and you said it was the trade-off for being able to follow your nose in your research, to go wherever the trail led you, because that wasn't possible except in a university? Because if you worked in industry you'd have to work on what the company needed or wanted? Can't you see that's exactly what I want to be able to do, follow my news nose wherever it takes me? And right now it's taking me into the pharmaceutical industry, not just drug promotion and cross-over ownership, but the influence the industry exerts on medical research. But here you are, the very person I thought might understand, urging me to erect walls and set limits, focus on

338

one area and stay with it, stop 'jumping all over the place, from flamenco to artificial hearts,' as you put it."

"I didn't mean it that way. And I only said that because I thought that's what you wanted to do, after all I've heard from you and Rachel about the raw deal women are getting from the medical profession."

"Well, I can't afford a studio like that, at least not yet," she added, going back to the money issue. Would Charles ever get it through his thick skull that she didn't give a shit how much money *he* had, that she could never let herself be financially dependent on any man, because that would close off all avenues of escape? She had to be able to make it on her own, which was why she'd been socking away every dime she could for the past six years. Because most female news reporters had a short on-camera lifespan, and only rarely did it run past thirty-five. The few who did make it past that age were either genetically blessed or had exceptionally good plastic surgeons.

"But I can, that's the point. You do things for your friends all the time. Why won't you let me do something for someone I love?"

She turned and looked directly at him, a look that was more sad than angry now. "You're willing to spend that kind of money on me, when you can't even stay awake for a few minutes, an hour, whatever it takes? I'd manage to stay awake, somehow, Charles, all night, all day, a whole week if that's what it took, for someone I loved. If you think that's irrational, fine—you can have your damned rationality or objectivity, or whatever you want to call it. But do you really think it's going to be enough, in the dark of the night when you're lonely, or sick? Or when you look back across the years and realize they're running out and you're still alone, because you were too timid, too spineless, to take anything personally? Your words, not mine!"

"What the hell is it you want from me—blood?" He combed his fingers through his hair, over and over again, a gesture of utter frustration and despair. "No, let me guess. I'll bet you want to see me on my knees, don't you, groveling, begging for your forgiveness. Just because I couldn't get it up one goddamn time!" He pushed away from the doorway suddenly, then stopped dead in his tracks when he saw her flinch and curl her body forward into a sort of halfway crouch. Neither one of them moved for one frozen instant, and then she straightened and left the room, turning her face away from him. But not in time to hide the look of naked terror he saw in her eyes.

Beginning to doubt his own sanity now, Charles moved like a robot, first to the bathroom to gather up his toilet articles, then to fetch his hanging suit bag from the closet. At last he had everything, and stood in her bedroom for a minute, glancing around one last time, to see if he'd missed anything. He carried his suitcase out to the living room and noticed that she'd cleared the table, so he went to the kitchen door. She was stacking the dishwasher.

"I think I'd better be going," he mumbled.

She just stood there, frozen, staring down into the sink.

Charles waited, but when she still didn't say anything, he moved closer to give her a quick kiss on the cheek, not touching her anywhere else. He didn't know what else to do, or say. So without another word he turned and made his way across the living room, opened the front door and left.

The road between Houston and Austin was so familiar it didn't demand anywhere near Charles's full attention. He'd just come off the seventy-five-mile stretch of I-10 and was leaving the coastal plain behind, beginning the gentle climb toward Austin on the old two-lane highway near Columbus, through wooded, hilly countryside. He tried to maintain his interstate speed, in a hurry now to get back. He also felt a certain relief at the prospect of dealing with the kind of problems waiting for him there, in the lab. Who the hell could even hope to figure out what the problem was, let alone a solution, when she wouldn't sit down and talk about it in a deliberate, logical way? It just wasn't like her to be so damned emotional! Or was it?

He zoomed past the chartreuse and purple Chez Paree, its peeling facade both garish and pathetic in the bright light of day. Typical of a dying breed that had dotted the Texas landscape from El Paso to Texarkana during the forties and fifties, the "roadhouse" probably looked far more inviting to the locals in the dark of night, with its beckoning neon lights and loud music. He flipped on the car radio to KMFA, the classical music station in Austin, thinking he should be close enough to pick it up, and forced his grip on the wheel to relax.

As far back as he could remember, his fascination with science had been a refuge, beginning with the hours he'd spent reading the *Book of Knowledge*. A few years later he'd discovered that his first rudimentary experiments in electronics were a way to escape the constant arguing and fighting, especially during those last couple of years before the divorce.

It was almost as if she'd set out to provoke him, on purpose, to trap him into doing or saying something she could jump him about. What the hell did she want from him, anyway? At times she seemed positively obsessed with all the injustices in the world, and seemed to believe that she alone could right whatever was wrong simply by exposing it to the light of day, on television. He remembered asking her why she was always angry, only to have her fling back a heated, "Because there's so much to be angry about!"

He stopped at a gas station in LaGrange, filled up and got a cold drink from the machine, then hit the road again. At least she hadn't resorted to tears, like Lupe, as if that could help anyone figure out what was wrong with a piece of equipment! It was enough to make you think twice, dammit, before ever taking on another female graduate student!

He passed the turnoff to Flatonia and slowed for Plum, a tiny community of mostly gray and crumbling frame houses, one of which housed Farrar's Faucet Beauty Shop. Something sure as hell had her wound up last night—and this morning—tight as a spring, ready to jump at the least little thing. Maybe it was something to do with the awards thing at the Hyatt, though she certainly hadn't seemed to mind being in the spotlight at the time—had reveled in it, in fact, just like his mother, flitting from one group of people to another with the greatest of ease, able to talk to anyone and everyone, whether about the food or artificial hearts.

Just before Bastrop the trees thickened to become an impenetrable forest of tall green pines, gum, scraggly oaks, and tangled underbrush—the Lost Pines of Texas, an unexplained outcropping that shouldn't by rights have found adequate nourishment from either the soil or rainfall in this part of the state. It was almost noon, and the sun was flooding in through his window. He turned up the air conditioner and redirected one of the vents to blow directly at him. Maybe that's just the way she got whenever she was nervous, only he'd never been around to feel the full brunt before. Did that mean the blush was off the rose, that the glow, the blinding sexual attraction, the blissful euphoria, or whatever the hell it was in the beginning, was gone?

He came down over the last hill, rounded the curve and caught his first glimpse of the university tower jutting up on the distant horizon. Most problems were solvable, even the ones that didn't look it at first, given a little unhurried analysis in the cool light of reason. Maybe the best thing now, for both of them, was to give it a little space and time.

Charles spent what was left of Saturday, and then all day Sunday and Monday, working late into the night at the university, shut up alone in his lab, until he was too tired to think, and could go home and straight to bed without even turning on the lights in the rest of the house—too tired to notice how empty the house felt. But it didn't quite work. Wednesday afternoon he was sitting in a budget-council meeting, listening to his faculty colleagues debate which junior-faculty members should get how much salary raise next year, when it suddenly hit him that he not only didn't want to be here, wasting his time on this kind of crap—he didn't *need* to be! He'd just signed a contract for a million bucks up front, plus an estimated half million more in royalties every year for the next God-only-knows-how-many years, an estimate he knew damned well was on the conservative side. But what the hell good was that going to be, if she wouldn't even accept a minor addition to his house?

With every passing day the frustration got worse, not better, because he still couldn't figure any way around her adamant refusal to let him use that money in a way to make it possible for them to be together—to get married and live like normal people! He called her Thursday night, but got her answering machine and hung up without leaving a message. What the hell! She was the one who'd torn up the house plan, threw the fit of temper! So why should *he* be the one to try to patch things up?

He left his own answering machine on for a couple of evenings after that, even when he was home, in case she called. Just so she would see how it felt, for a change, to get nothing but a recording!

Saturday and Sunday he stayed home, puttering around the house, which only reminded him again of how she'd responded to his plan to add onto it, but the phone didn't ring once. No one, it seemed, gave a shit whether he was even alive! He felt restless, as if something wasn't quite right, a feeling he recognized from the past, though he couldn't actually put a name to it. Dammit to hell and back, didn't she know or care that he needed to work, that Biomed was waiting on the new software for the Vampire, that she was messing with his peace of mind, interfering with important work? Is that supposed to mean hers isn't? Was she right after all—was he asking *her* to do all the compromising?

The following Monday was like any other except that he left the university early, to go home for a swim, to try to clear his head, because nothing was going right, even in the lab. He couldn't find the damned "bug" in the new program, which was somehow messing up the compiling function, and couldn't move any further until he did. Tuesday he considered calling her again, then remembered that she spent Tuesday and Thursday nights at one of the women's centers—another touchy subject with her, one that he couldn't even begin to fathom. He was sitting in his study, trying to decide what to do next, when his attention was caught by the spots of colored light dancing across the wall. The picture of her eager, smiling face appeared in his mind's eyes, as clear and fresh as it had been that day while she waited for the woman to wrap the pieces of faceted glass in old newspaper—remnants of a discarded, dismantled chandelier that was of little value to anyone. Except Mari.

Wednesday night he dug out the flamenco videotape, wondering why he hadn't thought of it sooner, put it in the VCR and sat in his dark, lonely living room, letting the sound of her voice wash over him. It opened with the view across the Strait of Gibraltar, looking toward Morocco and the Atlas Mountains, the home of the Berbers, "blood brothers of the Moors." Voice-over, Mari talked about

Orientalism, the "something extra" brought to the region by the Moslems, which made Spain different from all the rest of Europe, even today.

"More than a millennium ago the Moors invaded the Iberian peninsula and created a culture to rival Constantinople and Damascus, and revitalized the culture they found here by absorbing and enriching it, rather than destroying it—as the Catholics did seven hundred years later when they purged anything and everything they considered 'heathen.'" Charles recognized De Falla's *El Amor Brujo*—"Love the Magician"—without consciously realizing it, while watching the changing scenery—beaches, olive groves shimmering in the sun, ancient hill towns, lush tropical flowers and snowcapped mountains—until far more personal images began to impose themselves on the landscape, in spite of his effort to concentrate on what she was saying.

And then she was describing the *cante jondo*, or "deep song," that had grown spontaneously out of the African-Moorish-Hebrew cultures of the area, rather than originating with the Gypsies. Again the music crescendoed, but this time it was the sliding, quavering voice of a flamenco singer, pouring out a tale of love, sadness, and loss against the staccato beat of the flamenco guitar.

"Andalusia stretches across the Iberian peninsula from the Mediterranean north to the Sierra Morena. Oriental, pagan, ancient—a culture so steeped in antiquity that its history is still part of the sensibility of the Andalusian people, who possess a unique sense of history, or time." A shot of Picasso's *Demoiselles d'Avignon* flashed on the screen. "As we can see in the painting that announced the cubist revolution in 1907, shattering our Western vision of art as realism. An Andalusian view of reality." Then the scene was changing again as Tony's lens zoomed in on the shores of a rocky island.

"A civilization at least 3500 years old, as old as the Minoan culture on Crete and the palace at Knossos." She paused dramatically. "Which contained flush toilets and hot baths." Charles had to smile at that, but was duly impressed when he recognized Tony's hand again, transforming the ruins of the labyrinth on Crete into the walls of the

Alhambra, through a series of superimposed camera shots, while "The Gardens of Spain" played in the background.

"I'll never be able to listen to that music again without seeing the Generalife," she'd said, that night in the hotel. Even now he could feel her lips caressing his temple.

"The Alhambra, where the sound of water is poetry to the ear, even as it cools the air moving through its lacy chains of interlocking rooms and courtyards." Charles recognized the Royal Baths, and that other "curiosity" she'd shown him— the seats where water could run underneath. He wanted to look longer, to relive the memory, but already she was moving away, taking him back to Knossos, to the famous wall painting of the young gymnasts dancing with the bull god. They seemed to come to life as he watched, metamorphosing into a troupe of matadors filing into the bullring at Ronda. And then one of them was facing a charging black bull, only to step aside at the last minute in an artfully structured dance. "And so it is easy to see why there has been an intermingling of the famous flamenco and toreo clans in Spain.

"Choreographed expressions of sexuality and fertility, life, death, and resurrection—rhythmic, constant renewal —have been part of religious celebrations through most of human history. A joining of the spiritual and the sensual, the sacred and the profane, the salacious and the transcendental. Meant to excite within, to stir both the flesh and the spirit." The camera returned to Knossos for the third and last time, for a tight shot of the little bronze statue of the priestess to the snake goddess—her eyes staring, transfixed, arms raised to frame her head, bare breasts jutting forward above her flared, ruffled skirt. And then she, too, metamorphosed into the face and body of Galiana, the flamenco dancer he and Mari had seen in Torremolinos.

There was much more, most of it focusing on the forms and variations of flamenco—among them the *zambra, zarabanda,* and *siguiriya*—ending with the words of the poet Federico García Lorca—"a man proud of his Moorish blood, who was shot by the Falangists at the age of thirty-seven, whose presence still seems to pervade the city of Granada"—who saw in one small boy he found dancing barefoot in the dirt "the heroic rhythm of my whole people, of our whole history—the incarnation of the hot ashes of the Andalusian past."

But it was those three scenes at Knossos, which Mari and Tony had visually transformed into the here and now, tying centuries of history together without having to say a word, that stayed in his mind afterward, through the long hours of the night and into the next day. And the next night. That and her final wrap as the camera began to pull back, leaving the last scene fixed, looking across the vega from the Alhambra at twilight, the sky going dusty gold, violet, and rose.

"The Andalusians speak of *duende*, the spirit of flamenco, as a special kind of knowing. The intuitive side of consciousness. Perhaps because it enables us to recapture some of the awe and mystery we lost, that we gave up in exchange for rationalism."

The more he thought about it, the more sure he was that she'd meant those words especially for him, that the purpose of the whole package—words, music, and pictures—had been to send a message she'd been unable to convey to him any other way. "We not only don't live in the same world, Charles, you don't even know that my world exists." At the time he'd assumed she meant only that he didn't appreciate what it was like to be a woman, especially the kind of woman who needed her work as much as he needed his, who at times found herself powerless and discriminated against. But now he wasn't so sure.

In folk art Mari saw the striving of common people to "transcend having feet of clay," and in the Alhambra the unity of the human body and spirit with nature. He thought back to that day at the Alhambra, remembering how she'd seemed to "know" the place in a way that was completely foreign to him.

"The intuitive side of consciousness." The words, the thought, the idea, held a certain fascination, piquing both his imagination and his reason, a fascination that he couldn't possibly explain—except, perhaps, to Mari.

Friday morning Charles picked up the phone in his office and called Rachel, at the hospital clinic. "Hi, how's it going?"

"Charles? God, am I ever glad to hear from you!"

"Why? Something out of whack with the Vampire?"

"No. With Mari. I'm worried, was going to call you myself, but Tony said she wouldn't appreciate it. She's knocking herself out on that damned Pharmacol thing. But something is wrong, Charles. Bad wrong. She's dropped out of her music group, said she was missing too many of their practice sessions and it wasn't fair to them. Has even stopped going to the shelter, and you know how she felt about that. Refuses to see anyone outside of work, won't answer her phone, even when she's there. Keeps that damn machine on all the time."

"Tell me about it," he muttered. "I've been trying for a week. I can't even get her at the station."

"Tony says she's taking calls there, but he thinks she's got Sandy on orders not to put you through."

"That's great, just what I need to hear."

"She won't go out to eat even with us, or come to my place. No explanations, no nothing. Tony's worried. Said she acted like a zombie in New York. Since then, well—"

"He try talking to her?"

"Yeah, but she just says it's a personal problem. That she'll learn to live with in time. He thinks she's such a 'strong woman,' but dammit, I'm not so sure."

"Shit! That is one stubborn woman! If she won't answer her phone, then she'll just have to talk face to face." He was already thinking ahead. Semester exams were over, and all he still had to do was average grades and turn them in. After that he'd be full-time on research for the summer, which meant no teaching except for a couple of graduate students he'd continue to supervise, gratis, since his salary would be paid out of a research grant. So no one would be looking over his shoulder.

"I'm going to try to get away from here by noon. But don't mention it if you talk to her. Better not even mention it to Tony. She might know just from looking at him."

"What are you going to do?"

"Who knows? Camp on her doorstep until she gets home, I guess. After that I'll just have to play it by ear."

CHAPTER

18

It was almost eight o'clock when she got home, but still light enough for Mari to see him from the bottom of the stairs, sitting on the top step with his briefcase open beside him.

Charles rose to his feet as she started up, waiting for her to reach him. "Hi!" It was all he could think of to say as he took in her sky-blue dress with the full skirt gathered into a wide white elastic waistband. In spite of the soft fullness, it was obvious that she'd lost weight. She not only looked too thin, but fragile. Her whole body spoke of exhaustion as well as the dark circles under her pale eyes.

"Hi," she returned softly, refusing to meet his eyes. Her mind was still spinning, wondering why he'd come, but then she couldn't help herself. And when she saw the warm, welcoming smile, all her defenses collapsed.

"Oh Charles!" She threw her arms around his neck. "I'm so glad to see you!" He enclosed her body almost automatically, holding her close while she rattled on incoherently, laughing and crying at the same time. "I thought I'd never see you again, that I ruined everything, that you'd hate me for the way I behaved, even though I had to do it. I thought you'd never want to see me again, not that I'd blame you."

"Fat chance." It was all he could manage, with his throat

in a vise and his eyelids burning. And all he wanted to do was bury his face in her hair, breathe in the aroma of her hair and skin, immerse himself in her and never let go.

It was Mari who pulled away first, fumbling for his hand as if she, too, were unwilling to break physical contact completely. She started toward the apartment door, pulling him with her. Once inside she dropped her purse on the floor and turned into his arms again, needing to feel him with her body as well as her mind, warm and solid, not the product of wishful thinking or fanciful daydreams. In spite of all the endless dark hours when sleep refused to come, she knew she wasn't hallucinating now. He was real.

"Are you okay? You been sick?" Charles asked at last. "You don't look too—I mean—"

"I know what you mean," she interrupted, moving her head against his neck. "Just haven't been sleeping very well. But I'll be okay now."

"Rachel said you'd been burning the candle at both ends, trying to track that Pharmacol business."

"Rachel? She called you?" She leaned away, releasing him reluctantly, not sure she was ready for what she knew was coming next—questions.

"Uh-uh, I called her. Couldn't ever get you, nothing but that damned answering machine of yours. How come you didn't want to even talk to me, Mari?"

At the reminder, she started toward her study to turn the machine off. Charles followed right behind her, not willing to let her out of his sight yet. The little red light was flashing, but Mari didn't bother to listen to the messages. She turned around, leaned against the edge of her desk and looked down at her hands, instead of at him.

"I didn't think you'd want to . . . call, or anything, only I didn't want to know that, for sure. I suppose you think that's silly." She flashed him a quick glance to see how he was taking it.

Charles nodded. "Yeah. Not much like you to turn tail and run, either, refuse to face the music. I get the distinct feeling there's something going on I don't know about, Mari. And I'm not very happy about that, I have to admit. But, well, I think maybe you need to spit it out, in black and white, straight, so I can at least try to understand. And maybe I can—now." She watched his face, trying not to let herself hope he might mean what she wanted that to mean. "Yeah, I watched the tape, finally. Several times, in fact."

"And? What'd you think?" she asked, anxious to know still more.

"I guess I'm still working on that. No, not just what I think. I'm not sure how to explain. How it made me feel, what I'm just beginning to understand—about your world. But at least I know it exists now." He moved closer, to frame her face with both hands, and this time her eyes didn't flinch from his. "I'm not too sure about too much anymore, in fact. Except for one thing, Mari honey. I love you enough to chance staying awake, enough to stay and fight, if that's what you have to do." He leaned forward to brush his lips across hers, back and forth, slowly, persuasively.

"I love you, too. I didn't want to believe it at first. You were too good to be true, or almost."

"Just what the hell is that supposed to mean?" He tried to sound gruff, then ruined it by grinning when he saw her lips begin to lift at the corners, and the smile in her light blue eyes.

"It means that I've loved you from the start, couldn't you tell? But, well, do you remember what I tried to tell you in Torremolinos? It's wonderful, isn't it, the feeling that comes with being in love, of loving and being loved? At first. But what about later, when one problem after another keeps cropping up, problems you don't want to face but can't avoid, questions you can't answer or answers you can't live with? What happens then?" She stopped, leaving the question hanging in the air between them.

And then the phone rang, causing them both to start. Mari reached across her desk, lifting the receiver to her ear without even half thinking about what she was doing.

"Mari? It's Jackie. I tried to call you earlier but—"

"Hi, Jackie. What's up?" She recognized her sister's voice, even though it sounded sort of thick, as if she might have a cold.

"It's Mom. She—I don't know how to tell you. She's gone."

"What do you mean, she's gone? Where?"

"Oh Mari, I, she . . . she just laid down for her usual nap this afternoon, and, and . . . never woke up."

"No, she couldn't have. I talked to her just last night and she was perfectly all right, said she was feeling good." Mari kept her back to Charles because the tears were suddenly flooding her eyes, and then overflowing, running down her cheeks, and she had to sniff and swallow to get a breath.

"I know, she called to tell me that she'd talked with you. She always did that, knew I'd want to hear about you, what you were doing." Jackie paused, and Mari knew she was trying desperately to keep control. Poor Jackie. Her sister had always been much closer to her mother, and was used to seeing or talking to Janet every day or two.

The sun had gone down, and it was almost dark, so Mari leaned over the desk to turn on the lamp. "What . . . what happened?"

"Dr. Richardson thinks her heart just stopped, that she didn't have any pain. Or suffer."

"When?" What difference does it make to know that now? Her eyes were hot and swollen, her nose was all stuffed up, and all she wanted to do was lie down and cry, until she couldn't cry anymore.

"I tried to get her around four-thirty, then again at five, but she still didn't answer. I was worried, so I called Mrs. Henderson, asked her to go see if she was home."

"You want me to try to come on tonight, if I can get a flight out?"

"No." Jackie just barely managed to get the word out, and Mari could hear her sniffling and gasping for breath.

And then Nick's voice came on the phone. "You okay, Mari?"

"Yes. And Charles is here." She turned around when she said his name, expecting to see him standing just behind her, but he wasn't even in the room. "Tell Jackie I'll be there sometime tomorrow, earliest flight I can get. I'll call, soon as I know."

"Sure, I'll pick you up. Any time, Mari. Talk to you later, then."

Mari replaced the receiver, slowly, and stood there staring into the dusk outside the window, not quite able to make herself believe that just what she'd been dreading for the past two months had actually come about. At last she wandered out to the living room, looking for Charles. And found him sitting in the nearly dark corner, in the leather lounge chair. She made no attempt to turn on a light, but as she moved closer, she could see that he had a hand on each knee and was staring down at the floor.

"That was Jackie." She stopped, unable to find the words to continue for a second, then looked at his face for the first time. He looked perfectly normal, except for the quivering lips and the silent tears pouring down his cheeks. And the pain in his dark wet eyes when they sought hers, pleading for help.

Her heart went out to him and she crumpled to the floor between his knees, to take him into her arms and hold him, the only thing she knew to do to give comfort. He leaned forward to accept her, wrapping his arms around her, then began rocking her back and forth from time to time, like a child, while dusk silently turned to night.

It wasn't until later that they began to talk. Even then the words came in bits and pieces, as the memories returned one by one, demanding expression out of the need to share their deepest thoughts and feelings. What at times might seem a non sequitur in the beginning, in the end was revealed to relate in some way or other to Janet, because she was never really out of mind or memory, every minute of every hour during the nights and days that followed.

They were on the plane to Denver when Charles said, "I never told you about Roy, did I?" Mari didn't answer, only waited for him to tell her. "He was a real honest guy, the voice of reason, the calm after the storm. That's what the divorce was, you know, like a storm, leaving everything scattered and broken." His hand was tight around hers all of a sudden, so tight the ring on her finger dug into the one next to it. But she didn't want to complain, or to interrupt. "I was sure it was hopeless, that I'd never be able to swim. Hell, I couldn't even bend my knee on my own. But he showed me how to start exercising the muscles, in bed or sitting in a chair, then got me into the water. It took months, but he never complained about all the time and trouble it cost him, hauling me back and forth to the Y. Even stayed with it later, when I got stronger, started coaching me on how to improve my speed. I've always suspected he may have figured all along that that might be the only way I'd ever get to the university. I can still hear him. 'Smart kid like you, Charlie,' he'd say, 'would be bored out of your gourd slinging drilling pipe. That's not what you were put on this earth for. Anyway, I doubt you'll ever have the muscle for it.'" He glanced at Mari with a little grin. "You should've seen me when we started, scrawny as the runt of the litter, one leg like a toothpick."

After that he was silent for several minutes, looking out the window of the plane, lost in thought. "'Go to school,' he was always saying, 'learn how to do some good in this world.' Even after they separated he used to come up to Austin once in a while, for a swim meet. We'd go out after, drink beer, talk."

"You don't see him anymore?"

Charles shook his head. "He was killed in a rig accident, a couple of months before I graduated. Always hated that. The timing, I mean. I know he knew, but it just didn't seem fair, somehow." He squeezed her hand. "Your mom understood, right from the beginning, why I do the kind of research I do. It was a little like having Roy back, someone who really understood. Having someone in your corner again, cheering you on."

That was something of a revelation to Mari, reminding her of how little she'd appreciated or really understood her mother. "I know what you mean about it not seeming fair. That's the way I feel, too, because I was just beginning to really know her, as a woman. And now she's gone. I can't help thinking about all the wasted years, when I couldn't see her except as a child. Why did it take us so long to become friends?" The ever-waiting tears welled up again to interrupt her emotional confession. She dug in her purse for a tissue, determined not to break down under the load of sorrow and guilt she was carrying. Would it be like this for the rest of her life, she wondered, because of what might have been?

"I feel ashamed now. Because I envied you, you know, when I saw how even-handed your relationship is, with your mother," she admitted, wanting to purge herself of this last disloyalty. "The atmosphere is so different when you're together, not all 'loaded' or whatever you want to call it. Like two adults who respect each other, don't invade each other's territory or come across as judgmental. I'd almost given up hope that Mom and I would ever be like that, get to where we didn't have the conflicting vibes or the emotional electricity between us that kept rubbing my fur the wrong way. Until that last weekend I spent with her in Denver. I don't know, but I think something started to change for us in Spain."

Charles straightened in his seat and dropped her hand, visibly shaken. And then he began to laugh—a dry, humorless burst of derisive disbelief. "That's really a laugh! My God, I wouldn't wish my mother on my worst enemy!" She wondered if he were joking, until she saw his face. "Amy Merrill doesn't love anyone but herself, never has, never will. Doesn't even know the meaning of the word." He expelled the same dry chuckle again. "All my friends used to envy me, too, the kids I played with, because *my* mother never said no to anything I wanted to do—hardly ever reprimanded me, in fact, unless we got in her way, were too noisy or something—which only made me feel 'dumb,' because I wished she would." He grabbed Mari's hand, as if fearing he might be set adrift, alone, which was exactly how he remembered feeling back then.

Mari could only gape at him in disbelief. Charles shook his head a little, glanced out the window for a minute, then back at her. "Your mother cared so much, you felt she was interfering in your life, drove you to rebel," he continued finally, "while I wanted mine to throw a screaming fit about what I was or wasn't doing, just once, so I'd know she cared, even if it was only a little bit. It's easy to be civil, never have a heated exchange about anything, like you had with Jan, when you don't really care—when what one of you is doing, or thinking, doesn't matter to the other. I suppose I'm my mother's son, because what I really meant earlier, about it not being fair, well, was that except for Roy, there's never been anyone who cared about me or what I did—whether I succeeded or failed—until you. And Jan." When he looked at her this time, the tears were glittering in his eyes again.

"One thing I do know for sure, Mari honey. You can

succeed beyond your wildest dreams, get all the awards in the world. And it still isn't enough—if you don't have anyone to share it with who really cares."

They stayed at Jackie's, but Mari and her sister spent hours at Janet's house, going through her personal belongings, a wrenching task that threatened to destroy what little control Mari could muster. When she did break down and cry, it was because Jackie was crying, or the reverse, and she learned that that, too, was an intimate kind of sharing as well as catharsis. Nick and Charles came with Nick's pickup truck and took several pieces of furniture to Jackie's, leaving what Mari wanted to keep in the house. Unable to face parting with the home they'd both grown up in, Mari and Jackie agreed to share the cost of upkeep, taxes, and insurance for the time being, and leave the decision as to what to do with it for later.

Though the Church had never been an important part of Mari's life, which was another thing she and her mother had disagreed about, it was comforting to see all of Janet's friends there. Rather than a formal eulogy, her friends told stories about Janet, about her sense of humor and her tolerance, the way she lived what she believed, putting her money and her hands to work to help others. And her equanimity in the face of crisis—the latter by Etta Henderson.

Tony and Rachel came for the memorial service. Janet wouldn't hear of a "funeral," had always insisted that she wouldn't be there anyway, except in the memory of those she left behind. They spent the night at Janet's house and then returned to Houston the next morning. And just before they left, Tony pulled Mari aside, and she knew immediately, just from the way his speech changed, that he, too, had been deeply touched by her mother.

"We came because we want to, Mari. For Rachel and me, your mother was a special lady. I see you in her, too, the first time I met her, even there, in the hospital. The same strong feelings, about fairness, what is right. She loved you very much. Let that be enough. For her, and for you."

It was the day after the service that Mari began to feel the finality of her mother's death, with the first vague realization that she was an orphan now, a little as if she'd been cast adrift without an anchor. She began to wonder how Charles had managed to deal with those feelings when he was only a child. Worse than being alone, though, he'd had to find a way to live with the knowledge that the one person in the world he should have been able to count on to love him, didn't. Perhaps that was because she was too much a child herself, though Mari doubted Charles would have been able to understand that then. Even today his mother didn't really value Charles except for what he could do for her, for how his reputation might enhance her own. And that thought brought sudden hot tears, of rage at Amy, and then of unutterable sadness for Charles.

Mari jumped up from Janet's desk, where she'd been going through papers in preparation for the meeting with the lawyer later that afternoon, and went looking for Charles, needing to hug and comfort and love him. All the cabinet doors stood wide open and he was methodically emptying them of food, sorting it by type into cardboard boxes, canned goods in one, dry boxed things in another. She ducked under one of his raised arms, insinuating herself between his chest and the counter, and put her arms around his waist. He stopped what he was doing, surprised by the unexpected show of affection.

"I was sitting in there, thinking, and I decided I needed to come tell you something." She paused and he waited, wondering what "confession" was coming. She seemed to be carrying so much guilt about her mother, yet he couldn't think of any way to help, except maybe to listen.

"What do you need to tell me?" he urged, cupping the back of her head with one hand. Her hair wasn't as silky as he remembered, but at least it no longer had that fuzzy, coarse feel.

"That I love you."

He squeezed her tighter, then waited. When she didn't say anything more, he asked, "That's all?"

Mari nodded her head against his chest. "I wanted to make sure you know, don't want you to forget."

For answer he laid his chin against the top of her head and held her close, rocking her in his arms in time to his words.

"Never, I promise. As long as I live, maybe longer." And then they just stood there like that, for several minutes, not talking, not kissing, not anything. Just holding each other.

At last Mari broke away with a long satisfied sigh. "I'm almost done. Just have her check stubs to go through, and then I'll be ready to leave. How about you?"

He cast a quick glance at the cabinets. "About fifteen minutes should do it, plus loading the boxes in the car."

"I'll be on the sun porch. Let me know when you're finished. I suppose I could take the rest of her papers with me, go through them at Jackie's."

Charles completed packing the boxes, then took the first one out to the car. He'd just stepped back inside when he heard her.

"Oh God, no! Oh no! No!" She was crying, and kept moaning the same thing over and over. She must be hurt!

Charles sprinted for the porch, his heart in his throat, fear and worry already fogging his brain. He found her sitting on the floor, cross-legged, arms folded across her chest, hands clasping her elbows, rocking back and forth, sobbing. Bits and pieces of paper were scattered all around her on the floor, which didn't tell him a thing.

"What happened, Mari? Are you hurt?" She just shook her head and continued wailing and rocking. He crouched down beside her, feeling frantic and helpless. "For God's sake, Mari, tell me what's wrong, so I can do something to help!" he demanded.

Something in the tone of his voice got through to her and she stopped rocking, then looked up at him, letting the tears stream down her face. One hand shot out, and he looked down to see what she was holding out to him. The stubs from what looked like one of her mother's checkbooks. He looked back up to her face, trying to understand what she was trying to tell him. And then she began to speak, in a voice so torn with pain it almost broke his heart.

"Ah God, Charles, she knew . . . all along . . . all this time. She knew."

He pulled his handkerchief from his hip pocket, sat down on the floor next to her and began dabbing at her tears. But they kept coming. "It'll be all right, Mari, whatever it is.

We'll work it out, together," he murmured, trying to comfort her as a parent would soothe a child awakened by a bad dream. "Tell me what it is, please?"

"Oh no, because then you'd hate me too . . . you'd know . . . how I . . . what I let him do to me." With each word she sounded more incoherent, and disturbed. Charles hesitated, unsure what to do, afraid she might go into hysterics, so he grabbed her by the shoulders with both hands and shook her a little, gently, just enough to get her attention.

"What did your mother know, Mari? What did you find in her checkbook? Please tell me, so I can help you. You know I won't hate you, no matter what it is."

She looked at him, blinking her reddened eyes, calmly took the handkerchief from his hand and began swiping it across her eyes. He waited, trying to be patient, while she sniffled and fought for breath. And then she dropped her hands into her lap, still working at his handkerchief, wadding it into a tight little ball, and began to speak.

"It's all here." She pointed to the little books of stubs scattered around her. "She's been sending a check, to the Denver Battered Women's Center." She drew in a deep breath, then let it out in a long sigh. "Every month for the past ten years. Ever since——" He watched her face begin to crumple as she struggled to hold on to her hard-won composure, and felt his gut wrench in pain.

"Ever since I lost my baby. Since Phillip . . . since Phillip hit . . . knocked me into——said I was clumsy, stupid . . . couldn't do anything right. Because I miscarried." She turned and looked at him then, and he knew she could see the tears in his own eyes now. He wanted to put his arms around her, but didn't. "But I never told her, never told anyone . . . I was too ashamed. Except Nick. He was the one I called, from the 7-Eleven on the corner——" She had to stop for a second, and he knew she was reliving the pain and horror all over again. "Blood running down my legs . . . so embarrassed . . . didn't know what to do. And then Nick . . . came . . . took me to the hospital. And found me a place to live . . . so I could hide." She looked startled for a second. "I mean recover. But he'd never tell. Even Jackie doesn't know."

She turned away from him then, to look out at the

mountains, the view her mother had loved so much. "It wasn't the first time—that he beat me, I mean. He always said he wouldn't do it again, promised he wouldn't. I guess I wanted to believe him. Thought it was as much my fault as his, that if I could change, things would be different. That I needed to try harder. I should never have gone back, so he could do it again—to me . . . and to my baby. It was my fault, and I'm going to have to live with that for the rest of my life."

Charles was too shocked to even speak—and so blindly furious he could hardly keep from lashing out at something, anything, even an inanimate piece of furniture. But he still had enough sense to know that any display of physical violence would probably send her over the edge. Even so, some primitive instinct—hormones, call it what you will— cried out in him for physical retribution. For vengeance. What he wanted more than anything in this world was to find Phillip Ashmore, and to beat him to death!

"The hell it was your fault! Dammit, Mari, how can you even think that? The shitty bastard should have his god-damned balls kicked off."

"No. It's true. That's the really hard part. A man can batter only one time and have it be only his fault. After that it takes two, the batterer and his willing victim. Oh, I'm not saying the woman *wants* to be beaten, though lots of battered women have such a poor opinion of themselves, they think they probably deserve it. I've worked with enough of them to know."

Somewhere on the fringes of his mind he realized that she was beginning to sound more like her usual self, but Charles felt completely impotent, helpless to do anything to change what had happened to her, which left him so frustrated, he felt like he just might explode. "How can you stand working with battered women, after—"

"But that's why I do it. Most of the time I can seal off my own personal feelings, use what I've learned to help others. And God knows, there are plenty of them out there who need it!" She sat there quietly for a few minutes. "I don't know if you can ever understand, Charles, because some-times even I think my head is a hopeless mess. But I can't ever go back, can never live with the feeling of being trapped, again." She turned to face him. "I do love you, Charles, so much that sometimes I think I'm going to die of it. But I'm enough of a realist to know that the doors have to be open for me. And if you can't deal with that, well, I guess I'll find some way to get over that, too—eventually."

Charles thought he knew what she was talking about, but maybe she meant it literally. "That's why you tore up the house plan?"

"I suppose, in a way." She smiled, remembering that morning. "I'm sorry about that, Charles. But I had to do it, had to find out, before—"

"Find out what? What the hell are you talking about? Will you please stop with the riddles?"

"I really was angry with you, the night before, when you fizzled out on me and then played dumb, wouldn't even talk to me about it."

"Nothing like you, right?"

"Okay, maybe I deserve that, but—"

"Okay, okay. But it sounds so goddamned Freudian, you're going to laugh your head off." He scooted over, closer, so he could reach a hand up to cup the back of her neck and fondle the edge of her hair. "What really upset me, I think, was seeing what you'd done to your hair." Mari looked puzzled. "Yeah, well, I like it better smooth, straight, like it was. And then, when I saw how well you fit in with that crowd of phonies, flitting around like the rest of the social butterflies, like my mother, I began to wonder . . ." He had the grace to look a little chagrined. "On top of that, after we got home, in bed, well—I reached up in the dark, expecting to feel your smooth, silky hair—which really turns me on, by the way, in case that has escaped your notice up to now. Anyway, instead it was all fuzzy and rough. And . . . well, you know the rest."

She drew back to look at him, her eyebrows raised in question. "That was the final straw?" What she thought he was really trying to say was that she'd reminded him *too much* of his mother.

"Yeah, I know. Sounds weird, doesn't it?" She thought about that for a couple of minutes, nodding her head understandingly. "Was that what you wanted to know?" he asked finally.

"Yes. No, not really. The next morning, at breakfast, I was trying every way I could think of to make you angry. Really angry. To see if—oh God, don't you see, Charles, I had to find out if you would—" Charles just looked at her, his mind whirring in confusion for a second, and then he leaped to his feet, suddenly too angry to even stay in the same room with her.

He strode through the kitchen, swooping up a box of canned goods on his way through the kitchen, then out the door to the car.

He was unusually quiet the rest of the afternoon, and even through supper at Jackie's, though it wasn't as noticeable then because Kitty and Alan kept up a constant barrage of chatter, mostly with Mari and Nick.

"Do you think Charles might help me with my arithmetic homework?" Alan asked Mari, as if Charles weren't even there. "If he's a whiz at it, like you said, I could be finished in no time and we could all have a game of that trivial stuff you like to play." Mari looked at Charles, but before he could respond, Nick jumped in.

"Go bite the bullet, Al. You better get at it, too, Kitty. After that, if you have a problem you can't figure out yourself, you might consult Charles, if he doesn't mind. But only one or two questions. I don't know about playing games. It's getting kinda late." Nick pushed his chair back and started stacking dinner plates.

"Okay, girls, your shift is over. Charles and I will clear the table, clean up the kitchen." He grinned at Jackie. "And leave it just the way you like it, *Mother*. You and Mari go on into the other room, watch TV, read the paper or whatever. We'll bring you a cup of something, maybe a little brandy to go with it, soon as we finish up."

Charles carried the supper dishes to the kitchen while Nick stacked them in the dishwasher, then stood in the kitchen watching Nick finish up.

"She told you, didn't she?" Nick asked after a couple of minutes.

Charles just nodded. What was there to say?

"Just the fact that she told you oughta mean something. You planning to stick around?"

Charles looked at Nick sharply. "Come hell or hot water.

Don't really have a choice. Did you?" Nick smiled and shook his head, knowing exactly what he meant. "But Jesus, Nick, it makes my skin crawl, just thinking about what that bastard did to her. Couldn't you have done something to stop it?"

"Didn't know it was goin' on. She'd sort of hide out, say she had to work, or something. She worked waiting tables till all hours, and he was at the hospital most of the time, so it wasn't particularly unusual for us not to see her for two, sometimes three weeks at a time. Wasn't until that night she called me that I started putting two and two together, figured out that probably wasn't the first time. Just the last. That's what she said, that it was the last time. I made damned sure of it."

"How, what do you mean?"

"He went to see her, once, in the hospital. I hunted him up, told him face to face if he ever tried to even talk to her, in person or on the phone—or anybody else in the family, for that matter—I'd see to it there wasn't a soul in Denver who didn't know what he'd done—how many times he beat her, every damn blow he ever landed, how she lost the baby, bring charges against him for manslaughter, maybe even murder, the whole goddamned ball of wax!"

He gave the counter a final swipe with a wet sponge, then swung around and looked straight at Charles. "Hope to hell you don't have a temper you can't control!"

"You too, huh? My God, it must run in the family! You know what she did two weeks ago, just before she took off for New York? There we are, eating breakfast, and I'm showing her a plan I had drawn up for an addition to my house, for her, including a TV studio. All I did was ask her what she thought of it, and all of a sudden she jumps up and tears it in half, throws it down in my eggs and says that's what she thinks of it!"

"What'd you do?" Nick was grinning already.

"Told her she was behaving irrationally. You won't believe what happened then. She threw a shoe at me!"

"Testing you, was she?" Nick guessed, his voice quiet.

Charles stared at his feet for a second, then nodded grudgingly.

"Think about it," Nick suggested gently. "She marries a

guy she thinks she's in love with, good-looking, smart, going to be a doctor, has a lot going for him. Then discovers there's dirt under that clean white coat. Can you blame her for wanting to see what you might be hiding under your nice clean coat?"

"Listen to this," Mari said, then read aloud to Jackie from the article she'd just run across in the *Denver Post*. It was yesterday's paper, which didn't really matter for the kind of stories and columns the Sunday Contemporary section usually carried. " 'The genetic makeup of a child is a stronger influence on personality than child rearing, according to a recent study of 350 pairs of identical twins.' Back to the old nature versus nurture debate. Do you ever think about that with your kids—they're so different, aren't they? A lot of it's got to be in the genes. Let's see, says here that 'Researchers at the University of Minnesota were trying to determine to what extent eleven key personality traits are inherited.' "

"What traits?" Jackie asked. "I really don't see how you could ever determine something like that. Whether you have a particular trait, yes, but not how much of it is inherited. Sounds like poppycock to me."

"Do you think it's possible that we could've inherited a cliché gene from Mom?" Mari teased. "Only it was our home environment that determined exactly which ones we learned to use? Poppycock! Where else could that have come from?"

Jackie laughed a little, in spite of the fact that there were sudden tears in her eyes, and nodded understandingly. "Okay, let's hear about a couple of those traits. We'll put 'em to the test."

"First one is social potency. That's psychological jargon for leadership qualities. Sixty-one percent of this trait is inherited, and a person who has it is 'masterful, a forceful leader who likes to be the center of attention.' I know plenty of guys who fit that description, don't you? Jack Lunsford, for one."

"But not many women, because 'leadership,' quote-unquote, is mostly in the eye of the beholder, and men do not see women as leaders, except at home, where they get to take the 'lead' whether they want to or not—in cleaning the toilets, getting sick kids to the doctor, making sure the beer is always cold."

"You got it," Mari agreed with a wry smile, eyeing her sister with a new respect. "Let's see, oh yeah, the second trait is traditionalism. Means a person follows rules and authority, has high moral standards and strict discipline. And they think that sixty percent of this one is inherited."

"You mean a person can't have high moral standards and be creative at the same time, be an innovator? Somebody like Charles, for instance? Judging from what I've seen, I'd say his moral standards are right up there. Of course, I never did agree with Mom about a man and woman sleeping together before marriage being 'immoral.' That's a little too black or white for me." Jackie was only halfway teasing. "But I'll bet you anything that he doesn't buckle under to authority very often, because it's just part of his nature to question things. What does it say about that?"

Mari scanned the article, searching. "Closest they come is one called absorption. Fifty-five percent of that one is inherited. Means, 'Has a vivid imagination readily captured by rich experience; relinquishes sense of reality.' Which doesn't work for me. Maybe it's just the definitions that are flawed, not the traits themselves. Lots of this stuff probably is inherited, though, through the genes, and the biochemistry. Charles thought Mom and I were a lot alike, said so right from the first time he met her." She looked over at her sister with eyes suddenly blurry with tears. "I just can't . . . can't *believe* she's gone, that she won't walk into this room any minute, or that I'll never hear her play the piano again." She shook her head apologetically and dabbed at her eyes with the back of her hand, even though the pocket of her jeans was bulging with wadded tissues, then saw that Jackie was crying too.

"We had to have inherited this trait from Dad," Mari mumbled, trying to make light of their ever-ready tears. "I remember one time when I'd been home for a visit and was about to leave, and he was in tears. You know how he could do that, smile and cry at the same time, when it had anything to do with his kids, or his mother? And I asked Mom how come she never cried. You know what she said?"

Jackie shook her head. "No, but I can guess."

"She looked at Dad, then back at me, shrugged her shoulders and said, 'Someone has to be strong.' Sounds just like her, doesn't it? I've thought about that a lot, though, lately. Especially since Spain. I used to believe it was just a physical thing with her. But now I think crying probably was a luxury, one she wouldn't allow herself to indulge in because it was a sign of weakness—it was womanly, which to her generation was synonymous with being weak."

"Maybe, but I suspect the real reason was more mundane, or pragmatic, if you wish," Jackie replied. "Because most mothers learn early on, from the first day they bring a baby home from the hospital, to do what's necessary, whether they want to or feel like it or whatever. I remember once when Kitty was about three and cut her finger on one of my kitchen knives—I don't know how she got it, but I always felt it was my fault, that I wasn't watching her closely enough—having to stand there and watch the doctor stick a needle in her soft little finger, not once but two or three times. The fat was exposed, and it was bleeding all over the place—you know how I used to be about things like that—and she was screaming and crying, and I was trying to hold her. And then while he was stitching it closed, Nick comes rushing in, takes one look and turns positively green. The nurse happened to notice and ushered him right out of the room. Thought he was going to faint. I didn't have a choice, couldn't indulge in the 'luxury' of fainting, or crying, or running away—which is what I really wanted to do. That's probably the one fantasy we all have in common. Running away."

She looked at Mari with a self-deprecating smile. "Now let me finish this article I was reading, or you're going to have me bawling all night."

Mari went back to her newspaper, too, but she hardly saw the print on the page, because she was still thinking about what Jackie said, and all the times her mother had had to bandage her knee, or her toe, or a finger. And Janet's comment to her, just a few weeks ago, that "You were always getting into something."

"Oh my gosh, Mari," Jackie blurted suddenly, startling Mari out of her reverie. She jumped up from her chair and started toward Mari, folding the open newspaper section back on itself and then creasing it a second time along the fold before handing it to her. "Here, you'd better read this for yourself."

Mari accepted the paper from her, reading the headline she pointed to in one glance—UBC SELLS TWO STATIONS—then quickly scanned the first few paragraphs of the story.

New York (AP)—Universal Broadcasting Corporation today announced it has completed the sale of two network owned and operated television stations to Bertrand/Petrocorp for $200 million. The stations are KPOC-TV in Houston and WXIT-TV in Kansas City.

Industry sources say the plum in the deal was KPOC-TV, the network's leading profit-maker for the past two years, in spite of the recent economic downturn in Houston, which is the fourth-largest television market in the nation. Last year the station generated cash flow of $16 million on revenues of $40 million.

Formerly an independent oil and gas company, Bertrand/Petrocorp has, after a decade of mergers and diversification, become a multinational conglomerate with headquarters in Paris and holdings in electronics and communications as well as petroleum products.

According to media critic Ben Bagdikian, author of *The Media Monopoly,* the sale is further evidence of the trend toward concentrating the ownership of news sources in the hands of a few giant corporations. Bagdikian, Pulitzer Prize–winning reporter and former assistant managing editor of the *Washington Post,* was in Washington yesterday to testify before a House Appropriations subcommittee looking into . . .

CHAPTER
19

It was almost two o'clock before Mari managed to get to the station Tuesday afternoon, after a reluctant farewell to Charles. She was sure he'd been away from Austin longer than he'd originally intended, and probably really needed to get back, but she couldn't help dragging out the leave-taking—finding one more thing to tell him, giving him one more kiss, needing to touch him one more time—even out in the blacktopped parking lot under the midday sun. Somehow the Houston heat and humidity always came as a shock after the dry Denver air, sapping both her energy and enthusiasm.

She hunted for Tony first, and then Ron, but couldn't locate either one, which probably meant they were out on assignment, and was just heading back toward her office when she heard Jack call out her name.

"Mari! Glad I caught you." He rushed toward her and caught up just short of his own office. "Come on in a minute. I need to talk to you. Hope everything went okay in Denver. Sure am sorry about your mother." He kept up a steady stream of patter as she followed him into his office. "Sit down," he urged, waving to a chair, then sat down behind his desk. He leaned forward, put both elbows on the desk and steepled his fingers, then let them slide in and out between each other, a nervous gesture she recognized for what it was.

"You hear about the deal?"

"That the network sold the station? Yes." She waited, watching him slide his fingers in and out, up and down, avoiding her eyes.

"I hate to tell you this, kid, especially now, right after— but, well, we're buying up your contract. It's belt-tightening time, which shouldn't come as a big surprise to anyone who knows shit about this business. Hell, you know we're looking at the softest network economy in the past fifteen years! It's getting to everybody. Team was in here Saturday, from the new owners. We'll continue our association with UBC as an affiliate, but Jesus, with the level of affiliate compensation what it is these days, we already know we're going to have a cash-flow problem. Everybody's bitching since that last reduction, 'cause there's no way you can make up the difference by increasing ad rates—especially in this market, with the local economy what it is." Once he got started, he couldn't seem to stop, maybe because he was hoping to squelch any arguments before she had a chance to voice them. So he droned on and on, about the current cost-conscious mentality in the business, and ratings problems. "Those damn people meters are going to do us all in, kill the goose that laid the golden egg, divvy the ad dollars so many ways between on-air and cable that nobody'll be able to mount a decent operation." At last he seemed to just run out of steam, drew in a deep breath and gave her "the bottom line."

"So I know you'll understand why we have to grab the bull by the horns, do what we're doing. But I want to assure you that it's nothing personal, Mari, strictly a business decision. We just can't afford you any longer."

Mari really didn't know what to say. What *could* she say? There was no breach of contract to protest, no complaint to try to defend herself against, no nothing. It was a business decision, nothing to do with her professional performance, which was entirely within the new owner's right to make. She tried to keep her face as neutral as possible, bland, noncommittal, because she was determined not to give Jack the satisfaction of knowing he'd taken her by surprise or knocked her off her feet. Not that he had. It was just so damned sudden.

"You've done a good job here, Mari. Shouldn't have any trouble finding another spot," Jack continued, uncomfortable when she didn't respond. "We know you'll do well, wish you well, wherever you go."

Platitudes, nothing but empty platitudes, she thought. Jack may not have been the one to initiate this, but down underneath he must be feeling a certain satisfaction after all the times she'd argued with him over what she thought were ill-considered judgment calls or policy decisions, not to mention that she'd rejected him personally, as a man. In the end he'd left her nothing she could say, since KPOC was complying with the terms of her contract. So she nodded her head and rose from the chair, ready to go back to her office, where she could mull everything over in private. "When?" That was all he'd left her, the only thing she didn't know.

"Officially, yesterday," he answered, also rising from his chair, grabbing at the chance she was offering to have it over with quickly. "So we'd like you to clear out your desk right away, be out of here by the end of business today. Any questions about payment on your contract, have your lawyer take 'em up with Jake Tolbert, our business manager."

She'd just been given the coup de grace, a quick and painless death, was all Mari could think about as she walked out of Jack's office and back down the hall to her own, closed the door behind her, walked straight to her desk, as usual, dropped into her chair and swiveled it around to look out the window, as much out of habit as need.

An hour and a half later she dropped her keys on Sandy's desk and walked out of KPOC-TV for the last time.

She'd already loaded all the personal things from her office in the trunk of her car, which mostly amounted to a box of medical references, her DAT recorder, makeup mirror, and a couple of pictures, because she wasn't one to "decorate" her office with personal mementos. What she valued most of what she was carrying away with her were the floppy disks and computer printouts containing all the notes in her futures file, and an up-to-date listing of names, addresses, and phone numbers—information sources she'd been accumulating over a period of years. She was leaving behind a computer whose memory was squeaky clean—pure as the driven snow, unsullied, immaculate, virginal—a thought that brought a grin of pure self-satisfaction to her face as she got into her car and drove west, toward Loehmann's.

"Charles? It's me."

"Mari! Where the hell have you been? Are you okay?"

"Of course! Why shouldn't I be?"

"Tony called, told me what happened, that's why! Said he couldn't locate you anywhere, went by your place several times but you never showed up there. He and Rachel have been calling around, but no one's seen or heard from you since you left the station. You had us all out of our minds—and wondering whether we ought to call the police and the hospitals."

"Oh Charles, I'm sorry, I didn't have any idea—" She looked down at her watch. It was only ten o'clock. "I'll call them, right away, soon as I hang up, okay?"

"Where were you?"

"I—" She really didn't want to tell him. "I went shopping. Remember, this morning, I mentioned, well, that it's too hot for most of my clothes, that I needed some cooler things?"

"Yeah, but Jesus, that's the last thing I'd expect you to do after—"

"Well, if there's one thing I've learned in this business, it's to stay cool, take the time to think things through, not to panic, in spite of the constant pressure to squeeze down the length of a bite or to meet a deadline. Time. There's never enough time. And this afternoon, when I walked out of the station, it was like being let out of school early. I felt free."

"Okay, I get the picture." She could hear the smile in his voice now.

"So I went out to Loehmann's, spent a couple of hours trying on blouses, skirts, dresses, pants, everything. One of the best places in the world to put things in perspective, it's like a meat market in that big common dressing room, with mirrors lining the walls, seeing yourself from all angles. All the other women, too. I'm always surprised by how friendly they are, makes me feel good to have perfect strangers help me find an earring that popped off when I pulled a dress off over my head, or to have someone ask my opinion about how a skirt looks on them." She paused, but Charles didn't say a thing. Maybe he thought she was being frivolous or hysterical, or something, but didn't want to say so. "After that I stopped for a hamburger, because I didn't feel like cooking, and then, as I was coming back this way, I happened to notice that *Manon of the Spring* was on at the Greenway Three. And I thought to myself, 'Why not?'"

"A movie! You went to a movie?" he blurted, disbelief replacing the earlier smile in his voice.

"Yes. The sequel to *Jean de Florette*. I missed it the last time around. Have you seen it?"

"I can't believe this! Two minutes ago I was on the verge of listing you as a missing person, and here we are chatting about some damn French film. Is that why you called, to tell me about the movie you just saw?"

"No. I called because I wanted to hear your voice." She paused, suddenly feeling tired. "And to tell you about what happened, that the new owners are buying up my contract, so I'm out of a job. Nothing personal, Jack said, just can't afford me anymore."

"Yeah, I know. He told Tony the same thing."

"Tony? They let him go, too? But why? He's the best cameraman they've got. And they can't lay off everybody." She knew Tony didn't have the contract protections she did, which meant he was out of a job *and* a paycheck, as of yesterday!

"They're not. According to Tony, only you and him." That hit Mari like a physical blow, leaving her speechless. "Tell me something, Mari. How much longer did you have to go on your contract?"

"About a year, maybe a little less," she mumbled distractedly.

"Then you tell me—how is it more economical to buy up your contract instead of just letting it run out, get their money's worth out of you? If that's the real reason for letting you go? I can see cutting back on your expenses, travel, stuff like that, but . . ." He paused to give her time to think about that. "I suppose there could be other reasons for letting Tony off, too. Maybe they think he'd be too loyal to you, give 'em trouble, who knows what. But it sure as hell smells fishy from where I sit. Can you think of any reason why they might just want to be rid of you? Both of you? Besides Tracy and Lou Slocum, I mean?"

"I don't know. I guess the possibility just never even occurred to me, but—listen, I've got to talk to Tony. Maybe I'd better do that right now, especially if he's as worried as you say. Let me think it through, sleep on it, okay? I'll call you tomorrow." She started to hang up, then swooped the receiver back up to her mouth. "Charles?"

"Yeah, I'm still here."

"Uh, I just wanted to say thanks."

"What for? Worrying about you? I'd just as soon we didn't do that again any time soon."

"I meant for being you, someone special I can talk to, who cares."

Mari was the first one through the door when the downtown branch of the Houston Public Library opened the next morning. Parking was a bitch in this part of town, so Tony just dropped her off and began circling the block, or blocks, since most of the streets were one way. She headed straight for the reference shelves and within minutes had just what she was looking for—Standard & Poor's *International Directory*, Dun and Bradstreet's *Principal International Businesses*, and another one she happened to see on the shelf, *International Corporate Affiliations*—and took them to an empty table. She began flipping the pages, searching for what she wanted in the index, while rummaging in her purse for her notebook and a ballpoint. There it was—"Bertrand/Petrocorp, pages 221–24." She lifted big sections of pages, turning back toward the front of the volume, watching the top of the pages until she found 221, then scanned the page quickly, knowing exactly what she was looking for. Her eyes moved down the next page, quick-reading the subheads, and then the next, until—"Bingo!"

The whispered exclamation came out like the break shot in a game of pool, sudden, fast, and hard, but rather than scattering her thoughts in all directions, the name on the printed page brought all the mental churning and pieces of fragmented evidence together. She started scribbling in her notebook, hurrying like crazy now, hardly able to sit still, she was so anxious to get back outside to tell Tony. Bertrand/Petrocorp was a holding company.

And one of the companies it was holding was *Pharmacol!*

"Charles? It's me again. Don't talk, just listen." She began spilling it all out, about the Pharmacol-Bertrand/Petrocorp relationship, everything she'd been able to learn about Pamezine so far, and what she now believed to be the real reason behind KPOC's decision to buy out her contract.

"I have to admit it does seem to fit, though it sounds wild—no, stupid—to me, that a company would actually think they could get away with something like that. That they wouldn't get caught!"

"Maybe to you and me," she replied, "but if the stakes are high enough . . ." She left the statement hanging. "It wouldn't be the first time. Look at what Pfizer was willing to risk. There they are, the fourth-largest pharmaceutical in the country, with eight billion dollars in sales, and Feldene is their most lucrative product. People were dying all over Europe by 1979, which Pfizer knew but didn't tell the FDA, until six months after it was approved. Even then, the fact that Feldene could cause massive bleeding in the bowels, and heart failure, didn't get mentioned in the package for two years, and it still hasn't cost them anything in the way of punitive action by the FDA, even though they broke the law. They've been hit with some personal-damage suits, but nothing like the numbers Robins is getting because of its Dalkon Shield. Big companies, like people in high places, often are too arrogant to believe they'll get caught. Or if they do, that they can't control the damage. That's exactly what I think may have happened with Pamezine. When I started nosing around, looking like I might make trouble, posed a threat, they reached out their all-powerful arm and simply knocked me out, shut me up. Or thought they did!"

"So what are you going to do?"

"Get the rest of the story, and then try to make sure it gets to the public, one way or another. And I've already got a couple of ideas about how I might be able to do that. Tony and I are leaving for Washington in the morning, this time with a minicam. But I just talked to Rachel, and, well, I need to ask you some questions."

"Shoot."

"Wait a minute. The three of us are all here, at her place, brainstorming this thing. Let me get her to pick up the other phone, so she can hear what you say straight from the horse's mouth." He could hear muffled voices, and then Rachel picked up a second phone.

"Okay, I'm on," she confirmed.

"Supposing we could get blood samples from women who are on Pamezine, Charles," Mari began, "what do you think it would take to get at the adverse effects of this drug, when—if my whistle blower is right—it's confounded by another drug plus smoking? Rachel says she can run all the standard blood-chemistry stuff, plus sedimentation rate and clotting factors, things like that, but she wondered if maybe looking at the viscoelasticity would tell us—"

"Wait a minute, let's start at the beginning," he suggested, understanding where she was headed and grasping the problem immediately. "Get blood from women who are on Pamezine alone first, if that's possible. See what that tells us. And that means donors who are healthy otherwise, at least as far as we know, not patients in the hospital—if that's where you had in mind getting the samples, Rachel. We've got to assume they're in for some disease condition that could be the real reason behind any abnormalities we'd see."

"How many samples would you need?" Mari asked.

"Oh, maybe a half dozen to start with. Then, if we got any kind of consistent evidence from those, we'd know we're on the right track, could decide how to proceed next. But listen, Mari, don't get your hopes up too high, that we'll be able to pin this down conclusively. Your whistle blower could have had all the best intentions in the world and still be wrong, because sometimes even the guys working with the drug don't really understand what's going on. And he sort of admitted as much, as I recall. Best we can do is take one step at a time, see what we find. How long do you plan to be gone?"

"As long as it takes. But I just had an idea. Rachel, you know Barbara Amaral, don't you?"

"The gynecologist? Yeah."

"I called her when I was trying to find physicians here who prescribe Pamezine. She doesn't, but one of her partners does. A family-practice guy named Obregon. I bet you anything that with a little help from her we might be able to persuade him to cooperate, get him to have his nurse draw enough blood from a few of his patients for our tests, especially if we promised him anonymity, and maybe an early warning if we find anything, so he could warn his patients off before anything hits the fan. Maybe you could call in the morning, talk to her, explain what we're doing, and why—before you talk to him."

"And I could be there as soon as you can get them, Rachel, or before," Charles injected. "Let's close all the potential loopholes, set up to do all the tests at the same time in the same place, so there won't be any doubts that whatever we find has nothing to do with aging or temperature variations. I'll bring my latest update of the Vampire, with the faster software, and plug it into your computer."

"Wait a minute, Charles," Mari interrupted. "Rachel, I can't ask you to do anything that might jeopardize your job. So maybe we need to try to get a commercial lab to run—"

"Jeopardize my job! By trying to determine whether some damn drug is killing people? What the hell am I here for, if not that? I say if anybody really thinks anything like that, let 'em speak up loud and clear, so we can all identify who the bastards are!" Her voice crescendoed enough for Tony to hear her all the way out in the kitchen, where Mari was using Rachel's other phone. He just grinned happily and shrugged his shoulders when Mari glanced around and raised a quizzical brow at him.

"What about you, Charles? It could get messy. Couldn't Rachel do the—no, I take that back. I want you to, need you to do this. That's enough, isn't it?"

"There may be hope for you yet," he chided, but with a smile in his voice. "At least you're learning. Call me tomorrow, Rachel, here or at the university, day or night, soon as you know anything. You too, Mari. You got me into this, now don't leave me hanging out in the cold. I'm already beginning to feel like a damned detective. I can see how you might get hooked on this sort of stuff."

When Mari put down the phone, she turned to Tony with a crooked smile and gave him a barely discernible nod.

"Venceremos, mi compañera," he assured her quietly. "We will overcome." Then his lips split in a mischievous smile. "Maybe."

Wednesday morning Mari and Tony left for Washington. They were no more than off the ground when Rachel got on the phone to Barbara Amaral. Wednesday afternoon she called Charles, and when the first blood samples began arriving Thursday, shortly after lunch, he was at the clinical lab with his equipment set up and ready to go. Dr. Obregon had requested an extra draw from all of his patients who were on only one drug—Pamezine. So they had plenty of blood to work with in spite of the fact that they intended to run several tests on each sample. Small sample size was one of the beauties of the Vampire, and Charles had even managed to carry out reliable measurements with only a drop of blood. Most of the time, though, he worked with a half milliliter, just to be on the safe side, which was what he planned to do today—play it safe, leave no room for question. Each sample was numbered, and what was left over put in the refrigerator, in case a rerun was needed.

Rachel ran the hematocrit, cell and platelet count, prothrombin time, partial thromboplastin time, sedimentation rate, and all the chemical factors, while Charles drew a complete viscoelasticity profile on each sample, which meant "looking" at the flow characteristics under different levels of pressure. Elevated viscoelasticity would indicate either an enhanced tendency for the red cells to aggregate or loss of deformability.

They took a thirty-minute break for a quick bite, then went back to work on the new bunch of blood samples that had arrived only a few minutes before five. By eleven-thirty, when they finally closed down for the night, all the tests were complete. Most of the clotting times had come up normal, which meant that the "thickening" Mari's informant had claimed was causing "sluggish blood flow" wasn't due to any triggering of the clotting factors. On the other hand, both the deformability and aggregation-tendency curves showed strong abnormalities. The values were so far off normal, in fact, that Charles couldn't help wondering if his equipment was malfunctioning in some way. Standing in the dimly lit hospital parking garage, he and Rachel reviewed everything they'd done to prepare the samples, rechecking each other and themselves.

"We'll just have to double-check everything in the morning. I'm going to recalibrate the instrument, check out a couple of other things, maybe also try running a few samples at different hematocrits and see what that does to the values. We're getting more samples tomorrow, aren't we?" Rachel nodded, then climbed into her car. "Well, I'm off to dig for the house key," he said, sighing, watching her fasten her seat belt and lock the car door. Mari had sent word to him through Rachel that the key to her apartment was "in the pot of cilantro."

"I'm betting they'll be back tomorrow night," Rachel said through her open window. "Because whether they got what they went after or not, I can't see Mari sitting in Washington over the weekend with nothing to do." He grinned and nodded, then started to walk away. "Charles?" she called, stopping him. "It's at least possible, isn't it—for the values to be that high? That what we're seeing isn't necessarily due to some experimental artifact?"

"Yeah, it's possible." He nodded, but refused to draw any conclusions at this point. "Call me if you hear anything. I'll do the same. See you bright and early, right?" He stood there for a second, watching her drive away, recognizing in her his own inability to turn loose of a problem until it was solved, and knew he wouldn't be the only one who would keep mulling it over tonight, even in his sleep.

More blood samples were delivered late Friday morning, and again around four that afternoon. There was an undercurrent of excitement in the lab, as if everyone could sense something unusual was in the works. The other lab technicians strolled over to watch from time to time, or to ask a question. But all they got from either Rachel or Charles was that they were testing for sedimentation rate, clotting factor, and viscoelasticity correlations. One of Rachel's assistants brought sandwiches in for lunch, which they stopped to eat only because it was unthinkable to handle food with the rubber gloves they wore while working with the blood. Even then they used the time to report what each had found since the last time they talked, and to plan their next moves. It wasn't until ten minutes after eight Friday night that they finished with the last blood sample.

"That's it, Rachel! Let's close up shop, forget about it for a while," Charles decided, finally satisfied that they'd done everything they could. He began stacking all the curves and scattered data printouts together. "Why don't you go call home, see if they're back or left us any messages, while I clean up this mess." When he looked up again, she was standing beside him.

"Still no word?"

"You might say that," Rachel answered with a wry smile. "Just 'See you soon, gringa bebé.' But he did sound sort of bouncy, up, almost smug. So they must be getting something."

"Okay. Then why don't we go find us some dinner? Someplace decent, no more sandwiches or deli stuff. I'm buying, you pick the place."

"Anyplace?" She waited for his confirming nod. "Even Nick's Fishmarket?"

"Sounds good to me." In spite of the name, Nick's was one of the better restaurants in Houston, combining exceptional seafood with a lush but quietly understated decor. The high-backed, overstuffed leather booths, each one equipped with adjustable lighting and its own telephone jack, provided both sound isolation and visual privacy, even from the piano music emanating from the darkened cocktail bar, which was separated from the dining room by a glass wall. In short, the food was good and it was also a good place to talk.

Rachel ordered pompano and Charles a swordfish steak, but they both started with a shrimp cocktail. And a bottle of French Chardonnay. And then they began to let down, talking all around the subject they both were so keenly aware of after two days of thinking and talking about nothing else. Rachel told him about her work and why she was thinking about going back to graduate school for another degree. Charles told her about the company he was starting, to do both research and development of scientific instruments, to be supported at least initially by income from the Vampire. He even mentioned he was thinking about leaving the university, which came as no great surprise to her. They dawdled over coffee, neither one in any hurry to get home to an empty bed.

"I have to confess I wish they'd get back. I'm more than a little worried, aren't you?" It was the first time she'd even mentioned something that had been bothering her for the past few days.

"About what? That we don't have enough cases?"

"No, not that. It's just, well, I don't see how there can be any doubt anymore that Pharmacol has known all along—even if they didn't know exactly why, they had to know that *something* was wrong with this drug, even if we can't prove for sure just when they knew. Otherwise why buy the television stations to shut her up? And if they were willing to spend millions of dollars to do that, why stop there? Why not finish the job, make sure she . . .?"

Charles was in the process of signaling the waiter for the check, and it took him a few seconds to catch on to what she was suggesting. And then it felt like his heart simply stopped for an instant. He looked at Rachel, understanding for the first time what Tony had really meant by his parting cryptic remark—"Not to worry, I will be riding shotgun."

The smell of bacon woke Charles the next morning. He climbed out of bed and headed straight for the kitchen, to see if his imagination was still playing tricks on him. Mari turned to greet him with an impish "Hi!" and a matching grin, then came and slipped her arms around his neck. When she would've moved away, though, he held on tight, needing to actually feel her presence as well as to know it with his eyes and ears.

"So that was really you in my bed last night after all," he said, smiling the quiet words into her ear. "Why didn't you wake me?"

"It was late, and you didn't even budge when I crawled into bed, so I figured you must've been pretty beat. Anyway,

I wasn't much up to any wild and wicked amorous antics myself." She kissed his neck and then pushed herself away. "Breakfast is almost ready. Why don't you go shower, get dressed, while I call Tony, see how soon they can haul it over here. I want all our heads together when we start laying out all the pieces, because we can't afford to have anything fall through the cracks at this point. Talk about sitting on pins and needles! I'm so anxious to hear what you and Rachel found out that I probably won't be able to eat a thing, or if I do, keep it down."

"Okay, but tell 'em to bring their swimsuits along," he tossed back over his shoulder as he left the kitchen. "After two whole damn days and nights slaving over a hot Vampire, I've gotta get some exercise somehow—and it sure as hell doesn't look like I'm about to get any in bed!"

She chased after him, caught him before he'd gone even a few feet and grabbed him in a bear hug that ended in a long, passionate kiss. "That's just to hold you for a little while," she murmured against his lips, then broke away and hurried back to the kitchen.

They'd just finished breakfast when Tony and Rachel arrived. Mari put on a fresh pot of coffee, and then the four of them settled down around the cleared dining table.

"Briefly," Mari began, "what we know for sure is that the FDA was under a lot of political pressure to approve this drug, both in Congress and from a big-shot Washington lobbyist hired by Pharmacol, who also was threatening to appeal the case to the Commissioner of Food and Drugs. The agency had already turned them down once, and when they applied again, the company simply reanalyzed the old data, from studies that were flawed in the first place because the test subjects also took aspirin, which the FDA admits may have ameliorated the adverse effects of Pamezine. So it looks like Pharmacol fudged their test results to befuddle the FDA, which already was under the gun to speed up the approval process in order to get new drugs to the public faster."

She hunted through a stack of papers until she found the one she wanted and then handed it across the table to Charles. "This is a copy of an internal memo, from one of the agency's group leaders."

Charles held the memo so Rachel could read it at the same time:

"The company's computer file didn't allow retrieval of the data broken down the way we need it. No data was available on the usual case-report forms. Therefore, the safety data base is softer than we are accustomed to."

Charles glanced quickly at Rachel, before looking across the table at Mari, amazement written all over his face. But then his lips broke into an admiring grin as he shook his head in wonderment that she'd actually managed to obtain such damning evidence.

"Don't look at me," Mari told him. "We'd never have known it even existed, except for Rachel's Latin lover, here, who just happened to be 'passing the time of day' with one of the consumer-safety officers—female, of course—while I was off chasing down a couple of documents."

Tony beamed a toothy grin at Rachel and murmured, "If you've got it, you have to use it, else it may just—"

Rachel reached over and ruffled his hair playfully, then leaned the other way, toward Mari. "I should have listened," she whispered, pretending to speak in confidence, "when you warned me not to trust a man with short legs, 'cause his brain is too near his bottom." She slipped out of her chair and went into the kitchen to refill her cup, with Tony in hot pursuit.

"We've got more," Mari continued, ignoring them both, "but that's the gist of it. Now, did you two find anything at all that we can use?"

"Amaral and Obregon came through for us with blood from thirty-six donors on Pamezine, and twenty-four normals to use as a control group," Charles replied, just as Rachel and Tony returned with their arms around each other. He described every test he and Rachel had carried out, how they'd changed one variable at a time, all the cross-checking they'd done to eliminate or account for every possible variable except the effect of the drug itself. Then he deferred to Rachel, letting her describe the results of the clotting tests. When she finished, Charles did a quick summary.

"The viscoelasticity values for all the Pamezine donors are up, some so high they've got to be living dangerously.

The flow profiles indicate that both the aggregation tendency and loss of deformability are way up, a one-two punch. I'd guess from these figures that there's got to be more involved than imparied perfusion in the limbs. Some of the vital organs probably are being starved of blood, too."

"Just on Pamezine alone—you're sure?" Mari queried, surprised.

He nodded. "God only knows what happens when you add heavy smoking besides. The only thing we forgot to ask for was where the donors were in their menstrual cycles, but even that wouldn't account for the values we got."

"I don't understand. What difference could that make?"

"Well, we know that both the viscoelasticity and the volume of blood flow in the limbs varies during the monthly cycle, with the lowest levels of flow in the limbs generally occurring just before and during menstrual flow. So that kind of information might help account for some of the minor variations in the values we found. It's not likely to really change anything significantly, only show that we took everything into consideration."

Charles had a reputation for thoroughness in his work, so it was reassuring to know that she wasn't reading more into his data than was actually there, out of her desire to nail Pharmacol to the wall.

"I'm sure we could get Dr. Obregon's nurse to call the patients and get that information for us," Rachel pointed out. "But I don't think we really need it, since the higher sedimentation rates support Charles's enhanced red-cell aggregation data. I realize that sedimentation rate is nonspecific, doesn't necessarily indicate any particular disease condition, only an abnormality, like pregnancy. Don't forget, sedimentation rate was one of the first pregnancy tests."

"Wait a minute," Mari objected, confused now. "You're saying that blood flow is more 'sluggish'—let's just call it that for want of a better description at the moment—in pregnant women, and also just before and during menstruation? Then what would you expect to happen when you add the pill to Pamezine?"

"As I recall, though I'd have to recheck the literature to be absolutely sure, there's a fall in limb blood-flow volume mid-cycle in women on oral contraceptives. Aside from that one brief period during the month, flow volume in women on O.C.s is about the same as in men, which means the pill should help bring the V.E. levels down some, but—"

"You mean the pill does *not* make the problem worse? May even make it better? But my caller, the guy at Pharmacol or whoever he is, said that in their tests the most adverse effects showed up in the group of women who were both heavy smokers and on the pill as well as Pamezine."

"Could be just a statistical fluke, I suppose. That's the problem with correlations, where you're dealing with chance associations, probabilities. Doesn't tell you a damn thing about cause. You know that, Mari. But find a correlation, and everyone starts deducing all sorts of stuff from it, a lot of it unfounded. Your caller also said Pamezine tends to block the action of anticoagulants, which means they believe they've got a clotting problem. But they don't, and an anticoagulant—to prevent clotting—isn't going to do much good when you don't have any clotting going on in the first place!"

"That's just great! Wonderful!" Mari beamed at him, then Rachel and finally Tony. She jumped up from her chair suddenly and started twirling in circles in the middle of the living room floor, unable to contain herself any longer. "Don't you know what you've just done?" she asked, noticing the puzzled expressions she'd left behind at the table. "You not only managed to come up with what looks like enough evidence to hang Pharmacol from the highest limb, but in the process exonerated the pill."

She danced her way into the kitchen, took a package of croissants out of the freezer and yelled "Reward time!" as she put them in the microwave. "But first we take time out for a swim, get the blood circulating to our brains. Can't afford any sluggish flow now, right?"

In the end, the croissants served as dessert, along with a jar of Janet's homemade peach jam, to a hastily prepared mid-afternoon lunch of salad and soup. And then they started all over again, from the beginning, going over and over every piece of data, every document and every statement Mari and Tony had collected on tape in Washington, and pored over Charles's flow curves, examining each little bump and squiggle—questioning, looking for any flaw or weakness in the case they were building.

When Tony and Rachel left Saturday evening, it was only to repair the physical and mental exhaustion, because Mari wanted to start all over again the next morning, just to be sure.

By Sunday night she intended to have her strategy all sketched out in detail, starting with the "deal" she would offer to Sam Downey, the network's evening news anchor in New York, when she called him Monday morning.

CHAPTER
20
~~~

It was exactly nine-fifteen Monday morning, Houston time, when Mari picked up the phone in her apartment and put in a call to Sam Downey in New York. He was "in conference," which she knew could cover a multitude of sins, even a trip to the men's room. But she did get through to his chief editor, Frank Lawson, who remembered her instantly without any reminder that they'd talked before at the time of the Paris hotel bombing. He took the opportunity to congratulate her on the DuPont-Columbia award, which didn't do anything to hurt her credibility—and right now she needed as much of that as she could get.

She mentioned right up front that she was no longer with KPOC, then told Frank that she had a major story, one that ought to be of special interest to UBC since the network was part of it, which—just as she'd expected—really got his attention.

"How about you give me the gist of the story, I'll talk to Sam soon as he's free, then get back to you?"

"Sure," she agreed readily, "so long as it's no later than noon, New York time. This isn't one I can sit on, Frank. Too many people could be hurt. Besides that, well, maybe I'm getting a little paranoid, but I'm not sure how many more big guns might be pulled into the fray once I tell you what

I've got." She knew he'd understand exactly what she meant—that she didn't trust the network not to try to bury the story. "So I'm going to have to go elsewhere with it if I don't hear from you pronto, okay?"

"Okay. What've you got?"

She quickly sketched the bare bones of the story, then wrapped it up with a punch line that drew the conclusions she really wanted him to come to.

"B.P. and Pharmacol have knowingly been distributing a highly profitable drug with potentially deadly side effects, the FDA caved in under pressure and approved it, and UBC apparently was an unwitting dupe in Pharmacol's attempt to keep the public, the government, everybody, from finding out. Buying the second station was nothing but a smoke screen to cover the real purpose—to muzzle me, stop my investigation!"

"You can substantiate all that?"

"Enough. My 'authority' on the side effect has a tag line a mile long, and you're not going to find anyone who knows more about blood than him, anywhere in the world." She knew she had Frank interested, but she wanted to set the hook. "I wanted you to be the first to know, give you first chance to air the story, to show that UBC wasn't a knowing accomplice in the attempt to commit criminal fraud."

There was a moment of silence on the line, then, "Okay, gimme the number there where I can reach you, let me see if I can find Sam. And for God's sake, Mari, don't even look at anyone else until you hear from us!"

She waited until she heard the click, then put the receiver down and, for the first time, looked around at Charles, who'd been standing in the doorway to her study the entire time, listening to her end of the conversation.

"Anywhere in the world?" he commented with a crooked grin. "How can you be so sure?"

"I just am." She raised an eyebrow. "Now comes the really hard part, the waiting."

They talked odds and ends for a few minutes, speculative, desultory sort of comments that neither one of them paid much attention to, knowing it was just a way to pass the time. "Should I make another pot of coffee?" Charles wondered finally.

"Sure, but use the decaf this time, will you? I've already got the shakes." Mari got up and walked to the living room with him, then began pacing the floor, just to get rid of the tension in her muscles.

"Sure wish I could take a swim. Which reminds me, are you sure you don't need to get back——"

"Forget it," he interrupted, watching her through the kitchen pass-through. "I'm not letting you out of my sight again until all this shit is out in the open. Thought you understood that."

"But it already is, now."

"Yeah, but they don't know that yet."

"They?" She tried to laugh but couldn't quite pull it off. "What do you think you or anyone else can do, C.B., if they really want to hurt me? Inspect my car, make sure there's no bomb under the hood?"

"Maybe. Hadn't thought of that, but it sounds like a good idea." She couldn't tell if he was serious or not.

A sudden shrill noise ripped the silence, startling them both even though they were waiting for it.

Mari dashed for the phone on her desk.

"Hi, Mari. Sam Downey here." She mouthed "Sam" to Charles, who'd taken up position in the doorway again. "I want to hear it from the top, everything you've got."

This time she used the notes she'd organized over the weekend, to explain the what, how, and why of every test Rachel and Charles had performed, and then the results and what they meant. "We've got the goods on them, Sam, because I also have copies of everything Pharmacol filed with the FDA, plus an internal memo from one of the agency's group leaders." She read the memo verbatim.

"Then why the hell did the FDA approve it?" Sam shot back.

"Thought you might ask that, so I put a few bites on audiotape for you. Wait a sec while I plug you in." Charles was there, ready and waiting to make the connection for her, then stood listening and grinning at her while the tape played. Mari's voice came first, identifying the source of the first statement, the director of the FDA's Bureau of Drugs. "Pamezine was just one of several drugs being used in the political arena as examples of agency inefficiency."

387

There was a short silence, and then Mari's voice came again. "The next one is Nathan Richardson, with the National Council of Senior Citizens."

"From a consumer point of view, this is the worst FDA in the last twenty-five years. Career employees have been replaced by political people, and there's been an ideological change at the FDA, especially since 1980. They've created an anticonsumer environment, made it into a different kind of organization, one that wants to please business."

After another brief silence, Mari's voice on the tape said, "This is the last one, the director of the Public Citizens Health Research Group."

"The FDA has been outgunned by multinational companies that have more resources—money, power, and influence—than the regulating agency itself."

"There's more," Mari said, speaking directly into the phone now.

"You got those guys on videotape?" Sam asked.

"Yes. In Washington. Three days ago Friday."

"What makes you so sure the tests your experts did on the blood samples will hold up to scrutiny by medical authorities and pharmaceutical research people? Because I've got to warn you, Mari, that's exactly what we'll do if we decide to go with this—line up the experts, see if we can pull the rug out."

"I know. S'fine with me. Rachel Widener has a master's degree in biochemistry, is head clinical lab technician at Hermann Hospital, with ten years of experience. I'd trust her to do those standard blood tests in her sleep. Charles Merrill is a professor at the University of Texas, in Austin, and . . . well, go ahead and drag in your experts, by the dozen if you want. But let me give you a friendly warning too—if you happen to find someone who doesn't know about Charles Merrill's research, throw him back in, 'cause he's too small to keep."

"Okay. Let me talk to my producer, a couple of other people, see what they have to say. You want to give us a little more time?"

Mari glanced at her watch. It was 10:45, New York time. She hesitated, debating with herself. "No, I don't think so. Sorry."

"You say it's mostly women who are affected by this drug?"

She'd expected him to either argue for more time or else simply end the conversation, so his question surprised her a little. "Yes. We're not entirely sure why, except for the fact that it's mostly women who get the prescriptions for tranquilizers. Dr. Merrill thinks it could have something to do with amplifying a condition that's already present at certain times during the menstrual cycle. Why?"

"My wife takes some damn tranquilizer. Don't remember what it is. I think I'll give her a call, just tell her to lay off of whatever it is, without mentioning any names."

"Sure. And one other thing, Sam. I probably should have mentioned it up front, but I wanted you to know what I have first. Bring in all the experts, get statements from other sources, whatever you need, but if you decide to go with the story—and want the evidence I've got to back it up—you'll have to take it without any substantive changes. I mean, without censoring an inconvenient piece of information here or there."

He hesitated for no more than a fraction of a second. "Okay. Stick around. I'll get back to you soon as I can."

After she hung up, Mari repeated Sam's questions for Charles, speculating on what his various comments might mean, and then called Tony, to let him relay everything to Rachel. It wasn't likely that Sam would call back right away, but she wanted to keep the phone free, just in case.

She'd left the network little room for an end run around her, and they must know it. There wasn't time to go back and develop the story themselves, even given the fact that they now knew what to look for—at least not before she gave it to someone else. News-value considerations aside, they had to realize they would have a better chance of controlling what was said and how it was said, about their own role in the affair, than if the story went to a competing network. Still, she couldn't help worrying, wondering if she might've overlooked something.

Charles tried to help pass the time while they waited by telling her about the research and development company he was starting, but by quarter to twelve, New York time, Mari was ready to decide that all their carefully planned strategy had gone awry. The UBC news team was going to "pass" by letting the deadline slide by, which she found irritating and disappointing, not to mention a spineless way to say no. By five to twelve she was sure of it.

And then the phone rang.

"Okay, we're on," Sam said without preamble. "We've got a couple of people in Washington ready to run with the ball, see what they can pick up. You get to the station, transmit everything you've got—documents, taped interviews, with voice-overs, whatever else there is. Then get on the phone to Frank. But one other thing, Mari. We've got to insist that—"

"Wait a minute," she protested, trying to stop the headlong rush of instructions. "What station? KPOC?"

Her question was met with complete silence while he thought that over. "Yeah, you're right. I wasn't thinking. Maybe we could—hold on a minute." She heard muffled voices in the background. "Okay, we're on the line to KUHT right now, your public television station there. They've got a satellite hookup, everything we need. I'll let you know before we sign off. If not them, we'll have to move you to another city. But listen, like I was saying, we're all agreed here that we need to have your two experts available for questioning on camera, by anybody we designate. Otherwise, well, I gotta be frank, Mari, it's probably not going to fly, at least not as a major story."

"I'll have to talk to them."

"That mean you think they won't do it?"

"No, I didn't say that. I just can't commit without asking them first. Give me fifteen minutes, okay?"

Mari hung up and then told Charles everything. "Great! Sounds like they're going to do it just the way you want. I'm game, but I guess you'd better call Rachel, ask her, just to make sure, huh?"

"Listen, Charles, I want you to think carefully about this. It's possible to make anyone look bad, you know, by not giving you enough time to state your case. And you probably won't know beforehand what they're going to ask or who they'll get to question you. They're up there searching for people who might be able to throw doubt on your procedures or conclusions, and if they let some real jerk babble on endlessly, then cut you short, you could be the one to come off the loser, no matter how strong you think your case is."

"I'm willing to take my chances." He was adamant. "Now hurry up and get on the phone to Rachel."

She gave Rachel the same warning, and got pretty much the same answer. But when she questioned Rachel about possible repercussions in her job, she got a reply she wasn't expecting. "I don't know how much longer I'll be here anyway. Depends partly on what Tony decides to do. But I've got another job offer, something I've wanted to do for a long time. So if the people here turn up the flak over this, it'll just make it that much easier for me to leave."

Mari called New York, gulped down a carton of yogurt, and then gathered up all her notes and documents and cassettes. Charles said he needed to "consult" with Rachel at the hospital, where she could reach him if needed, but he assured her, more than once, that they'd both be at the studio in plenty of time. Tony was already on his way.

The traffic was relatively thin as she cut through Hermann Park to MacGregor Way, which wound along the edge of Brays Bayou, then turned left onto Cullen. From there it was only a few blocks to the University of Houston campus and the KUHT studios.

The afternoon passed in a blur of activity, and somehow between phone conferences with editors and reporters in New York and Washington, she managed to script and coordinate her own segment. As the time grew shorter and shorter, Mari could sense the excitement building in New York as well as in the studio around her, and by the time Rachel and Charles arrived, she was so tense she could hardly sit still.

Charles took one look at her flushed face and started to grin. "What do you do with her when she gets like this?" he asked Tony, trying to joke to relieve the tension.

"Considering how much the two of you have riding on the next few minutes, Charlie boy, I can't say as how I blame her. It's a wonder she isn't dancing a damned jig."

Charles went to Mari and gave her a big hug, then took her face between his hands and held her still, watching her eyes as he spoke. "Anything new happen I ought to know about, that's got you worried?" She shook her head. "The guys in New York haven't found any holes that you know of?" She shook her head again, keeping her eyes glued to his. "Think you did the best you could?" That cued a flash of memory, and she could hear Janet's voice, but she only nodded. Charles watched her eyes a little longer, then leaned forward to brush his lips across hers—once, twice, three times, whispering a couple of words between each caress.

"Don't forget . . . I love you . . . Mari berry."

The Pamezine story was second from the top that night, but even Mari was surprised when she heard Sam Downey's lead-in.

"The Food and Drug Administration announced today that it has issued an order to halt the sale of Pamezine, a prescription tranquilizer manufactured by Pharmacol, pending further investigation of allegations that the drug causes severe adverse side effects. Here now with the story in Washington is Klaus Miller."

Mari watched the story unfold on the studio monitor, muttering comments to Tony about how the network was integrating their taped interviews into the updated report, using them to flesh out the information on the FDA's decision to approve the drug, and then reading the agency's internal memo.

When Sam bridged to her in Houston, she began with a quick summary of what the blood tests performed by Rachel and Charles had shown, then directed a question to Rachel about the sedimentation and clotting tests she'd done.

Sitting only a few feet away from her, Charles couldn't help admiring the calm exterior Mari managed to present in spite of how nervous he knew she'd been just a few minutes earlier. And that was when it first registered with him that she was wearing a red knit top. It looked sort of tweedy, as if some contrasting color was mixed in, so it wasn't exactly fire-engine red. But it *was* red. And it looked great on her. He knew without even asking that she'd bought it that day she went shopping at Loehmann's, after learning that she no longer had a job, the day she'd suddenly felt free! Her hair was shorter, too, barely reaching the edge of her jaw now. She'd brushed it back from her face in a smooth, flowing curve, and he had to consciously stifle the urge to reach out and touch it.

Sam came back with a follow-up question to a professor of clinical medicine at Johns Hopkins, and then used an identifying tag line to bridge back to Houston and Charles.

Charles spoke a little more rapidly than usual—explaining how and what his measurements showed about the effect of Pamezine on red-cell aggregation and deformability—partly because he didn't want in any way to convey the idea that he had doubts or didn't know what he was talking about. But he also was careful not to pause, because he'd taken Mari's warning to heart, and didn't want to chance an interruption before he'd completed what he wanted to say.

As soon as he finished, Sam picked up another "expert," a Chinese-American medical doctor from Boston University, whom he identified as having just received the gold medal of the International Society of Clinical Hemorrheology, then explained that hemorrheology was the study of how blood flowed. Dr. Chou made a few general comments about the importance of the deformability of the red cells to normal blood flow, noting some of the problems researchers had run into trying to measure red-cell rigidity. "Dr. Merrill's experimental work in this area is, of course, well-known. It is quite elegant, in fact, because of the precision of his measurements. Now that his instrument is to be available to other researchers, I would anticipate that we will quickly know a great deal more about blood flow in vivo than we do at the moment. I cannot vouch for what Pharmacol's tests may have shown in this regard, and of course they would not have had access to Dr. Merrill's instrument, either, so I suppose it may be a question of what it was possible for them to know at the time they were testing this drug, given the available means to measure what we have now learned from Dr. Merrill's tests."

Mari hated the appeasing tone he took, just as she hated even the idea that Pharmacol might get away scot-free, but the ball wasn't in her court anymore. And she couldn't help feeling relieved about that. As the broadcast wound down, she began to feel lighter and lighter, as if she might just float right up off her chair if she didn't hold herself down.

And then Sam Downey cut back to Houston to pick up Charles one more time, to ask if he had any recommendations to make as a result of what had just been revealed about the Pamezine case.

"Well, I suppose there's not much anyone can do about the political pressure, or the bureaucratic foul-ups," Charles sort of drawled, with a little smile. "One thing we could do, though, is not let the company that develops the drug conduct, or even contract out, the clinical tests. Aside from that, well, I guess I'm pretty much of the opinion that physicians ought to be looking for the causes of complaints rather than being so ready to cover their own diagnostic failures by prescribing tranquilizers. And if they did that, I suspect we wouldn't see much need for anyone to be taking tranquilizers. The medical profession needs to start listening more to patients, and less to the drug companies."

The on-camera monitor picked up Sam in New York, who did the wrap and then was followed by a commercial break. Charles and Mari just sat there when the studio lights dimmed, grinning at each other.

Mari slept until noon the next day, then ate breakfast and read the articles in the *Houston Post* and *Chronicle* about KPOC and Pamezine. Charles told her everything he'd heard on the morning newscasts, while she put her dishes in the dishwasher and loaded it with soap. After that she opened the refrigerator door and stared inside for a couple of minutes, moved a few things up into the freezer, then filled a plastic container and went out to the balcony to water all her potted plants, mumbling something about not understanding how she could've slept so late. He thought she seemed oddly preoccupied, but didn't say anything until she went into the bedroom and got her suitcase from the closet, plopped it down on the bed and began filling it with clothes.

"What's wrong, honey?" He was really worried now but trying not to hit the panic button.

"Nothing. Why?"

"Then why are you packing? Where are you going?" he asked quietly, not even sure that she knew what she was doing.

Mari looked up at him, a little puzzled. "I thought we were going home, to Austin. I was sort of hoping if we hurried, we could get there in time for a swim while it's still light." Intuitive as she was, Charles was never crystal clear to her—any more, she suspected, than she was to him. In the end a kind of ambivalence always remained, an echo of the child.

Charles turned her to face him, gently, letting his hands slide up from her shoulders to cup her neck, so his thumbs could caress the line of her jaw.

"Home?" he asked, remembering how much he'd taken for granted about her in the beginning, how little he'd really listened to her, wanting not to make that mistake again, ever. Much as he prided himself on his open-mindedness, which he'd always known was his greatest asset in the laboratory, he hadn't really been open to or with her.

"Yes, home. Though it's not really the place, you know, much as I love all the trees and animals. Wherever you are, Charles, is home for me."

He looked into her eyes, understanding exactly what she meant, unable to keep the tears from welling in his own and unashamed that they did.

She knew now that he wasn't as self-sufficient, or assured, as he seemed on the surface, that he was just as vulnerable and needful of love and understanding as she was. Perhaps even more so, since he'd had so little of it as a child, while she—well, whatever else might come and go, or change, she'd always known that her mother and father loved her. With the suddenness of an unexpected flash of lightning, Mari realized that it was her mother's constant, unwavering love that had made it possible for her adventuresome spirit to roam free. And knew, too, that she could never really be in control of her own life as long as she acted out of unthinking reaction, even to a person who loved and wanted only the best for her, rather than deliberately, according to what *she* thought was right, which was one of Charles's most endearing traits—at least most of the time.

"Don't misunderstand me. I don't mean that I want you to be a substitute father, or mother. You can't shield me from everything bad or disappointing that's going to happen to me, any more than they could. I've thought a lot about what you said—you know, about how all the awards in the world don't matter if you don't have someone who really cares about you to share them with."

He wrapped his arms around her then and held her close. "I swear, Mari, I'd sell my soul to change how I behaved that night, make it different for you if I could."

"Sssshhh, that's not what I meant," she whispered, her breath stirring the hair alongside his ear, sending an involuntary shiver of sensation racing across every nerve synapse in his body. "Do you remember Alhamar?"

Charles nodded his head against hers, nibbling her ear with his lips at the same time.

"Do you think maybe I could be your friend and slightly irrational companion?"

The unexpectedness of it brought a burst of laughter from his throat, and then he was lifting her feet off the floor and twirling her around, and she was laughing, too, until they fell together across the bed, just barely missing her open suitcase. But the laughter ended when his lips hovered over hers, whispering every form of her name he could think of, even adding a few new ones no one had ever called her before, then breathed kisses into her hair, down into the hidden curve below her ear, and across the tops of her breasts.

It was nearly five o'clock by the time they arrived in Austin, which meant no more than a quick swim before the evening newscasts. Charles recorded one network on his VCR while they watched another, so they could keep up with what the others were doing with the Pamezine story, which mostly was a repeat of what UBC had aired the previous night. The only new development was that a House subcommittee was launching an investigation into drug approval procedures and standards at the FDA.

Every day for the rest of the week Charles stopped on the way home and picked up a variety of newspapers, always including the *Washington Post*, so they could monitor the story as the news wires, newspapers, and television news programs around the country began picking it up. By the end of trading Wednesday, Bertrand/Petrocorp's stock had fallen twenty points, losing nearly a third of its value. And by Friday, members of both parties in Congress were beginning to talk about legislation to separate end-stage testing of drugs from the companies who manufacture and distribute them.

It was the following Tuesday, at exactly ten minutes before three, that Mari found out that the Corporation for Public Broadcasting was going to fund her women's health series. She was alone in the house when the call came, and afterward she sat in Charles's study, where she'd taken the call, thinking about how everything was beginning to come together in her life. And wondering why it couldn't have happened just a little sooner, so her mother could have known. A rush of emotion brought tears to her eyes, but she didn't care, just let them run down her cheeks unheeded—until the phone rang again and she started guiltily, swiping at her face with the back of her hand.

"Hello?"

Charles picked up on the tremulous waver in her voice instantly. "What's the matter, honey?" She could hear the concern in his voice.

"Nothing. Just the opposite, in fact." She started to smile through her tears. "I just now heard—CPB is going to fund the programs, all of them. They even want me to do a book to go with it, to be issued at the same time the series airs, late next fall."

"Hey, that's great. I really like the book idea, don't you? That way anybody who wants it would have all that information instantly available, like a reference. You were crying happy tears, huh?"

"No, not really. I was just wishing Mom could've known. Oh, God, Charles"—the tears started flowing again—"I never imagined I'd miss her so much!"

"I know. Me too." He paused and swallowed, feeling a sympathetic surge of sadness and regret. "Look, I can be home in about thirty minutes. Let's take a swim, then go somewhere and celebrate, okay? You think about where you'd like to go while I'm on my way."

"Kate's," she answered without hesitation, "except I wish Tony and Rachel were here, don't you?"

397

"Have you talked to him yet?"

"No, I wanted you to be the first to know, but I'm going to call him now."

"Okay, tell 'em if they hurry, they can go to Kate's with us," he teased. "I'll see you in a few minutes."

Rachel answered the phone on the second ring.

"What are you doing home?" was all Mari could think to say.

"Oh, well, mostly trying to make a baby!" she answered, seizing the opportunity to shock Mari. "Tony just heard, Mari. Isn't it great, wonderful? I'm so glad, for both of you."

"So I'm not the first one to interrupt you, then, right? That makes me feel better. You got married, didn't you?" Mari guessed, not at all shocked.

"Yeah. Hope you don't mind that we went ahead without you. Tony said you'd only cry anyway, and I had some vacation coming, before I leave the job for good."

"You *did* run into trouble, didn't you? I knew you shouldn't have gotten involved with those tests, that they'd say it wasn't a proper thing for the clinic to be doing!"

"Whoa, hold on a minute, will you?" She sort of laughed. "You're way off in left field. I'm taking that new job I told you I was thinking about, that's all. I may even go back to school, if I can manage it along with everything else, at U.T. Because I'll be working in Austin."

"Where—how? I don't understand."

"Ask Charles. He'll tell you about it. Talk to you soon, okay? Here's Tony."

"You must close your tender ears to this woman, no?" Tony teased. "She is already full of ideas for the programs. Only one way to shut her up." He laughed, and she could hear them sort of scuffling, even over the phone.

They talked on for only a couple of minutes, mostly about what each of them had heard from CPB, then agreed to talk again tomorrow.

"Rachel says she's taking a job in Austin, and I should ask you about it," she told Charles as soon as he got home. "So give."

"Yeah," he drawled, pleased with himself for keeping it from her this long, "she's coming to work with me, in the company. I'm taking leave from the university, to give it my full attention for a year, see how it goes. I need a biochemist, somebody with a medical background, and she's a natural for research, has all the right instincts."

"Instincts?" Mari repeated, letting her voice rise skeptically.

"Instincts," he confirmed, grinning, "and I don't need any smart remarks from you."

Two weeks later they were sitting out on the back deck late one afternoon, having a glass of wine and mulling over the day, when the phone rang. Charles went in to answer it, then was right back.

"For you. New York."

When she returned a few minutes later, she didn't say a word, not even who it was calling, just sat there staring off across the valley.

"Kind of late for a call from New York, isn't it?" he asked finally, curiosity getting the better of him. Mari just nodded, so he waited, giving her the time she apparently needed. He picked up both their glasses and went inside for a refill, pouring the white wine over a cube of ice, because even at this time of day, with the sun down behind the ridge of hills to the west, it was close to ninety degrees outside.

She accepted the refreshed drink without meeting his eyes. "That was Reed Gilbert. UBC News Division."

"And?" he asked when she seemed reluctant to continue.

"And they want me to come to New York, to talk about doing a one-hour documentary."

"On what?"

"The big pharmaceutical companies, international. The extent and kind of influence they exert on medical practice and research."

"Hot damn! That's just what you've been wanting to do, isn't it?" He jumped up from his chair, so excited he couldn't sit still. Mari nodded. "Then how come you're not dancing with joy?" She just shrugged.

There must be some kind of hooker in what they were asking her to do, something she didn't feel right about, otherwise she would've jumped at the chance. Charles recalled her encounter with Jack Lunsford that night after the broadcast, when Tracy had butchered the story about the contraceptive sponge. Angry as a mother defending a helpless child when it came to getting out the full story—the essential truth, she called it—she'd also learned to temper her idealism with pragmatism, so had offered Jack a compromise they both could live with. Mari had a strong sense of where to draw the line, and what lines were worth defending to the death—unlike most of the compromisers he knew at the university, "educated" men who didn't begin to understand the difference between negotiating for a principle and selling your soul. Hell, most of them didn't have any principles, so had nothing to sell out!

"What's the problem, then? Some kind of joker in the deck, something they won't give in on that you can't live with?"

"No, not that I know of, at least not at this point."

"So what'd you tell him?"

"That I need some time to think about it."

"What's to think about, for God's sake?" He couldn't help shouting, astounded that she would even consider turning down the opportunity to do exactly what she wanted to, and for national television.

"You. This. Us. I'm already committed to do the PBS programs, and the book. Adding the documentary would mean spending even more time away from you, traveling all over the place, probably even to Europe. Delaying starting a family even longer."

Charles got up without a word and disappeared inside the house, but was back in less than a minute with a brown-paper-wrapped package, which he dropped in her lap.

The sense of déjà vu was nearly overwhelming. Everything was exactly as it had been the day he'd given her the silver bracelet, even his "Go ahead and open it," causing her to doubt her sanity for a second. And again the rough paper revealed a brilliantly colored jewel. This one was woven of deep red, blue, orange, and sea-green wool in an intricate geometrical pattern which was embellished with scattered tufts and tassels of yarn, some with sequins attached that shook and glittered in the dying light.

"A pillow cover? Moroccan?" she asked, looking up at him in wonder. Actually, she knew without asking. The weaving was nearly six feet long, but the half intended to cover the back of the pillow was more simply woven, in multicolored stripes.

Charles nodded, grinning. "From the Middle Atlas Mountains. For my seraglio, my harem." He shoved a book at her, which she hadn't even noticed he was carrying. She took it and read the title. *From the Far West: Carpets and Textiles of Morocco.* "You can read it later," he said as he pulled one of the deck chairs close to hers, sat on the edge of the seat and reached over and took one of her hands between both of his.

"Let's build our own Alhambra, Mari. In the mountains, in Colorado. I want to learn to ski, for you to teach me. About a lot of things. A place without doors, only openings to the mountains and valleys and high plains, where we can go to renew and replenish the spirit. Openings that work both ways, in and out. We can keep this place, or go wherever you need to, but it would always be there, waiting for us, whenever or for however long we want and need to be there. Like the Moors, we can create harmony out of contrast and variety—out of our own energy and love. You saw it, you know what I mean." He squeezed her hand. "I know you want to do this, so grab your chance, Mari, or you may regret it for the rest of your life."

"But—Well, I'm afraid it might turn out to be sort of like going down a cafeteria line when you're hungry, ending up with more than you can eat, more than I can manage and still be everything else at the same time."

"Don't play games with me now, Mari. Tell me what everything else means."

"I know I can't have everything, Charles. You and a real home, and children, and all the other things I want to do. But, well, it's so hard to decide. I guess I've never really grown up, maybe never will be able to face the reality that I have to give up something." She paused, but he waited, knowing she wasn't finished yet. "Because I'm not sure, well, that what we have, the way we feel, can survive, unless—if I don't. Maybe you'll think I'm old-fashioned, or just egotistical, but I don't think I could turn a baby over to

401

a sitter or day-care place, at least not full-time. It seems so—oh, I don't know—impersonal, I guess, to be so uninvolved as a mother.

"So I've been trying to think of ways to either taper off or change the kind of work I do, but that's not very satisfactory, either, because it calls for the same thing—to uninvolve myself. And I guess I've never been very good at doing that, as you've pointed out more than once."

Charles had finally come to recognize that the shell of noninvolvement he'd wrapped himself in for so long, that he'd even convinced himself was necessary to his work, was a form of self-protection, a way of denying the reality that he was unappreciated and unloved by the man and woman who had given him life. He also realized that Mari probably was the stronger of the two of them, because in spite of what Phillip Ashmore had done to her, she'd never closed herself off. Instead she'd reached out to help other women, even though it must have been a constant reminder of what she, too, wanted to forget or deny.

"If that's what you think, you're right, you are old-fashioned. And in the worst possible way. Buying into all the old myths, about what women are supposed to be and do, and the corollary, too—what men are and aren't supposed to do. If you want to do what other people expect, instead of what's right for us, you'll have to do it without me. Either you agree to give me full partnership rights—whether it's blood tests or babysitting—or the deal's off."

She saw his lips begin to twitch with humor as he issued his ultimatum, but tried not to respond in kind. Instead, she kept him in suspense a few seconds longer, nodding slightly, trying to keep a straight face. "Okay, I'll take your request under careful consideration."

"Come on, Marilyn," he shouted finally, so agitated he had to jump up from his chair again. *"Where the hell's that adventuresome spirit I love?"*

The words she'd never used except in the privacy of her own mind fell into place like the last piece of an intricate jigsaw puzzle, with a sense of recognition akin to a light going on somewhere inside of her, illuminating who she was—her true self.

"Okay, okay." She laughed happily, agreeing. "But only on one condition."

Charles held his breath for a second. "What?" The word came out like a small explosion.

"No matter how many children we do or don't have, that *you* will never, ever, even think of calling me *Mother!*"

Author's Note

Mari McNichols's experience during her marriage to Phillip Ashmore is, unfortunately, all too real for many American women today—with one out of five emergency room visits by women the result of domestic violence, and half the women who go to shelters reporting battering during pregnancy. Two million women were battered in 1988 alone, and more than half the women who were murdered were killed by a former or current partner. Yet battering severe enough to put a woman in the hospital, at least in the State of Texas, is no more than a third-degree felony—a crime equivalent to stealing a pig, owning a slot machine, using an expired credit card or bypassing your gas meter. Even then, the charge must be pressed by the victim herself.

Statistics cited for the incidence of certain surgical procedures, and for tests and medications prescribed for women compared with men, are a matter of public record. The drug Pamezine is pure fiction; that blood exhibits the flow properties described here is not.

History suggests that it is often where diverse disciplines and research approaches come together that we see significant advances in knowledge, and certainly biomedical engineering has proven to be such a convergence. While Charles Merrill is the product of my imagination, he does exhibit some of the qualities I've observed in "real" scientists I've met over the years of being married to one. Among them have been a chemist who works with blood all day in his laboratory, yet is apt to keel over at the sight of his son's cut finger; a physicist who likes to brag that he can do nothing with his hands (even adjust his hi-fi), and one who repairs everything from the family dishwasher to delicate shutter mechanisms in the old cameras he collects; a Nobel laureate who talks about "higher order concepts" and a geneticist adept at manipulating even the most innocuous conversation into a discussion of the relative merits of the vaginal muscles of the women he has "known." If they have anything at all in common, it is an irreverent set of mind and an addiction to the endlessly fascinating game they play, which drives not only every waking hour but often their dreams as well.

Finally, my inspiration for the flamenco segment was María Benitez, the fiery American Indian in whose veins must surely run the blood of the Spanish-Moorish Gypsies, for to watch her dance is to feel racing through your own blood what Andalusian poet Federico García Lorca called "the heroic rhythm of my whole people, of our whole history."